A DISTANT DRUM

BOOKS BY
CHARLES BRACELEN FLOOD

LOVE IS A BRIDGE
(*A Houghton Mifflin Literary Fellowship novel*)

A DISTANT DRUM

A DISTANT DRUM

by

CHARLES BRACELEN FLOOD

HOUGHTON MIFFLIN COMPANY BOSTON

The Riverside Press Cambridge

1957

The Riverside Press

CAMBRIDGE · MASSACHUSETTS

PRINTED IN THE U.S.A.

To the members of the class of 1951
at Harvard College who died in the Korean War

A DISTANT DRUM

1

PATRICK KINGSGRANT stood under a warm spray in the shower room on the fourth floor of the Indoor Athletic Building at Harvard, letting the hot water carry the tiredness and the stiffness out of his muscles. He had a cake of soap in his left hand, and he was soaping his chest slowly and absent-mindedly. His right arm had been hurt when he was born, an injury that left it as long as his left arm but a little less developed and considerably more awkward, and the result was that Patrick unconsciously did most things, other than handwriting, with his left hand. He had always gone out for sports, despite his bad arm, and at Harvard he had done a good deal of noncompetitive swimming, and then gone out for football, until a knee injury had stopped him. Now he contented himself with an occasional long session with the light bag and the heavy bag in the boxing room, and that was what he had been doing this afternoon.

He moved his left hand with the cake of soap up to his thinning brown hair, and began to give himself a rudimentary shampoo. Back in the fall of 1947, when he had begun to swim as a freshman, mainly because his friend Bill Bench was out for the freshman swimming team, Patrick's father had warned him that swimming would make him lose hair. Now it was the spring of 1950, and Patrick's father was absolutely right.

Patrick put the soap back in its dish near the shower knobs, and stood in the rush of warm water for another couple of minutes. There was so much to be done once he went outside this shower that he just wanted to stay here. The final examinations of his junior year were bearing down on him like an express train, and he had to produce some more work for his short-story writing course, and he had to dream up something in the way of a story for the year's last issue of the *Lampoon*. And under that there was another problem, a problem that had nothing to do with college, but a problem that went right to the core of a lot of things.

The water went off with a snap as he turned the knobs simultaneously, and Patrick went out into the locker room, drying himself with a towel. He stepped on the scale, was pleased that it said 177, the same weight that he had been last fall when he had reported back early for his ill-fated football venture, and went on toward the locker where his clothes were hanging.

The sun was sparkling on the Charles River, and Patrick walked along the bank on a detour back to his room at Leverett House, only half aware of the scene around him. It was a bright May afternoon, and on the river there were single sculls and eight-man crew shells, with coaches following the long shells in motorboats, wearing battered fedora hats and yelling through megaphones. There were some Harvard men and Radcliffe girls sitting on the green banks, pretending to themselves that they were studying, and, off to Patrick's left, the real paraphernalia of Harvard rose into the sunshine: the Houses, and farther in from the river, the buildings and libraries of Harvard Yard. It was all red brick and white windows and white towers, and the coxswains kept shouting at their crews on the river.

In the middle of all this Patrick was not smiling. He was twenty years old, and his problem seemed big to him. In its last analysis, the problem was an island in Maine. It was called Kingsgrant, and Patrick's father, Jacob Kingsgrant, had been born on the island, as had a great many Kingsgrants before him. Patrick had been born there too, but Jacob Kingsgrant had moved to New York shortly after Patrick was born, so that Patrick was essentially a New Yorker. He had grown up in New York, in a world of private schools and Central Park and a military drill class for little boys which was called the Knicker-bocker Greys. His mother, who had been an Irish beauty from San Francisco, had died when he was eight, leaving Patrick and his younger sister Eileen to be brought up by Jacob Kings-grant. Jacob Kingsgrant was a tall, strong lawyer who loved his half-Celtic children and believed that life was work. He had sent Patrick to Tabor Academy, where he had received a good education in English, sailing, and close-order drill, and here he was at Harvard.

Except that the island still remained. It still belonged to Jacob Kingsgrant, and the three of them had often gone back there in the summers. Two years before, Patrick had had the best summer of his life by going off on a project of his own and teaching horseback riding at a camp in Vermont. He had been planning to do the same thing again this summer, but yesterday a letter had come from his father. It was a firm, fair letter, pointing out that if Patrick should be away this summer it would be quite a while since he had worked in the blueberry factory, since Patrick had preferred to scythe down fields at Kings-grant the summer before to get in shape for football, instead of working in the cannery. Jacob Kingsgrant's clear handwriting said that he did not have to repeat the importance of having one member of the family make occasional appearances in the fac-tory. Both he and Eileen were hoping very much that Patrick would change his mind, and then they could have a good time together this summer at Kingsgrant, Very sincerely, Father.

Patrick came up the steps of D entry in Leverett House and on the third floor he turned to the right to go to his room, D-32. There was a muffled sound of conversation coming from the room, and Patrick opened the door and went in.

"Listen," Snowjob Porter was saying, "you give the Germans some foot soldiers, and then you'll give 'em some tanks to go with the foot soldiers, and then you'll give 'em some planes, and then you'll wonder why they're handing *us* ultimatums."

"But we don't have any *choice*," Bill Bench said. "Hi, Pat."

"Hi." Patrick looked around the living room of their suite. He and Bill Bench lived in the bedroom off to the right of the living room, rooming together as they had at Tabor, and Snowjob Porter and David Tall Man lived in the other bedroom, separated from the living room by the bathroom. Right now the gang were all there. Bill Bench was sitting in his armchair, looking like a rugged fair-haired sheepdog with a temporarily forgotten stack of notes in his lap, and Snowjob, looking like all the crew-cut Princeton men in the world put together, was perched on the edge of the round table that sat in the middle of their faded green carpet. Dave Tall Man was lying on a couch over by the open window, studying some group theory equations in a notebook.

"These comedians have been on this thing for the last hour," Tall Man said, not looking up. "A man with less patience would get up and go somewhere quiet."

"You don't have to study, Tall Man," Snowjob said. "Mathematicians don't have to study. You just sit around contemplating zero. We know that."

Tall Man turned his long muscular body so that he had his prominent jaw propped up by the palm of his hand. "I'd just as soon contemplate it quietly."

"You must have a view on this, PK," Snowjob said. "What do you think about arming the Germans?"

Patrick smiled. On the *Lampoon* they signed their stories with their initials, and it gave him a kick when somebody occasionally called him PK.

"I don't trust the Germans very far myself," he said, heading toward the door of his room, "but it's going to happen. I just hope we can keep them pointed the right way."

"I'd still rather be killed by a Russian than a German," Snowjob said. "At least we haven't had the Russians down with our foot on their chest twice this century."

Patrick went on into his room. Outside he heard Tall Man saying something about Snowjob's being awfully particular about who killed him, what difference did it make who killed you, and Snowjob saying it made a hell of a big difference to him whom he was killed by, but most of Patrick's attention was concentrating on the piles of papers on his desk. There was just one desk in their bedroom, sitting underneath the one good-sized window, and by some unspoken agreement the desk was Patrick's, while Bill did all the work for his Government courses in the big armchair in the living room. Right now, staring down at the desk, Patrick winced at the accumulation. There were the notes on Merle Fainsod's course in Dictatorship, and some of the short stories to finish out his quota in Clark's writing course, and the optional paper on the Oxford Movement that he was doing for Owen's course in English History. Somewhere underneath the top layer of papers were his notes for Levin's full year of Shakespeare. Patrick's mouth tightened.

"Hey Snowjob?" Tall Man's voice said in the other room.

'What is it?"

"Why don't you go take a run around the river? Look at Patrick. He gets on the verge of cracking up, he goes over to the IAB and beats up on a punching bag."

Patrick fished the keys to his car out of his pocket, still lost in his contemplation of the papers on his desk. The car was a

'41 Ford convertible, called Chrissy from the Saint Christopher medal on its dashboard, and the four of them used it equally. "Do you want to take the car anywhere?" he said, opening the door into the living room.

"No thanks," Snowjob said. "I know damned well I can't get Tall Man to get off that couch and come with me."

"You're so right," Tall Man said, his eyes still on the lines of symbols and figures.

"I guess I'll go down to the House Library," Snowjob said. "Thanks anyhow, Pat."

Patrick closed the door and sat down at the desk. He heard Snowjob and Tall Man mutter a couple of parting remarks, and smiled. They were such an unlikely pair, the Groton alumnus from Philadelphia and David Tall Man of Flagstaff, Arizona, one quarter Navaho Indian and the grandson of Chief Jonathan Tall Man. Their conversation consisted mainly of Tall Man's asking Snowjob to shut up, please. But there was something good between them.

He stretched his arms out to the side, yawned, and put his roommates out of his mind. The afternoon sun was shining in through the leaves of the tall tree that stood in the corner of the Leverett courtyard outside Patrick's window, and several ragged-edged sunbeams were putting a leafy pattern across the photographs on Patrick's bureau. He sat there, leaning back in his chair, and let his eyes wander from one picture to the next, while he thought about how to write the director of the camp in Vermont to tell him that he could not come and teach horseback riding this summer after all. The first photograph was an exceedingly conventional one. It was of Eileen in a white dress, taken the year before, when she had graduated from the Brearley School in New York. It showed a pretty girl with dark hair who looked perfectly capable of telling you to go to hell if you presumed too far upon that good-natured smile. The next picture was of Jacob Kingsgrant at the time he came back as a captain from the First World War. It was a small photograph of an unsmiling, magnificent-looking man, and even though the picture was just of Captain Kingsgrant from the waist up, looking dead on, you knew that he was a tall man who walked erect, and that the boots you could not see were every bit as shiny as the Sam Browne that sparkled in the picture. His father had never liked the picture, but it was Patrick's favorite.

The next picture was right to the point. It was a big un-framed glossy print, eight inches by ten inches, and it was still not big enough for its subject. It was an aerial view of Kings-grant Island in Penobscot Bay, a not particularly well focused shot, which nevertheless conveyed a clear idea of the place, the woods, the marshy fields that Patrick had scythed down last summer, the servants' quarters for the Negroes who were the de-scendants of slaves who had arrived up here in the Underground Railway, the pier, and finally the house, Kingsgrant itself, hunch-ing down under the lee of the North Bluff. The picture had been taken while the plane was banking in from the direction of Bar Harbor, cutting over the woods at the southwestern end of the island, so that the house was farthest away from the cam-era. In a little stand of birch not far from the house there was a graveyard in which lay the Kingsgrants of many generations. You could just barely see it in the picture; but what you could not see at all was the bare space among the spruce trees on the Bluff, where Patrick's mother was buried. When she had found out that she was going to die, Maude Buckleigh had picked out her spot, and that was where she lay.

Patrick stared at the picture in the filtered afternoon sunlight. Another thing you couldn't see, off some six hundred yards of water to one side, was the little town of South Harbor, on the mainland, where Patrick's father had practiced law before he came to New York, and the road that moved on from there, to split and move in one direction past the cannery with its syrupy blue smell of berry juice and steam, and to move in the other direction to Ellsworth and the outside world.

So that was Kingsgrant. Jacob Kingsgrant and Eileen Kingsgrant and Patrick Kingsgrant were the descendants of fishermen who had settled on an island because it was safer to put six hundred yards of water between themselves and the Indians. There had been quite a few Kingsgrants, but they had died at sea, first off Matinicus and the Grand Banks, and then in places like the Indian Ocean and the Sargasso Sea and a hospital in Shanghai. A few of them had managed it on land, one younger son from wounds received at Saratoga, another younger son at Vicksburg, until all that was left was Oliver Kingsgrant, Justice of the Supreme Court of Maine and no wanderer he. His son was Jacob, and Jacob's son was Patrick. They came back during the summer, and the colored servants kept up the house and even made some money out of the truck gardens, but if you asked Patrick where he lived, he would have said New York. If he had been asked what was his family seat, he would have said, Kingsgrant Island, it's an island up in Maine. And he would have said up in Maine, not down in Maine.

The heir to Kingsgrant began rummaging around in the center drawer of his desk for some writing paper. He got it out, shoved Shakespeare and the Oxford Movement out of the way, and picked up the dark green Parker '51 that Eileen had given him this past Christmas. He balanced it all in his mind just once more, but he already knew what he had to do. His father was not forbidding him. His father was asking him, and putting it fairly. He had not used the words "duty" or "responsibility" once in his short letter, but that was what they were talking about. He smiled a soft remembering smile as he thought about that independent summer in Vermont, cantering across a field by a lake, and then he began to move his pen across the paper, telling the director of the camp that he was terribly sorry, but he would be unable to work there this summer after all. As he wrote, he could already smell the damned blueberries.

II

At just about the same time that Patrick was finishing his letter in Cambridge, Eileen Kingsgrant was changing from the blouse and skirt that she had worn at Barnard that day into a turquoise silk print dress. She finished zipping the dress up the side and stood there for a minute, alone in her big bedroom twenty-one floors above Park Avenue at Ninetieth Street, looking out of one of her windows, across the Avenue and the blocks of tenement houses that stretched off to the East River. It was a lovely afternoon, and the sunlight was dancing on the steel span of the Triborough Bridge.

Eileen turned away from the window, walked past the desk at which she studied, and sat down at her little dressing table. There was a pair of black leather high-heeled shoes sprawled beside the skirts of the dressing table, Delman shoes that were her favorites, and she bent over and slipped them on. Then she picked up the pair of loafers that she had worn to school today, and went over to her closet and put those away.

She heard the elevator door on this floor open and close again, and she looked at her watch. It was just five. Her father was home early. Eileen went over to her dressing table, picked up a silver bracelet, put it on in one quick motion, and went out into the hall. Her father had just put away his hat in his room, and now he was coming down the hall, the *World-Telegram* under his arm, headed for the library.

"Hi, Daddy," Eileen said, and Jacob Kingsgrant stopped in the dimness of the inside hall and smiled at her.

"Hello, dear," he said, smiling even more as she kissed his cheek. "How was school?"

"Fine. You tired?"

"Not too."

"How about some tea?"

"Sounds good," Jacob said. "Good idea."

"I'll be up with it in a couple of minutes."

"Don't hurry." Jacob smiled at his daughter again, and then went on down the hall, past the door of her bedroom, and into the library.

Eileen went down the stairs to the lower floor of the apartment, walked through the dining room, and came out into the pantry. In the kitchen she could hear Eleanor, the maid, talking to the cook, but she decided that she would just as soon fix things herself.

"Eleanor," Eileen said, pulling a tray out from beside the sink in the pantry, "could you boil some water for tea, please, or have Mary do it?"

"Yes, Miss Eileen."

Eileen set out the tea things on the tray, and then she peered into the breadbox. She knew perfectly well that her father never ate anything with tea, never ate anything with a cocktail, never ate anything from noon until dinner, but still a tea tray without some cookies or bread of some description on it always looked naked to Eileen, and besides, she was known to nibble an occasional nibble. She found a few cookies, spread them out decoratively on a plate, ate one right there, and about five minutes later she was carrying the whole business upstairs.

The door to the library was open, and Eileen came in and headed for the low table near the armchair that sat on the right side of the fireplace. Jacob was sitting in his own armchair, near the door, his feet up on his big footstool and his eyes riveted to the paper, but when the jingling of the tea things penetrated his concentration he stood up and made a gesture toward coming over to help Eileen put the tray down.

"Never mind, Daddy. I've got it."

Eileen sat down and began to make the tea, and Jacob sat back down in his chair. He rubbed his eyes once or twice, turned on the light beside his chair, and went on reading.

Eileen stood up and took a couple of turns around the room while the tea was steeping. There were windows at either end of the room, one set looking out on the same view toward the east that she had from her bedroom, and the other pair of windows looking out past the other wing of 1120 Park, out over Central Park and the Reservoir, and even allowing a glimpse of the George Washington Bridge way up the West Side in the distance beyond the Park. Eileen was feeling restless, and she hoped that her father would suggest that they go up on the roof after they had their tea. For the moment, all she did was look out one set of windows, and then out of the other set of windows, while Jacob Kingsgrant read his paper with the furious concentration that characterized any Kingsgrant in contact with the printed word.

"You know this is a hell of a thing," Jacob said suddenly, putting down his paper and standing up. He walked over to the mantelpiece. "These congressional investigations have got to be taken out of the hands of the legislators and put in the hands of the judiciary in some form or another."

"But Daddy, weren't most of these congressmen lawyers themselves somewhere along the line?"

"My God, you'd never know it," Jacob said. He turned and stood there in front of the fireplace, a tall, powerful man in a gray suit with a vest. He thrust his hands into his pockets.

"I think the tea's about ready," Eileen said.

"At the very least, they've got to get some sort of standard procedure about these things," Jacob said. "This is like shooting at the side of a barn with a shotgun. It's not accurate enough. It's not good enough. It's not good investigation, and it's not good justice."

Eileen held out a cup of tea to her father, and Jacob pulled his hands out of his pockets and took it. He looked down at the steam rising from the cup of tea, and his expression softened somewhat. "Have you heard from Patrick?" he said quietly.

"No, Daddy." Eileen sat down. In the back of her mind, she had been waiting all day for this conversation, and here it was.

"Don't you think he ought to be in Kingsgrant with us this summer?"

"I guess so, Daddy. I know I'd like it."

"So would I." Jacob took a sip of his tea. "And I think he might bang up his knee very badly if he does this riding thing."

"Well, he walks all right." Eileen leaned forward in her chair. "He can run all right."

"Do you know what the doctors said?" Jacob walked over toward the windows nearest Eileen and stood there, outlined against a panorama of sky and city and the river half a mile away. "They said no skiing, no ice skating, no wrestling, and no more football. Do you know what Dr. Harris said to me? He said, 'Did you encourage that boy to go out for football up there?' *Encourage* him!" Jacob glared at his tea, and then drank it all down.

"All right, Daddy, but that was last September, and I think Patrick has made up his mind that he isn't ever going to try skiing or any of these things. More tea?"

"No, thanks."

"And anyhow, I think Patrick can ride pretty well."

"The boy can ride a horse." Jacob's voice was quieter now. "Not particularly well, but he can ride a horse. But here he's proposing to spend the whole summer around them, feeding them, lifting children on and off them, riding all over the countryside — you can't be sure a horse couldn't manage to fall squarely on top of his knee somewhere in there." He shook his head. "Let's go up on the roof."

"Good."

They left the library, went on down the hall past the stairs that led down to the dining room, past the elevator, past the doorway to Jacob's room, and, just before they came to Patrick's room, they went through a door to the right and came out of the apartment onto the back stairwell. The whole fireproof back stairs of the building were concrete and steel, and the concrete walls were painted gray. They went up the stairs, the sounds of their feet echoing under the giant skylight overhead, and came out at the top of the steps, just a flight above.

Jacob opened the door that said ROOF, and Eileen walked out under the blue sky. Then she waited by the wire fence a few feet away, sniffing in the spring breeze, while Jacob brought out the key that unlocked the gate in the fence. Eileen had her own key to it, but she knew that her father enjoyed fussing around with the key, as if he were each time opening a present for her. She had her roof garden up here, with lattices on the brick walls of the towers that housed the elevator machinery, and big boxes of earth set along the low walls at the side of the roof. The iron railings that had been put up to protect Patrick and Eileen when they were children were still there, looking like crowbars set into the marble ledge that formed the ledge of the low brick walls. Out in the air Jacob seemed to relax, and he took his daughter's arm as they strolled around the roof together. Only a few flowers had come up thus far, but Eileen was pleased with them.

"You see, Eileen," Jacob said after a few minutes of walking around remarking on the flowers, "it's a parent's duty to stop a child from its own destruction, if possible." He stopped and stood by the railing, letting Eileen's arm go and putting one foot up on the low sill while he looked out toward the East River. "I would have loved it if he could have made the team up there."

Eileen looked at her father, and nodded. She was thinking that her father, with his powerful shoulders and his rangy body, still looked like his pictures when he had been substitute left end on the team up there in the fall of 1915. Last summer, during the weeks that he was at Kingsgrant on his vacation, Eileen had seen him watching Patrick as Patrick scythed down the fields. Jacob had watched in a pained silence, never encouraging Patrick and never forbidding him to go, and when Patrick had come back on crutches after two weeks of pre-season practice, Jacob had nodded and never said anything more about it, except to ask how the knee was healing.

"I don't see why he has to go out and break his neck all the time," Jacob said.

"I don't know, Daddy." Eileen stood there.

"Let him take the job, Daddy. Don't force his hand."

"I am letting him take the job. I'm letting him take the job." Jacob took his foot down off the sill. "Speaking of self-destruction," he said quietly, as if he were anxious to dismiss the thought as quickly as possible, "has he ever said anything to you about this notion of his that he wants to be a writer?"

Eileen blushed. This conversation was involving her a good deal more than she wanted to be involved. She could hear Patrick's voice right now, home on any vacation, talking over his stories in the copies of the *Lampoon* that he had sent her, and showing her some of the stories he had done for whatever writing course he was in at the time. It's the only thing, she heard him saying, it's the only thing I've ever done where I lose all track of what time it is. Maybe these aren't any good, but if you feel like that, don't you think it'll work out, Eileen?

Sooner or later you'll make your writing as good as it makes you feel? And every time, Eileen had ended up somewhere between agreeing with him enthusiastically and telling him to take it easy, Patrick.

"I think he writes very nicely, don't you, Daddy?"

"Oh, sure." Eileen always smiled at the way her father said "sure." That pronunciation tacked straight upwind from Maine every time. "Very nice little stories. With his command of the language he can go a long way in the law." He nodded his head emphatically. "A long way."

"Well, supposing — just supposing — he wants to think things over when he gets out of Harvard next year?"

"What's there to think over? Come to Kingsgrant, get a good summer's rest, and start off at the Law School in the fall."

"Well, suppose now, that he really wants to write as a career?"

"A career." Jacob pressed his toe hard against one of the flower boxes. "Eileen, Patrick is a lawyer. I know what it takes, and he's got it. Assuming that he applies himself, he has everything for it."

"Miss Eileen!"

Eileen turned around. The maid was standing next to the gate in the fence.

"What is it, Eleanor?"

"There's a Mr. Woodhart on the telephone."

"I'll be right there." Eileen turned to her father. "Well, let's not worry about it any more right now."

Jacob nodded. "I'll be along in a little while. Who's Woodhart?"

"Columbia. Not very interesting." Eileen turned and started walking quickly toward the gate in the wire fence.

After Eileen had gone downstairs, Jacob Kingsgrant stood with his foot on the ledge, staring out over the humming canyon of Park Avenue. All right, Maude, he thought as he looked out over the traffic running twenty-two floors below. We'll let him go ride the horses. You still have a full vote, darling. If he keeps on wanting to, we'll let him go ride the horses. Then Jacob straightened up, brought his foot down off the marble sill, and turned away from the ledge.

2

A LOT of the people had already left the examination room, and the remainder were either writing frantically or reading over their bluebooks. Patrick sat there, the point of his pen moving down the margin as he checked over his answer to the last question. He inserted a comma in the last sentence. Well, he said to himself, that's the ball game. You may not know much about Dictatorship, but you got everything you do know in here one way or another.

He slid the second bluebook inside the cover of the first one that he had done, and stood up. His seersucker jacket was lying on the next seat, and Patrick pulled the penny postcard out of its inside pocket. He had addressed the card to himself at Kingsgrant, and on the back he had written:

> *Gov. 130 Could you please send me*
> *Exam Grade____*
> *Term Grade____*
> *Thank you.*
>
> *P. Kingsgrant*

Patrick stuck the postcard inside the bluebooks, put on his jacket, scooped up his bottle of ink and the pile of filing cards that he had been studying even on the walk up to the exam, and went down the aisle as if he were in a daze.

"The examination is now over," one of the proctors announced in a self-important manner. "The examination is now over. Please turn in all bluebooks immediately." Patrick found the pile labeled "A–K" and put his contribution on it. Then he left the room, still numb from the three hours of constant thinking and writing.

Outside, it was a beautiful afternoon, and Patrick walked along slowly under the green trees, suddenly realizing that he had just handed in the last examination of his junior year.

"Hey, hold up!"

Patrick turned around. Bill Bench was coming up behind him.

"What'd you just have?" Patrick asked.

"Economics." Bill shook his head. "As far as I'm concerned that stuff is medicine. It may be good for me, but I certainly don't like the taste."

"I don't blame you."

They both walked past Memorial Hall and on into the Yard, two young men in seersucker jackets and khaki trousers.

"That was your last one, wasn't it?" Bill said after a minute.

"That's it. It's all over."

"I wish mine were."

Patrick looked at a pretty Radcliffe girl walking by.

"How many more have you got?"

"Just one. Day after tomorrow. How do you think you did in your Dictatorship thing?"

"All right. I got everything down. Pretty fair exam." Patrick watched another girl go by. This one was wheeling a bicycle. "Too bad you can't blast with us tonight."

"Where're you going to go? Cronin's?"

Patrick nodded his head. "Tall Man got through this morning, so I guess he's game, and Snowjob's finished, and I guess there'll be a couple of guys from the club." Patrick thought of something. "Listen, Bill, I guess I'd better go over to Warren House and pick up my stuff from my writing course."

"O.K. See you back at the room."

"Check." Patrick swung off to the left, on the walk that led out of the Yard past Lamont Library. He crossed Quincy Street slowly, went through the gate beside the Freshman Union, and a minute later he was walking up the wooden steps of Warren House, the old yellow frame house that served as the headquarters of the written word at Harvard College.

"I'd like to see Professor Clark," he said to the secretary in the first room of the hall.

"I'm sorry, he's out. Are you in his course?"

"Yes."

"He left some of the grades and papers here. What's your name?"

"Kingsgrant. Patrick Kingsgrant."

"Uh-huh. Yes." The girl handed Patrick a manila folder, and Patrick mumbled "Thank you" and went outside. He didn't look at the manila folder until he was down the steps. Then he got ready to look. He could feel his heart beating. Then he looked. There was a big blue-penciled B on the folder. Patrick smiled, relaxed, and began reading the comment written underneath. "I have remarked on your stories in a more detailed way along their margins," the blue handwriting said, "but my over-all impression is that you have a gift, although I think it is early to judge it with any hope of accuracy. Although your efforts to experiment in the handling of time are interesting, they are not too successful. Also I rather dislike some of your patent sentimentality, and your addiction to happy endings. Again, you will never be truly successful until you are willing to revise more than you have in these stories. But I've enjoyed having you in the course, and if you acquire a suffi-

ciently determined attitude about developing your talent, I
think you could be a true contender."

Patrick opened the folder and looked at what Professor Clark
had given the various stories. He stood there for quite a while,
paging through the various typewritten stories, and then he
closed the envelope and walked on out to the street. The academic year was finished, and now he started thinking of the
things he had to do before he drove down to New York the next
morning.

Patrick looked at his watch. It was almost six o'clock, and
Bill had probably gone down to dinner. There was no point
rushing. Then Patrick realized that he probably would not get
a chance to drop in at church in the morning, so he walked down
Bow Street to St. Paul's and went through the little side door
down to the basement chapel.

It was dark and cool. Patrick dipped his finger in the font
by the door, made the sign of the cross, and went forward to
the pew that he always sat in when he came here alone. On
Sundays he went to High Mass upstairs, but often in the evenings, or at odd hours, Patrick came here. He would say a few
prayers on his knees, but mostly he just sat in the pew, the
fourth pew from the front, over against the right-hand wall,
and felt the comfort of the darkness and the silence and the
candles burning in their red glasses before the altar.

After he had said an Our Father, a Hail Mary, and an Act of
Contrition, Patrick got off his knees and sat back in the pew,
his right hand resting lightly on the manila folder. A true contender. It was a surprise to Patrick that Professor Clark considered him a true anything. All year he had thought that Professor Clark considered him as someone who had no business
being in a serious creative-writing course. More than once
Patrick had seen Clark's eyebrows go up at some comments
that he had made in class, as if he were about to ask, "Are you

sure you're in the right room, Mr. Kingsgrant?" But he never had done anything more than raise his eyebrows, and the remarks he made on Patrick's stories always helped him see something he had not seen before. And now Professor Clark said that he could be a true contender.

Patrick got down on his knees again. The last weeks were still one swirl in his mind, reading and typing and taking exams, but it was over. Patrick said a few more prayers, and then he gathered up his manila envelope and the bottle of ink from the exam, genuflected, and walked out of the church.

II

Eileen came into the library and found Jacob pacing slowly across the floor, looking at his watch.

"I imagine they ought to be here pretty soon," Eileen said. Her father nodded his head and kept on moving.

"Pretty bad day for driving down," he said, stopping at the far windows and looking out into the drizzles and fog that hung over the Park. "Have you figured out where they're going to sleep?"

"Well, I thought I'd put Patrick in the other bed in your room, Daddy, and then Snowjob and Tall Man can sleep in the two beds in Patrick's room."

"Sounds fine," Jacob said, and Eileen sat down, watching her father as he stood at the window staring out into the rain. He was almost pathetically eager to see Patrick again, Eileen thought, and yet almost every time that Patrick came home, he and Jacob would be at each other's throats about something within twenty minutes after he came in the house. It was almost like a custom; they would both blow sky-high about something, and then the rest of the vacation or the week-end or whatever it was would go off pretty smoothly. They loved each other, but there were moments when you would never know it. As she sat there, watching her father awaiting Patrick's arrival, one scene from the past came into Eileen's mind. It was an unpleasant scene, but sometimes, when Patrick and Jacob were about to meet again after an absence, it would come into her mind, with all the high relief of human tension against a peaceful lapping evening at Kingsgrant. It had been a simple thing. The summer that Patrick was twelve he had taken to rowing the tender for the launch out around the point of the North Bluff. There was a certain amount of groundswell out beyond the North Bluff, and on top of it all, Patrick got caught out there in a couple of squalls. Jacob had told him in just so many words that if Patrick went out there alone again he would punish him. Patrick was to stay on this side of the North Bluff, in sight. Patrick had nodded, and all had gone well for a week or so. Then, one night just after supper, Eileen had been sitting down near the dock when she saw Patrick give in to his impulse, and go out of sight around the tip of the Bluff, the wake of the little rowboat spreading out on the glassy sunset waters. Eileen had stood up and raised her hand, but before she could wave or yell to him to come back, he was gone. Eileen had sat down on a rock, her face worried, and a minute later she had seen her father coming down the road.

"Hi, Eileen," Jacob had said. "Where's Patrick?"

Eileen had opened her mouth and closed it again. "I don't know," she said after a minute.

Jacob had stood there, still quite cheerful, and then he had noticed that the rowboat was gone.

"Is he out around the Bluff?" he had said, his face getting red, and his voice sounding choked and harsh.

Eileen had begun crying. "Daddy," she had said, "it's a calm night, he's all right, he'll be back in a minute, Daddy?"

Ten minutes later, Patrick came back into sight. Patrick

looked over his shoulder, and Eileen could see him stiffen up when he saw Jacob. The whole scene had unfolded with a terrible slowness, Eileen sitting huddled on the rock, Jacob advancing down onto the pier, and Patrick rowing on in.

Jacob had been on the pier for about two minutes when Patrick tied up at the float and came walking up the ramp. Patrick looked at his father, standing there at the top of the ramp, and then he smiled. Back on her rock, Eileen winced. That smile of Patrick's could be a maddening thing, and the trouble was that he didn't ever mean it as a gesture of defiance. He just smiled when he didn't know what else to do.

Jacob's hand had lashed out and slapped the smile off Patrick's face. Patrick had looked at him for a second, tears in his eyes and his lower lip rolling up tight, and then he had sailed into Jacob with both his fists. Jacob had got around behind Patrick and held him with his arms to his sides, and Patrick had begun kicking him in the shins, twisting and struggling, both of them breathing hard and neither of them saying a word. After about two minutes Patrick stopped kicking.

"I'm sorry I hit you," Jacob said. He was almost crying. Patrick just shook his head, and when Jacob let him go Patrick ran across the field and into the woods. The next day Patrick had not said a word, and then the day after that, when Jacob asked him a question, Patrick had called him "Father" when he answered. Eileen had assumed that Patrick would go back to calling Jacob "Daddy," as they both always had, but Patrick had never called him Daddy again.

Now, eight years later, Eileen looked at her father, standing by the window, and then she started going over the meal in her mind. It was five-thirty now, and assuming that they had left Cambridge by one o'clock, they ought to be here any minute. An hour to let them get unpacked and washed up and have a drink, and dinner at seven ought to be about right, because they probably would be pretty hungry. About the meal she had no worries. It was fried chicken, with white wine to drink and a dessert of vanilla ice cream that had slices of fresh fruit on it, and some crème de cacao in each dish. After the House dining halls, Eileen had an idea that this meal was going to compare favorably.

The elevator door opened, and Eileen got up. Jacob almost bowled her over, he had come across from the window so quickly.

"After you, dear," Jacob said, and they both walked down the hall toward the elevator. The three of them were shuffling in from the vestibule to the hallway, carrying suitcases and clothes on hangers. Patrick put his clothes over the top of the suitcase and stepped around the suitcase to kiss Eileen, and then he shook hands with his father.

"Hi, Tall Man. Hi, Snowjob," Eileen said, shaking hands with them and smiling. Jacob came forward.

"Hello, David. Hello, Snowjob. Good to see you." For some reason Jacob could never quite call Tall Man "Tall Man," but "Snowjob" didn't seem to phase him. "Have a good trip down?"

"Sort of rainy, sir," Snowjob said.

"Well, it's good to have you here," Jacob said.

"It's good to be here," Tall Man mumbled, and then Eileen was dispatching them to their rooms.

"You're in with me tonight," Jacob said, and he carried Patrick's clothes in while Patrick followed with his suitcase.

Half an hour later they were all gathered in the library. It was a marvelous sort of feeling in the room, the release of the end of the college year, and the happy chatter and speculation about the summer ahead. Not even the gray sky at the windows could put the slightest damper on the glow within the room. Eileen had taken her last exam just that morning, so she joined in with laughter every bit as heartfelt as the others'. From time to time she let her attention wander from her conversation with Snowjob, and stole a look at Jacob and Patrick. They were both standing by the mantelpiece, glasses in their hands, and Patrick was talking animatedly. Jacob was nodding his head, and occasionally he chuckled. Eileen sighed. It looked as if everything was fine. She smiled. Standing there, they looked less like a father and son than an uncle and a nephew. Jacob was a full four inches taller than Patrick, but Patrick had a broad strength about his back and shoulders that gave an impression of power. There was an awful lot of energy standing by that fireplace, a lot of strength and energy, and Eileen smiled happily as she felt them both here in the room.

"How's the Order of the Concrete Kimono?" she said, turning back to Snowjob and Tall Man.

"It's all right," Tall Man said.

"Any new members?"

"One or two, but I think the quality is falling off," Snowjob said.

"That's just because we don't know them as well," Tall Man said, and they were off, debating the merits of the newest members.

Eileen smiled as she thought about their club. About a year before, Patrick had come across the phrase *concrete kimono* in an article he had been reading on Murder, Incorporated. A concrete kimono was what the gangsters called the block of cement in which corpses were dumped into the river, and Patrick had howled at the name. He had told Snowjob, and Snowjob had loved it, and they had decided to form a club. It was called the Order of the Concrete Kimono, and it had started out with just the four of them in Leverett D-32, and then gone on to include about eight more of their friends. It had been Snowjob's idea that the Order should have a tie, and they had trooped down to the Crimson Men's Shop and designed a tie, which was duly executed for them and delivered. It was almost a parody of a club tie, a string tie of fire-engine red with evenly spaced sets of twin gold horizontal bars, and when they went up to Cronin's en masse to drink beer, the neckties caused a minor sensation among those who prided themselves on knowing every organizational tie in Cambridge. The only rule of the Order was to be vague about the Order. One or two of Patrick's friends in his final club, the Seneca, had tried to take him to task about wearing another tie, and Patrick had told them exactly what they could do about it. Snowjob had encountered the same sort of problem in the exalted heights of the Porcellian, and his reply had been that Pig Club, the original name of the Porcellian, was not one whit more dignified than The Order of the Concrete Kimono. All in all, the Order had been a great, if limited, success, and the only people with a legitimate complaint about it were the members of the Spee, whose colors were also red and gold.

"Still don't drink, Eileen?" Tall Man said with a friendly smile, indicating the ginger ale in Eileen's hand.

"Only wine, Tall Man," Eileen said.

"I ought to give up drinking," Snowjob said, staring lovingly at the scotch and soda in his hand.

"Let's not waste time talking about something that isn't going to happen," Tall Man said. "When are you going up to Maine, Eileen?"

"Well, I think Patrick and I are going to drive up in about a week," Eileen said, "and then Daddy'll fly up a couple of days after that for a week-end, and then I guess he'll come back up a little later for his vacation."

There was a knock on the library door, and Eileen turned her head. Eleanor was in the doorway, wearing her plum-colored uniform and a white apron.

"We'll be right down, Eleanor," Eileen said as she rose. "Why don't both of you bring your drinks along to the table?"

Jacob came into the library, mixed himself a drink over at the little table near the fireplace, and sat down in his easy chair. Down below him he heard the piano playing in the living room, and every now and then Eileen's clear laugh came through. They had all had coffee in the living room tonight instead of up here, because it was an occasion, and Jacob had had coffee, and then about half a brandy, and finally, when Tall Man had begun to play, Jacob had felt that the party was going very nicely, and that he would just as soon retire upstairs.

He sat here now, looking at the ice in his glass and listening to the sounds of conversation and piano music as they floated up the stairs. It was good to hear that piano being played. His wife had played the piano, not nearly as well as Tall Man, but pleasantly, and all that Jacob had ever asked of music was that it be pleasant. When he heard piano music, and gaiety, particularly here, Jacob's mind would find itself still yearning hopelessly for Maude. It was thirteen years since she had died, and twenty-three years since he had met her, but every time he thought about her, as he was thinking about her now, it began with a happy smile, and then the smile faded because she was dead and he didn't want her dead. It hurt when he thought about her, and in a far larger sense than either his colleagues or his children would have guessed, Jacob's memories of Maude were all that he had.

Jacob had been twenty-four when he came back from France, and twenty-six when he had finished his interrupted Law School career. Jacob's sister Emily had died when she was a little girl, and Jacob's mother had died of influenza while he was with the A.E.F., so this left Jacob pretty much in charge of the island, since his father was in Augusta a good percentage of the time, sitting on the Supreme Court of Maine. Jacob went into South Harbor every morning by power boat. He and his friend Roland Grindall composed the entire junior partnership and clerical staff of his father's law office, Oliver Kingsgrant, Esq., Attorney-at-Law, and so Jacob's day broke itself up into the silence of Kingsgrant, and the practice of law on the mainland. In 1924 his father had a heart attack during a session on an income tax case, and Jacob was left really alone, eating dinner by himself in the white-paneled dining room at Kingsgrant, and crossing to South Harbor every morning, no matter what the weather.

So this was the way that matters stood for three years. On the rough afternoons, Bertram, the oldest and huskiest of the Negroes, would pick him up at the wharf in South Harbor, and on the calmer days it would be Benjamin. Benjamin was only fourteen when he started bringing the launch over by himself. Jacob would get off at the pier and walk up the long driveway between the elm trees. The winds out here discouraged almost everything but the fir trees, which clung, short and thick, to the rocky sides of the islands of the Bay. They were damned if they were going to grow straight up into the wind as long as they could grow sidewise. The Kingsgrant elms were in the most protected part of the island, and they had grown up exceedingly arrogant, tall, and beautiful, framing the white house that sat at the top of the drive. Jacob would walk up this drive, smelling the crisp air, and if there was still enough light, he might change into heavier shoes and a sweater, and stroll around his island. He had a wound in his knee from the war, a queer wound that had seemed to heal up perfectly, allowing him to go back into the lines, and had only stiffened up when Jacob was out of the Army and back at the Law School, and if he took the right-length walk before dinner, he could get the stiffness out almost completely for a few hours. He would stride back to the house with a high, healthy pink in his cheeks, almost a boy again, and the sight of him would bring a motherly joy to the heart of Harriet, the colored cook, as she saw him walk past the kitchen and around to the front of the house. Jacob would bathe and change and have his whiskey before dinner, and then he would sit quite alone at the head of his beautiful mahogany dinner table, eating the soup, the entrée, and drinking the wine, as if it were quite unheard of for a person to eat in the company of other people. The hideous portraits of his ancestors stared out at him from their places on the wood panels of the white-painted walls. To a man, they approved of Jacob. One or two of the earliest ancestors, really the ugliest portraits, had been destroyed when the old Kingsgrant, the farmhouse, burned in 1818, but there were still quite enough bony faces left to accompany Jacob through the meal. Then after dinner Jacob would read, and it would be the law that he read, because Jacob loved the law, and loved it more every year. By midnight every weeknight, he was in bed, and not even the stoutest winter storm could shake him from his sleep.

Once a week, usually on Saturday evenings, Jacob would take the launch over to Bar Harbor to have dinner with Henry Wintridge. Henry was a man of about sixty who had retired to his estate, and somehow he was under the impression that Jacob, who was thirty, was his exact contemporary. Jacob did not bother to disabuse him of the idea, since it hardly affected their relationship, which was based on a mutual appreciation of good food, good wines, and chess. Occasionally Jacob would go to one of the balls given in Bar Harbor during the summer, but more often Saturday evening would find his straight back inclined slightly forward as he studied the chessboard.

. . .

One Saturday evening in the spring of 1927 Jacob appeared at Henry Wintridge's little dock, dressed in dinner clothes, and helped Ben make the boat fast. Ben was eighteen now, and Saturday night at the movies in Bar Harbor was the high point of his week. Jacob often suspected that Ben never saw a movie and went straight to the servants' entrance of a house down the road where there was a colored maid, but he was never certain, and would have approved in any case. All he was sure of was that Ben would be on the dock when he wanted to go. Now he smiled and pushed Ben up the ramp ahead of him.

There was a girl at the top of the ramp. She was wearing a suede coat and no hat, and she had her elbows planted on the railing of the pier.

"Hello," she said. The breeze was just moving her hair.

"Good evening." Jacob took off his hat.

As nearly as he could see in this light, she had hair the color of dark honey. Honey-colored hair, and a quite definite tan on her cheeks and her firm, pert nose.

"I'm Maude Buckleigh," the girl said. "Unless you're a pirate, I think we're bound to meet sooner or later this evening."

Jacob smiled in the twilight. Henry had said there would be a few other guests, but Jacob had imagined a roomful of old people more dead than alive. "No, I'm not a pirate," he said. "My name's Jacob Kingsgrant."

"I'm delighted to meet you, Mr. Kingsgrant." Her eyes in this last spark of sunset were an Irish gray, as if the blue in her eyes were trying to turn ever more blue, diamond blue-white, and had settled for this sharp gray. Then she looked at Jacob's black tie. "I haven't dressed yet. Let's go up."

They walked up the wide lawn toward Henry Wintridge's house. The sky was a wonderful luminous blue now, and there was a star out, off to the right. The Bay stood quiet behind them.

"How old are you?" she said, looking up at him.

Jacob missed a step. "Thirty-two."

The girl looked down for a moment as they kept walking in step. "I'm twenty," she said. "I've never met anybody thirty before, I don't think."

Jacob smiled again and looked over at her. "Are you sure?"

"Well, most of the men I meet are boys my age, or else they're *ancient* — you know, parents."

They walked on for a minute.

"Where were you coming from in that motorboat?"

"My house. It's on an island."

"What's it called?"

"Kingsgrant Island."

"Is it all your island, Mr. Kingsgrant?"

"Yes. Unless some pirates have landed this evening."

Maude laughed, a lovely clear laugh on the evening air. "You know, you really *did* look like pirates. Sneaking in — you know, so quiet and sort of businesslike."

"We've been at it a long time," Jacob said. They were at the house now.

"I think I'll go in over there," Maude said, pointing at a door off to one side that would take her upstairs without going past the living room. Through the window, Jacob could see several people in dinner clothes sitting and talking.

"I'll see you in a few minutes?" he asked.

"Yes. You might spill a drink or do parlor tricks or something to give me a little more time to get dressed."

"All right," Jacob said. "I'm a little rusty, but I'll see what I can do."

He grinned and walked into the hall, handing his hat and coat to the butler.

After dinner Jacob was mixing himself a scotch and soda over by the sideboard when he became aware of Maude Buckleigh standing beside him. They had been seated fairly far apart at dinner, and this was the first time they had spoken since she had gone upstairs to dress.

"Will you take a drink?"

"No, thank you," Maude said. She looked around the room. "What does one usually do here after dinner?"

"I don't know about other people," Jacob said, taking a sip of his drink, "but Henry and I usually have a game of chess."

"Can't you have one this evening?"

"Well, usually it's just the two of us for dinner."

Maude looked over to where Henry Wintridge was sitting with the others, her mother among them. He seemed to be entertaining them largely by listening, and occasionally emitting a monosyllabic term of appreciation or endorsement. "Poor man," she said. "I wish I could give you a game, Mr. Kingsgrant, but I don't know how to play."

"Well, perhaps there's something you'd like to do," Jacob said.

"I can play the piano. Do you think it would bother them?"

The piano was a full forty feet away, across the living room, and Jacob decided that half the elderly guests would be too deaf even to know that a piano was being played at all.

"I don't think it would bother them a bit," he said.

"Let's go," Maude whispered, as if they were conspirators, and a minute later she was sitting at the piano. "What do you want to hear?"

"Anything you want to play."

"Here's a new one," she said, and began playing "Sometimes I'm Happy." She looked up at him in the middle of it. "Don't you love it?"

"I've never heard it before."

"You must have. It's all the rage in New York." She started singing it, sweetly and teasingly. She had a pleasant, natural voice, and a warm smile.

"Is New York where you live?" Jacob said when she had finished. He was leaning over the piano, unaware that he was doing so, and his smile had moved on up into his eyes.

"Well, I live there now. I've lived in quite a few places since my father died." Her fingers stroked a few notes from the piano. "I used to live in California."

"Where in California?"

"San Francisco." She looked at Jacob sceptically. "Are you really interested, Mr. Kingsgrant?" .

"Yes, I am."

"Well, I lived in San Francisco, and I went to school out there, and I used to come East for dances and things, and when my father died my mother wanted to get away, so we went to Europe, and then we've been all up and down this coast the last year or so. Maybe you've heard of my father. His name was Donahue Buckleigh."

"I certainly have. . Are you really his daughter?"

"That's what they've always told me." Maude smiled, and then she began to play "Thou Swell." Jacob was fascinated to find the daughter of Donahue Buckleigh here in this quiet evening. He had been one of those minor American legends, a strong man in California. He had helped to build California, and he had built himself a fortune. Everybody had heard of names like Vanderbilt and Rockefeller and Carnegie. You might or might not have heard of some of the California names like Fair and Mackay and Donahue Buckleigh. Jacob had come to know about Buckleigh because of the terrific and classic legal wrangles that he had been forever getting into, and if he had ever imagined Donahue Buckleigh's daughter, he would have pictured a tough old girl of about forty-five.

"I like the way you play," he said.

"Thank you." She gave the keyboard a half-sad, half-loving look, and then she raised her head. "What do you do with yourself, Mr. Kingsgrant? I mean, if you don't mind telling me."

"It's just that there's so little to tell," Jacob said, and then he began telling her. He told her for about ten minutes, about Kingsgrant and going to Harvard and the Army and practicing law in South Harbor, and all the time Maude Buckleigh kept nodding her head and playing softly.

"That sounds like quite a bit to me," she said when he had finished. "All I've ever done is just what you see me doing, and tennis and swimming and things."

"How about school?"

"Don't remind me." She shook her head and closed her lovely eyes. "I was the despair of my teachers. The despair, the despair, the despair. And they were stuck with me because Daddy was practically supporting the school. The only person who thought my diploma was worth anything was Daddy."

Jacob laughed. He had started out thinking that she was an innocent, simple girl. It wasn't innocence, particularly. It was just straightforwardness, and if you didn't like it, too bad. Jacob liked it.

"Well, what are you going to do in the future, Miss Buckleigh?"

Maude stopped playing. "I'll probably get married pretty soon."

Jacob's eyebrows raised slightly, and the girl laughed. "Oh, nobody in particular, Mr. Kingsgrant," she said. "But it seems to be happening to all my friends, and I don't suppose I'm an exception."

Later that evening she insisted on walking down to the dock with him so that she could see the boat pull away. A moon had risen in the sky, and Jacob swung over the gunwale of the launch, his pipe making an ashy orange coal in the darkness.

"Don't get lost," she said. She had put on a black taffeta cape, and it was rustling in the evening wind.

"Don't worry," Jacob said. "It's been a great pleasure, Miss Buckleigh."

"I've enjoyed it too."

"Well," he said. "Let her go, Ben. Good night."

"Good night," Maude said. They backed away and turned out into the night, and she watched the launch spread its wake in the moonlit water.

Jacob went back to Kingsgrant, and once or twice that week, sitting drinking his whiskey before dinner, or standing near the wheel of the launch as it put out from South Harbor, he thought about the girl, and when he thought of her a smile would cross his face. It was not until he came back the next Saturday evening and found Henry Wintridge alone and Maude and her mother gone that he knew he had to see her again.

The library door opened, and Jacob looked up. Patrick had come in, a glass in his hand.

"Everybody happy down there?" Jacob said.

Patrick sat down in an armchair and nodded his head. "I still think it's fantastic that Tall Man never touched a piano until a year and a half ago. Mathematics or no mathematics, I don't see how he got it so quickly." He let his head go back against the chair and looked up at the library ceiling.

"I didn't want to ask you this when the others were around, but how do you think you did for grades?"

Patrick brought his head forward, and straightened up in his chair.

"All right. I think I got four B's. It's hard to tell. I know I got a B in my writing course."

Jacob studied Patrick as he sat there. In this light he could see that Patrick's hair was going right on thinning on top, even though Patrick had stopped swimming a long time ago. Although most of it was gray, his own hair was pretty much intact.

He decided not to say anything about it right now. He had one or two more important things to talk about.

"When do you and Eileen want to go up there?" he said.

Patrick looked down at his glass for a moment.

"I think about Thursday."

"Fine." Jacob hesitated. "I got the impression that you were fairly keen on teaching riding at that camp again this summer."

"I was." Patrick took a sip of his drink.

"Well, I keep having the feeling that there's some reason for your reluctance to spend the summer at Kingsgrant. I mean some reason I don't understand. I'd just as soon have it out."

"If you really want to know what's itching me, it's going into the blueberry factory."

Jacob stood up, leaving his glass on the table by his chair, and walked over to the windows on the west side of the apartment.

"Patrick," he said after a few seconds, turning at the window, "I take seven thousand a year out of there before income taxes. That's my share of the profits, and when I die that'll be your share, give or take a thousand. I think that's worth having one of us be there during the harvest, don't you?"

"All right, but what purpose do I serve by being there? Now, Eileen and I get up there next week. O.K. Then I'll start going over there a good two months before they start canning and start helping them with making boxes, and loading up boxcars for odd loads, and all the rest of it."

"But that won't be every day."

"Maybe not. But my point is, what am I really doing over there? I can operate every machine in that factory right now. I can't fix them but I can operate them. Believe me, Father, you don't have to make boxes for seven weeks to learn how to make boxes." Patrick scratched his cheek. "I knew as much about that job, or the winnower, after one week as I did after seven. I mean, it sounds fine to say one of us ought to be there, but what good does it do?"

Jacob held his hands out in front of him.

"You don't understand, Patrick. Neither one of us thinks you're going to end up working in that factory. It's just that when you're there, you're *there*. You know what's going on. You get the feel of the place and the feel of the business, and later on, when you're practicing law, nobody is going to be able to sell you a bill of goods about what's going on in that factory. You'll *know*. I haven't worked in that place since the summer of 1920, and I still know how things are running the minute I stick my nose in the door. Isn't that something worth having?"

"All right, Father, but you know all these men. Who's going to try to cut you out of your share? You can't stand over every investment you make."

"You can damned well stand over an investment when it's as easy to stand over as this one is," Jacob said. "Your Grandfather Buckleigh did very well out in California as long as he kept his eye on what he was building. Then when he started going into syndicates and losing money right and left he kept thinking there was something wrong with the methods they were all using. His trouble was that he was too trusting. It never occurred to him that some of those syndicates were formed in the first place just to fleece him. When it did occur to him, it was pretty much too late." Jacob sat down and took a swallow of his drink.

"All right, Father," Patrick said. "I'm going to do it."

"I know you're going to do it." Jacob stopped looking so serious, and smiled. "It's just that I wish you could see the reason for it. An absentee landlord can get into some very unrewarding positions."

Patrick smiled. "All right, all right, all right. When are you coming up?"

"I think about the Thursday after that. I'll stay over that week-end and fly down that Monday."

"That sounds good," Patrick said. "Think I'll see how they're doing downstairs."

"I'll probably be in bed pretty soon, so I'll say good night."

"Good night, Father. I'll tell Tall Man to knock it off."

Jacob pulled his watch out of his vest. It was five minutes past ten.

"It seems a little early to make him stop playing," Jacob said.

"No. He's probably had enough anyhow. Good night."

"Good night, Patrick," Jacob said. Patrick went down into the conversation and music. The piano stopped after a minute, and Jacob looked at his glass, decided that he did not want what was left in it, and carried it over to the table where the bottles were. He found himself wondering whether Patrick would ever fully appreciate the value of money, and how much of it he consumed, and then he went out of the library and down the hall to his bedroom.

III

"Well — " Bill Bench said, and he and Patrick shook hands. Eileen was already in the car. She and Patrick had broken up their trip to Maine by staying overnight at the Benches' in Pride's Crossing, and now they were about to leave the whole Boston area behind and pick up the turnpikes that would take them into Maine.

"Thanks again, Bill," Eileen said, "and thank your mother and father again for us."

"Right," Bill said. "Don't break your necks getting up there."

Patrick got into the car. "Thanks a lot, Bill. Take it easy."

"Don't worry," Bill said, smiling. There was a big New-foundland standing beside him, and he bent down and patted the dog's shoulders. "Have a good summer, Eileen."

"I will. You too."

Patrick pressed the starter button, and Chrissy's astoundingly durable engine leaped into action. Patrick waved once, and then moved out.

Eileen looked back and waved as they turned out of the driveway. Bill was in front of the white house, one hand patting the big dog and the other hand waving to them. She smiled and waved once more before she turned her face forward and composed herself for the long pull ahead. She always enjoyed seeing Patrick and Bill together. Bill was an even six feet, almost two inches taller than Patrick, and it was funny to see the way the two would look each other in the eye when they were talking, standing up. Patrick would grudgingly tilt his head back just the slightest bit, and Bill would exaggeratedly tilt his head forward, as if he were talking to somebody a full head shorter. They would stand there, and the whole thing would be a remarkable example of fair skin. Bill had blond hair and blue eyes and clear English skin that tanned well, and Patrick had brown hair and green eyes and one of those pink Irish complexions that left the area just under the eyes noticeably white. They both had straight noses, but one was an English straight nose and one was an Irish straight nose, and you would never mistake one for the other. They were true friends. They had roomed together at Tabor, and at Harvard, and they never worked at being friends. It was just that somewhere in those years of living together they had come to understand that each had a standing offer out to the other to give him the shirt off his back, or, a bit more practically, to loan him one of the clean shirts in the top drawer. Bill was a staunch Episcopalian, and occasionally they would lace into each other about religion, but except for that they backed each other up and down the line.

"Could you put your side vent out?" Patrick said. "I know

it seems silly when the top's down, but I think it does make a difference."

"Sure," Eileen said, coming out of her thoughts about Bill and Patrick, and the car went on toward Maine.

IV

On Saturday morning Jacob found a telegram sitting at the breakfast table. It was resting on top of his *New York Times*, and Jacob drank his orange juice and then opened the telegram. It said ALL WELL KINGSGRANT   PATRICK CHECKED CANNERY STARTING PRESEASON WORK THERE SOON   CAN YOU BRING MY BROWN EVENING DRESS   TURNS OUT EVANS PARTY INVITATIONS WERE HERE   EXPECTING YOU FLIGHT 104 THURSDAY   LOVE FROM ALL   EILEEN.

Jacob put the telegram back in its envelope, stuck it in his inside pocket, and sat there. All well Kingsgrant. And he was glad that the children had been invited to the Evanses' party after all. The Evanses were giving a ball for their granddaughter Sarah, and evidently it was going to be the biggest thing in Northeast Harbor since the Twenties.

The maid came in with his soft-boiled egg. Jacob went after it methodically, ate two pieces of toast, and then began reading the *Times* as he started on his coffee.

Halfway down the right-hand column of the front page he laughed out loud. Jacob went through periods of being bored with the *Times*, but every now and then it put its musclebound tongue in its cheek, and the result was usually delightful. They were describing the President's trip out to a reunion of the Thirty-Fifth Division in St. Louis. There was a picture of President Truman talking to a sailor on his early morning walk. That was at the top of the page, but what had Jacob beaming was nearer the center of the page. In the afternoon, the *Times* said, President Truman drove a coach and four on the estate of Gustavus Busch, of the noted brewing family. The estate encompassed the land farmed by Ulysses S. Grant when he failed as a farmer before going on to be a general and President.

Jacob took a sip of his coffee and stared thoughtfully at the tablecloth. All well Kingsgrant, he thought, and then he went back to the *Times* as it quietly took President Truman apart.

3

PATRICK PARKED his car on the gravel near the siding for freight cars and got out. He put the ignition key in his pocket and started walking toward the office. Nothing had changed. The weather-beaten shingled buildings stood quiet in the early morning, and Patrick could hear his footsteps echoing against their sides. The whole thing looked more like a set of connected barns than the popular conception of a factory. Patrick had never forgotten Bill Bench's disappointment when he first saw the cannery. Bill had evidently been expecting Willow Run, and instead he had seen some barns and sheds that looked as if they might topple over in a storm.

Patrick went up the wooden steps to the office. Luther Allen was sitting there on a wooden chair, studying a piece of paper. Patrick looked at his watch. Luther was early, as he always was. The day that Luther Allen was merely on time, the world would stop revolving.

"Good morning, Mr. Allen," Patrick said.

" 'Lo theyah, Patrick," Mr. Allen said. He stood up, and they shook hands. Patrick smiled at him, and kept his mouth shut. It was hard for Patrick to keep his mouth shut, but Luther Allen was the plant manager, and every time in the past that Patrick had had a bright idea, it had meant that he ended up working hours longer. You don't know it, Mr. Allen, Patrick thought, standing there at a quarter to eight in the morning, but this summer I have no suggestions. Pile the boxes your way. Stack the cans your way.

"Have a good year?" Mr. Allen said.

"Fine thank you, Mr. Allen. How about you?"

" 'Bout the same." Mr. Allen ran his hand across his chin. "Got Myron Grey comin' ovah. The pickin' tables are wiggly. That's the first thing we've got to fix."

There was a wild roar of machinery outside, and Patrick went to the window. Myron Grey was arriving in his souped-up Model A coupé. Myron eased himself out of the car and came strolling toward them. He had on a gray workshirt like Patrick's, and bluejeans, while Patrick had on khaki pants.

"Hi theyah, Patrick," he said, coming up the steps in his relaxed bounce. "How's it goin'?"

"Fine, thanks. How've you been?"

"Pretty good, I guess." They shook hands. "They teachin' you much up theyah?"

"Some." Patrick smiled. "You just graduated, didn't you?"

Myron nodded. "Only thing I'll miss about high school is playin' basketball."

"What are you going to do now?"

"They've got some construction jobs over to Ellsworth. Might get one of them."

Patrick nodded.

"Let's take a look at those tables," Luther Allen said, picking up some keys from the surface of the desk, and they followed him out the door and down the steps.

II

Eileen came down the stairway into the white-paneled hall. Harriet was standing by the door with a raincoat.

"It's clouding over, Miss Eileen," she said, holding out the raincoat so that Eileen could slip into it.

"Where's the wind coming from?" Eileen said, standing just inside the door and buttoning the tan raincoat over her dark green plaid wool dress.

"From the southeast. Sure you don't want Bertram to take you down to the landing in the car?"

"No." Eileen smiled as Harriet opened the wide white door for her, and looked at her watch. "Daddy's plane gets in at four at Bar Harbor, so we ought to be back here by five-thirty easily. Let's have supper at seven." She stepped out onto the top step and nodded as she looked at the gray clouds piling low.

"I'll have it ready at seven. Mind you don't drive too fast, Miss Eileen."

"Don't worry." Eileen smiled and then turned down the front steps. She took one more look at the sky, and then started walking down the gravel drive that ran between the two rows of elms to the landing four hundred yards away. She walked quickly, with her hands in the pockets of her raincoat, but there was a peaceful expression on her face. When she came around the bend in the drive she could see the pier framed at the bottom of the arch of trees, with the powerboat, the *Ethan Kingsgrant*, tied to it, and Ben kneeling on top of the cabin, doing something to the searchlight. Eileen moved toward it, looking at her watch again and trying to figure out if there was time enough to swing past the cannery on her way over to Bar Harbor and see if Patrick had finished work. She decided that there wasn't quite enough time.

" 'Afternoon, Ben," she called as she passed the last of the elms and crossed the few remaining feet of gravel onto the dock.

"All set to go, Miss Eileen," Ben said, and as if to prove his point he crawled to the side of the cabin roof and leaned over its edge and into the window, pulling the engine throttle. The engine immediately stopped idling and roared.

Eileen went down the ramp and onto the float. "Engine sounds fine, Ben," she said, stepping over the gunwale and onto the seat of the cockpit. Another step took her to the floor of the cockpit. Ben jumped from the roof of the cabin to the dock, landing with his knees bent and looking for a moment like an ape in denim clothes.

"Engine's fine," he said over his shoulder as he went forward and cast off the bowline. Eileen cast off the stern line, and a second later Ben swung into the cockpit and started backing the *Ethan Kingsgrant* away. "Engine's got a new exhaust hose, cabin's got a new coat of varnish, searchlight's got a new bulb, everything's just right," he said half to himself and half to Eileen, who was sitting on the red-cushioned bench that ran the length of the port side of the cockpit. In a moment the launch's bow fell out toward the mainland, and Ben started accelerating the engine. They picked up speed and when they were out in the open water, with the spray flying and the engine at three-quarters speed, Ben turned around and smiled at Eileen, his white teeth brilliant in his strong black face. She smiled back, both of them enjoying the bounce and buffet of the run in the wind, and the beginnings of groundswell in this part of the Bay. Then Ben turned back to the spray-covered window of the pilot house, beaming when he thought of Miss Eileen in the wind, with her hair flying and the smile on her face.

They came alongside the landing at South Harbor and Eileen nodded when she saw that the garage had brought the station wagon down to the pier for her.

"Don't bother tying up!" she yelled, and was standing on the float before Ben knew what had happened. "Remind Bertram to have the car at the landing a little before five-thirty, and you'd better be here about five."

"Five o'clock. Yes, Miss Eileen. Mind you don't drive too fast." The words came from across a little distance of water as Ben idled the engine and the powerboat sat with her bow again pointed toward the island.

"Don't worry," Eileen called, and then she started up the ramp toward the car. There was a note on the dashboard. "Eileen. Car is washed, greased, oil changed, tires rotated and checked, gas, oil, and batteries. Everything else is O.K." Eileen smiled as she read the note, and then she got into the car. I can hardly wait until he asks me if I've had the car looked at, she thought, and a few moments later she was on her way to meet the plane.

Eileen had parked the station wagon at the airport, and now she stood by the wooden railing at the edge of the landing strip. There was a good-sized hangar to her left, and a half-dozen small private planes sitting on the concrete near her. To her right was the small building that combined being an office downstairs and a control tower on top. Other cars were arriving now, and their occupants were coming up to the rail too, all of them looking up at the tan clouds that hung quietly above them. It was the sort of silent summer brittleness that comes before a thunderstorm, but Eileen was not the least bit worried about her father. If Jacob Kingsgrant was on a plane, the plane would come in on schedule. Eileen stood there, more formally dressed than the vacationers from Bar Harbor and Northeast, an erect figure by the rail. She had unbuttoned her raincoat, and her green wool dress was a sharp contrast to the shorts and shirts around her.

The sound of a plane came out of the sky, and a few moments later the plane slid through the beige clouds. It touched down smoothly, and a minute later there was her father walking toward her in a felt hat and a gray business suit, with a briefcase under one arm and a raincoat just the shade of Eileen's hung over the other.

Eileen went up and kissed him on the cheek.

"Hi, Daddy."

"Hello, dear." Jacob smiled down at his daughter. He had taken off his hat just as they came together. "I've got your dress checked with my suitcase."

They went into the little building and a couple of minutes later they were walking toward the station wagon, with Jacob carrying his suitcase, and Eileen holding the big blue box that had her dress in it.

Jacob took one look at the station wagon.

"Car practically sparkles," he said as he got in behind the wheel of the car. "Well, tell me everything."

As he drove along the roads he knew by heart, Eileen told him. The house was fine, and the corn looked as if it was going to be unusually good this summer, and Harriet and Bertram and Moonstone, Ben's Richmond-born wife, were all fine, and Ben was fine too.

"That's good," Jacob said, his eyes on the road. "Now, how are you?"

"Just fine."

"How's Patrick?"

"Fine. He started over at the factory today. I guess I told you that in the telegram."

Jacob nodded. "Do they know yet how much work they've got to do before the harvest starts?"

"I don't think so. Patrick said something about Mr. Allen's wanting him every day for two weeks anyhow. Daddy, I don't think Patrick likes the idea of working on Saturdays very much."

"Well, maybe by working Saturdays they can straighten up the place in a hurry." Jacob smiled. "You know, everybody in this country used to work on Saturdays. The Bible says to take the Sabbath off. It doesn't say anything about week-ends."

"Yes, Daddy, but the Sabbath was Saturday, wasn't it?"

"I guess it was," Jacob said. "All I'm trying to say is that they were not specifically against the six-day week. I work at home on Saturdays."

"Daddy, as far as that goes, I think you work a nine-day week," Eileen said, and the car kept shooting along the tar road toward South Harbor.

They came into town, and Jacob started to wave to the people he knew. He was smiling again as he pulled the car to a stop outside his old law office. The office was upstairs, over the grocery store, and on the window it still said "Kingsgrant and Grindall, Attorneys-at-Law," although it had been a long time since a Kingsgrant had worked there.

Jacob got out of the car. "Rolly!" he cried out, just once, in the way that a man trained in public speaking can shout without seeming to raise his voice, and a few seconds later the window flew open.

"Jake! Eileen told me you were going to be here."

Jacob stood in the street, his hat tilted a little bit back on his head, and looked up at his old partner. "How's it going?"

"Pretty busy, Jake." The bushy head of hair pushed back inside the window for a second and then reappeared. "Say, Jake," Roland Grindall said, gesturing toward the station wagon with the stem of his pipe. "I read your brief in that antitrust suit. That was damned smart work."

Jacob beamed. "Thanks, Rolly. But there were a lot of people in on that."

"That's all right. I heard your voice talking all the way through that thing."

"Well — how's Marjorie?"

"Fine thanks, Jake."

"I'll be in to see you tomorrow."

"Be expecting you. 'Bye, Eileen," Roland Grindall said, this being his first acknowledgment of the fact that Eileen was in the car, and closed the window.

"That's a fine office," Jacob said, getting back in behind the wheel. "Think I'll ask Rolly tomorrow morning if he'd consider taking Patrick on for a while when he gets out of the Law School." He looked at his daughter. "Think he might?"

"Do I think he might! Grandfather started the office, and then you — I think there'd *better* be room for Patrick." Eileen had been caught up in her father's enthusiasm, and then, just as Jacob pulled the car to a stop at the dock, and Ben came toward them, beaming at Jacob, Eileen thought of Patrick in that office. She couldn't imagine Patrick's spending the winter in that office as Roland Grindall's law clerk.

"Come on, Eileen, you don't want to spend the night in the car, do you?" Her father was holding the door open for her.

"Sorry, Daddy. I was thinking about something else."

They stood near Ben as the *Ethan Kingsgrant* slammed through the waves. It had started to get really rough, but Jacob stood there in his raincoat, with his hat in his hand, and as Eileen watched him looking out toward his island, smiling as it came nearer, it was as if the years were being washed from his face by the wind and the salt spray, leaving the young man who had been content to live at Kingsgrant and practice law in South Harbor until something happened that took him away.

Bertram was standing on the float, and the '38 Ford station wagon that served mainly as a truck around the island was sitting down at the bottom of the drive.

Jacob waved, and then he and Eileen stepped off the boat even before Bertram had tied up the bowline that Ben had tossed him.

"Hello, Mr. Jacob," Bertram said as he secured the line.

"Hello, Bert. How are you?"

"Fine, thank you."

Jacob stood there on the dock, watching Ben as he made fast the stern line. "She's going to blow tonight, Ben," he said casually, looking up at the gray scudding clouds.

"Yes, sir. I'm setting out extra fenders."

"That's the stuff." Jacob watched Ben hand the suitcase and the box that held Eileen's dress over the gunwale to Bertram, and then they started toward the car. "I'll drive it up, Bert," he said, getting in. "You just put those things in the back, and then you can help Ben batten the boat down."

"Yes, sir."

Jacob started the car. The engine coughed and the starter whined and whinnied and the engine puffed into life.

"Let's go, Eileen," Jacob said. "If this car's going to fall apart, I'd rather have it fall apart up by the house."

Eileen looked over at her father as the car made its way up the drive between the elms. She felt happy to see him sitting here again, and there was no doubt that he loved being back. She saw his face light up as the house came into view, framed in the arch of elms at the top of the drive, and in another minute Jacob was home.

III

"It's a fairyland," Eileen said. "It's really a fairyland."

Patrick nodded as they looked over the water. Ben was bringing them in to the Evanses' pier at Northeast Harbor, and Patrick was in complete agreement that he had never seen such a beautiful man-made effect in this part of the world. It was half-past eleven, and the lights from the big house and the gardens played out golden on the still water as they came sliding in closer to the shore. Ben was trying to keep his mind on his work, but every now and then he looked with a

child's stare at the myriad Japanese lanterns in the gardens.
There were several other launches tied up to the float, and
there were two men there to make fast the lines that they
flung out.

Patrick helped Eileen over the side in her gold stole and
brown tulle evening dress, and then he turned to Ben.

"I guess they'll probably bring you a drink or something
down here, Ben," he said. "I'll bring you one anyhow. I'm
afraid it's going to be a long wait."

"I don't mind waiting here, Mr. Patrick," Ben said, smiling,
and Patrick followed Eileen as she went up the ramp. They
walked up through the formal gardens to the house. There
were Japanese lanterns all over the place, casting down a lovely
golden glow, and here and there in the soft light there were
boys and girls wandering around, some of them with glasses of
champagne in their hands. Ahead of them they could see a
marquee for dancing just beside the house. There were dozens
of couples turning on the polished floor under the big striped
tent, and the sounds of the orchestra came down to them.
They were playing "It Was Just One of Those Things."

They went into the house while Eileen left her stole, and
then through the receiving line. Finally they made their way
to the marquee and began dancing. After about ten steps a
Princeton friend of Eileen's who was spending the summer at
Blue Hill cut in. Patrick did a couple of his least promising
duty dances, the ones he always did early in the evening to
avoid being stuck later on, and then he and Eileen and another
friend of Eileen's found themselves sitting at one of the small
white-covered tables on the lawn.

"Good champagne," Eileen said, tasting her first sip of the
evening.

"Damned good," Patrick said, swallowing about half the
glass.

A girl came walking out of the house and crossed the terrace.

She had a tall young man in a white dinner jacket with her, but neither Patrick nor Eileen nor anyone else noticed the young man. The girl was a blonde, a striking girl with a lovely, intelligent face that had a full mouth and high cheekbones. She was tanned, and she was wearing a pale blue satin dress.

"What a girl," Patrick said.

"What a dress," Eileen said. They sat there as the girl went by, moving simply and gracefully. "That's about the five-foot-seven category you like, Pat," Eileen said.

"I think I used to see that girl at dances in New York."

"Why didn't you cut in on her, Pat? She certainly looks worth it."

"As I recall, I was rather awed," Patrick said, taking another sip of his champagne, his eyes following the girl as she and her partner went out onto the dance floor. "A lot of those beautiful girls used to scare me, particularly if I didn't know them from somewhere else."

"Still awed?" Eileen said, smiling.

Patrick looked out toward the dancing. "I guess I probably am," he said, still looking out there.

"Have some tiger juice, tiger," Eileen said, and took two more glasses from a tray that was being passed by a waiter.

Patrick circled around the edge of the dance floor a couple of times, pretending to himself that he was just looking around, but his eyes kept coming back to the tanned blonde in the blue dress. She had wonderful-looking shoulders, and a dignified way of carrying her head, and after a minute or so Patrick began to know that he was going to cut in on that girl, no matter what happened, and no matter how big an ass he made of himself.

All right, if you're going to do it, do it, Patrick said to himself, and he strode out onto the dance floor and tapped the shoulder of the tall young man with the blonde. The young man wheeled and disappeared, and Patrick and the young lady in the blue dress were facing each other.

"Hello," Patrick said.

"Hello," the girl said, and they began dancing. "I think you may have done yourself a disservice," she said after a second, and smiled. She had a cold expression when her face was in repose, but when she spoke, her face lit up, and her voice was surprisingly low and warm.

"How do you mean?" Patrick smiled back.

"Well, I mean I don't know many of the people here."

"That was before this evening," Patrick said. "Where do you come from?"

"New York. Usually I spend the summers in Tuxedo, but this summer I decided to take a job up here."

"What kind of a job?"

"Taking care of kids. It's all very informal. There're these friends of my family over on Walker's Pond, and I sort of hang around and take care of their two children."

The orchestra had just switched to a samba, which was high on the list of steps that Patrick had never learned.

"I'm not very good at these South American things," he said. "Do you mind if we sit down?"

"Not at all," the blonde answered, and they went off the dance floor in the direction of the champagne bar. On their way off, Patrick passed Eileen, and Eileen gave him a wink and a broad smile. Patrick picked a glass of champagne off the white cloth and handed it to the girl, and then picking up a glass for himself, followed her as they made their way to an empty table.

"Well," the girl said, sitting down. "I don't think we ever found out each other's name."

"I'm Patrick Kingsgrant."

"I'm Anna van Neerdaam."

Patrick nodded, and offered her some cigarettes that were in a glass in the center of the small round table.

"No, thanks," the girl said. "I don't."

"Neither do I."

"My father thinks that smoking is a messy habit, and that drinking is a clean one," Anna van Neerdaam said, and smiled.

Patrick grinned. "I never thought of it that way."

"Well, it doesn't hold up too well if you go in for drinks that have a lot of garbage in them."

"What's your idea of a clean drink?"

"Beer," the blonde said.

Patrick looked at her. "Do you really like beer?"

"Um. Don't you?"

"Yes, but —"

"I drink other things," she said, holding up the glass of champagne, "but beer and I get along pretty well. Did you think I was the sherry type?"

"I don't know."

The blonde smiled. "I suppose I don't like sherry because I've had a lot of it thrust at me here and there." She dismissed the subject with a turn of her hand. "Where do you come from, Patrick?"

"Well, we own a place up here, and in the winter I live in New York, and I go to Harvard."

"What class?"

"I'll be a senior next year."

"So will I, at Bryn Mawr," Anna said. "Do you know Snowjob Porter? I think he's in your class."

"Do I know him!" Patrick exploded. "He's one of my roommates! How'd you know him?"

"Well, he used to go around with a girl at college. Kitsy Townsend."

"Sure, I've met her. That was quite a thing."

"I'm glad he thought so," Anna said, and took a sip of her champagne. "How'd he ever get the name Snowjob?"

"I don't know," Patrick said. "He arrived from Groton with that name hooked to him. He could never shake it."

"I don't think he wanted to shake it, anyhow. What kind of things do you do up there?"

"Well, I major in English, and I'm in a couple of clubs and things, and I'm on the *Lampoon.*"

"What do you do for them?"

"Well, I write things."

"Patrick Kingsgrant," the girl said to herself. "You're PK," she said, suddenly, turning her face toward him. "You wrote the thing about the rabbits, and the one about the calculating machine."

"That's right," Patrick said, beaming.

"Well, I've read all those things," the girl said. "Some of the girls get it down at school."

"I'll be damned," Patrick said. "I never knew anybody really read the magazine." He was grinning from ear to ear.

"I liked your things." Anna said. "Are you seriously interested in writing?"

Patrick involuntarily smiled down at the tablecloth. He had heard that tone of voice before when something like becoming a poet, or a painter, or a writer was mentioned. It was a combination of the curious and the dubious.

"Well, I've been taking writing courses all the way through. I don't know how interested I really am, to tell you the truth. And then there's the question of supporting yourself on it."

"Couldn't you get some help from your family when you started out?"

"Not *my* family," Patrick said. He was still smiling. "My father wants me to be a lawyer, and that's that. I think there's about a fifty-fifty chance I'll go to the Law School when I get out of Harvard."

The girl nodded approvingly. "Well, it's good training no matter what you do."

"That's what I hear," Patrick said. "What do you major in?"

"History," the blonde said. "I know it sounds awful, but it really isn't."

The music had switched back to a foxtrot.

"Would you like to dance?"

"Love it," Anna van Neerdaam said, and they made their way back to the dance floor.

The local team knew a good thing when they saw it. Patrick danced exactly six steps with Anna before someone cut in, and Patrick made his way to a table where Eileen was sitting with three other people.

"You won't believe this," Patrick said, pulling a chair up next to Eileen, "but she's a *fan* of mine. I didn't think anybody read the *Lampoon*, and she's a fan of mine."

"She certainly is attractive," Eileen said, handing Patrick what was left of her glass of champagne. "Have some more tiger juice."

At a quarter past six the next morning Patrick was in a kitchen on Walker's Pond watching Anna van Neerdaam, in her evening dress, make scrambled eggs, and he still didn't know quite how it had happened. Somewhere during the course of the evening he had discovered that Anna had come over to Bar Harbor in her own car, and that the young man she had first walked in with had just been her partner at a dinner, and nothing more. At about a quarter to four Patrick had gone over to Eileen.

"When this thing breaks up, I'm going to take her home."

"In *what?*" Eileen had said.

"Her car."

"Well, what happens to the boy that brought her?"

"He was just somebody from a dinner party before the dance. She got invited because she knows Sarah Evans's married sister, you know, that one that isn't here, but she doesn't have anybody really with her."

Eileen had looked out at the dance floor. "She seems to be doing all right." She turned to Patrick. "But how are you going to get back out to the island? How are you going to get to work? How are you going to get anywhere if you're over there by Walker's Pond somewhere?"

"I'll work it out," Patrick had said, and Eileen had pointed toward the coffee urn on the buffet table.

"I'd suggest about a gallon of that," she had said, and started talking to somebody else.

Now Patrick was sitting on a stool in the kitchen of this lodge-like house at the edge of the lake, and he was not feeling the least bit sleepy.

"So what happened then?" Anna said.

"Well, the jury acquitted her."

"Even after all the eyewitnesses?"

"She was a pretty woman, and after all, the man had promised to marry her."

"And what was her name again?"

"Laura Fair. You sure you don't need some help?"

"No, thanks." Anna's hand kept moving the fork in the frying pan. "And this was all in San Francisco?"

Patrick nodded. "My mother had a lot of stories like that. They weren't very conventional stories to learn at your mother's knee, but I always enjoyed them. I never *have* thought the jury was wrong, really."

"Well, if your father's a lawyer, what did he think?"

"He thought they should have strung her up. But after all, she wasn't a murderess, she was just a woman who'd been given a bad deal."

"Laura Fair," Anna said, starting to scoop the scrambled eggs from the frying pan onto the two plates. "What a wonderful name. You can pour the coffee if you want to, and I'll butter the toast."

They went into the living room, which was a high-ceilinged room made of polished yellow timbers. There was a huge stone fireplace, and there were still a few ashes smoking from the fire that had burned there all the evening before.

"It gets awfully cold on this lake at night," Anna said, putting down her plate and throwing some kindling onto the ashes with a series of deft motions. "Could you bring one of those logs over here?"

Patrick got a log from the opened woodbox and brought it over, setting it down on top of the smoking remnants of the fire. Anna stuffed in some newspapers from the pile that sat to the left of the fireplace, and in a minute they were both sitting in front of the beginnings of a fire.

They sat there and ate the eggs and drank the coffee and talked. Patrick didn't have to ask her where she had been all his life. The more she talked, the more he knew very well where she had been all his life. She had been to Chapin, a shy girl at Chapin, and then she had gone to Bryn Mawr, and the shyness had disappeared somewhere along the line.

"I think it's the History that got me over it," she said, taking a sip of her coffee. "It gave me that habit of asking questions, but it got me out of my shell. But I really do care about the answers to the questions I ask. I have a passion for information."

A passion for information, Patrick thought. That wasn't a bad phrase. He loved her voice, and a lot of the things she said. She had the New York accent that rose above that pretentious product with the slurring and the *r*'s turned on their sides, she had the real thing, and she was the real thing. She had told him about her family coming to New York from

Holland in the 1600's, and over the years, marrying a considerable number of other burghers and patroons like themselves. When she said she came from New York, she meant it. Only those worst of realtors, the Manhattan Indians, could mean it more.

"Where do you live in New York?" Patrick said, after they had been silent for a minute.

"West Eleventh Street. Seventeen West Eleventh."

Patrick beamed. That really tied it up. No Park Avenue, no Fifth Avenue, no Sutton Place. West Eleventh Street, and the hell with it.

Anna studied the look on Patrick's face. "We had the house there when Eleventh Street was pretty far uptown, and then we decided ——"

"You decided what the hell," Patrick said.

"Well, yes." She looked at Patrick's face in the combination of firelight and gray dawn, and then she smiled. "You really *do* understand, don't you?"

"Yes," Patrick said, "I understand."

They talked about politics and discovered to no one's surprise that they were both Republicans, and they talked about people they both knew in Tuxedo, and they talked about people that Patrick had known back in the Knickerbocker Greys, and suddenly Patrick looked at his watch.

"It's five after seven," he said. "Look ——" he stopped. It was suddenly hitting him that he was here in his dinner clothes, and in fifty-five minutes he was supposed to start work at the factory, twenty miles away. "Look, Anna, do you think you could lend me your car until lunchtime? Then I can get somebody from the factory to follow me over here in his car, and bring yours back to you."

"Don't be silly," Anna said, standing up and picking up both of their empty plates. "I'll take you over there. I've been planning to, the whole time. Just give me a minute to change out of this dress."

Patrick opened his mouth to make some polite protest, but his sense of humor came to the rescue. It was obviously the best solution.

"All right, if you don't mind. I promise you I appreciate it."

"And I appreciated your bringing me back here. I think my chances of being robbed are slimmer in broad daylight than they were then."

"I think your chances of being robbed around here are small to begin with." Patrick said.

"Maybe you're right, but some of those stretches where you're just going through woods give me the creeps." She piled the coffee cups on top of the plates, and disappeared out to the kitchen.

Anna's car was a Chevrolet convertible, and she had put the top down before they started over. Now they came bouncing into the area by the siding, and Patrick got out. He could see Luther Allen and Myron Grey standing on the platform outside the warehouse, looking at him. There were a couple of other men there, too, which meant that they were going to load the boxcar that had been brought in yesterday. Patrick thought of a day of loading cases of cans from last year's harvest on box-cars, shrugged his shoulders, and got out.

"Well, thanks again," he said. He couldn't help staring at her, even after all these hours. She had changed into a simple sweater and skirt, and even after staying up all night her cheeks had a healthy glow. If she was beautiful now, she was a beautiful girl.

"It's been good meeting you, Patrick," Anna said.

"Can I come over and see you sometime?"

"Come over anytime you want to," Anna said, and then she

gestured toward the loading platform with her head. "I think we're attracting attention."

Patrick looked up. The men on the platform were not even pretending to do anything else. They were just staring.

"Good-bye," Patrick said.

"Good-bye, Patrick." She put the car into reverse, turned it around, and moved out. Patrick watched the car go, and then, dressed in his black trousers, white dinner jacket, and with his bow tie still in place, he came walking toward the loading platform.

"You got some overalls there, boy," somebody said, and Patrick smiled. He took off his dinner jacket as he walked toward them, and took off his tie.

"Good morning, Mr. Allen," he said, coming up the steps. " 'Morning, Myron."

" 'Mornin'," Luther Allen said, with little pellets of dry ice in his voice, and started talking to one of the other men.

"I've got a shirt you can use in my car, Patrick," Myron Grey said. "It's beat-up, but it's better'n workin' in that thing."

Patrick looked down at his white shirt front. It was wet through and wrinkled, but the onyx studs were there, and the onyx links in his cuffs.

"That's a damned good idea," he said.

"I'll get it out of the car," Myron said, and then he came closer. "Listen, boy," he said, smiling, "Don't let Luther bother you none. If I'd been out with that, I never would have got here at all."

That evening Myron dropped Patrick off at South Harbor. Ben had the launch waiting for him, and Patrick flopped down on the seat and stared at the sky as the boat moved across the water. There wasn't much left of him after working at the cannery the day before and staying up all night and working all today on the boxcars, but he felt peaceful. When the boat pulled in at the island, Patrick came walking up the drive, his white dinner jacket slung over his shoulder and a smile on his face.

He came in the front door and there was his father.

"I'd like to talk to you for a moment," Jacob said, quietly, and Patrick followed him into the living room. The living room was white like the dining room, but in here the furniture and the decorations had been relaxed.

Jacob sat down on the edge of the desk that sat over by the inside wall, near the fireplace.

"I hear you made quite a display of yourself at work today."

Patrick sat down. His heart was beating faster, as it always did when he heard that note come into his father's voice.

"What did you hear?"

"I heard that you arrived for work this morning dressed in dinner clothes, in a convertible driven by some blonde."

"That's substantially correct," Patrick said.

"What kind of an impression do you think that made on the people over there?"

"I don't know," Patrick said. "Did anybody say that I didn't work just as hard as the next man?"

Jacob opened his mouth, and then he closed it. "No," he said after a few seconds. "But something like that doesn't look well."

"All right," Patrick said. "It won't happen again. It's never happened before, and it won't happen again."

"I just don't think it looks well, at eight in the morning. Did you ruin your dinner clothes?"

"No, I don't think so. Myron Grey gave me a shirt to wear, and the only things of mine I wore working were the pants and shoes."

"How are they?"

"Pretty sweated up. How did you think they'd be?"

"You get that fresh tone *out* of your voice!" Jacob stood up. "You're on the carpet, not me."

"Yes, Father," Patrick could feel himself breathing hard.

"I never thought I had to tell you that besides learning over there, you're supposed to be a credit to us, but now consider yourself told. Do you want to be a joke over there? You know, men don't work better for somebody they're laughing at, no matter what you think. That story is all over the county right now."

"All right, Father. I can't do anything about it now."

"No, but you can profit from the lesson. That's one thing about you, Patrick, I'm not sure you profit from lessons."

"Have you been sitting out here all day just building up to hit me with this?" They both stayed there, Patrick sitting stiff and Jacob standing, both of them staring right at each other.

"All right," Jacob said after a minute. "I've said everything I have to say."

"I'm going to wash up," Patrick said. He stood up.

"Fine," Jacob turned away and walked over toward the bookshelves at the far end of the room.

4

PATRICK SWUNG his car into the drive of the house on Walker's Pond where Anna van Neerdaam was staying. He didn't have the faintest idea of whether she'd be there, and whether there would be other young men calling on her if she were, but anyway, he was there. It was Sunday afternoon, and it had been nine days since the evening of the Evans party. In that time his father had gone back down to New York, and work at the cannery had stopped, not to start up again for a few weeks, until the farmers began bringing in their berries. Patrick had not mentioned Anna in the three days after his run-in with his father, and Jacob had left without bothering to ask Patrick or Eileen her name. Now, with the unexpected bonanza of work being over, Patrick was coming up the drive, a little curious to see if the whole thing had been an illusion, but convinced that a certain amount of good fortune was on his side. His father had evidently forgotten the dinner-clothes-in-the-cannery incident, work was over for probably a month, and this afternoon the sky over his top-down convertible was a lovely blue. If only there would *not* be four Princeton men sitting around Anna van Neerdaam. There was no way of calling up, since the Prestons, who owned the house, did not have a telephone, so he was coming in blind. Blind, and interested.

Patrick parked the car in front of the big log lodge and went up to the front door. He knocked on it, and a pleasant-looking woman came to the door.

"Yes?" she said.

"I'm a friend of Anna van Neerdaam's," Patrick said. "I was wondering if she was in."

"I'm Louise Preston," the woman said. "Come on in. I'm sure Anna's around here somewhere."

"I'm Patrick Kingsgrant," Patrick said, and followed Mrs. Preston through an open corridor that led between the kitchen and the living room, out to a terrace.

"I think you'll find her down there," Mrs. Preston said.

"Thank you." Patrick saw a couple of figures on a tiny strip of beach about fifty yards away, and went down off the flagstoned terrace and picked up a trail that led along the shore, twisting among birch trees.

Anna was sitting on the sand in a red bathing suit. There was a little girl sitting with her, in a bathing suit too, and the two were talking and laughing at something.

"Hi," Patrick said, and they both looked up.

"Hi, Patrick," Anna said, and Patrick stepped down onto the sand beside them. "This is Mary Preston, and that's her brother Joe out there in that rowboat."

"Hi, Mary," Patrick said.

"This is Patrick Kingsgrant," Anna said to the girl, and the girl nodded gravely.

"Hi," she said after a couple of seconds.

"I hope I'm not interrupting anything," Patrick said.

"We're just spending a typical afternoon," Anna said, and then her face became serious for a second. "Except there was one thing on the radio. I don't know anything about Korea, but anyhow, the North Koreans have attacked the South Koreans."

"That's out near Manchuria, isn't it? What is it, some kind of civil war or something?"

"I guess so. It was just a bulletin. It didn't say very much." Anna stood up, and Patrick could not help looking at her figure in that red bathing suit. She had a generous body, fuller than it had looked in the evening dress. "How about a swim?"

"Sounds good."

"We could get you one of Mr. Preston's suits."

"No, I've got one in the car. I'll get it."

"Do you want a drink or anything?"

"No thanks, Anna," Patrick said. "I'll get my suit, and maybe I'll take you up on the drink later. Where can I change?"

"Oh. Mrs. Preston'll show you. O.K.?"

"Perfect," Patrick said, and went off down the path, after his bathing suit.

II

Jacob was strolling around the roof in the afterglow of the sunset, one hand hooked in his vest pocket and the other curled around the bowl of his pipe. He came to a halt for a moment, looking out toward the Triborough Bridge. It was the Fourth of July, Jacob had not been able to get up to Kingsgrant because of a sudden press of work that had developed while the other two senior partners were taking their vacations, and so he stood here, listening to the firecrackers going off in the city below him and thinking about this thing in Korea.

Jacob took the pipe out of his mouth, and his mouth reformed itself in a hard, tight line, as it always did when he thought about warfare. It had made him angry when he had heard some of these fellows at lunch the past week saying there wouldn't be a draft. Of course there'd be a draft. It didn't make any difference what they called it, it was a war. Jacob sighed once, and straightened up to his full height. Thank God Patrick's arm will keep him out of it, he said to himself for the thirtieth time. Jacob had been thinking about this war all through his solitary dinner in the apartment, and now, with the evening closing in and an occasional skyrocket going off over Long Island, it was with him all the more.

He was not as cheery about the First World War as most of his contemporaries that had lived through it. The Monday after the news first came in about Korea he had been having dinner with his partner Henry Lee, who was about to go off on vacation.

"What do you think about it, Jake?" Barbara Lee had asked him as she poured them coffee after dinner. "You're an old soldier."

"I'm not an old soldier," Jacob had said harshly. "I'm an old man who happened to be in an army once." Then he had tried to smile, but that was how he felt. He hated war, and yet, without ever saying it in so many words, he felt that any single young man worth his salt who was out of college in 1917 should have been with him in the first wartime camp at Plattsburg. That was the way they had all felt in the first wartime camp. There was a war on, and the thing to do was stop thinking about anything else and hop in right up to your neck.

Jacob almost hopped in over his head. Even though he was never convinced, as most of the others seemed to be, that they were going to get to play in some bigger, better, Harvard-Yale game, the realities of it when he got there were a terrible shock, particularly in view of the fact that he got along very well at Plattsburg. He had that graceful precision which momentarily soothes the rage in a drill sergeant's heart, and he had an intuitive feeling for weapons. On his last leave before they sent him over, Jacob occasionally stole a glance at himself in a mirror, checking his glassy-leather puttees, his Sam Browne belt, the crossed rifles at his high collar, and decided that he was not at all a bad figure of a man. When he got on the transport he commended his soul to God, and told himself he was not going to worry. He would do his best, and let God do the worrying.

But one morning there he was, a platoon leader in the 308th Infantry, Seventy-Seventh Division, and God handed him back all the worrying. They were about to make their first attack, and Jacob walked up and down his platoon's sector of the trench while the preliminary barrage was going out, trying to remember what he was supposed to do. He could not remember anything, except that they were supposed to go forward. His mind closed to everything else. When the moment finally came, Jacob went over the top like something shot out of a cannon.

The next thing was that he seemed to be running along in a great hush. He had expected a hail of bullets, and instead he and his platoon seemed to be running in a vast vacuum. He felt more alone than he had ever felt in his life, and stark naked. Then the vacuum broke. There were bullets snapping, and several years later Jacob saw the enemy wire going past and the trench ahead of him. As he jumped over, raving ready to kill anything in there, he saw the last Germans running away down a communications trench.

Later that morning Jacob was sitting there eating some of his rations in the captured trench, beginning to feel his stomach unknot, pleased with himself and his platoon, when there was a flash, a blast of heat, and the last thing that Jacob felt was himself actually rising above the edge of the trench. After that he seemed to be a long way away for a while, and there was a terrible screaming going on somewhere in the middle of a great silence, outraged, horrible, desperate screaming, and then the screaming died down and the clouds up in the sky came into focus. Jacob tried to move, but he couldn't. He was lying outside the trench somewhere, a lot of stuff was flying back and forth over his head, and he didn't like it at all. Then he saw Corporal Kelly's face, under a helmet, floating in at him. There was blood streaming down the side of it.

"You're wounded, Kelly." Jacob said. "Go to the rear."

"There ain't no rear right now, Lieutenant," Kelly said. He started crawling back across the ground, dragging Jacob behind him. Jacob kept trying to move, and at the same time he was thinking about the blood on Kelly's face, how there was nothing as red as blood. Then Jacob went into darkness and never felt the pain from the leg wound until he woke up in the hospital.

When he was up again he did not put in for convalescent leave. He got back to the Division, which was at rest, and found that Regimental Headquarters was in a stone barn. He went in and reported, and the colonel shook his head.

"Kingsgrant," he said, "I'd put you in a company in a minute, but you look to me as if you'd fall on your face if you had to step over a brick."

They made him liaison officer to the British next door. All it entailed was for Jacob to get on a horse nicknamed "The Hobby-horse" for its slow, dignified canter, and ride over to the British brigade's mess two or three nights a week. This was no chore for Jacob, since the British mess had a more than adequate supply of whiskey. There was only one custom that invariably tripped him up. The British all hung their Sam Browne belts on the wall before sitting down to eat, and the penalty for sitting down wearing your Sam Browne was to buy a round of drinks. Jacob invariably forgot, and by the end of the second week he had bought five rounds for the mess. One evening Jacob came in with a proud glow in his eyes. The communiqués that day had been terrible, by and large. Bad news in Italy. The French pushed back. The British pushed back. But down near the bottom of the communiqué had been the information that the

First Division had captured Cantigny, the only bright spot of the day and the first clear-cut American action since the A.E.F. started entering the lines. Jacob forgot again, and sat down to dinner wearing his Sam Browne.

The English brigadier general beamed. "I see our American has forgotten again. Drinks 'round, Lieutenant?"

Jacob looked him in the eye and smiled.

"Tonight, General?"

Without a word, every officer at the table stood up, went over to the wall, and buckled on his Sam Browne. Then they all sat down again and began to order one round of drinks after another. At the end of the evening, Jacob had to be lifted onto his horse.

It was getting dark on the roof now. There were lights on everywhere across the city, and there was one really big display of fireworks across the river. Jacob took another puff on his pipe. There were moments, he said to himself, there were moments, all right, but they weren't worth the wounds and the deaths, and you shouldn't get too sentimental about it because you lived through it. He knew only one thing; you might have to fight, for independence, or against men who attacked you, but fighting was a pretty miserable experience. He had to admit that it looked as if Truman was right in going into this war, but every war was a tough war for the men in the holes. Jacob turned in the darkness and went through the wire fence and on downstairs, leaving the roof silent between the firecrackers on the streets and the evening stars above.

III

Patrick came down the wooden steps of the post office and sat down on the bottom step. He was wearing sneakers, khaki pants, and a gray workshirt, and there was a smile on his face. There was no more work to be done at the factory the rest of this Saturday afternoon, and there was a letter from Snowjob in his hand. Patrick passed one hand across the top of his head, smoothing down his hair, and then, sitting there in the sunshine on the wooden step, he tore open the letter.

CONCRETE KIMONO NEWSLETTER struck his eye, and he chuckled. Trust Snowjob to think of something like this. He glanced through it quickly. Tall Man was working on a construction job in Flagstaff, and "our numerous other correspondents in Flagstaff tell us that he is terrorizing the female population, as usual." Patrick grinned. There was no doubt about it, Tall Man was thoroughly and cheerfully experienced, and he made the other three members of D-32 look like the complete novices they were when it came to women. "Brother Bench is leading the good life at Pride's Crossing, and PK's prayers for his conversion from the Anglican heresy are still evidently of no avail. PK, on the other hand, has been voted Mr. Blueberry of 1950, and remains the least letter-writing English major your Secretary has ever heard of."

Patrick put down the letter and smiled. He wondered what Tall Man and Snowjob had to say to each other in their letters. It had always been a relationship that had charmed Patrick, and someday he wanted to write at least a short story about it. Tall Man was sparing in information about himself. All Patrick knew was that he was an orphan with not much money and a guardian who did not seem to care about him, and that he had a devastating mathematical mind that embraced the piano as a hobby. There was no squaw marriage involved in his Indian blood. His grandfather was Chief Jonathan Tall Man, who had married a white schoolteacher, and you could take it or leave it. Patrick had the impression that quite a few people in Flagstaff had left it. That was all he knew about Arizona Tall Man, but now, sitting on the post office steps in the sunshine, he was thinking about Harvard Tall Man. By chance, in his freshman year, Tall Man had roomed across the hall in Stoughton from Snowjob Porter. Snowjob had been fascinated by Tall Man, and particularly at the thought of how well Tall Man's magnificent shoulders and back would look if they were got out of windbreakers with capital F's on them and into good-looking suits with natural shoulders. The rest was history. They ended up rooming together. It was the biggest live-and-let-live situation ever seen, and Tall Man began to enjoy his occasional extravagances on Cambridge-type clothes. Snowjob kept on going to Porcellian punches to look over prospective new members, and Tall Man, who had once played a vicious game at tackle for Flagstaff, sat on the couch in D-32 and got better and better at space-time continuums, with a little modern algebra thrown in. In his spare time he helped sharpen up the music for the Hasty Pudding Show. It was a perfect thing.

There was a sudden screech of brakes, and Patrick looked up. Myron Grey and his Model A were suddenly there.

"Know anybody wants to buy a car?" Myron said.

Patrick stood up and went over, putting his elbows on the door of the Model A. "Your car?"

"That's right, boy. Won't be needin' a car for a while, I guess."

"Where're you going?"

"Marines. Accepted and everythin'."

Patrick stared at him. "What'd you do, just enlist?"

Myron nodded. "Over to Bangor. Fixed me right up. Give me the physical and everythin'."

"When do you leave?"

"Tomorrow. You don't know anybody needs a car, do you, Patrick? Tell 'em I'll sell it cheap."

Patrick was dazedly silent for a moment, and Myron smiled. "Why don't you come along, boy?"

"I don't know. I've never known if I could get in."

"Never had a physical?"

Patrick shook his head. "I just registered, and they've kept me classified as a student ever since."

"I bet you could pass it easy. Why don't you come along? The Marines are the best thing there is. You see anybody wants a car, let me know."

"Well, when did you decide all this?" Patrick said. Myron's car engine was idling with its usual racket, and they had to speak pretty loudly.

"Well, I got thinking. These Communists want to take over the world, right?"

Patrick nodded his head.

"Well, I'm just as happy with what we got. Got to stand up to the bastards some time."

"I wish you luck, Myron," Patrick said. "Did you think of selling the car to the garage?"

"They won't give me more'n twenty dollars for it. I want to get a little more'n that."

"I don't blame you." Patrick stepped back. "Good luck."

"We'll be seein' you," Myron said, and he roared off.

Patrick stood there in the road, the Concrete Kimono letter hanging down in his hand. He looked at his wrist watch. They had finished too late at the cannery for him to get over to Bucks Harbor and try to get in the Saturday afternoon race and crew somewhere, so he supposed the thing to do was to go out to the island and start getting dressed to pick up Anna this evening. He was supposed to meet her at the Prestons' at five-thirty, and by the time he got out to the island and back here and then over to Walker's Pond it would probably take a good two hours.

He started walking down toward the pier. The road was

quiet, and there was the summery salt smell on the air, and the rustle of leaves in the breeze from off the water. A funny expression set in around Patrick's eyes as he thought of Myron's going. There was something right about going, even if it was true that they would always call you if they needed you. He thought about how his father had told him about the Minute Men, and the guns and bells ringing all the way up the coast when the British marched on Lexington, and way up here men turned out on the village greens. Get out of bed. Get your gun and bring some food. The country is in trouble. Never mind why. Get out of bed.

IV

Anna ducked under one spruce bough, pushed another lighter one aside, and walked out onto a shelf of rock high over Eggemoggin Reach. Patrick had brought her here on a walk one afternoon a week before, and today she had felt the impulse to drive over here and then take the trail that eventually led up to this private lovely view from what had once been a granite quarry. The trees and the moss had covered over most of the harsh angles of the abandoned quarry, but here and there an outcropping still stood forward high above the blue water.

Anna stood on the rock, feeling the wind in her hair and the lukewarm sea sunshine on her face. Admit it, she said to herself. Get it over with and admit it. You think about him all the time. She stood there, looking straight and trim in the shirt and bluejeans she was wearing, and smiled ruefully. Here it was, the end of July, and he had not kissed her yet. Maybe the summer would end and he would not have kissed her even then. They talked all evening, or they went to the movies, or they danced at the Hancock House, and then there would be that moment when they were standing at the door of the Prestons', and they would both stand there, and then he would say good night. He would say good night, and then there was nothing she could do but say good night, and then she would close the door and hear his car go away.

Well, all right, Anna said, sitting down on the granite and wrapping her arms around her doubled-up legs. It's probably better this way. In another month it'll all be over and he was terribly nice and that's that. She sat thinking about that square white house out there on the island, with the white-painted hall and the stairway leading up to where she had never been, and the white dining room to the right, and the living room to the left. She was going there again for dinner tonight, and this time Mr. Kingsgrant was going to be there. She had never met Mr. Kingsgrant, and she and Patrick and Eileen were in a conspiracy to keep him from knowing that she was the dinner-clothes-at-the-cannery blonde, at least until after she had made her good impression.

The smooth skin of Anna's forehead moved into a vertical wrinkle. Now Mr. Kingsgrant was going to be up here for three weeks' vacation, and Patrick was probably going to have to spend some time with him, and nothing would ever come of anything and it would be September and they would go back to college and they might exchange Christmas cards. Maybe Patrick didn't care at all. After all, she was about the only girl his age around. Maybe he didn't care. It was probably all convenience.

Anna shook her head. Every morning there was at least one letter from some beau of hers, asking her to come somewhere, go to some Race Week, and these days she barely had the interest to open them and skim through. She smiled as she thought of what they all looked like, the boys she knew. All fairly thin, with crew cuts and snub noses, and very predictable. And then there was Patrick, no snub nose, no crew cut, and not too darned predictable.

I don't know, Anna said to herself. I just don't know. Then

she lay back in the thin gold sunshine and tried not to think of anything at all.

"Well," Anna said, putting down her dessert spoon, "don't you think it's probably always been that way? I mean, if people weren't saying 'Where's Korea?' then they were saying 'Where's Pearl Harbor?' or 'Where's Fort Sumter?' "

"I think you're right," Jacob said, although Anna's remark had been addressed to Patrick across the table in the candlelight.

"She's got you on that one, Patrick," Eileen said. "There may be differences in this war, but I don't think that's one of them."

"All right," Patrick said, "but in those other wars everybody knew who the potential enemy was a long time in advance. My point isn't so much that nobody ever heard of the place where we were attacked, but nobody ever heard of the people who did the attacking. Even if people didn't know exactly where Pearl Harbor was, they certainly knew about the Japanese. This time I don't think anybody knew there was such a thing as a North Korean Army."

"Well," Jacob said, "I think you've amended your pleading a bit." He sat there listening to the three of them go on with the discussion, and there was a pleased look on his face. He was charmed with Miss van Neerdaam, and he enjoyed watching the faces of Eileen Kingsgrant and Anna van Neerdaam in the candlelight. They were both lovely examples of their types, and sitting here eating his dessert after the good veal and the red wine that Eileen had planned for them, listening to the laughter and the semi-serious voices saying "Oh, well, now *come on*," it was hard to remember that other Americans were being torn to bits at the opposite side of the world.

A while after they had all finished their coffee, Jacob excused himself and stepped out onto the lawn near the driveway. He lit his pipe and then strolled around, finally coming onto the driveway and walking slowly down it in the night, hearing the leaves of the elms rustling above him in the darkness. In his mind he saw the picture just as clearly as if he were still in the living room, Eileen on a chair with a volume of the *Britannica* open in her lap looking for something that had come up in the conversation, and Anna leaning forward talking to Patrick, both of them intently discussing a point. Jacob decided that neither Patrick nor Anna was aware that they were just on the brink of falling in love. It was a queer feeling to sit there in a room that had a portrait of Maude set in the large white panel above the fireplace, and look at her face in the picture and then look at her son, sitting there intently talking to a girl whose eyes were soft when she said "But look, Patrick" as their conversation wove in and out.

Jacob had come to the end of the driveway, and he stepped onto the pier and stood there, hearing the water move lightly against the shore. So Patrick was in love. If he wasn't in love tonight he would be in love tomorrow morning, and if he wasn't in love tomorrow morning, he would most certainly be in love by the end of the week. And since that was going to happen, it was just as well to consider him in love right now. Jacob smiled into the darkness. Anna van Neerdaam was a charming girl, and she had beauty, and she evidently had brains. He knew that she was spending the summer over near Walker's Pond, but he wondered how Patrick had met her. Then he stopped wondering about that. His mind slid away from the picture of Anna and Patrick sitting there, and back to his long-ago love.

Once Jacob had decided that he really had to see Maude Buckleigh again, he had found himself in an agony of inadequacy. He did not know where to begin. He did not even know where she lived. His work at the office began to suffer.

"You seem pretty jumpy lately, Jake."

"I'm not jumpy."

"All right. You're not jumpy." And Roland Grindall would address himself to the papers sitting on his roll-top desk, while Jacob pursed his lips and tried to concentrate. Jacob kept pointing out to himself that this was ridiculous, he had only seen the girl for one evening, where would Kingsgrant be if every Kingsgrant just took it in his head that he had to go off and find some visiting girl he had met one evening? Having pointed all this out to himself he went over to Henry Wintridge's house for dinner. All through dinner he kept trying to get around to asking Henry where Mrs. Buckleigh and her daughter Maude lived, or where they could be found. His chess game fell apart completely, and finally he sat back.

"Henry," he said, "for God's sake tell me where I can find Maude Buckleigh."

Henry Wintridge looked up from his contemplation of the chessboard.

"Check," he said, pointing at the board.

"I know. I know."

Henry Wintridge nodded. "Emma Buckleigh and her daughter. Think I've got their newest address around here somewhere." He stood up and padded off toward his den, while Jacob went over to the sideboard and mixed himself a drink.

"Jake," Roland Grindall said, "that's the most preposterous idea I've ever heard in my life." He was sitting forward in his swivel chair, his thumbs hooked into the pockets of his vest, and his slightly graying hair looked more touseled than usual.

"You've got to do it, Rolly. You've got to help me."

Roland Grindall stood up, looked at Jacob, and almost fell back onto the top of his desk.

"Look, Jake," he said, as if he were speaking to a small child, "I don't mind if you go to New York to see this girl. I mean,

I think it's a pretty damfool thing, but that's your business. But why should I have to come with you?"

"Rolly, I'll never be able to do it without you." The look in Jacob's eyes was one of absolute pleading. "Besides, we haven't had a vacation in a long time."

"I go fishing on my vacation."

Jacob suddenly sensed that the jury was with him.

"Not this year, Rolly," he said, and then he smiled.

Maude Buckleigh was having tea with her mother when the maid walked into the room bearing a card on a small silver tray. The card looked perfectly clean but fairly old, and it said "Jacob Kingsgrant."

"Mother," Maude said after a moment of staring at the card, "wasn't that nice man I met at Mr. Wintridge's named Kingsgrant?"

"I don't know, dear," Mrs. Buckleigh said, and continued to sip her tea. At first, when Maude had begun to go to dances, she had been quite interested in her daughter's beaux, but the last few years the thing had gotten entirely out of hand. If you tried to keep track of Maude's suitors you would go crazy, and Mrs. Buckleigh was having none of it. She took another sip of her tea.

The maid was still standing there. "Just a minute, Ann," Maude said to the maid, and went over to the door that led into the hall. She bent down and peeked through the keyhole. Two men were sitting there. It was the same man, all right. He and this other, shorter, bushy-haired man were sitting there, and neither of them was saying a word to the other. For a moment Maude had the strange feeling that they had come to take her away. Then she straightened up and opened the door.

Rolly went back the next day, and Jacob stayed in New York two weeks. He looked up his friend Henry Lee, and Henry and his wife Barbara had Jacob and Maude to dinner, and he and Maude saw Harvard play Princeton, and Maude enjoyed it all thoroughly. She felt almost as if she were playing some sort of trick on her contemporaries, as if she had a real man whom people took seriously, instead of a boy. One or two of her friends told her that Jacob was very good-looking.

"Oh, I don't think he's so *good*-looking," she said, thoughtfully. "I think he's more *distinguished*-looking." She enjoyed showing Jacob this New York autumn of 1927. At first he had been horrified that she should frequent speakeasies, but after he had met one or two of his classmates and their wives in them, he began to relax and think it might be permissible after all. There was only one thing of which he was absolutely certain: it was a good thing that Maude had some common sense, because her mother didn't have the faintest idea of where Maude was, or whom she was with, or what she was doing. There was no one in the world to say Maude nay. By her own code, she decided that if Jacob had come to New York for two weeks then she would give Jacob two weeks of her time. There was only one engagement that she could not break, and Jacob spent that afternoon sitting with Mrs. Buckleigh, having a nice long talk about herbs.

Finally, one evening Maude stood on a platform in Grand Central, her hair pretty well out of the way under a cloche, and looked at Jacob as he took off his hat.

"It's been wonderful for me," Jacob said, holding out his hand. He was wearing a new coat that she had helped him buy, and for a second she thought she could smell that nice clean smell of him that she knew from the times they had danced together.

Maude brushed aside Jacob's hand and kissed him firmly on the cheek. She had to raise herself up on her toes to do it.

"I've loved it," she said, and then Jacob nodded, put his hat back on his head, and took his suitcase onto the train. Maude walked home, feeling the October air beginning to get really crisp in the night, and then, just as she closed the door at home, she realized that she was going to miss him terribly. Maude took off her coat and walked to the mirror in the hall. She looked at herself, in the mirror, her face serious and sober. She swallowed. This was terrible. This was not part of the bargain at all. She knew right then that if Jacob Kingsgrant asked her to fly to the moon with him, she would put her hand in his and fly to the moon. She did not like it, but that was the way it was.

5

PATRICK KNELT beside his bed, saying his prayers before he went to sleep. The light from the lamp on the table beside his bed cast up a pattern of light and shadow on the walls that Eileen had had painted blue-gray the summer before, and his head was pressed down into the warm wool blankets. Patrick's prayers were often more than a repetition of given devotions, and tonight he was thinking about Anna, and praying about Anna. A picture rose in his mind as he knelt there with his hands clasped, a picture of himself as a lawyer in New York, coming home and finding her there. Always there. Always. When they talked about writing she was interested, as if he were talking about a safari that would never take place, but when he talked about going to the Law School and being a lawyer, she was there. It clicked when he talked about the Law School.

Patrick raised his head from the blanket, but he kept staring down at it. He was thinking about a more immediate picture, that of Anna in her red bathing suit. And he hadn't even kissed her yet. He wanted to kiss her, in all their conversations he wanted to reach over and kiss her, but if she wasn't thinking that way he hated to foul it up by making a pass at her.

All right, snap out of it, he said to himself. These are prayers, not some sort of a sexual reverie. He said an Act of Contrition, and then he began thinking about the religious situation that they would have to face if she ever conceivably, possibly, wonderfully — The thing is, Patrick said, I can imagine myself being so carried away that I would consent to be married in a civil ceremony or something. But I know I'd wake up, and once I woke up I'd be unhappy the rest of my life. So that leaves it up to her, and I certainly don't blame her if she'll be damned if she'll sign on the dotted line. It's just that I can't do anything else. I think she knows that already. Patrick shook his head a couple of times, and then he said three more Acts of Contrition, turned out the light, and got into bed.

II

"You wouldn't really shoot McCarthy, would you, Patrick?"

"I don't imagine I'd have the guts," Patrick said. "But all I'm trying to say is that you can be against the Communists *and* be against people like McCarthy at the same time, that's all. And I think maybe somebody is going to have to do something pretty desperate to bring people to their senses before they become too acquiescent."

Anna looked out over the water. They had borrowed a Seventeen and tied a dinghy behind it, and sailed out here to Hog Island for a picnic. They had gone in swimming in the icy water first, and now they were sitting on the pebbly beach of the deserted island eating chicken sandwiches and drinking beer. Patrick had put on a sweatshirt over his bathing suit, and Anna had a blanket around the red one-piece suit that Patrick liked.

"I don't know, PK," she said. "What would it prove to assassinate a man like that?"

"It would demonstrate that we're not going to let our freedoms be taken away from us, no matter in what cause." Patrick took a sip from his can of Budweiser. "That's all. Never mind about phrases like academic freedom. Either you've got freedom or you haven't, and when people in this country start clamming up about what they think, it's a damned sad day."

"Well — " Anna smiled at Patrick. They had been on this for about twenty minutes now, and she wasn't sure what she thought, and it was awfully clear that he had reached his conclusions on this subject some time ago. "Let me think about it," she said.

"Sure." Patrick took a bite out of his chicken sandwich. He was feeling pretty much at peace with the world. They had been speaking seriously for the last few minutes, but before that there had been the kind of talk that was always there with Anna, talk and agreement on a hundred different things, talk that nobody thought was important, but the kind of talk that made men happy, and made the world go around. Just a few nights before, he had started writing something about Tall Man and Snowjob, and he had started out hoping just to make a few notes, or a short story at best, and the thing had instantly moved ahead twenty pages, carrying him with it. He had decided not to tell Anna about it, to wait until he had some more pages and then let her read it, but coming out here, he hadn't been able to resist it, and he had told her. As always, she had been right there, interested in the idea. He had told her how he had set it up, with the main theme being a love story between Tall Man and a Boston girl, and the name Snowjob Porter being changed to Technical Jones and David Tall Man being Henry Leapingdeer. He had explained how the alternate names had just come to him, and Anna had loved it, and said that he ought to call the whole thing "Technical Jones," and maybe he would.

"Patrick?"

"Urf?" Patrick said through his sandwich.

"What did you mean when you said before that you were anti-intellectual?"

Patrick finished the last of his sandwich. "I didn't mean to say that, exactly. I mean I'm non-intellectual. I mean, I think it's fine to engage in intellectual pursuits, but don't be an intellectual."

"Oh." Anna looked puzzled. "In other words, don't be a mental person."

"I mean don't be exclusively a mental person." Patrick took a long sip of his beer and looked at Anna as she sat beside him. She had worn a bathing cap while they were swimming, and now she had taken it off, and her blond hair was moving in the breeze. She turned and looked at him, and Patrick swallowed once more than the amount of beer he was drinking required. He had still not kissed her, and now, looking at her in the red bathing suit, the blanket around her shoulders and coming in a V down her front, he felt everything rising in him. He could feel the desire to do it, to hold her, right in the top of his mouth, and tight in his throat. He put his hand on hers. She was still looking at him, a serious expression on her face. That's all, brother, Patrick said to himself, and he leaned forward, and found her leaning forward just as fast, and they kissed, and then he was rolling the picnic basket away with one shoulder, and they were lying there, kissing hard and desperately on the rocks and pebbles of the beach.

It was like no other kiss that Patrick had experienced. The six weeks of looking at each other, of being close to each other, broke and splintered around them, and neither one of them would break out of the kiss. It went on in a gold haze, and Patrick could feel and hear her breathing, and feel her clean skin still wet from the water, and there was nothing more in the world, and he thought he said something, and he was sure she said something, and then, still tense, they were sitting up, looking at each other, with dazed looks on their faces.

Anna stood up.

"Where're you going?"

"I think I'll go in swimming again," Anna said.

"But it's so damned cold, Anna."

"I know. But I think I'll just go in for a couple of minutes."

"All right." Patrick started to get up too.

"No. Just let me go in," Anna said. She let the blanket slide off her shoulders and onto the sand, and then she was walking away from him. Patrick watched her move, watched her arms and her golden legs and her back in the red bathing suit. He felt breathless, and it seemed to him that time had become meaningless and the only thing that was moving anywhere on prehistoric earth was Anna walking toward the water. He sat there watching her as she walked in and swam around and waded around, and then, five minutes or five hours later, she was coming back toward him again. She came toward him, her feet stepping gingerly on the stones of the beach, and she sat down next to him and put her head on his shoulder.

There was one good long tack back toward Bucks Harbor, and they both sat on the floor of the cockpit, on the windward side. They had left the island without kissing again and without saying another word, and now Patrick had one hand on the tiller, and the other arm around Anna. They kissed, and smiled at each other, and Patrick kissed her eyes, those wonderful blue eyes with the crystals of gold in them, but in a way they were sad. Something was gone, and neither of them knew what it was. What had come in its place was more important and more interesting, but once or twice, when they smiled at each other in the spray and the wind, there was a shadow of sadness in their smiles.

III

Jacob sat on the edge of his bed, about to put the lights out and go to sleep. It was August 10, his birthday, just four days after Eileen's birthday, and he and Patrick and Eileen had had dinner together. Rolly and Marjorie Grindall had come over to the island for a while after dinner, and at about nine-thirty Ben and Bertram and Harriet and Moonstone had come in for a few minutes. Ben had given him a pipe, and Harriet had given him a sweater that she had knitted for him, and Ben's wife Moonstone and Bertram had both given him neckties, each a little embarrassed to discover that they had had the same idea, and got him almost the same tie from Eaton's in Ellsworth. But Patrick had given him the present that mattered, and Jacob was sitting here, turning that present, that one wonderful present, not meant as a present, over in his mind. After they had all had a drink together, and Margie and Rolly had gone down to the boat with Ben, Eileen had gone off to bed. Jacob had kissed her good night and thanked her for the smoking jacket that Patrick and Eileen had given him jointly, and then he and Patrick had been left sitting there in the living room. It was a chilly night, and there was a fire in the fireplace under the portrait of Maude.

"Father," Patrick had said, "I've been thinking a lot about the law lately — " he stood up and went over to the fireplace. "I think I ought to try it."

"Well, I thought you would," Jacob had said, his voice calm, but his heart had beaten faster. "Patrick, promise me one thing. Try it for a year anyhow, will you? Go to the Law School for one year anyhow."

"All right," Patrick had nodded his head, his legs outlined by the flames in the fireplace. "I want to do it. I think a lot of things would make sense this way."

"I've always thought that."

Patrick had nodded again, and kept staring down into the flames, while a smile, a happy and contented smile, came onto Jacob's face and stayed there.

Jacob switched out the light and got under the covers. For so long he had been worried about Patrick, about what was going to happen to everything, and now he was coming through, right on the dot, before his senior year. He would go through the Law School, and if there were more time, perhaps he should work with Rolly for a while, but maybe it would be better if he came down to New York and started right in with Cutter, Kingsgrant, and Lee. Joe Cutter had been acting strangely this summer. He had been setting all his affairs in order, and he had stayed home during his vacation instead of going off on a fishing trip, and he had been avoiding taking on any matters that might run on for years. When a man started doing that you knew that something was happening to him, in his bathroom or his bedroom, that he wasn't telling anybody about. Jacob stared up at the dim ceiling of his room. Cutter was sixty, and as of tonight, he, Jacob, was fifty-six years old. Henry Lee was fifty-five, and all three of them, Cutter, Kingsgrant, and Lee, were agreed that none of the junior partners was terribly exciting. One or two of the junior associates were pretty good, but there was more than enough room for Patrick, and Patrick might come through with the goods, the same stuff that it had taken to start Cutter, Kingsgrant, and Lee in 1931, when nobody knew what was coming next. Patrick was a religious person, and a person of loyalties, and for a time loyalty was all that had kept Cutter, Kingsgrant going. It was funny, Jacob thought, lying there in his bed. When people spoke about unemployment in the Depression, you thought about factories shut down, but you didn't think much about law offices shut down. But they had been shut down all right, all over the place, and he and Joe Cutter and Henry Lee had kept at least twelve people employed, not including themselves, right through one after another of those slow, nightmarishly slow years. There had been some paydays in Cutter, Kingsgrant when he and Joe Cutter had arrived straight from their own banks with cash from their own pockets to fill out the payroll, and more than once Henry Lee had had to put in an IOU and let Jacob and Joe take up the slack. That was how they had come through, backing each other up, and if the offices of Cutter, Kingsgrant didn't look much like a conventional breadline, there were still days there was so little real work to be done that Jacob and Henry Lee had made up fictional requests for memoranda to keep up the morale of the junior partners and the associates and the secretaries.

Jacob turned over. Well, those bad times had passed, and if the smart boys downtown wanted to say that they never would have made it if they hadn't had a good deal of money of their own to put into it, that was fair enough. They'd used their own money, all right, but still it was better than putting your head in the sand like an ostrich. By now he and Joe and Henry were each taking between thirty and thirty-five thousand a year out of there, after every single salary and office expense had been paid, and if that was a lot less than some of the partners in the bigger and older firms took home, that was all right too. They had built up a damned good reputation in a damned short time. If there was something wrong with Joe Cutter, they would have to bring up Nash whether they liked it or not, and put Harrison up into Nash's place, and nobody thought that either White or Martin had much of a future in the firm, so there was going to be all the room in the world for Patrick if he came in at the end of his three years at the Law School.

His eyes closed. Fifty-six years old. He had never been much of a believer in heaven, and the only reason he sometimes believed in the possibility was that Maude had been so sure they would be together again in heaven. But still, most of the time he assumed that at the end of his life he would simply become unconscious. Fifty-six. It was no use pretending that fifty-six was a young man's age. At fifty-six most of it was over, and if you were ever going to amount to anything people knew it right now. You were on the other side of the slope, and if you weren't too sure about immortality in heaven then the only approximation of it was living on through your children. Jacob lay there, his eyes shut, thinking about Patrick as a lawyer. Patrick's mind was as good as anybody else's, his voice was good, he had an excellent way with words. He would be all right. He could write briefs that ticked it off, one two three four, and there would be judges who would appreciate it, the whole thing, the voice and the manners and the words. And Patrick looked honest. That was always a help.

Jacob smiled from halfway into sleep. He was thinking that Maude had only been in his life ten years. It had been ten years and four months from the moment that he had met her until she had died, and Jacob could never believe that there had been forty-five other years without her, spread out on either side of those ten happy years. Maude and New York were somehow inseparable in Jacob's mind; Maude encouraging him to start off with Henry and Joe when they left Kingsgrant after the business about Patrick's arm, Maude at the other end of the table at 1120, always there, always saying the right thing, always backing him up, and always giving him a wink just as he began wondering whether she was really interested in the man she was talking to. She had taken him away from Kingsgrant because what happened to Patrick's arm had happened there, but she had paid him back one thousand times over for taking him away, and he still could not believe that she had stood still in his life only ten years before she went to a heaven in which she believed as surely as if you could turn on the radio and get the harp music direct.

I still love you, Maude, Jacob said, his lips just moving while his eyes stayed closed, and Patrick's all right. Patrick is all right.

IV

Anna had just finished helping with the dishes after lunch, and Mrs. Brown, the woman who came in to cook and clean for the

Prestons, had started to mop up the kitchen floor, so Anna got out of the way. She walked onto the flagstone terrace by the lake, trying to think of something to do, and then she remembered the catechisms that Patrick had brought over last night. They had got into a discussion about religion a couple of days before, and Anna had said she didn't know much about the Catholic Church. Patrick had just nodded, and last night he had handed her two little pamphlet-like books. She had been meaning to look at them after Patrick left, but he left pretty late, and then the kids had taken up all her time this morning. Right now she couldn't hear them, which meant that they were either asleep or dead, and Anna had stopped worrying about their drowning a long time ago.

Anna went into her bedroom, took the paper-backed books from the table beside her bed, and went back to the terrace. She pulled up one of the white wicker chairs and sat down, studying the titles of the two books. They both had green covers, and both said *Baltimore Catechism*. One said *No. 2*, and the other said *No. 3*. Anna took a deep breath and opened up *No. 2*. The first page seemed to be all questions and answers, and Anna began at the top of the page.

Q. Who made the world?
A. God made the world.

Anna nodded her head. So far so good. She went ahead.

Q. Who is God?
A. God is the creator of Heaven and Earth, and of all things.

Anna nodded again, and kept on going. She read for about ten minutes, and then she sat there, the catechism still open on her knees, looking out over the lake. It was far less frightening than she had thought it was going to be. If you accepted their premises, every conclusion was perfectly logical, she supposed, but the thing was that one of the premises was the direct presence of the Divinity on earth, and the direct presence of the Divinity in daily life. She had always believed that there was a God, and that God was good, and that morality and God and goodness were all properly and inextricably tied up. That had always seemed to Anna to be one thing, and something like the presence of the body and blood of Jesus Christ upon the altar to be another. But this book said it was not enough to believe in a distant, good God. Every page of the catechism insisted that God was right here right now.

Anna stood up, put the book down carefully on the wicker chair, and walked over to the low wall of the terrace. The sunshine was sparkling almost blindingly on the lake, and she wished that Patrick weren't working at the blueberry factory these afternoons. She wished that they were out sailing, and then maybe he could talk to her about all this. No matter what she finally thought about it, she wanted to understand it. Evidently it was an all-or-nothing proposition. Anna sat down on the low wall and looked at the green book on the white wicker chair. In any other kind of a conversation, politics or literature or history, Eileen and Patrick might compromise, but they didn't compromise on what was in that book. Whenever religion entered the conversation, Patrick and Eileen were ready to say that anybody was entitled to his opinion, but they never said "Well, you might be right" or "I may be wrong about this," as they did on every other subject. It was obvious that this was a subject on which their convictions were fixed.

Anna sat on the wall, looking at the green book in the white wicker chair. All right, Patrick, she said to herself, we'll try some more, and then she walked back toward the book.

v

Patrick sat on the stern thwart of the little tender, his hand on the tiller of the whining outboard motor. There was moonlight on the water, and he had just driven into South Harbor from seeing Anna, his headlights the only bright thing in the town except for the streetlight by the tiny post office. There was a cold wind on the water, but he didn't feel it. The moonlight sparkled silver, and ahead of him he could see the light that Ben had left on for him out at the float. He was thinking about what had happened tonight. They had been sitting in front of the big stone fireplace, and Anna had been wearing a skirt, and a man's shirt. They had been kissing, and he had unbuttoned the top two buttons of the shirt, and she had kept her eyes closed and made no move to stop him. He had started for the third button, and then he had known, with his hand there on her clothed chest, that with Anna he wanted it right. He wanted everything like this to be married, and he was willing to wait until that was the way it was. But now, sitting on the hard wooden seat, he twisted as he thought about it, and he twisted again. He was getting pretty tired at work these days, but he couldn't stop himself from going over there every night that she let him. It was more important than being all that great in the morning. It was more important than anything.

6

LUTHER ALLEN shook his head and kept on looking at Patrick, who was standing by the labeling machine.

"I still don't see how you did it," he said.

"I don't either, Mr. Allen." Patrick was trying to be serious, but the nature of the mistake he had just made was so ridiculous that he was afraid he was going to laugh.

"There's no gum on the front of the labels," Mr. Allen said. "I don't see how it could happen."

"Neither do I," Patrick said. He looked over at the pile of cans that had just gone through. They entered the machine as plain shiny cans, and came out with the label on them. The only thing was that the last three hundred that Patrick had sent through had come out with the blank side of the label on the outside.

"I've never seen it in twenty years," Mr. Allen said. "Them labels just *can't* stick on backwards." He pointed at the mountain of offending cans. "You didn't notice what they was doin' any too damn fast, Patrick."

"Well, they come through pretty quickly," Patrick said.

Luther Allen ground one heel on the concrete floor of the warehouse.

"You've been lookin' pretty sleepy lately," he said. They

both stared at the labeling machine again. All the labels that had been in the machine were used up now, so it was impossible to tell whether they had been gummed on the wrong side, or whether Patrick had put the whole batch in upside down and near some other gum, or what. "It's goin' to take somebody half an hour to tear the labels off them wrong ones."

"Do you want me to do it, Mr. Allen?"

"Nope. I'll tell you when I want you to do somethin' different." Luther Allen clicked his false teeth and walked away. Patrick shrugged his shoulders, grinned at the idiotic-looking pile of incognito cans, and carefully and correctly lowered a new pile of labels into the machine.

II

"Absolutely not," Jacob said, a shadow of a smile on his face. It was Sunday afternoon, and Eileen and Patrick had driven him to the airport. His vacation was over, and on top of it all Patrick was trying to persuade him to use his influence at the cannery to get him out of the office job that they had stuck him into two days before.

"Look, Father," Patrick said, "I explained about the labels, didn't I?"

"You certainly did," Eileen said, giggling, and Patrick glared at her.

"But look," Patrick said, "we've agreed that it could have happened to anybody, aren't we?"

"Of course, Patrick," Jacob said. "But I'm not going to stick my nose into it. It can't be all that bad working in the office."

Patrick stood there, frustration on his face. For the past two days, for eight hours a day, he had been taking the weight of the filled wooden boxes of blueberries that the farmers were bringing in, and subtracting five pounds per box as the weight of the box.

And that was all. A man came in from the scales with a list of weights, Patrick multiplied the number of boxes by five, subtracted that figure from the total weight, and that was it.

"I'm going to go crazy doing that," Patrick said, "I'll do *anything* else over there. I didn't even know they had a job like that."

"I don't think you'll go crazy, Patrick," Jacob said. He was standing by the railing at the edge of the field, and most of the other passengers were already aboard the plane. "I think I'd better get going. G'bye, dear." Jacob kissed Eileen's cheek, and then he straightened up and shook hands with Patrick. "Sometimes you've got to do things you don't like to do," he said. "If they put you in the office making up lists saying two and two equal four, just take it for a while. You'll be through next week anyhow."

"Yes, Father." Patrick nodded and tried to smile.

"I'll be seeing you two in New York on the tenth, right?" Jacob said.

"That's right, Daddy."

"Good." Jacob fixed his hat more firmly on his head, and strode out toward the plane.

III

"That's looking a lot better, Patrick," Anna said. She had discovered that he had never learned how to do the Charleston during its revival the last couple of years, and she had set about remedying it at once.

"Thanks." He smiled at her and took out his handkerchief to mop his brow. She had him posted behind a chair, with both his hands on its back, and then, when she turned on the one Charleston record with which the Prestons' victrola was supplied, he hung on to the chair and flailed away at the steps she had taught him.

"All right," Anna said. They were both out on the flagstone terrace, and the sun was setting behind one of the hills that circled Walker's Pond. "Now take your hands off the chair and do it when I put on the music. I'll teach you what to do with your arms later, but right now just swing them any way that helps you keep your balance."

"O.K."

Anna bent over the victrola, and the music began again, ringing out over the silent sunset lake. Charleston, Charleston, it's not a back number, bumdedumdedum, bumdedumdedum, bumdedumdedum, bumdedumdedum, dumdum — Patrick kicked away at it, his face a picture of concentration. This dance wasn't particularly good on his loose knee after the first few minutes, but he was bearing up all right, and she seemed delighted that he was learning how to do it.

Suddenly Anna came veering in toward him across the flat slate of the terrace, doing the step herself. They smiled at each other again, facing each other, about four feet between them as they swung their feet forward and back. The dance ended, and they both stood there, laughing and gasping.

"That's enough for the first lesson," Patrick said. "I'm pooped."

"I imagine you are," Anna said, turning off the vic. Patrick picked it up and took it inside, and then they both went out to the kitchen.

"Beer?" Anna said.

"And how."

Anna got two cans of beer out of the icebox. Patrick opened them, and then they wandered back out to the terrace. The sun was down, and the sky was a dark luminous blue. The air was cool, but neither of them noticed it. They stood in the dimness, looking at the flat evening lake, and they looked at each other, warm and flushed from the Charleston. Patrick tilted up his beer, feeling the can cold in his hand, and feeling the beer cold and foamy in his throat.

"I finished the *Catechism* yesterday," Anna said.

Patrick put his can of beer down on the stone ledge.

"What's your reaction?" he said, sitting down on the top of the low wall beside his can of beer.

"Well, I don't know, PK." Anna sat down too. "Do you really believe that the body of Christ can be on the altar, or a thousand different altars, all at the same time? I mean, do you *really* believe it?"

"Yes," Patrick said. "Look, Anna. If you really believe in an all-powerful God, who created the world —" He stopped and looked at his can of beer. "Let me put it this way. If you believe in a God who can do anything, things you can't even imagine, then everything else is perfectly possible. If you believe that God can do anything, then there's nothing tough about believing in miracles. You may not understand them fully, but you can believe in them."

"Well, look, Patrick. Assuming you have this belief, I mean that complete a belief, still, why does it specifically have to be the Catholic Church?"

"Well," Patrick said, picking up his can of beer again, "you're the historian. If you believe that Christ is the son of God, then you study His life and His statements, and I think you come up with the conclusion that He started a church, and entrusted it to a few specific men. Then you study the men that these first men taught, and on down through the centuries, and I think you come to the conclusion that the Catholic Church is the one that was started by Christ, and if that's the one He started, then I think it's pretty likely that's the one He wanted."

"Well, you think there's just one true faith?"

Patrick nodded his head. "So does anyone think he has the one true faith, Anna. No matter what religion it is, you probably think you have the best way of worshiping God. Leaving the spiritual things aside, I think we have the best historical support. That is, if you believe in the divinity of Christ."

"Oh, I believe Christ was the son of God, all right," Anna said. "But you aren't going to say that other churches don't do some good, are you?"

"Of course they do some good," Patrick said. "Nobody said that they're evil because they aren't Catholic. God loves everyone, and He has a lot of devoted servants in a lot of places, but I still believe that one of the reasons His son came to earth was to found one church, one Christian Church, and I think the Catholic Church is the one He had in mind." Patrick took a sip of his beer. Anna's blond hair was still bright in the increasing darkness.

"I don't know," Anna said. "I think it's got a lot, but you have to *feel* some of these things. You see, you feel them, Patrick."

"You mean faith." Patrick nodded his head in the darkness. "The Church will go along with that, all right. You've got to have faith in these things." He stopped and thought for a moment. "Supposing you were going to marry a Catholic? I mean, supposing you didn't have to believe the articles of faith right down the line yourself, but you had to agree that your children would be brought up as Catholics?"

There was quite a long silence. "I don't know," Anna said after a while. "Suppose one of the children wanted to be a priest or a nun or something?"

"There would always be that possibility, I suppose." Patrick looked over toward Anna in the dusk. The lights were on in the house now, and he could see the golden reflection on the beer can that she was holding in her hand.

"I don't know," Anna said. "I think I'll have to look into it some more."

"I don't blame you," Patrick said.

"Of course this is all purely hypothetical, isn't it, Patrick?"

Patrick sat there, and then he felt her hand take his in the darkness, and then her head was on his shoulder, and she was chuckling.

"Purely," Patrick said, kissing her forehead and feeling that wild joy that she sometimes brought up in him, as if he wanted to burst out laughing or crying or something. "Purely."

IV

The afternoon before they were to leave Kingsgrant, Eileen took a walk around the island, pausing to look at each thing that she would not be seeing for another winter. Finally she ended up sitting on the North Bluff, looking out over the slate September water. From here all you could see was the water, and a few trees, and a good many rocks, and you had no idea that there was a house tucked down on the other side of the bluff. About fifty feet away, in the spruce trees, the body of Maude Kingsgrant was buried, but Eileen was not thinking about her mother. For once, she was thinking of herself. She had this whole coming sophomore year in Barnard, and before she ever got to Barnard she had put in twelve years at the Brearley. It had been a long time in New York, and during the last few months she had been thinking of the possibility of taking her junior year in Paris. She weighed it again as she sat on the Bluff, staring out at the gray sky that hung over the faintness of the Camden Hills in the distance over the water. One of the things that she didn't like about it was that if she went, she would want to take the whole summer in Europe, too, so she would probably only be at Kingsgrant for a few days next June before she left. Eileen's right hand slid down over her navy wool skirt and touched the ground. It seemed a long time to be away, but still, ever since she was a little girl, there had been a certain magic when somebody said France, or Italy. Just the names themselves had always stirred her up, and when she had seen the pictures of some of those cathedrals and castles in her textbooks, she had promised herself that someday Eileen Kingsgrant would go and look at them, and they wouldn't be just pictures any more.

Eileen stood up. It was still a long way off, but she thought she would probably go. She already knew that she was going to miss this place, and she would miss her father and Patrick, but the way the world was going, with the Russians about two days' drive from the English Channel, and with Malik filibustering about Korea in the U.N., you didn't know how long there would be a Europe left to go and see. Eileen walked slowly into the grove of spruce trees, and stopped at the edge of the little cleared space where her mother's gravestone stood. It was a simple piece of marble, and the epitaph said MAUDE BUCKLEIGH, WIFE OF JACOB KINGSGRANT, 1907–1937. Then, over on the trunk of one of the trees, there was a small crucifix. The cross was made of iron, and the body of Christ was of white marble. Eileen stood there. Her hand came up and made the sign of the cross, and she said the Lord's Prayer silently. She gazed down at the grave for a minute or so, and then she turned and walked away through the spruce trees.

V

Patrick got off the Fifth Avenue bus and started looking for 17 West Eleventh Street. He had been back in New York for several days. Anna had come down the day before, and after spending her first evening at home alone with her parents, she had invited him for dinner tonight. It was a lovely September evening, just chilly enough for Patrick to break out his tweed topcoat for the first time this fall, and everything seemed right with the world. Patrick had found that he could not even speak to the bus driver without grinning.

Patrick studied the numbers on the doors of the houses. Three, five, seven, nine, eleven. Patrick stood on the sidewalk, looking at Anna's house. It was a brownstone, more polished-looking than the ones he had just passed. Patrick smiled, a funny tingling in his stomach, and turned around once to look at the sky. The streetlights had just gone on, and the sky was letting the daylight lower its sails into the west. Patrick went up the stairs and rang the doorbell. There was that feeling of somebody coming toward the curtained inner door, and then it opened, and Anna was standing there in a black dress, smiling at him.

"Hi," Anna said.

"Hi."

"Come on in."

"Thanks."

Patrick followed her through a hall that had a stairway, and into a living room. Patrick had expected to find the furniture old, and instead most of it looked new but not modern.

"Mother," Anna said, "this is Patrick Kingsgrant."

"How do you do, Patrick," a handsome woman said. She was sitting on a sofa, and at first Patrick had not seen her. She had gray hair, and a string of pearls around her neck, and she was a good-looking woman.

"How do you do, Mrs. van Neerdaam," Patrick said, coming over and shaking hands.

"Daddy's still upstairs," Anna said. "How about a drink?"

"That'd be fine," Patrick said.

"What would you like?"

"I think a scotch and soda," Patrick said.

"Fine." Anna disappeared through a door. Patrick had a glimpse of a dining room beyond, and then the door was closed.

"Sit down, Patrick," Mrs. van Neerdaam said.

"Thank you." Patrick sat down in a chair near the sofa and looked at Anna's mother again. It wasn't hard to see where Anna got it. Her mother had very much the same features, although her eyes were brown instead of blue.

"Anna was very enthusiastic about her summer in Maine," Mrs. van Neerdaam said.

"I'm glad she liked it."

"We usually spend a few weeks at my sister's place in Tuxedo, but I think this was probably more fun for Anna."

"I thought the Prestons were awfully nice," Patrick said. "I don't think she could have been with nicer people."

"I've known the Prestons for ever," Mrs. van Neerdaam said. "They said some very nice things about you too, Patrick."

There was a *harrumph ing* sound by the door, and Patrick stood up without even bothering to look around first.

"This is Patrick Kingsgrant, dear," Mrs. van Neerdaam said to her husband. Patrick turned and saw a bald man bearing down on him. He looked younger than Patrick had expected him to be.

"How do you do," the man said.

"How do you do, Mr. van Neerdaam."

"Sit down, sit down," Mr. van Neerdaam said, dropping down on the sofa beside his wife. He was wearing a well-cut dark smoking jacket, and Patrick suddenly noticed that he had on evening pumps Then Patrick saw his eyes. That was where Anna got the eyes.

"When'd you get down from Maine?" Mr. van Neerdaam said.

"A few days ago. My sister and I drove down."

Anna came through the door, bearing a tray with several glasses on it.

"Hi, Dad," she said. I hope this is all right, Patrick."

"Looks wonderful," Patrick said, taking his drink off the tray.

· · ·

By the time dinner was over and they were out in the living room again, drinking coffee, Patrick was feeling happy. For a young man Trying To Make An Impression, he thought he was doing pretty well. And there was no doubt that the van Neerdaams were pleasant. They were pleasant, and they ate very well, and he had no idea of why Anna did not turn into a plump young thing. He looked at her as she came around, passing brandy in snifters. There was no doubt about it. Everything in that black dress was filled out, but it wasn't plump. Patrick set down his empty demitasse and took the brandy.

"Would you like a cigar?"

Patrick looked up. He hadn't noticed Mr. van Neerdaam getting up from his seat on the sofa but there he was, with an opened box of cigars in his hand.

"No thank you, sir," Patrick said, rising.

"Keep your seat, keep your seat," Mr. van Neerdaam said. Patrick sat down. He almost wished that he'd taken the cigar. Sometimes after a formal dinner at the Seneca, or any exceptionally good dinner, he smoked a cigar. But just now a cigar didn't seem like such a suave move. Patrick took a sip of his brandy.

"Do you play billiards, Mr. Kingsgrant?" Anna's father asked after they had been sipping their brandy for a couple of minutes.

"No, sir, I'm afraid I don't," Patrick said.

"I suppose you two are going out," Mrs. van Neerdaam said to Anna. Patrick had thought that the question about billiards was just one of general interest, but suddenly he sensed that there was a billiard table in this house somewhere, and Mr. van Neerdaam wanted a game. And he wanted a game right now. Mr. van Neerdaam was staring down into his brandy snifter, and he was not looking pleased.

"I'll play you, Dad," Anna said after about five seconds. "Patrick and I don't have to go out for a while."

"No, indeed," Patrick said, letting out his breath.

"Fine," Mr. van Neerdaam said. He began smiling. "Let's go downstairs." He stood up, the cigar in one hand and the brandy snifter in the other, and Anna and Patrick stood up too.

"Perhaps Patrick isn't interested," Mrs. van Neerdaam said, as she remained firmly seated on the sofa.

"No, I'd like to watch, if it's all right," Patrick said.

Mr. van Neerdaam led the way down some steps into what once must have been simply part of the cellar. It was a wood-paneled room, with a good many books on shelves that were set into the paneling, and there were a couple of leather easy chairs and reading lamps over in one corner. In the center of the room, on a maroon carpet, was the billiard table, complete with a lamp that hung down from the ceiling, and a scoring wire that ran overhead. Cut into the farther wall there was a bar. Mr. van Neerdaam walked over to the bar and pressed a button on its surface. A minute later the man who had served dinner appeared on the other side of the bar, pulling on a black jacket.

"Roger," Mr. van Neerdaam said, "we'll be playing here for a while. What will you take to drink, Patrick?"

Patrick looked down at his empty brandy snifter. He didn't like brandy all that much.

"Scotch and soda'd be fine," he said.

"I think I'll join you in that. Do you want some beer, Anna?"

Anna nodded her head. She was busy taking the cover off the billiard table, and Patrick hastened to help her.

Patrick stood there, a respectful distance away from the two players, and sipped his drink. Just now Anna was making a difficult two-cushion shot, and Patrick watched her as she stretched out over the table to make it. Her arms were tanned from the summer, and her hair caught every possible light from the lamp suspended over the green cloth of the table. Her right arm moved, the cue flashed, and the cue ball spun down, hit the cushion behind the first ball, hit the first ball, spun into the side cushion, reversed its spin, and came to rest just short of the second ball.

"I'll have to teach you a little more about thinking ahead," Mr. van Neerdaam said. "That was all right, but if you'd put some more steam on it you could have knocked that second ball way down there." He pointed toward a spot far away from where the second ball and the cue ball were standing. "You left me too good a shot." He bent over, and took position. Suddenly it was if everything was being run by machinery. The cue flashed, there was a knot of clicking balls, and then the balls rolled away from each other and ended up resting in different corners. Mr. van Neerdaam took a little of his scotch and soda, and looked at Anna over the top of the glass.

"I think you just might have me," Anna said, and bent down to study the shot.

"That's the thing about being an only child," Anna said as they came down the steps of the house and started strolling toward Fifth Avenue. "I can shoot skeet, too."

Jacob was still up when Patrick came in the door that led from the elevator vestibule on the upper floor of the apartment. Patrick saw the light on in the library, and started down the hall in that direction, getting out his handkerchief and feverishly rubbing away what lipstick might still be left on his mouth. His father was sitting in his easy chair, surrounded by papers. Patrick looked at his watch. It was two-fifteen.

"Hello," Jacob said, standing up and stretching. His tie was loosened, and over his shirt he was wearing his vest open in front.

" 'Evening, Father."

Jacob sat down again. "Have a good time?"

"Wonderful."

"What did you do?"

"Well, I had dinner at the van Neerdaams, and then we went to the Stork Club for a while."

"You young people and that Stork Club," Jacob said, shaking his head. "Listen, Patrick, do you want to marry that girl?"

Patrick's jaw dropped. Then he realized that he still had on his coat, and took it off and sat down.

"I guess that's about it," he said.

"How're you working it out about religion?"

"Well, look, Father," Patrick said. "I mean we haven't actually said we're going to marry each other. But she's going to go to the Catholic church down in Bryn Mawr, and explain that she wants to know more about it, and then maybe they'll give her some instruction or something."

Jacob nodded. "But if you can work that out, you'd like to marry her."

"If she'll have me."

"All right." Jacob straightened up in his chair. "I think she's a very fine girl, and I'd just as soon see it happen. But I want you to get some idea of the size of the responsibility. You're going to need money." Jacob stopped and nodded his head. "You're going to need a lot more money than you can imagine. Now here's my idea. If you do all right at the Law School and seem to be making a go of things, I don't see any reason why you shouldn't get married after your first year of law. I'll see you through."

Patrick sat there. "Well, that's very nice," he said after a minute.

"I just want you to get some idea of the realities of this thing," Jacob said. "You've always had this idea that there's always more money somewhere. Maybe I gave you that, but I can't believe it. Just wait until you have to buy baby shoes. You won't believe how often you're paying for new shoes for your children." Jacob smiled. "You just won't believe it."

Patrick stood up. He felt there was an awful lot more to say, but he didn't know what it was. "We'll, we'll see what happens," he said.

"We certainly will." Jacob picked up a blue-covered brief and opened it. "Don't worry about it all at once. Just try to start thinking about it, that's all."

"I'm thinking about it, all right." Patrick looked at his watch.

"I hope you get some sleep some time tonight."

Jacob smiled. "This is my job. You'll be at your job when you get back to college."

"Well, good night. God bless you."

"Good night, Patrick. Anytime you want to talk this thing over, just bring it up.

"I will, Father," Patrick said. "I will."

7

BILL BENCH smiled across the table in Cronin's.

"Well, she sounds like quite a girl," he said.

Patrick nodded his head. Tall Man had dragged Snowjob off to a get-acquainted dance at a secretarial school, and Patrick and Bill had decided to settle for a few beers at Cronin's. So here they sat, on the first night of their last year at Harvard, swapping stories about their vacations, as they had done for the past seven years at school and college. They had both put on their Concrete Kimono ties, and they were working on their second bottle of Budweiser.

"I think this one's going to work out," Patrick said.

"What does she think about religion?" Bill said.

" I don't know, exactly. At least she seems to be judging the thing on its own merits. We talked about it quite a bit up there — I don't know. I gave her a Catechism, and now she's going to go to the Catholic church in Bryn Mawr and see if she can get some instruction."

"That sounds reasonable," Bill said.

"She's been terrific about it," Patrick said. "You're really going to like her, Bill."

"I'll bet I will."

Patrick took a sip of his beer. "This is just between us, but I think maybe she and I could get married after my first year at the Law School."

"Boy." Bill sat looking down at the beer in his glass. Patrick had mentioned the Law School half a dozen times since he had unpacked today, and it bothered Bill. I don't know, Bill was thinking as he studied the edges of foam on the surface of the beer. Patrick goes away not at all sure about law, and he comes back sure he wants to go to the Law School. And the only thing I can make out that's changed about Patrick is this girl.

"Are you going to take any writing courses this year?" Bill said after a minute, raising his eyes and looking across the table at Patrick.

Patrick shrugged his shoulders, and Bill noticed that Patrick was tearing the label off his bottle of beer. Patrick always did that, tearing the label off neatly and systematically. "Maybe I should, just to round it out," Patrick said after a minute.

"Why don't you try to get into Allston Hunt's course?"

Patrick stopped tearing at the label.

"What do you know about him, Bill? I always thought he just gave a lecture here every year, but I guess he's really on the faculty, isn't he?"

"Of course he's on the faculty," Bill said.

"Well, I just didn't know," Patrick said. "I know he's a famous writer and everything, but I just didn't know how much time he spent here."

"Well, it's your field," Bill said, taking a swallow of his beer, "but I should think it would be nice to be able to say you were in a course with him, even if you end up on the Supreme Court or something."

"Well, what do you know about him?"

"I don't know. The guy's a fabulous character, that's all I know. He was in the Foreign Legion in the First World War, and then I guess he knocked around, and you know as much about his writing as I do."

"I don't know a damn thing about his writing, except that I've always heard his name."

"Haven't you ever read *The Hellheart?*"

"Uh-uh."

"Well, it got a Pulitzer Prize and a couple of other things. It's just a short thing."

"A novella."

"You're the English major, buddy," Bill said. "I'm just a guy who reads. Call it a novella or anything you say. I think I've got it in an anthology back at the room."

"Maybe I'll try to get into that course," Patrick said. He hadn't thought about "Technical Jones" for a couple of weeks, but now it came flooding into his mind. He had brought it up from New York with him, along with all his short stories from the past two years, and all the copies of the issues of the *Lampoon* that he had had stories in, and now suddenly he was trying to pick out which things to bundle up together, along with the forty pages of "Technical Jones," to show to this man Allston Hunt. "I'll never get in that course," Patrick said after a minute. "The guys in the senior course are real pros."

"What the hell," Bill Bench said, finishing his beer. "You might as well try." He looked at the electric clock over the bar at the end of the big smoky hall. "Let's get out of here."

"O.K.," Patrick said, standing up. "I've got twenty cents. Think that's enough to leave her?"

Bill put his hand in the pocket of his khaki trousers and came up with a quarter. "I'll put this down, and take one of your dimes, and you keep the other one."

"Yeah, I guess you're right."

They both walked toward the front door, past the rows of booths filled with laughing, talking boys and girls, and then they

were through the two sets of glass doors and out on the street.
It was suddenly quiet out here, and the coolness of the evening
came onto their brows. They stood there for a second, looking
at Dunster Street just outside Cronin's, with a girl sitting in an
MG waiting for somebody, and the sound of laughter in the
distance, and a beer can bouncing on the pavement. Patrick
nodded his head at something, and if you had asked him why he
nodded he could not have told you. They began walking back
slowly toward Leverett House.

II

Anna van Neerdaam came out of her dream with a start and lay
on her side, looking at the dimly lit wall of her college bedroom.
After a few seconds she sat up in bed, straightening her pajama
top, and looked over at the luminous dial of the alarm clock on
her bureau. It said that it was four o'clock.

Anna got out of bed, put her feet into a pair of mules, and
slipped on her old maroon wool dressing gown. Then she went
into the big middle room that she and Pam Jackson shared as
their living room, and put on the light on her desk.

She sat down in one of their two easy chairs. The halls of
Pembroke West were dead-quiet, and the only sound was that
of their two alarm clocks ticking, and Pam's breathing in the
other bedroom. Anna sat there, thinking over the dream that
she had just had. She and Patrick had gone over to the Blue
Hill Fair just before the summer ended, and in her dream just
now she had been back there. They were standing by the rail
watching the trotting races, and then she walked away from him.
That was all that had happened, but it had been enough to wake
her up.

Anna stared down at the blue carpet on the floor for a couple
of minutes, and then she rose from the easy chair, turned off the
light, and went back into her bedroom.

III

Patrick stood in the line of perhaps thirty students who were waiting in an upper corridor of Warren House to see Allston Hunt in his office. There was sunlight coming in one of the windows and falling on the wooden banisters of a stairway, and most of the boys and girls were tanned from the summer.

"What's your major project, Kingsgrant?"

Patrick recognized a young man who had been with him in John Ciardi's course two years before.

"Hi. What do you suppose they mean by a major project?"

"I don't know, but that's what the catalogue says. Must be engaged in work on a major project."

"Well," Patrick said, "I've got about forty pages of something. It's too long to be a short story."

"I'm working on a verse play," the young man said.

"Sounds interesting," Patrick said, and that was the end of that conversation.

A few minutes later Patrick was the next in line. The door opened, a short Radcliffe girl in a skirt and blouse came out looking unhappy, and Patrick took a deep breath and walked in.

It was a long room, sparsely furnished. There was a table surrounded by chairs near the door through which he had just come, and a desk set at right angles to the one tall window at the far end. A man was sitting there beside the window, leaning back in a swivel chair, and Patrick walked toward him. My God, Patrick thought as he came closer, he looks just like Raymond Massey.

The man in the chair looked at him. There was an impersonal expression on his face when he looked up, and then he smiled. It was the darndest smile that Patrick had ever seen. It was a little-boy smile, and it said, just as if the man was speaking,

Don't let anybody kid you, son, nothing in this world is a very
big deal.

"Sit down," Allston Hunt said.

Patrick was still standing there, struck by that smile that had
exploded in the room, and finally he sat down.

"What's your name?" the man said. He asked it as if he was
sorry to have to bother Patrick, but they both knew that there
were a certain number of these little details in life.

"Patrick Kingsgrant, sir."

The man wrote down Patrick's name on a sheet of paper, and
then he stopped and stared at it. "Did you ever have a relative that
played football here?"

"My father played here, sir. He was in the Class of Nineteen-
Sixteen."

The man nodded. The smile had disappeared, and that cold
serious look was back on his face as he studied the sheet of paper
in front of him. Patrick was still trying to get over that smile.
When the man smiled, they were equals. When that look
came back on his face, he was a full professor and Patrick was
an undergraduate.

"Why do you want to be in this course, Mr. Kingsgrant?"

"Well, I've been trying to get an education in writing,"
Patrick said after a minute, "and I've taken Ciardi's course, and
Clark's course, and I've been on the *Lampoon* since I was a
freshman, and I think this is the next logical step."

"So do I," Allston Hunt said, not looking up as his pen moved
across the sheet of paper on his desk. "What do you want to
do when you get out of here?"

Patrick straightened up in his chair. The moment had come
to tell a lie, and he didn't like it, but either he was trying to get in
this course or he wasn't.

"I'd like to get a job on a newspaper or a magazine," Patrick
said.

The man nodded. "You in a club?"

"Yes, sir."

"I can always use somebody from that milieu," the man said, half to himself, and then he sat there looking Patrick over. His eyes were brown, and there was something just a little bit funny about his right eye. "Got an idea for a novel?"

"Yes, sir."

"Tell me about it."

Patrick told him about Technical Jones, and Leapingdeer, and how Leapingdeer fell in love with a girl from Boston, and the girl's family did not approve, and eventually the girl broke up with Leapingdeer.

"Sounds as if it's more about the one from Arizona and his romance than his friendship with Technical Jones," the professor said when Patrick was through.

"I'm afraid you're right, sir. Maybe I can get it back into proportion."

"Maybe I can help you," Hunt said. "Who do you think is the most important American writer? Contemporary American writer."

"Ernest Hemingway."

"What do you think of him?"

Patrick suddenly remembered something that Luther Allen had said to him the day he labeled the cans backward.

"Lot of brains and not much sense," Patrick said.

Hunt smiled, and there it was again. He seemed like a person you'd really like to have a beer with. "What do you think of Faulkner?"

"Well, I don't know much about him. I haven't liked what I've read."

"What writer do you think you're most like? Any period."

"Scott Fitzgerald. That's the one I want to beat."

"So you think you're in competition with Scott Fitzgerald,"

the man said, looking at Patrick. He was grinning.

"He's my favorite writer," Patrick said. "I think Hemingway's better, but I like Fitzgerald more."

"So you don't necessarily enjoy the best writing the most?"

"I think you can be fond of a horse that's slower than another horse you don't like quite as much."

"That's all right as long as you're not betting," Hunt said. "Leave your stuff with me. I'll send you a card about whether you're in or out."

Patrick handed him the big manila envelope that he had with him. It contained "Technical Jones," a couple of *Lampoons*, and two short stories from Clark's course.

"What's your address?"

"Leverett D-Thirty-Two, sir. I've got it there on the envelope."

"Right."

Patrick walked across the long room and went out into the hall, knowing that there was a line of students, but not really seeing them. He was playing the conversation back over in his mind, word for word. Anyhow, Patrick said to himself, you're not going to get in. They've got graduate students and Nieman Fellows and everything else in that course. But he's a nice guy. Patrick went out the door of Warren House and walked across the asphalt space in front of the Union. He kept thinking about Allston Hunt, and he decided that he'd read *The Hellheart*, even if he wasn't going to get into the course.

IV

Anna came out of the archway that joined Pembroke East and Pembroke West, and started down the street under the leaves that were just beginning to turn brown. She was wearing a navy blue coat cut in the coachman style, with white slashes at the pockets, and a black velvet beret. The two Catechisms were in her right hand, and Anna had a thoughtful look on her face as she walked down the sloping street away from the gray stone tower of Pembroke. She had an appointment at the rectory of the Catholic church in Bryn Mawr, and as she walked along, she was wondering how much they would expect her to know. She had switched over from the No. 2 book to the No. 3, and read every question and answer in it carefully, thoughtfully. Now she was going to go over there and explain to the priest she was seeing that she was interested in a boy who was a Catholic, and that she would like to learn more about the Catholic Church.

Anna turned the corner at the bottom of the hill, and went to her right. Her feet started slowing down, and then she stopped for a minute, under a low-hanging maple branch, her eyes looking down at the sidewalk. A sudden vertical wrinkle formed on her forehead. It had just hit her that she was not at all sure that she wanted to marry Patrick Kingsgrant. She stood there under the tree in the sunshine of late September, and a breeze passed through the leaves over her head, and tugged her golden hair a bit away from her neck. When Anna looked up from her contemplation of the sidewalk, the expression in her eyes was one of blank horror. All her life she had known what she was doing. She had sometimes been wrong in her estimates of other people, but she had always known how she herself felt about any given thing. And now here she was walking toward a church to take up their time teaching her a religion because she was interested in marrying a person of that religion, and suddenly, just walking along the street, she was not at all sure she wanted to marry him.

"Hi, Anna. Don't you look nice."

Anna nodded. She didn't even see who it was. It was somebody on a bicycle. I love him, Anna said to herself. And if I love him then I want to marry him. That's why I'm here. She tried to say it to herself again, but it wouldn't take. She tried to tell herself she was sure of what she was doing, but a little voice had started up on the other side of her brain. She couldn't hear what it was saying, but it was jabbering away to beat the band.

Anna shook her head. If that's the way it is you better not go up to that church right now. You must be just nervous or something today. She shook her head again, violently, and pressed at the sidewalk with her heel. You'd better get back there and call up the church and say you're sick or something. A look of sadness was coming across her face, as if it were some sort of poison that was being pumped into her. She felt sick at her stomach, and sick in her throat. Slowly, as if each step required concentration, she started back toward her room.

v

Professor Allston Hunt put down a section of "Technical Jones" and smiled. He was sitting in the swivel chair at his desk, and he turned in the chair and put his feet up on the window sill. His right eye was a glass eye, and many years ago he had moved his desk so that its left flank was against the window. He would read for a while, and then when his one good eye tired, he would just push his chair back from the desk, turn to the left so that he was facing the window, and put his feet up on the window sill.

He stretched once as he leaned back in his chair, staring at the leaves that brushed against his window. The room was quiet. His mind was quickly and expertly going over the rhythm of Patrick's prose, and after a minute he smiled. It was so funny, he thought. You read so many efforts, by so many students, and every now and then you picked up something and there it was, perhaps raw and redundant and immature, but there it was, with the spark of life in it, as different from the others as night from day.

Hunt stretched again, and then he took his feet down from the sill and stood up. He paced the length of his office, past the table around which his class would sit, and past the bookshelves that held the printed words that were the instruments of his art. It was all there on the bookshelves: dictionaries, anthologies, novels, books of poetry, and manuscripts, his manuscripts and other people's manuscripts. It was all there on the bookshelves except for one thing, and that one thing was the curious combination of brains and heart that made a man a good writer. Everything else was on the bookshelves, but that one thing was what the communicating individual carried around with him, and either you had it or you didn't. If you had it, it could be developed, but if you didn't have it, there was nothing anybody could do for you.

Allston Hunt turned at the door, and paced back slowly toward his desk. He had to pick the twelve people who were going to be in his course, and he had to let them know by tomorrow, so they could sign their study cards. Hunt sat down and pulled the list of applicants for the course toward him. He put a check behind Patrick's name, and sat there for a second, looking at the forty-page pile of "Technical Jones." Hunt pulled a big manila envelope toward him across the top of the desk, and began putting Patrick's things into it. A couple of short stories there were not particularly well focused, two well-done but superficial things in the *Lampoon*, and the forty pages of "Technical Jones." He closed the envelope and stared at it for a minute. He was feeling tired this afternoon, and it was no afternoon to be feeling tired and dreamy. But still, looking at all the envelopes around the room, the work of hopeful applicants for the course, he could not be the totally cold-blooded judge that perhaps he should be. Eventually he would get twelve people out of this mass of envelopes, but now, looking at the silent bundles of words, he felt an impractical desire to protect all of the youthful compulsions that these manuscripts represented. He was a bachelor, and he was fifty-nine years old. When he had been the age of these boys and girls, he had been in love with something, just as these people were, and he had not known what it was, just as they did not know what it was. He often thought that he felt more closely bound to his students than they did to him, because he was standing down nearer the finish line, and he could see what a tough course they still had to run, while they could not see anything ahead but the next page, and then the next chapter.

Allston Hunt knew what it was to be young and yearning to learn and to express. He loved his work today as much as he ever had, but he loved now from the knowledge of how to communicate, and he had loved then from the hunger to learn everything, and to express everything. He had paid more for his passion than most of the glib, comfortably dressed young men who came to sit in his classes, and, sitting there staring at his desk top, his heart went back to his first flirtations with his lifelong love.

Cambridge, Massachusetts, was a long way from Crannon's Mill, Oregon, in 1910, and it was even farther away for a boy who had no money. John Hunt was not an unkind man, but sometimes in the evening when he and Allston were washing up at the pump in the shed he would look at his son with a reproachful sadness in his eyes.

"I don't see why you want to go to that place," he would say, slowly. Allston would keep washing his forearms and hands. "Why?" John Hunt would say, a little louder.

"It's a good school, Father. I'm going to go if they take me."

"And what do you think you'll use for money?"

Allston would shake his head. "I don't know," he would say, drying his hands with a towel. He had tried once or twice to explain to his father about the way reading Shakespeare made him feel, and how they had this fellow Copeland at Harvard, and Kittredge, and what Miss Sterns at the high school had told him about Harvard, but none of those things meant anything to his father. John Hunt cared about his apple trees and his two cows and his fields, and that was all right with Allston, but he was damned if his father was going to stop him from doing something that his father didn't even understand.

Finally the day came. It was the first of July, and Allston figured that if he started now and worked where he could, he ought to be in Cambridge all right when school started in September. His mother and father stood there while he put his one suitcase up on the buckboard in which Jeff Morton was driving him in to town. His mother knew perfectly well that it was going to be a long time before she saw Allston again, but it was easier for her than it was for John, because she had an idea that he was doing the right thing.

"Well, I wish you luck," John Hunt said.

"I know you do, Father." Allston was an inch or two taller than his father, and just then, with his hat on his head, he looked much more like a man than a boy. Then he took his hat off and kissed his mother.

"I know you'll make us proud, Allston," his mother said, and she held the tears back until the buckboard was out of sight.

Allston got there with two weeks to spare, and without touching the money in the bottom of his suitcase, the money he had saved toward his tuition from odd jobs in the last two years. Before he even tried to find a room he walked around the Yard, a tall boy from Oregon with a suitcase in his hand. Most of the buildings were shut for the summer, but Allston stopped in front of Sever and Boylston and one or two of the others, looking at the walls and wondering how many books there were inside them. He was excited just thinking about how many books were inside there. Finally he went off to look for a place to live. He figured that if he could find a room in a house where he did the chores, he might be all right. Then if he could get a job in the afternoons, he might even be able to get up the rest of the tuition money.

As usual, Allston was a pretty good figurer. A Mr. McCann took one look at this obviously healthy specimen and said he'd give him room and board if he did the chores, which was a lot more than Allston had been hoping for, and then he got a job clerking in the afternoons in a warehouse in Cambridge, and things got along. It was hard work staying ahead of what it cost him to go to Harvard, but he did it. On Sunday afternoons he would walk along the Charles and up through Mount Auburn Cemetery, and his main thought would be how lucky he was. He didn't have a friend to walk with because he had been too busy to make any friends, but it didn't bother him. Allston was humble about the education at Harvard, and this was what kept him from getting bitter about the boys with money, boys who had all the clothes they wanted and a servant in their rooms on the Gold Coast and access to the swimming pool in Westmorly Court. Allston saw all those things and thought the boys who had them were very lucky, and when he had enough money he went up to Max Keezer's and bought a secondhand suit that looked just like the suits those boys wore. He thought it was a lot better looking suit of clothes than the one he had arrived in, and he was right.

And on top of it, money didn't count in the classroom. Before long his professors knew that there was a brilliant, polite, reserved young man named Allston Hunt sitting in their classes, satisfying a ferocious hunger for knowledge, and they were all for him. He had come a long way, and he had been right to come.

Allston Hunt's pen moved across the back of a penny postcard. "Dear Mr. Kingsgrant," it wrote, "Delighted to have you in English R. First meeting next Wednesday, this office, 7.00 P.M. A. Hunt."

VI

"Can we come in now?" Snowjob asked.

"Sure," Patrick said, smiling. He had just finished calling Anna in Bryn Mawr, and as he put the receiver back on the hook, Snowjob and Tall Man and Bill came parading back into the living room from their temporary exile.

"How was she?" Snowjob said. He was much impressed with the fact that Patrick was going around with Anna van Neerdaam.

"Fine," Patrick said.

"That's good," Tall Man said, sitting down on the couch and promptly collapsing backward into the standard Tall Man Reclining Position.

"How'd your class go?" Bill Bench asked. Patrick had come straight back from Allston Hunt's seminar at nine o'clock in the evening, and promptly pushed the three of them into the bedroom that Snowjob and Tall Man shared, while he made his call.

"It was all right. Some girl read something out of her novel. I think she needs to have a baby, instead of writing a novel."

"How does the class work?" Tall Man said, staring at the ceiling.

"Well, each week a different person reads his stuff for about an hour, and then during the second hour they tear it apart."

"You mean anybody can tear it apart?" Bill Bench asked.

"And how."

"Well, what does Hunt do?"

"Oh, he sort of guides the discussion. He says nine-tenths of being a writer is what goes on when you're by yourself with your typewriter, so I don't think he worries too much about the class meetings. It just gives you a few new ideas, that's all."

"What's this novel of yours about, anyway, Patrick?" Tall Man was still lying there. If his lips hadn't moved, you would have thought he was awaiting the embalmer.

Patrick smiled. For a month now he had been successfully avoiding this sort of question from Snowjob and Tall Man. He couldn't quite see looking Tall Man in the eye and saying, "I'm writing a novel about you, boy."

"Well, it's still pretty unformed," Patrick said. "You know, it's a little hard to tell."

"All right, so you don't want to tell us," Snowjob said. "Can Anna go to the Princeton game with you?"

"Uh-huh." Patrick nodded his head and smiled.

"How's she coming with the religious field?" Bill asked.

"I don't know. When I was down there last week-end she said she'd been pretty busy, and she hadn't been able to get over there yet."

"They really do work them like hell at Bryn Mawr." Snowjob shook his head. "You want to hit Cronin's, men?"

"Sure," Bill said.

Tall Man kept lying there. "I think I'll do some work."

"Don't kid me," Snowjob said. "You're just resting up to go over and see the newest."

"What's this?" Patrick was suddenly interested. He hadn't heard a word about Tall Man's amatory exploits in weeks.

"It's nothing," Tall Man spoke quickly. "Shut up, Snowjob."

"This is the deal our friend Tall Man has been coaching himself for for years." Snowjob smiled. "She's a buyer for a store in Boston, she has an apartment by herself, and it looks as if Tall Man is elected."

"Why don't you mind your own business?" Tall Man said. He was trying to sound angry, but he wasn't succeeding.

"What does she look like?" Bill Bench asked.

"Terrific," Snowjob said, slamming the fist of his right hand into the palm of his left. "She made us dinner last Sunday night. She's fantastic. I'm not kidding you."

"You said you weren't going to say a damn thing about it." Tall Man was still trying to sound irritated.

"How old is she?" Bill inquired, grinning.

"About twenty-five." Tall Man could not disguise the pleasure in his voice.

"What does she buy?" Patrick asked.

Tall Man sat up. "She buys corsets. She doesn't need one herself, but she buys them. Anytime you want any corsets, just let me know. I can get you one-third off the wholesale price."

"You're too kind," Patrick said, and laughed.

"Has she got a friend?" Bill Bench said.

"Friendless." Tall Man's face composed itself in its most deadpan expression. "I'm sorry, men, but I'm scalping this one all by myself."

"Let's get going," Snowjob said to Bill. "Don't forget your toothbrush, Tall Man." They went out, and Patrick went into his room, leaving the figure of Tall Man once again stretching out on the couch, awaiting the hour of assignation.

Normally Patrick got to sleep pretty quickly once he was in bed, but he was still awake after Tall Man had gone out, and he heard Bill and Snowjob come in from their tour of Cronin's.

"Don't bother being quiet," Patrick said when Bill tiptoed into their bedroom. "I'm awake."

"O.K. Mind if I put on the light?"

"No. Go ahead." Patrick turned over, facing the wall. He kept trying to tell himself that everything was all right, but something wasn't all right. He went over the week-end in Bryn Mawr again in his mind. He had picked Anna up at Pembroke West, and she had directed him to the guest house where he was going to stay, and waited outside in Chrissy while he shaved and changed. Then they drove into Philadelphia to an Italian restaurant that Anna suggested.

Bill turned out the light, and Patrick flipped over so that he was lying on his back, staring up at the pattern of leaves on the ceiling, thrown on it by the lights from the courtyard below. That restaurant had been a good place. They had had a delicious meal, and after dinner they had stayed there and a violinist had come around and played at each table. Anna had smiled. "Will you play 'A Kiss in the Dark'?" she had said to the man, and then she had turned to Patrick. "It's corny, but I like it." Patrick had mumbled something, and the violinist had begun to play. Anna had taken his hand under the table, and Patrick had sat there, his hand returning every pressure through Anna's hand, but worrying about how much to give the violinist. All the way through "A Kiss in the Dark" he worried about it, and when it was over he gave the violinist a dollar and the man was very happy about it and Patrick was relieved. Then the violinist had played some more, and Patrick had relaxed and enjoyed it and they had finished the evening on a road near the college, with Anna's lips and Anna's mouth and Anna's hair and the stars in the sky. And the next day they had gone over to Valley Forge, and wandered around the place all day, and had ended up eating by candlelight at an inn.

Patrick had said his prayers before he got into bed, but now he slid out from under the covers and knelt down beside his bed again, his elbows on the blankets. It had been a perfect week-end, but every now and then it was as if Anna was holding something back, as if she was not quite with him all the way. Patrick bent his head in the darkness, said three Our Fathers, three Hail Marys, and an Act of Contrition, and got back into bed.

VII

Jacob sat in the library at 1120, reading a letter from Patrick. He had just come home from work and the letter was waiting for him, so he had come straight into the library to read it without bothering to hang up his coat and hat in his room.

Jacob smiled. Patrick was asking him to call up some stable in New York and get two horses for about 9 A M. the morning of Saturday, November the seventh. Apparently he and Anna wanted to go riding in Central Park and then go down to her place, change their clothes, and grab the train for Princeton and the game. Jacob stared at Patrick's request, thought of writing back and suggesting that they go riding Sunday morning when they didn't have to rush to a game, decided against it, and went on to the next paragraph of the letter. Patrick said that he thought it was wonderful to think of having a party for him at Locke-Ober's when his twenty-first birthday rolled around in December, and that he was reserving rooms for both of them when they came up.

Jacob looked away for a moment, and then his eyes went back to the letter again. Patrick said that he liked Perry Miller in American Literature very much, and that Perry Miller had told them, "You don't have to hate Alexander Hamilton in this course, but it helps." Constitutional Law was proving to be tough, and Allston Hunt's course was marvelous. Signed, Patrick. Then there was a P.S. "She can come to the Yale game, too. P."

Jacob put the letter down. So Patrick's girl could go to the Yale game too. He stood up and went over to the window. There was a kindly, sympathetic expression on his face. He was thinking that this was a young romance, all mixed up with college and football games and horseback riding in Central Park, and then, looking out toward the East River, one of the memories of his not-such-a-young-love swept over him. It had happened after he had been down to see Maude in New York in the autumn of 1927. He had come back and stewed around. He wanted to write her, but he was sure that he would say the wrong thing. Not just one wrong thing. A million wrong things. Finally he had sent her a Christmas card, a scene of the Nativity that had a simple "Merry Christmas" as a legend, and signed it, "With all my best wishes, Jacob Kingsgrant," and back had come a card that looked almost exactly the same, with the same message. And that was the way that it stood until the day that he was thinking about.

Jacob had come into the office at South Harbor one morning in February of 1928 and found Roland Grindall sitting at his desk with an air of studied nonchalance.

" 'Morning," Jacob had said, taking off his sheepskin-lined coat and bending down to unbuckle his overshoes.

" 'Morning, Jake." There was such an undercurrent of excitment and amusement in Rolly's voice that Jacob straightened up again, still wearing one overshoe.

"What's up?" he said, taking his hat off and putting it on the antler hatrack.

Rolly finally condescended to turn from his desk and face Jacob.

"Friend of yours is in Bar Harbor."

"Oh?" Jacob bent down to take off the other overshoe. "Who?"

"Maude Buckleigh."

"Very funny." Jacob stood up, holding the overshoe dangling from his right hand.

"You might read the letter from her. It's on your desk."

Jacob walked to the desk slowly, put down his overshoe and picked up the letter that was sitting there. It was addressed to "Jacob Kingsgrant, Esq., Kingsgrant and Grindall, Attorneys-at-Law, South Harbor, Me." Jacob ripped it open. It was from Maude. She and her mother were in Bar Harbor, taking care of Henry Wintridge, who was sick. Maude wondered if perhaps she might take him up on his offer to show her the island some-time. Jacob sat down in his swivel chair heavily, as if he had been shot, and were toppling into it. His eyes were half closed, there was a silly smile on his face, and he opened his mouth once or twice.

"Too bad you live out there, Jake," Rolly was saying as he pretended to look through some papers on his desk. "Central told me last night they got up here yesterday morning. Whole town knew they were here by last night."

Jacob was still sitting there. He thought about telephoning her. He couldn't trust his voice. He thought about writing her. Too slow. Suddenly he realized that if he hurried he could catch Ben while he was still shopping for a few things before he took the launch back to the island. He picked up his overshoes, grabbed his coat, slammed his hat on top of his head, and paused for just a second by the door.

"Miss Buckleigh needs some legal advice," he said, looking Rolly Grindall dead in the eye. "I'm going over to Bar Harbor to see that she's properly advised by counsel. I might be gone all day."

"Certainly glad she didn't trust any of those hick lawyers in New York," Rolly remarked, smiling.

"So am I," Jacob said, and then he thundered down the stairs and out into the snow-packed street.

Maude was sitting by one of the tall windows in Henry Wint-ridge's bedroom, listening to him explain about the vertical wisps that were hanging over the water all around Penobscot Bay that morning. Henry refused to stay in bed and he was sitting bundled up in an easy chair by the second-floor window, looking over the snowy lawn that led down to the water.

"It's called sea smoke," Henry was saying. "Those wisps go up about twenty feet off the water, and anybody going through them in a boat gets covered with ice crystals."

"It looks weird," Maude said, staring out at the forest of thin vertical clouds over the slate-gray salt water.

"Yes, isn't it weird?" He sat back and looked at Maude. It was all very nice of Maude to come along with her mother to look after him while he had this damned flu, but he was worried about what there would be to amuse her in February. After a minute he took up the book in his lap, and began reading it again. Maude sat there, looking out the window, wondering if Jacob had got her letter by now. Suddenly she straightened up, her head turning to one side and her eyes opening wider.

"There seems to be a boat out there," she said.

"Quite possibly," Henry Wintridge murmured, deep in his book.

"He seems to be putting in here."

"I rather think not." Henry was still reading.

"Maybe not, but he's coming straight in here."

Henry put down his book, leaned forward in his chair, and picked up the binoculars that he kept on the window sill. "That's the damnedest thing," he said, squinting through them. "If I didn't know he was over in South Harbor, I'd say that was Jacob Kingsgrant's boat."

"Well, whoever it is, he's putting in here."

"No doubt about that."

"I think I'll go down there and find out what they want."

"You don't have to do that, Maude. I'll send one of the servants."

Maude stood up. "I think I'd like to do it," she said, and went down the stairway with quick steps. She took her coat and overshoes out of the hall closet, and a minute later she was making her way across the wind-blown snow of the lawn, down toward the pier to which the float was connected in summertime. Just as she got there the *Ethan Kingsgrant* came sliding in from the Bay. Jacob and Ben were standing in the cockpit, both looking as if they were encrusted with diamonds, and the whole boat gave off a silvery sparkle from the millions of crystals of ice that had settled on its hull.

"Well," Maude said.

Jacob looked up at her. "Hello, Maude." He and Ben worked for a minute or two, securing the launch to the rings on the concrete pierblocks, and then they swung up. "Better come up to the house and get warm, Ben," Jacob said, brushing the diamonds from his sleeves, and then he looked down at Maude.

"How are you?"

"I'm fine, Jake. Just fine. Can I come see your house?"

Jacob looked out at the Bay. "Wouldn't you rather wait for a better day?"

"I'd just as soon go now."

Jacob nodded his head. "We'll go out there for lunch. Just as soon as we warm up and say hello. How's Henry?"

"He's all right. Mother's really fixed him up."

They walked up to the house. Henry sat there at his window, watching them come across the lawn. He had forgotten that Maude and Jacob knew each other. Perhaps Jacob might keep Maude amused, at least for a few hours.

All the way out to the island, Jacob kept thinking that there was something he had forgotten, something that had to be changed before Maude could be shown around, but he could not remember what it was. Then he would look at Maude, who was standing there in the cockpit in a tan leather coat, her eyes sparkling and her cheeks pink, and he would stop worrying about it. They pulled up to the landing, and Jacob helped Maude up over the slippery side. The sun was coming out now, and the sea smoke was diminishing. There was only a tasteful sprinkling of diamonds on the leather of her coat, and Jacob brushed these off as she stood still obediently for a moment on the pier. No one knew they were coming, so Bertram was not there with the car. They started walking up the snowy drive, laughing, and then Jacob remembered what it was. Right in the living room, right on the wall, he had a framed Masonic emblem, the emblem of the local lodge to which he and Roland Grindall belonged. Jacob was not a very active Mason, and he didn't really know why it was that the Catholics were death on Masons and the Masons were death on Catholics, but he didn't want a test case right then.

"Are you feeling sick?" Maude asked, looking up at him. "You looked as if something hurt you just then."

"Oh, no," Jacob said. He paraded her past the front door and around to the kitchen, where he handed her over to Harriet to dry out. Then he charged into the living room, still wearing his big sheepskin coat. He skidded to a stop, grabbed the emblem off the wall, tossed it into his desk drawer, and walked back to the kitchen, a smile restored to his face.

Maude had taken off her leather coat and her hat, and she was standing by the stove, wearing a green wool dress, with Harriet beaming at her, and it was just then, seeing her standing by the stove at Kingsgrant, that Jacob knew. He had been pretty certain before, but now he knew.

"Can you give us some lunch, Harriet?"

"Sure can, Mr. Jacob."

"Good. Let's have a drink," Jacob said, and Maude followed him out of the kitchen.

She kept looking at him as he bent to light the fire in the living room, as he poured her a little whiskey, and the one thing she was certain about was that it had been no hallucination this past fall during those two weeks he had spent in New York. Jacob was real, all right, and somehow he looked even better here than he had in the city. He had a wonderful color in his face, that kind of deep healthy glow that comes from being outdoors a lot, and she thought he was quite the finest-looking man she had ever seen. There was a quality of purity about this man sitting at the head of the mahogany table in his own white-wood dining room. It was so quiet on this snow-filled island, a silence much more profound than anything Maude had experienced before. She felt terribly grateful to Henry Wintridge for getting these bouts of the flu and asking her mother to come up and look after him. It wasn't right to pray that Henry wouldn't get well right away, but since he wasn't in any pain she didn't see why she should pray that he would make an instant recovery.

"Potatoes?"

"Potatoes?" Maude came out of her thoughts. "Potatoes? Oh, no thanks."

After lunch, Jacob showed her around the house. Maude loved it all, the paintings and the framed newspaper items about different clippers in which the Kingsgrants had had an interest, and the big beds in the bedrooms upstairs. These austere New Englanders managed a few comforts after all. Then Jacob showed her the barns, and, well wrapped up, they walked down to the graveyard, while Jacob pointed at various snow-covered fields and explained what the summertime crops in them would be. Finally they came back to the house and had tea. It was somewhere in there, when Maude was asking Jacob whether he would have cream or lemon, that she began to realize what a happy few hours she had spent on Jacob's island. The only thing that gave her any discomfort was the fact that she could not keep her eyes off Jacob, and it seemed to her that this was an impolite way to behave.

At last Maude was bundled into the launch, with Jacob standing beside her, near the stern. They stood there for quite a while, watching the island shrink and Mount Desert start rising firmly ahead of them, and then Jacob said, quietly, "I'd like to marry you, Maude."

Maude looked down at the wintry water as it went past, her senses reeling and the sound of the engine and the thump of her heart.

"Well, Jake, we haven't seen very much of each other, and — "

"I've seen all I need to see," Jacob said, staring down at the water himself. Suddenly he felt terribly tired. Well, there it was. She was not going to have him. He had blurted it out, the way he had always known he was going to blurt it out when the moment came, and she was not going to have him. He had had it all wrong.

Maude looked at him again. "I guess I've seen all I need to see, too, Jake." She smiled, the warmest, most trusting smile that Jacob had ever seen. "I can't stand it when I'm not with you, Jake." She stood up on her tiptoes and pulled herself against him. Then Jacob kissed her, for the first time.

Ben kept his eyes to the front, toward Mount Desert. He had an idea there was something going on back there, but any two people wanted to kiss each other in the middle of Penobscot Bay in February, that was their business.

It was just getting dark when Maude and Jacob burst into Henry Wintridge's room. Henry had pulled his chair over by the fire and was reading, a glass of bourbon in his left hand.

"Oh, hello there," he said, looking up. "Isn't Kingsgrant interesting, Maude?"

"Henry," Jacob said, "we're engaged."

"Excuse me?"

"We're engaged to be married," Maude said, her voice quivering with excitement.

"Oh, come now, Jacob," Henry said, carefully putting down his glass, and then he took another look at them. "You're serious?" They both looked at each other, and Jacob nodded. "Well," Henry said, standing up, "I must say — well, congratulations, Jacob. Congratulations."

Maude looked around. "Where's Mother? We couldn't find her downstairs."

Henry sat down again. He looked overcome. "I think she's in the kitchen, Maude," he said after a minute.

"I think I'd better speak to her," Jacob said.

"Oh, I would, Jacob," Henry Wintridge said. "I definitely would."

Jacob looked at Maude, and Maude nodded. Jacob went down the stairs, not particularly quickly. His throat felt dry. Just as he reached the bottom step Mrs. Buckleigh appeared from the direction of the kitchen, carrying a tray.

"Hello, Jacob," she said.

"Mrs. Buckleigh —"

"Yes, Jacob?" Maude's mother stopped, and they looked at each other, both of them standing at the bottom of the stairs.

"Maude says she'll marry me," Jacob said.

Mrs. Buckleigh put her tray down on the step. "She does?"

"Yes." It crossed Jacob's mind that they were both scared stiff.

"Well — there aren't any secrets about you, are there, Jacob? I mean, nothing that would change Maude's mind if she knew?"

The Masonic emblem came blazing into Jacob's thoughts, but he shook his head at it violently. "No, I don't think so, Mrs. Buckleigh."

"Of course, there's the Church," Mrs. Buckleigh said.

"I'll do anything you want me to about it. I don't have to become one myself, do I?"

Mrs. Buckleigh laughed. "No, you don't have to become one, Jacob." She shrugged her shoulders. "I suppose that's it," she said, and then she kissed him on the cheek. Jacob thought she sounded relieved.

VIII

Patrick came along the wooden corridor in Warren House, with a funny, excited feeling in his stomach. He was about to have his first individual conference with Allston Hunt about his work, and he straightened his tie before he knocked on the door.

"Come in."

Patrick walked in, closing the door carefully behind him. Hunt had a typewriter out on his desk, and he was flailing away at it.

"Sit down," he said. "I'm just trying to finish a section here."

Patrick sat down. The professor was really hammering away, a completely concentrated expression on his face, so Patrick took the chance to study him. Hunt's jacket was hung over the back of a chair nearby, and he was wearing an unbuttoned waistcoat, and his sleeves were rolled up above his elbows. His forearms looked surprisingly muscular, and even though Patrick looked at him closely, he decided that he would never have been sure that Hunt had a glass eye except for the fact that the professor had told them about it at the first meeting of the class. "If I ever cut you dead on the street," he had said, his smile lighting up, "just come around on the other side of me and say hello again." Patrick moved around in his seat and began to wind his wrist watch.

"You know," Hunt said, taking two sheets of paper out of his typewriter and putting the top one on a pile at his right side, "my understanding with the University is that I teach during the winter and write during the summer. That's like telling a tiger he can growl only four months a year." He pushed the typewriter away from him, and pushed his swivel chair back a bit from his desk. "Well, I like your stuff," he said. "You like to play the big game, don't you?"

"I'm afraid I don't understand, sir."

"It's a tennis expression. It's really a sportswriter's phrase. I was a sportswriter for a while once. That surprise you?"

"Not exactly, sir. There's a lot of vitality in sportswriting."

Hunt nodded. "A lot of vitality and a lot of clichés. Who would you call the best American sportswriter?"

"Ernest Hemingway."

Hunt laughed out loud. "You may be all right," he said. "This gets me to a point. Now, I like all your descriptions of physical things. When you have Leapingdeer remember some of the episodes of his high school football career, it really works. Did you play much?"

"Well, I played JV at Tabor, and then I went out for it here."

"What happened?"

"Nothing much. I lasted one spring practice, and then I smashed up my knee in preseason practice the next fall, and that was the end. And then I have a bad arm anyhow, and that didn't help me any."

"How'd you get that?"

"It was hurt when I was born, sir."

"I see. Didn't it hold you up in football?"

"Yes, but there are lots of ways to compensate for it if you're willing to throw your body around."

"Were you scared when you used to play?"

"I suppose so, sir. I never used to be scared on offense. It was just the defense that scared me. I didn't mind being tackled myself, but I used to be pretty scared when I had to try and tackle one of the good backs."

"What position did you play?"

"I played JV guard in prep school, and then I switched to wingback here."

"How much do you weigh?"

"One seventy-seven."

"That's a little light for the line in college, all right. How did you catch passes?"

"Well, I'll show you. Do you mind?"

"I wish you would."

Patrick stood up and showed him how he could trap the passes and pull them in to him, even if it was a little awkward to always get the palm of the right hand into the right position for a straight fingertips-on-leather catch.

"That's damned interesting," Hunt said, as Patrick sat down again. "You know, there's one story I always liked. There were two men in a shellhole, or a foxhole, or whatever you want to call it, and one of them was a big man, a real fire-eater, and the other one was a little timid conscript. Well, the shells were bursting ahead of them, and there was a way out behind them, and the big man kept teasing the little man about how frightened he was, and finally the little man said, 'Listen, if you were as frightened as I am, you'd run away.'"

"I like it," Patrick said.

Allston Hunt pulled a manila envelope toward him and stared at it for a second. Patrick could see that it had his name on the outside of it.

"I'll tell you," Hunt said, "I think you're doing fine, but there's one thing I want to point out to you. You have some things in here that don't further the total action of the book. For example, this business about horseback riding. It's very good, but it isn't as integral a thing as the football flashback, for instance." He stopped and stared down at the manila envelope. "Kingsgrant," he said after a moment, "you don't intend to stride through the literary world in a pair of riding boots, do you?"

Patrick grinned. "No sir. But I don't think it makes too much difference what you're wearing."

"In other words your idea is that if you penetrate one segment of life accurately enough, you've touched all life?"

"Yes, sir."

"All right." Hunt stood up, thrust his hands into his pockets, and looked out of the window. "I'll agree with you, but you have to keep one thing in mind. When you write a novel about people that are well off, as most of yours are, you have to keep your eye on the ball. Keep after the people, and write a novel about the people, and not about their background, or their bank accounts, or what have you. That's if you want to get at the heart of the thing, and be a first-rate writer, and I think you do."

Patrick was silent for a few seconds. He wanted to tell Allston Hunt that he was going to apply to the Law School, but he couldn't do it. "Do you really think I could be a first-rate writer, sir?"

"I don't know, Kingsgrant." He had been looking out of the window, and now he turned and looked at Patrick. "I don't know. When you came in here and said you were in competition with Scott Fitzgerald, I was amused. I'm not laughing any more. But it's awfully early to tell. You have a lot, but I don't know if you've got enough. Only you can tell me that, and you can tell me through your work. And I mean *work*." He put his hands down on the table and leaned forward. "This is the hardest work there is. Most men that work in offices in cities don't have any idea of what this kind of work is like. They may put in more hours at their desks than we do at our typewriters, but that doesn't mean a damned thing. And a lot of those ulcers they get come from twenty-five years of three martinis at lunch. Do you like martinis?"

"I've only had a couple in my life, sir."

"Well, just don't have them for lunch, and you'll be all right." Hunt picked Patrick's manuscript off his desk and handed it to him. "I think that's all for now. I know you have your exams and everything, but try to dig in and do another twenty or thirty pages, and we'll talk some more. When do you read your stuff to the class?"

"December twelfth, sir."

"Oh, well, we'll get in another talk before that. See you next week."

"Yes, sir." Patrick picked up his manila envelope and walked out of the office. He went down the stairs, and there was a happy light in his eyes.

IX

Bill Bench caught the medicine ball that the man across the way in the exercise room had thrown to him. He swung the big heavy-stuffed ball over his head and threw it back, and for the tenth time this afternoon he cursed himself for coming out for swimming this year. He had been pretty good on the freshman team, and the last two years he had been in a few meets, but it was hard work. Bill had promised himself that he was not going to go out this year, but then the old magic had started again. He had come down for the first time just a couple of weeks ago, just to take a few laps in the pool for old times' sake, and it had started. Everybody had asked him why he'd quit, and Hal had had a chat with him, and then it had felt pretty good to be in the pool again, gliding into the wall and sinking down against the wall and pushing off again in the opposite direction, and here he was, throwing medicine balls and doing push-ups and plodding forty and fifty laps a day behind a flutterboard.

No Budweiser, no going down to Princeton this coming week-end, no nothing. But still it felt pretty good, when you were hanging there against the wall right after the finish of the two-twenty, beaten out and gasping, and then you looked over at the other guy hanging there in the water, and he smiled at you and the two of you knew something that not too many other people knew. Bill had played a lot of sports in his life, but for total commitment of every cell in your body, there was nothing like swimming.

"All right, on your backs!"

Bill dropped the medicine ball that had just thudded into his hands, and got down on his back. In a moment the cadence started, and Bill began doing sit-ups, occasionally smiling at the exaggerated moans and groans that some of the other members of the squad were emitting.

x

Anna could not sleep, and she got out of bed, put on her mules and dressing gown, and went slip-slapping up the stairs to the room opposite the guest room. The room in the cellar with the billiard table was her father's preserve, and this room was hers. She had studied here when she had been at Chapin, and now it was more or less of a playroom and private library, with her books on the shelves, a couple of chairs, a sofa, and an old victrola that the family had handed over to her. She had added an LP of her own, so now she could play anything except the businesses that came recorded on wire.

Anna switched on the light and walked into her den. She looked at the clock swinging its miniature pendulum on the mantelpiece, and smiled. It was two-thirty, Patrick had said good-bye a half-hour before, and she had to be up at a quarter to eight if they were ever going to get uptown and horseback riding in Central Park by nine o'clock. If ever there was a night when she needed sleep, this was it, but sleep seemed miles away. Anna went over to her shelves of records and picked out Liszt's *Les Preludes*. Patrick had told her that he liked it very much, and although Anna did not particularly agree with him, it had made her think better of the piece of music ever since. She had gone through an exceptionally musical phase when she was seventeen, and now she was left with the remains of her passion, like a man no longer interested in collecting butterflies but confronted with case upon case of neatly mounted reminders of his frenzy.

Anna put the record on her LP and sat down on the sofa to listen. Patrick said that the end of it reminded him of a young prince coming home across the seas, and then, in the last movement, striding across the flagstoned floor of a castle or a cathedral to be met by his aged father, the king. Anna had listened to it carefully, but she never saw a young prince, or banners and trumpets on the ramparts of the city as the young prince came riding down the narrow, many-angled cobblestone streets past the cheering people to the castle. Music gave Anna feelings, and yearnings, and joy and sadness, but it never brought pictures to her mind, unless it was something like a waltz, because she had seen the waltz danced, and the memory of the whirling dresses could rise before her eyes.

She sat there, trying to concentrate on the music, but slowly the music went away from her, and the unnamed feeling in her mind took over. Her face was an impassive mask, and her eyes stared blankly, but Anna van Neerdaam was facing some facts. This past evening with Patrick had been a nightmare for her. She still took in her breath when he first reached for her hand, and she loved the feel of his lips on hers, warm and sometimes quivering and always warm and strong and coming in on her, but the other minutes, when they were just chatting over dinner, she felt as if she were lying to him. Of course she couldn't be lying to him, all she was talking about was school and her courses and politics and what tomorrow's game would be like, but still she felt as if she was lying to him just by sitting there.

"How can it be?" Anna said suddenly, out loud, and she slammed her fist onto the cushion of the sofa. The music was thundering away, and Anna stood up and went over to the record, lifted the needle abruptly, and shut off the machine. She could hear the ticking of the clock in the sudden silence of the room. You can't go on, a voice said in Anna's mind. You can't go on.

"Shut *up!*" Anna said into the silent room, and then she sat down again. Her face looked suddenly drawn, as if she were in pain. Put on "A Kiss in the Dark," she said to herself. That'll remind you of Patrick, and that'll fix it. She went over to the old victrola, the one that she had had while she was in Chapin after her family had got a new one for downstairs, and put on "A Kiss in the Dark." For a minute Anna smiled, and then the smile faded and she was paler than before. It wasn't working. Nothing was working. I love him, she said to herself. Maybe you do, Anna, the voice said, maybe you do. Maybe you do, but you're not sure.

Please no, Anna said to herself. Please. She thought about the summer in Maine, the drives in the crisp starry nights, and her face looked as if blood were being drawn out of it. How can I let him down? How could it be that I *can* let him down? Please dear God, it's just something temporary.

The waltz had ended. Anna stood up and turned off the victrola. Then she snapped off the light in the room and went downstairs to her bed.

XI

Patrick cantered along behind Anna, smiling as he watched her head of golden hair bounce up and down in the morning sunlight. They were moving up the bridle path beside the Reservoir, near

the exit from the Park at Ninetieth Street. Anna slowed her
horse down into a more collected canter, and Patrick came
abreast of her, looking over at her in her tailored tweed jacket
and jodhpurs. She hadn't said much this morning, but Patrick
couldn't really blame her. He was pretty sleepy and tired himself. They both brought their horses down to a trot, and then
into a walk.

"You know, it's funny," Anna said, patting the warm damp
neck of her horse, "but when I was a little girl I always thought
you must get a lot more tired doing a canter, just because it's
faster. But it doesn't work that way at all."

"No," Patrick said. He wanted to reach over and take her
hand, but it was a bright sunlit morning, and he didn't think it
was such a good idea. He contented himself with saying, "I'm
awfully glad you're here."

Anna looked over at Patrick and she knew that now was
now. Her eyes went half closed, as if she was wincing from a
pain, and she wet her lips with her tongue.

"Patrick, I've got to talk to you," she said, her voice sounding choked.

Patrick stared at her, and the happy, trusting smile went off
his face as if it had been slapped off.

"No," he said.

"I didn't want to let you down, Patrick," Anna said. She was
leaning toward him. "You have to believe me, Patrick, I never
wanted to let you down."

"Please, Anna," Patrick said, and then he stopped and they
were both sitting there on their horses, staring at each other, both
of them staring at what was happening. "There must be a
reason, Anna," Patrick said. "There must be a reason."

"It isn't a reason, it's a feeling," Anna said. She had stopped
looking at him. "Maybe I'm in love with you, PK, but I'm not
going to go on. And don't ask me *why*," Anna half cried out.

Her voice had gone up high. "I don't know *why*."

"I can't stand it," Patrick said.

"You're going to have to stand it, Patrick," Anna said. She had her voice back under control, but she was still looking away from him.

Patrick closed his eyes, and then he heard her horse start away from him. His horse started up too, but he turned him around and halted in the middle of the bridle path. Anna was cantering away quickly, her golden head of hair bouncing above the tweed jacket. Patrick watched her disappear around the bend, and then he looked down at his hands. They were shaking, and the rein and the curb-rein were fluttering and jerking. He took the reins in his right hand, and then he brought his left hand up and put his face into it. His hand was still shaking, and suddenly Patrick hauled off and slapped his face twice, hard. Then he looked down at his hand. It had stopped shaking. Patrick got the reins back into both hands, studying them intently, as if it was a job of great skill to get the right reins between the right fingers, and then he started the horse walking slowly forward.

At the livery stable Patrick dismounted carefully and went into the office. He paid the man and said thank you.

"Thank you, sir." the man said. "The lady you were with has gone."

"I know," Patrick said, and walked out to the street.

XII

That afternoon Patrick went out into Central Park. When he had got home he had been surprised that there was nobody there, and then he had remembered that his father had gone down to Princeton with a couple of his friends, and that Eileen was at the game too, and that the servants had the day off. Patrick had taken off his riding clothes, taken a shower, and then looked for his suit. After a minute he had realized that he had left his suit at Anna's house, so that he could change there after their ride. He had changed into something else, and walked down Madison Avenue to Hamburg Heaven. Still numb, he had eaten a hamburger and washed it down with a cup of coffee. Then he went out into the Park.

He walked for a couple of hours. Once, earlier in the autumn, he and Anna had gone walking in the Park, walking around all of his old haunts, the Museum, and the obelisk, and the big stone weather station that looked like a castle. Patrick kept thinking that Anna would be here. She would be too proud to call up, but she would come out here, to one of these places where they had been together, and he would find her there, and things would be even better than they had been before. Patrick walked up the steps to the obelisk, butterflies teeming in his stomach, and there was nobody there. He stood around there for a few minutes, the skirts of his topcoat fluttering in the breeze, and then he walked along past the little lake and up to where the castle perched on massive rocks. He came up the walk to the big concrete terrace of the castle, the terrace that gave a wonderful view north over the Park, and there was a blond girl in a black coat. Patrick started to run toward her, and she turned around, and she was definitely not Anna van Neerdaam.

Later on Patrick found himself walking along the path beside the Reservoir, coming nearer and nearer to Ninetieth Street. Every time he heard the sound of a horse coming along the bridle path that ran along below him to his right, he turned to see if it was Anna. As he walked along, he had this feeling in his head and his throat as if he was on the verge of crying. He didn't cry, but his throat was choked, and the tears were right behind his eyes, and occasionally he closed his eyes for a second or two as he walked along.

At Ninetieth Street Patrick stopped and stared down at the bridle path. An impulse came across him to go down to Anna's house and get his suit, and Anna would be there, and everything would be all right, but then he shook his head. Suddenly he wanted to get out of New York. The wind was coming up, and the sky was gray, and there were dead leaves flying past him. He headed down Ninetieth Street to get packed and start back in his car.

8

MRS. VAN NEERDAAM happened to be in the hall when the front-door bell rang, and she went to the door and opened it. There was a pretty girl, looking like a thundercloud.

"Mrs. van Neerdaam?"

"Yes."

"I'm Eileen Kingsgrant. I got a letter from my brother, and he asked me to come down and pick up some clothes he left here."

"Oh, yes. Please come in." Mrs. van Neerdaam went to a closet under the steps and brought out a gray suit on a hanger. "I think this is Patrick's."

"Yes. That's his," Eileen managed a polite smile.

"Won't you stay for tea, Eileen?"

"No thank you, Mrs. van Neerdaam. I'm afraid I have to get back."

Mrs. van Neerdaam looked at this pretty brunette who was holding up her head proudly, sparkling with anger because her brother had been hurt. Anna had gone back without saying a word, and Mrs. van Neerdaam still didn't know exactly what had happened, but looking at this girl standing in the hall gave her a pretty good idea. "I'm sorry you can't stay," she said. She wanted to say something more, but the girl was already moving toward the door.

"Sorry to bother you," Eileen said.

"Not at all," Mrs. van Neerdaam answered. "It was nice to see you."

"It was nice to see *you*," Eileen said, politely, and went out the door and down the steps, carrying Patrick's clothes.

Jacob had eaten dinner at the University Club because Eileen was having dinner out and he wanted a change, and now he was sitting alone at one of the tables over by a window. He had finished eating, and he was having a brandy while he smoked his pipe. The smoke from his pipe moved up vaguely toward the elaborate wood-worked ceiling of the vast, quiet dining room, but his eyes were gazing down at the tablecloth. He was thinking about Patrick and Anna. Eileen had told him about finding a note from Patrick, asking her to retrieve his suit, and it was clear that he had not gone to the game, so something fairly drastic must have happened.

He finished the little that was left of his pony of brandy, and then he stood up. He wanted to write something to Patrick, but he still could not imagine exactly what it was going to be. Jacob walked out of the dining room, nodding good night to the waiters, and walked the three flights down to the library instead of taking the elevator.

Jacob's pen hung over the paper. As usual, he was going to write a draft first, and then copy out what he wanted, but still, even though this was just experimental, he could not find the words. He felt what he wanted to say, but he could not say it. "Dear Patrick," sat there, but there was nothing after it. Finally Jacob tightened his lips, and began. "Eileen told me about your note to her," his firm handwriting said, "and I am making the perhaps unwarranted assumption that you and Anna have had some serious troubles." Jacob paused. "That is just to tell you that I am very sorry if this is the case." Jacob's fist came down

on the table in his sudden frustrated rage at being unable to make
this sound the way he wanted it, and a bald old man in the corner
of this alcove of the library looked up, his eyes coming up a full
two seconds after his eyebrows had arched. Jacob put his left
hand over his left eye. He wanted to reach out to Patrick and
still leave his son's pride intact, and instead he was sounding like
a lawyer addressing a client. "From my own experience with
some of the less pleasant things of life," he put down, "I can tell
you that there is nothing that you cannot get over and forget."
Jacob sat there, and he thought about Maude. Then he took his
pen and scratched out his last sentence. "Please believe that I
love you," he wrote, "and if there is anything that Eileen and I
can do, we are at your disposal." He tried to think of something
cheering. "I am glad that you are agreeable to the idea of a dinner
party for your twenty-first birthday," he said. "I think that
you should feel free to have up to ten of your friends, in addition
to Eileen and myself." Jacob looked over what he had written.
He thought about other things to say, about the fact that life
moved on and you had to move with it, and so on, but he shook
his head. He had nothing more to say. Jacob's face relaxed
slightly, and he drew another piece of paper toward him and
began to copy out the letter.

II

Patrick sat on the edge of the long table in the Great Hall of the
Lampoon. The afternoon sunlight was coming in at the tall
window up by the large, improbable fireplace, and a ray of light
from one of the smaller windows high up was brightening the
back of his brown tweed jacket. Patrick was staring at the wall
of the vaulted brick baronial hall, but he saw nothing. All the
memories of laughter in this room, of Christmas dinners and
dances and milk punches before the Yale game, were lost on him
right now. It was Thursday, and five days had passed since

Anna had ridden away from him in Central Park. He had stopped feeling as if he were going to cry, but every time he thought of her, her hands or her ears or some moment that they had had together, his eyes half closed.

Patrick looked at his watch. It was five o'clock, and he was supposed to be at a Seneca punch. The punching season, that round of parties that was called rushing everywhere else in the United States, was at its peak, and it was supposedly the duty of every member of a club to go to a punch, take a drink, and meet the punchees, most of them sophomores who had been shaking hands steadily since the middle of October. Patrick stood up slowly. He was not going to go to that punch. He looked at his watch again, and decided that he had time to go down to the Indoor Athletic Building and work out before dinner. The room was not a particularly cheery place these days. Bill was swimming until about six-thirty, Snowjob was always off helping the Porcellian on to bigger and better punchees, and Tall Man was preoccupied with the values of zero.

Patrick buttoned the middle button of his jacket, and looked around. It was strange, how alone he had felt in the last few days. Bill in particular had been worried about him, and Patrick appreciated it, but there were moments, walking down the street or sitting in class, when he thought of Anna, and when that happened nothing was any good. Nobody could help him with this thing. You're still breathing, Patrick said to himself, looking at the afternoon sunshine as it fell onto the rows of past members' pewter mugs around the walls. You're still breathing, and you can still carry on a conversation. He went down the staircase and out through the little side door, onto the brick sidewalk.

III

Allston Hunt was in the dining room of his house on Ellery Street, drinking a cup of coffee and holding his *New York Times* up out of the way of his elderly housekeeper as she cleared away the remains of his breakfast. He was studying the communiqués from the Korean front, and, as usual, his thoughts were running along parallel to the accounts that he was reading. For Hunt, as for many another man, the black letters on the white paper translated themselves into thirst and hunger and men falling on their faces from bullets and exhaustion. After the one war that he had been in, Allston had always been surprised at how well the movies captured certain parts of warfare. He always thought the explosions and screams in the battle scenes jibed pretty well with what he had experienced, until they came to the part that must be labeled "Lull in the Battle." That was when the movies before the Second World War had the young hero saying "We can do it, sir," and even after the Second World War the young hero said "Let's go get those sons of —— Nippon," or words to that effect. The way Allston remembered it, when somebody told them what they had to do next, they just nodded their eyes in their heads and wet their lips.

He took another sip of his coffee, and went on looking through the communiqués. The big weapons changed, but there were still frightened little men out in front, killing other frightened little men. He had been one of them, staggeringly weary and desperately scared, and he could never read a phrase like "patrol activity" without remembering night on the desert.

The desert. Most mornings, sitting in Cambridge sunshine as it came politely through the window, he found it hard to believe that once he had been one of the sacrifices that made up a communiqué. The desert seemed a long, long way away, and the only reason that he knew for sure that he had been there was that he had left his right eye out there. And the thing about it was that he had set off on such a different quest.

It had been June of 1914, and Allston, by a combination of

his usual brutal saving, and by winning the Francis Royal Hutting Essay Prize, had enough money to go to Europe for the summer after his graduation. He spent all of June and July in England, traveling the Lake Country and visiting Stratford and London, and then, in August, he was in Paris. He was in Paris, and France was going to war. He stood around for a few days, watching Frenchmen being called up, watching Englishmen go home to enlist, listening to some Americans talk about joining the Foreign Legion for a fast crack at the Germans before the war was over, and one morning he woke up with the sudden conviction that the worst thing that could happen to him was death. For some reason it was a steadying and satisfying thought that morning, and although the thought never comforted him again, and although he was to see things that would make simple death seem like a panacea, the idea carried him up to the Place des Invalides, where they were recruiting for the Foreign Legion. He walked back and forth, looking at the different flags, and the knots of men clustered around them, and his face was a study. Half of his mind was Careful Allston Hunt, the boy who had always had to save, the practical young man who could see that something like this was madness. That half of his mind kept talking about his career, how hard he had had to work just to get where he was, and how this war wasn't any of his business, and how he couldn't afford to take any chances. The other half was a young man with a heart that responded to excitement and the sudden intuitive knowledge that these men under the flags were important. He did not know exactly all the ways that they were important, but he knew that he ought to be with them, and see what happened to them.

There was a bunch of men standing around the American flag. Allston looked at his flag, and he looked at the men surrounding it. He recognized one of them from Harvard. Then there were a couple of men wearing pea jackets, and a little

Negro wearing a jockey's cap, and a lot of others. Allston nodded his head, and walked across the gravel toward them.

Naturally he thought he was going to fight Germans. They were shipping men north from the Legion depot at Tours, loads of them every day, and one day it was Allston's turn to get on a train. He had been trained to march and fire a rifle, and now he was going to fight the boches.

The whole lot of them in his contingent ended up in Marseilles, and before they knew it, they were on a ship for Oran. The British in their muster were muttering that they had been promised a chance to fight *les sales boches* and here the bloody Legion was sending them to bloody Morocco. The crew of the rusty little ship shrugged their shoulders. It is a warmer place to die, they said. They told them that they were not the first English sent to the Legion en Afrique by mistake. And then bang, there they were en Afrique. Several times, marching along under his pack, with the firewood and the stove on top of it, Allston wondered if he had contracted a strange fever at the training depot at Tours, and that all this was a prolonged delirium. Here he had enlisted to fight the Germans on the Western Front, and he was marching along due east of Meknès, Morocco, surrounded by Germans who were bellowing German marching songs, all on their way to fight an entente of rebel chieftains who had their own private feuds with the French government. A couple of the men at Tours had wondered where the Legion was keeping all the Germans in its ranks. Allston had the answer, as he started to wabble and a German corporal kept cursing him along under the sun. They were right here, singing their damned songs and walking him off his bleeding feet by noon every day. In some units it was sixty per cent Germans and in other units it was eighty, but Allston had found out where they were keeping the Germans. He kept struggling across country with them, month after month, stopping to hold this outpost and take that hill and patrol this road and one day, in an attack up a rocky hill, Allston felt darkness and a crackling inside his head. When he woke up again he was in the hospital at Sidi-bel-Abbès, and his right eye was out of his head.

Allston finished going over the communiqués for the second time, and then put the paper down. He heard a noise of a door closing on the floor above him, and he smiled. That would be Billy Hennessy. Allston rented the second and third floors of his house to two young married couples every year. This year both the young husbands were seniors, and neither of them knew whether or not he was going to be in the Army.

Allston stood up from the table. None of these poor kids had the faintest idea of where they stood in relation to the draft, and none of them had any idea of what was waiting for them if they got to the place where the killing was done. Standing by the breakfast table, Allston was remembering how strange it all had seemed to him when the United States finally went into the war in 1917. He had been back two years, and his glass eye looked real enough so that nobody at the Boston *Globe*, where he worked as a sportswriter while he was saving up to come back to Harvard and get his M.A., ever knew a thing about it. The bands were playing and the boys were going, and Allston felt sick as he watched them go. He stood on the curb and watched them march past behind a hundred American flags, and it seemed to him as if he must have died and come back to earth, and he knew that he must have taken his solitary walk toward an American flag in the Place des Invalides at least a hundred years before.

IV

Anna was at a table in the Covered Wagon having a beer with a pleasant young man from Penn. He was very nice, but the only trouble was that she couldn't pay attention to what he was saying. Tomorrow Harvard was going to play Yale at Cambridge. Anna took another sip of her beer and said "Yes, I agree with you" to the young man, who nodded and went on with whatever he was saying. She had promised herself that she was not going to think about Patrick this week-end, but tonight she kept wondering who he was going to take to the game tomorrow, or if he was going to go alone, and if he went alone what girls he would meet at the cocktail parties after the game. Every day when she went to her mailbox she half hoped and half feared that there would be a letter from Patrick. There had been so many letters, all of them good letters and funny and warm, and when she closed her eyes before she went to sleep she could see his handwriting.

All *right*, Anna said to herself, but I still had to do it. If you're not sure you can't just go blundering ahead. He knew what he wanted and I wasn't sure. She took another sip. Anna was surprised that Patrick had not written. The least she had expected was a hurt valedictory note. He had a tendency to dramatize things, and she was sure that he'd call in the middle of the night, or show up down there, or something. But not a sound.

"And then *she* fell in," the boy from Penn said, and Anna smiled weakly.

V

The afternoon of Patrick's birthday party Tall Man walked into Patrick's room. Patrick was putting away his laundry from the

Coop, and trying to pick out which shirt to wear when they started for Boston in a couple of hours.

Patrick looked up from what he was doing. Tall Man had that really punchy look that he got after about four hours in the mathematical stratosphere. "Hey, Patrick, who's going to be there tonight?"

"Well, my father and Eileen, of course, and you and Snowjob and Bill and a couple of guys from the Club and a couple from the Lampoon. Did I tell you Allston Hunt was coming?"

"No kidding. How'd you get him?"

"I don't know, I was just thinking about it, and then I went up and asked him. He's a riot." Patrick stuffed a couple of shirts into an already bulging drawer. "I went up to him, and I guess I looked worried or something. He said, 'What's the matter? Mental block? Fall in love with your heroine?'"

"He sounds like a pretty good guy."

"He wants to meet my father. I think he has sort of a thing about ex-Harvard football players."

"I just hope I don't disgrace you," Tall Man said. "I'm so sick of work I feel like having sixty-five drinks." He walked out into the living room, and Patrick put the big tan cardboard box that had held his laundry into the waste paper basket beside his desk.

"Hey, Patrick," Snowjob said, sticking his head into the door, "have you got the cavalry alerted in case Sitting Bull goes off the reservation tonight?"

"Tell them to try another outfit," Tall Man's voice said from the next room. "The Seventh Cavalry didn't make out too well."

"I've heard," Patrick said, smiling. He looked at the work on his desk. He had started writing an optional paper on Jonathan Edwards for Perry Miller about a week after the Yale game, and he had hoped to get a little more done on it this afternoon before he had to go out, but at the rate things were moving around D-32 right now, that was obviously going to be impossible.

The party was on its way to being a great success. Jacob and Allston Hunt were chatting in a corner of the private dining room, and Eileen was surrounded by young men. Patrick was standing by Tall Man, who was giving the little bar that had been set up at the far end of the room quite a bit of business. The talk and laughter during this time before dinner was contagious, and the group shifted and reshifted. At one moment Patrick was talking to Allston Hunt and Eileen was talking to Tall Man, and Jacob and Bill Bench would be talking something over. Allston Hunt had at least four people around him at any given moment, and at least twice a minute he evoked a roar of young male laughter.

"He's quite a character," Eileen said, slipping out of one group and coming up to Patrick.

"Who, Hunt?"

Eileen nodded. "You know what he just said? 'Show me a man who was totally happy at Harvard, and I'll show you a man who would have been even happier at Dartmouth.'"

Patrick smiled, first at the thought and then at Eileen. "How are you, kid?" he said. They hadn't had a moment to talk.

"Fine, fine. How are you?"

"I'm bearing up." Suddenly he wanted to ask Eileen if she had heard anything about Anna, if she had seen her or anything, but he did not, and a second later Eileen had been caught up again in the small whirlpool around Allston Hunt. Patrick went over to the little bar and asked the waiter behind it for a drink, and then he felt his father's hand on his shoulders.

"Enjoying yourself?" Jacob said.

Jacob looked at his watch. "When do you think we ought to sit down to dinner?"

"Oh, I don't know. Another fifteen minutes?"

Jacob nodded. "David Tall Man certainly seems to be cele-
brating your birthday. I've never seen him half as expressive as
he is this evening."

Patrick looked over at Tall Man. He and Snowjob were in a
corner, and Tall Man was howling with laughter and pounding
Snowjob on the back. Snowjob was smiling weakly, and Patrick
thought that "expressive" was an exceptionally gentle way of
defining Tall Man's condition.

"Well, he's been working pretty hard," Patrick said. "Excuse
me for a second, Father." Patrick had seen one of the boys from
the Lampoon making unmistakable have-you-got-a-match fum-
bles to his neighbors, and they were tumbling back, gee-I'm-
sorry-I-don't. Patrick picked up a couple of packs of matches
from the white covered table that was serving as bar, and started
toward them. He never got there. The words "Law School"
came into his ears, and Patrick stopped dead. Eileen was talking
to Allston Hunt. Well, Patrick said to himself, as he turned
toward them, there goes the ball game.

Hunt looked at him. "Your very charming sister tells me,"
he said, taking a sip of a dry martini, "that you're going to go to
the Law School."

Patrick felt himself turning an even deeper shade of red than
two drinks and a fair complexion would warrant. "I decided to
try it, sir."

Eileen was looking at both of them, her head swiveling to
watch each as he spoke.

"Well, I'll tell you," Hunt said. "If you can be happy doing
anything other than writing, by all means do it. Don't you agree,
Miss Kingsgrant?" His voice was soft but his face had on its
fullest Full Professor expression.

"I've always thought that Patrick was a good writer, sir,"
Eileen said.

"You've thought right, Miss Kingsgrant," Hunt said, and then
he smiled a brief smile of excusing himself, and walked over

toward a couple of the boys at the bar. A minute later he was relaxed and laughing again.

During the ten minutes before he was going to propose his toast to Patrick, Jacob sat silently at the head of the long table, barely conscious of the laughter and conversation that was batting back and forth in front of him. He was thinking of what he was going to say, and he was thinking of what he would like to say, but would not say. What he would like to do would be to get up and tell them about how lovely and vivacious Patrick's mother had been, and that he had always known that they were different in many ways, despite their love for each other. And then he would tell them that he saw so much of Patrick's mother in Patrick, and that he was all too aware that he did not always understand it. That was what he would like to tell them; how the children had always loved their mother's bedtime stories, and how, when he had tried to tell them bedtime stories after she had died, it had been a complete bust. They had been polite but restless, and it just made him miss her more, and he had quit.

The waiter was coming around, pouring more champagne into their glasses, and Jacob waited until all the glasses had been filled. Then he stood up, and the table became silent instantly.

"Well, Patrick is twenty-one," he said, his eyes traveling over the young faces looking up at him. Patrick was sitting at his right, and Allston Hunt was on his left. Eileen was somewhere down the table. "I was given a dinner somewhat like this when I was twenty-one, and I hope that someday all of you have the pleasure of seeing a son reach his majority, ready to take on the responsibilities of life." Jacob looked down at the fine screen of bubbles coming to the surface of the glass in his hand. "I am a very satisfied parent," he said, looking at them again. He knew that it wasn't coming out the way that he had wanted it to be, gay and simple and brief. "One day you will have children, and you'll see how you recognize yourself in them, and how you can feel that they are you, projected into the future, carrying on what you've done, and, if all goes well, improving on it." He looked at them earnestly. "When you're standing where I am, you can fully appreciate the opportunities for young people your age. You people in particular are fortunate. You're in good health, and you've had excellent educations, and you live in a wonderful country. All you have to do is reach out and give your best efforts, and I sincerely hope you will, because that's the only way that life is worthwhile. Don't try to avoid getting into harness." Jacob stopped again and looked down at Patrick. He was afraid that he would see Patrick looking embarrassed at the pomposity of his remarks, but Patrick was looking up at him with a straight gaze, and an encouraging look on his face. "Let's drink to Patrick," Jacob said, and they all rose, with the Lampoon men saying "Hear, hear" and a polite buzz from everyone.

Patrick looked at all of them as they began to sit down again. He was wishing that Anna were here. Maybe if she were here it would be all right again. Then he saw Eileen looking at him, and he stood up, the butterflies stunting around in his stomach as they always did when he had to make even the simplest statement in the informality of the Seneca or the Lampoon.

"I'm very pleased that you're all here, and I know that I speak for my father and my sister when I say that," he said. He tried to think of something to say. "I feel immensely older," he said, and smiled. "But anyhow, I think I've always been fortunate in my friends, and I don't say it often, but I'm very grateful to my family. Here's to all of you." He took a sip of the champagne, feeling his face blushing, and sat down.

VI

The Concrete Kimono had pulled itself together to the extent of having a punch, and it was developing into a very punchy punch indeed. Snowjob and Patrick had spent most of the afternoon straightening up the room and setting up a bar, and now the room was beginning to fill up with members of the club, all wearing the red and gold tie, and the sophomores who were prospective members. Tall Man had built a fire in the fireplace, and one of the other members had brought a Christmas wreath, which refused to stay straight above the mantel. The sounds of conversation and ice clinking in glasses rose in volume, while outside the windows a gray sky hung over the stark trees in the courtyard, and a wind whipped over the winter river.

Patrick was talking to one of the punchees, smiling and being polite while he inwardly told himself that he'd rather see the Concrete Kimono go out of business than take this particular person, when he saw Bill Bench come walking into the room with an extremely serious look on his face. Bill often looked tired when he came in from swimming, with his hair fuzzy and his face flushed, but tonight it wasn't that. Bill went into their bedroom to drop his coat, and came out into the living room and walked over to Patrick.

"Have you heard the news?"

"No. What?"

"I heard it on the radio down in the office at the pool. The Chinese have come over the Yalu River. About half a million of them."

"My God," Patrick said. "Are they fighting us right now?"

"I guess so. It said they have jet planes and everything."

"That does it," Patrick said. "They'll have this place turned into an Army camp in three weeks."

"I don't know," Bill said. "I think I'll go have my big exciting ginger ale."

Patrick's face was serious in the middle of the chatting crowd. In his freshman and sophomore years he and some of his friends had said in bull sessions that they'd all be fighting the Russians on the Montana border before they ever got around to graduating. The Russians on the Montana border or the Chinese in Korea, it wasn't all that different. The Chinese. Holy God, the Chinese. Millions of them.

Patrick looked at the sophomore beside him. "Now we'll have to start bombing China."

The sophomore nodded his head. "There's an awful lot of Chinese," he said, looking down at his drink. "Wonder if we'll use the atomic bomb?"

VII

For about two hours Patrick had been trying to concentrate on what he was reading, but the impulse that he was trying to avoid kept jabbing at him. There was nobody else around in either bedroom or the living room, and Patrick kept wanting to make a call to Anna in Bryn Mawr. He sat at his desk, remembering how pleasantly surprised she had been the two times he had done it early in the fall, and he kept hoping that if he just called her up now somehow it might be all right. If he just said that he was coming down for his Christmas vacation in two days, and he was hoping that they might have dinner and go to the theatre or something some evening.

Patrick got up from his desk and walked out into the living room. He stared at the telephone, and then he sat down on the sofa. His heart was beating in quick thumps, and suddenly he picked up the telephone.

"I'd like to make a person-to-person call to a Miss Anna van Neerdaam," he said to the Long Distance operator. "The last name is small v a n, and the next word is capital n double e r d double a m." Patrick sat there, after he had given the operator the rest of the information, and when she asked him for his number he gave it to her in a dry-throated voice. He felt his heart beating and a prickling in his stomach. A voice in the gray of the distance said "Bryn Mawr," and then a minute later a girl's voice was saying, "Just a minute, I'll get her." Patrick sat there and then he knew it was going to be terrible and he put the receiver back on the hook and sat there for two seconds breathing hard. He got up, went into his room and got his sports coat, and went out of D-32 to walk anywhere in the night.

Anna hurried down the stairs toward the telephone booth in Pem West. Venus, the colored maid, had come in and told her that Boston was calling. She knew it was Patrick, and she didn't know what to say. She ran the last ten steps down the stairs, and picked up the receiver.

"Hello," she said. "Hello?"

VIII

As the clock struck midnight on Christmas Eve, Jacob came through the door of the library with an armful of gaily wrapped packages. He knelt down in front of the tree in the corner, placed the packages on the floor, and started to sort them out in two piles. Finally, when the two piles had been pushed apart and put back under the bottom branches of the Christmas tree, Jacob straightened up and stepped back to look at the effect. He smiled approvingly at the tree. Patrick and Eileen had trimmed it two days before, and once again it had been Patrick who had the eye for placing the silver ornaments. He had started off obediently letting Eileen tell him where to put things, but by the time half an hour had passed, Patrick was putting the silver peacock way out on the edge of the branch where it would perch most serenely, and telling Eileen to put a silver bell just under that branch, where it hung looking as if it might actually swing and ring. He always broke one or two of them, Jacob reflected as he sat down in his easy chair, but when he was through, it was a pretty tree.

Jacob looked at his watch to see how long it would be before the children got back from Midnight Mass, and then stretched his legs out onto the footstool before his chair. He yawned once, and his glance traveled down from the tree to the plain brown carpeting of the library. It was Maude who had had the oriental rug replaced with this brown one when she saw that Patrick loved to play with his toy soldiers more than anything else, more than with his electric train or anything else.

Because it *looks* more like a battlefield, Jake. You can't have him running the Seventh Regiment across a field of elephants, can you?

Jacob straightened up in his chair. He had remembered it so clearly that it was as if Maude had spoken in the room. He looked at the brown carpeting again, and this time he could see Maude and Patrick sitting on the floor, debating where to put the howitzers, while way at the farther end Eileen was occupied with her dollhouse, which was to be inspected only on her invitation. Jacob smiled as he thought about Patrick's army. At first he and Maude had bought Patrick a variety of soldiers, some Grenadier Guards in their scarlet tunics, and a box of knights in armor, and some cowboys and Indians, but pretty soon it became clear that what Patrick wanted was lots of Germans and Americans, dressed for the First World War, in realistic fighting attitudes, all the one W. Britain standard size, with as much supporting artillery and tanks as possible. One night in about 1935 Jacob had come upstairs after dinner to get a box of cigars out of the library closet to take down to their guests in the living room, and Colonel Robert Rueger, a West Pointer who had been Jacob's company and later battalion commander for a while in the First World War, had been standing there, looking down at the two opposing lines of papier-mâché trenches from F. A. O. Schwarz. Patrick and Maude had launched an attack on the German salient, and the first wave was almost at the barbed wire in front of the defenders' trenches.

"This is really very nice, Jake," he had said, pointing to the sweep of trenches and the artillery pieces behind each side. "You help him with it much?"

"Not a bit. Maude and Patrick are the two militarists around this place." Jacob leaned his tall frame up in the closet and brought a box of cigars down off the top shelf. "Eileen and I prefer the quiet life."

The Colonel stepped over the trenches and looked at them from behind as if measuring inches to hundreds of yards. "This is really *very* good, Jake."

"It costs enough," Jacob said, turning off the lights in the closet and closing the door.

"Well, the boy must have a feeling for it," Colonel Rueger said over his shoulder. "After all, you didn't do so badly at it."

"Well, it did pretty badly at me."

Jacob and his old C.O. stood there smiling at each other, as two men who are related to a woman understand why one loves her and the other hates her.

"Do you think the boy might be inter—"

"Patrick will not go to West Point," Jacob said, opening the library door and holding it open for the Colonel, "for a number of reasons."

"I'm sorry, Jake, I'd forgotten about his arm."

"That's all right. I wouldn't want him up there anyhow."

They had gone on down the hall then in 1935, and now the conversation faded in Jacob's consciousness. He was still staring at the brown carpet, and now he stood up, looked at his watch again, and decided not to wait for the children. If he went to bed now it would give them a chance to put his presents under the tree, and he would be seeing the two of them anyhow first thing in the morning. He turned once before he snapped off the light, and found himself hearing more echoes, this time of a fight that he and Maude had had one afternoon of a Christmas Eve. Jacob did not do much thinking about Christ as a person during the course of a year, and one afternoon of a Christmas Eve he had started talking about his ideas on Christ, thinking that Maude might like to see that he had been doing some thinking on the subject. He said that although he knew most sects had a different view, he had always been attracted by the idea that Christ was merely a human being chosen by God to propagate a new doctrine of which the world had been sorely in need, and suddenly he thought a buzz saw had been turned loose in the room. Maude had said at the top of her voice that that was a fine thing on Christmas Eve, to deny the Divinity of Christ, and why did he bother to celebrate Christmas anyhow if that was the way he felt about the Second Person of the Trinity? I've never once tried to sell you any articles of faith, Maude had said, but — she had almost choked, and then said in a cold voice that this was just the kind of thing that made mixed marriages such a ridiculous idea. That had done it. He had walked out of the house just as fast as he could and walked once around the Reservoir in his business suit, not even feeling the December cold. When he had come back to the Ninetieth Street entrance to the Park, his rage at least slightly spent, she had been there, in her fur coat, with his overcoat and his hat in her arms. She had mopped the tears away from her eyes, but when he kissed her she started crying all over again.

Jacob turned off the light and went on down the hall. It had been quite an experience, falling in among these Catholics, two of whom happened to be his son and daughter. One thing you had to say for Catholics, Jacob thought as he closed the door of his room behind him and started undressing, most of them were pretty damned Catholic.

IX

It was three days after Christmas, and Patrick and Eileen sat across the table from each other at dinner, while Jacob sat at the head. Jacob looked down at the brandied peaches that Eleanor had just put before him, and then he looked over at Eileen.

"You've spoken to Patrick about the New Year's Eve Ball at Tuxedo?"

"Yes, Daddy."

Jacob turned his head toward Patrick. "You're going then, Patrick?"

"No, Father, I'm not."

Jacob slid one of the brandied peaches onto his spoon and ate it. He looked down at the peaches again, decided that was all the brandied peaches he wanted and why the devil did Eileen have them anyhow, and then he dabbed at his mouth with his napkin. "I think your sister would like you to go," he said, and Eileen made an affirmative sound.

"Look, Father, it's just that I don't particularly want to run into Anna out there. I think she'll probably be there, and — I don't know. Eileen can certainly find somebody else to be an extra man."

"That's not the point, Patrick," Jacob said. "You don't just withdraw from the scene because of something like this, do you?" His eyes traveled over to Eileen, seeking confirmation and getting absolutely no reaction. Eileen was thinking that the brandied peaches had been a failure. Well, there was going to be an apple pie tomorrow, and there couldn't be any two ways about that.

Patrick shrugged his shoulders. "The fact that you don't go to the New Year's Eve Ball doesn't mean that you're a hermit."

"No, Pat," Eileen said. "But I don't see why it should be you that doesn't go."

"Well, I do," Patrick said, but he didn't sound quite as convinced as he had a few moments before.

Jacob stood up. "Let's have our coffee in the library," he said.

They trooped up the stairs, Eileen first, and when they got into the library Jacob went over to the fireplace and put a match to the newspaper that was under the logs and kindling. He straightened up and stood with one elbow resting lightly on the mantelpiece, watching the reflection of the flames in the Christmas tree ornaments. The fire began burning well, and Jacob stepped away from it and stood there, thrusting his hands into his pockets, watching Eileen as she took the coffee tray from the maid and began to apportion the cream and sugar. He could feel what was going on in Patrick's mind. Patrick was sitting down, outwardly calm, waiting for his coffee, but all he was thinking about was this New Year's Eve business. Jacob knew that Patrick wanted to see Anna again, and now Eileen had put it to him in such a way that pride did not seem involved. If he could go without seeming to be going just to catch a glimpse of Anna, he would go. Jacob stole another glance at Patrick, and just as if it were written on Patrick's forehead, he saw what was going on in there. Patrick was convincing himself that it would really be best to go. It was the more mature attitude. One had to face up to things. As Eileen said, why should he be the one to disappear?

"Here's your coffee, Father." Eileen had been holding out the cup toward Jacob, while Jacob had been staring at Patrick and Patrick had been staring at the wall.

"Oh, thank you, dear," Jacob said, and the tableau dissolved. Patrick stood up and came over to get his coffee.

"I guess maybe I will take you New Year's Eve," he growled, and sat back down again with his coffee, not looking at anybody.

X

As it turned out, Patrick did not have to wait until New Year's Eve to have the chance of seeing Anna. He went down to Brooks Brothers the next afternoon to buy some shirts, and on the way down in the elevator from the Sixth Floor Shop, he decided to stop at the tie counter on the first floor. It was an old habit with Patrick, almost a good luck charm. His shopping expeditions were rare, but whenever he did buy clothes, in whatever shop it was, he always let himself be tempted at their tie counter. He never bought a tie unless it spoke to him, and the result was that he really liked the ties that he owned.

Patrick came out of the elevator on the main floor, walked over to the tie counter, and there was Anna, standing bent over the glass-topped counter, looking at some striped ties. For a moment, before she knew he was there, he considered making a sharp left turn and bolting out of the store. He felt his heart pounding, and he felt cold. Then he walked up beside her.

"Anna?" he said. Anna stood rigid for a second after he had spoken, holding the same angle of looking down at the neckties on the brightly lit shelf under the glass, and then she turned.

"Patrick," she said, putting out her gloved hand.

"How are you?" Patrick said, and then their hands were apart.

"Fine. How are you?"

"I'm all right," Patrick said. "How about a drink?"

Anna looked at her wrist watch. He could have killed her for looking to see if she had time to have a drink with him. "Great," Anna said after a second. "But I've got to buy a tie. Can you help me?"

"I think so," Patrick said, looking down at the ties. "How old a man is it for?"

"About your age."

Patrick smiled despite himself. Leave yourself open for a left hook and you get hit with a left hook, he said to himself. His heart was still pounding, but he was beginning to be all right again. Not great, but all right. Another part of his mind was trying to figure out if Anna had any cousins his age for whom she might have to buy a tie. "Does it have to be striped?"

"No. Don't you like striped ties, Patrick?"

"Not much. I think figured ones are a little nicer." He leaned over the counter, trying to concentrate. After a couple of minutes he had a tie picked out for her. It might not fill the recipient's heart with joy, but he certainly would not recoil from it in horror.

They walked out onto Madison Avenue, their packages under their arms. The sky was going from gray into blue over their heads, and the coldness of the winter afternoon contrasted with the warm glow from the windows, the windows of the stores, the windows of the buses that mumbled by.

"How about the Biltmore Bar?" Anna said.

"Is that the Under-the-Clock bar?"

"Yes. Haven't you ever been there, Patrick?"

"I don't think so. Anyhow, let's go."

They waited for the light that held up the crowd of buses and taxis and cars, and then they crossed and walked down to the Biltmore. They came out of the December street into an atmosphere of intense geniality. Everybody from out of town was meeting everybody from in town under the clock. Cousins from Scranton were meeting cousins who had been working in New York for a year now, and some of the cousins who had been working in New York for a year now swept them off to a quieter place, and some of them marched into the Palm Court, toward which Patrick and Anna made their way. At the many little tables there were college girls and college boys, with a few ensigns' and lieutenants' uniforms here and there. It was Christmastime in New York, and it was five o'clock in the afternoon. The waiters were overworked.

They sat down at a little table against one of the walls, and after Patrick had looked around at this spectacle that he had not seen before in his twenty-one years in New York, he began trying to attract a waiter. His eyes kept swiveling back again and again to look at Anna. He couldn't help staring at her face, prettily flushed as it was from their brief walk in the cold, her eyes, the blue eyes with the golden flecks, it was all there. Nothing had changed and everything had changed, and Patrick was grateful when someone came and took their order.

The waiter was back with their drinks in three minutes.

"This is fantastic," Anna said, raising her glass. "It always takes them longer than this."

"Well, we always do things differently," Patrick said, and took a good-sized swallow of his scotch and soda.

"What have you been doing with yourself?" Anna asked.

"Oh, you know — a few parties, a little Christmas shopping and unshopping, that sort of thing."

"How's your novel?"

"All right. It keeps coming. Not very fast." Suddenly Patrick heard the conversation as if he were a third person, and he felt himself starting to grow angry. He wanted to break up her poised, polite handling of him, shake her up — and then again he wanted terribly to kiss her, to take her hand and walk out into the night with her and never leave her, ever. The one thing he didn't want was this polite, restrained conversation, and that was the one thing he had.

"Are you going to be in Tuxedo New Year's Eve?" Patrick said after a few minutes.

"No. I think I'll be at Piping Rock that night."

Hit me again, Patrick thought. Hit me again, I can't feel anything.

"How about another drink?"

"No thanks. Honestly, PK, I have to go pretty soon."

"All right. Waiter!" The waiter came over. "I'd like the check, please."

A few minutes after that they walked down the steps, through the revolving door, and into half past five of late December. Patrick was about to suggest walking up the Avenue, or doing something, anything to hang on to her a little longer, a chance to take her arm as they crossed a street, when Anna hailed a cab. "I'm going downtown. Can I give you a lift?"

"No thanks, Anna." Patrick stepped down off the curb and opened the taxi door for her. They were facing each other, and Patrick was clenching his teeth to keep from asking her to lunch the next day.

"G'bye, Patrick," Anna said, and she put one gloved hand, a black glove, on his left cheek, and then she kissed his right cheek, a quick dove of a kiss.

"Good to see you, Anna," Patrick said. There was a flash of her silk-stockinged leg as she got into the cab, and then Patrick slammed the door and turned away, walking up the street.

Anna sat in the taxi. She took off her glove and looked at her hand. It was shaking. All right, she said to herself, all right, all right. It has to be some way and if you can't be sure the other way it's got to be this way, it's the only fair way.

"Did you say something, miss?" the driver asked.

"I hope not," Anna said, and put her glove back on.

9

EVEN AFTER she had got into bed and stayed there for a few minutes, Eileen's heart was still pounding. She knew that some of her friends had had several proposals of marriage, but she had had her first proposal tonight, and she was very much shaken up about it. She wished that her father were home, so that she could go into his room and tell him about it, but he was in Washington, and that was that.

Eileen sat up in bed, feeling her heart still pounding and her breath coming fast, and she shook her head as if she were sick. She still could not quite believe the whole thing, mainly because she had not known the young man three weeks before. His name was John Runder, and he was the first man she had ever met who did absolutely nothing. She had met him at a cocktail party just at the end of Christmas vacation, and he had driven her home in his car. It was a gray Jaguar sports car, and he had double-parked it outside 1120 and come on up for a nightcap. Over the drink he told her about his life, which consisted of an education terminating in a Bachelor of Arts from the University of Virginia, and a year in the Army just after the end of the Second World War. He also managed to convey the fact that he was a Catholic.

That had been an evening three weeks ago. Since then they

had had dinner together three times, and, from a remark here and a remark there, Eileen began to piece together the life that he had been leading since he finished with the University. He did nothing, in an organized way. In the morning he got up about ten, and went over to his club after breakfast and played a game of squash. Then he had lunch with one of his many acquaintances who worked in the midtown area, in advertising or television or publishing. The afternoon was something of a problem, but he filled it with a combination of reading magazines, playing backgammon, and throwing in another game of squash before meeting a young lady for cocktails and dinner. Once a month he had an appointment with the broker who handled the sizable amount of money his parents had left him, and on Sunday he went to Mass. Thus John Runder.

Eileen swung out of bed and turned on the light. Then she went over and flung herself down in a chair. She was thinking about the evening just past, going over it piece by piece. She had met him at the New Weston, and then they had gone on to dinner at the Brussels. It had been an evening just like the others, with John taking a lot to drink and not showing a sign of it in his healthy-looking face. He was just as he had been before; telling her mildly amusing stories, spending money as if he manufactured the stuff in his basement, and being distinctly friendly, rather than romantic, in his approach. After dinner they had gone to see *Annie Get Your Gun* and after that he had taken her dancing at the Algiers. Eileen had heard a lot about the Algiers, but she had never been there before. Now that she had been there, she never wanted to go back again. The place was mainly populated by a breed of men that seemed indigenous to it, swarthy types who looked as if they had been faced with living a life of crime or a life of living off women, and had chosen the latter. The women were either deathly pale or tropically tanned. John had moved among them all with perfect ease, kissing the cheek of one fading beauty after another, and, with his fair hair and his fair face, looking vastly different from most of the other men.

He had driven her home at about one-thirty, and when she had turned at the front door to thank him for a spectacular evening, he had asked if he could come upstairs for a minute. He looked earnest when he said it, and Eileen said of course.

Just as soon as he had taken off his overcoat and they were sitting on the sofa, he had asked her to marry him.

Eileen had tried to open her mouth. She knew that the answer was no, but it was about twenty seconds before she could say anything.

"John," she said, and then she shook her head. "I think it's wonderful of you to feel that way about me, but — no. Thank you."

He had looked down at the floor. "You see," he said finally, his voice sounding slow and tired and resigned, "I think you could straighten me out. I've never asked anybody to marry me before, Eileen." He kept looking down, and Eileen found that she was looking at the floor too. "I think I could make you happy, and I know you'd make me happy, and I think you could straighten me out."

Eileen almost said, without thinking, but I don't want to straighten you out. She sat there, horrified at what she had almost said, and telling herself that what she meant was that she didn't want to straighten him out that much.

"Could I see you again?" he said after a minute.

"I don't think so," Eileen said softly. "I'm awfully sorry, John. But I don't think there's any point, do you?"

"No, there's no point," he said, standing up. "There's no point at all." He looked down at her. "Would it make any difference to you if I got a job somewhere?"

Eileen stood up too. "Well, I think it might make a difference to you. But for what you mean, I don't think so." She shook her head again.

"Well — " he said, and then he smiled. It was a good loser's smile, and Eileen smiled back. She had never liked him more. A minute later he was gone, and it was only when she heard the elevator door close behind him that she felt how cold she was, and how her heart was pounding at the surprise and bigness of what had happened.

Eileen got up out of the chair in which she was sitting and went into the bathroom. She usually took her shower in the morning, but she thought a warm shower right now might calm her. She looked out of the bathroom window before she pulled the curtain down over the unfrosted top panes. It was a clear January night, and the lights were silver in the distance, silver on the oily surface of the East River. Everything was the same, but a man had just asked her to live with him for the rest of his life.

She pulled down the curtain and took off her nightgown. Her fingers seemed stiff as she put on her shower cap, but finally she was in the warm water. Her knees were shaking, and she hung on to the handle of the shower. The thought was sliding around in the back of her mind that she had been giving him ten points for being a Catholic. She had had very few beaux who were Catholics, and she wanted to marry a Catholic when she married. So she had had a proposal from a man who was a Catholic, and who could support her. And a man with whom you're not in love, Eileen said, so that's that. Her knees were steadying a little bit in the warm water and steam of the shower bath. I think you could straighten me out, she said to herself. Uh-uh. Nothing was going to straighten him out. He would go on playing squash until he was too old to play squash, and then he would have the magazines and the backgammon to fall back on, and one day he would hit one of the little silver bells in the tap room of his club, and when the waiter came to ask Mr. Runder what he wished to drink, Mr. Runder would be dead.

Eileen looked down at her knees. They had stopped shaking.

II

Patrick sat alone in the pew downstairs in St. Paul's. It was evening, and he had to go over to the Seneca for an election meeting in a little while, but right now he found that he had a few things to think over, and he had always found this a good place to think things over, as well as to pray specific prayers. Just this morning a letter from the Law School had come, saying that he was accepted. Some of Patrick's friends who had also applied had not heard yet, and one of them had said, "Well, that means you're in the first group. How to go!" Patrick had smiled. First group. It sounded good.

Patrick went forward in the pew, down on his knees. He said one Act of Contrition, and then, while he was still kneeling, a frown came onto his forehead. He had written his father, and he knew how happy it would make his father, and he had sent in his acceptance in the afternoon mail, and now he was kneeling here, not as happy as he had thought he would be. As he stayed on his knees, one picture kept coming back to him. The night that he had been initiated at the Seneca two years before, he had ended up, quite drunk, talking to one of the graduates who was about thirty years old, and all Patrick had talked about was whether he was going to be able to get into the Law School. That had been just two years ago, and before then, and since then, when people had asked him what he was going to do after he graduated, he had always said, the Law School, if I can get in.

And now he was in. Patrick slid back from kneeling, so that he was sitting again. Will you promise me to go for a year? his father's voice said in his memory. Yes, Patrick answered from the middle of the summer before. I promise.

III

It was the second week in March, and Anna was walking along a country road near Bryn Mawr, her hands thrust deep in the pockets of her polo coat, and no trace of lipstick on her mouth. It was a glorious day. In one of the pockets of her coat there was a letter from Patrick, a polite note telling her that he had been admitted to the Law School, and he thought she would like to know, since they had discussed it so often. Anna's face did not look happy.

"All *right*," Anna said out loud, almost convulsively. No one heard her but a bird sitting in a bare branch just off the road. All right, she said to herself. You miss him. Of course you miss him. But I haven't seen you wishing that you were married to him.

Anna kicked at a pebble that was sitting in the road, and kept on walking with her hands in her pockets. Patrick receded to where he always was these days, an unhappy pressure that could spring forward when she read something that sounded like Patrick talking, or when she saw somebody who looked even remotely like him. Patrick receded to that place, and she began to think of the examinations coming up ahead of her, the comprehensives and the last finals. They were still two months away, but she had a tremendous amount of work to do. Anna had always thought that it was a bit extreme of Bryn Mawr not to have a chapter of Phi Beta Kappa, because they claimed that any graduate of Bryn Mawr was the equivalent of a Phi Bate, but there was no doubt that they were pouring it on. Four academic years, from September of 1947 to this spring of 1951. An awful lot of books. Anna felt a sadness filling up inside her when she thought about it. It had been an awful lot of work, and right now, nearing the end of it, she was not at all sure that it had been worth it.

She came to a big elm tree at a bend in the road, and then

she turned and started back toward Pembroke West and her books. This afternoon she had been reading about the Entente Cordiale, and somehow this afternoon she could not get very worked up about the whole thing. She thought about everything for another minute, and a couple of wrinkles appeared on her forehead. She was glad that she was getting out this June, and she had never realized it more fully than this afternoon. She could never have stood it for another year. Whenever she thought about what she had done with her life thus far, she found that she had two consolations. One was her conviction that she had always tried to do the right thing, and the other was her conviction that most of the things she would be good at were still ahead of her. She had been a good student, but she thought she would be much better at being a woman than she had been as a student. She had always been good with children, and this year, for the first time, she had started to feel a yearning to have children, as if it had been there for a while but was only now beginning to announce itself, not the generalized feeling that it might be nice to have children, but a real desire to have a child.

Anna sighed as she walked along the road. She was remembering that first autumn here as a freshman, with all of them living from week-end to week-end, with conversations about who was going to take you to the Yale-Princeton game, and who you had for the Grosvenor Ball, and a vague worry if maybe you'd flunk out at the end of the term. If you went out for field hockey, you played hard. Things had Mattered. Anna smiled a tired, thin smile as she walked on back toward her books. It seemed a long time ago, and the afternoon was getting cold.

IV

Jacob stood in the crowded subway car, one hand on the enameled handle of the strap over his head. His face was composed in the patient boredom of the subway passenger. Some of his friends had cars and chauffeurs, and there was a whole bunch of men who shared a school bus to go downtown every morning, but Jacob went down to work on the Lexington Avenue subway. It was quick and it was efficient and it was cheap, and all those things appealed to him. It was also hot and crowded and smelly and dirty, and it was hard to love your fellow man during the rush hour on the I.R.T., but Jacob usually managed to think of something else.

This morning as the express hammered along in the darkness from Eighty-Sixth Street to Grand Central Station, he was thinking about how pleasant it would be to have Patrick down in New York after another three years, working in the firm and riding down with him every morning. They could have breakfast together, and then they would stroll down to Eighty-Sixth, past the unopened morning façade of RKO Eighty-Sixth Street, and go down into the subway, Kingsgrant and Kingsgrant, attorneys-at-law. Jacob's face remained motionless, but there was a sparkle in his eyes. He had been thinking a lot about Patrick lately, and he knew that he was boring Cutter and Lee about Patrick's having been in the first group accepted, but he couldn't help it. The boy had a brain, and now he was going to use it, and Jacob had stood here on the subway in the mornings this last couple of weeks, thinking over Patrick's life, seeing it now as one unity, all leading to the first group accepted at the Law School.

The train rushed into the roller coaster turns just before Forty-Second Street, and came braking in to the platform. A million people got off and a million people got on, and Jacob just stayed tight, and a moment later they were back thumping through the darkness again. And the thing was, Jacob thought, he almost didn't make it. Right at the beginning, he almost didn't make it. His eyes softened as he thought about how it had been when Patrick was born. He didn't think about it often, and when he did, the whole memory still scared and moved him.

Maude had been happy in her pregnancy on Kingsgrant Island. Jacob could not quite get used to the fact that Maude, who had gone from San Francisco to New York for a specific dance, who knew the shops in Paris and the restaurants in Cannes, really wanted just to live on an island in Penobscot Bay, but it was true. Jacob went off to South Harbor and the office every morning, and sometimes in the evening he brought back Dr. Field with him, and Maude would make them tea, smiling and happy and great with child. "She's a wonderful girl, Jacob," Dr. Field would say when he had finished his examination and Jacob would take him down to the landing. "She's going to have a hard time of it, but she's got me certain she can do it." And Jacob had nodded. If Maude could do her end of it, Dr. Field could do his. Harold Field had delivered every baby in the area in the last thirty years.

There was a hitch. The plan had been to bring Maude over to Rolly's house about two weeks before the baby was due, and then take her on over to the hospital in Blue Hill when the first pains began. But Maude begged Jacob not to take her off the island until a week before the baby was due, and Jacob looked into her pleading gray eyes and agreed. So they were still at Kingsgrant when the storm hit. It was a howling gale, half snow and half sleet, and as if nature had not created enough violence, Maude began to have her child, a good ten days before Dr. Field had thought it could possibly arrive. The

Bay was being torn apart, and Maude was having her child, not tomorrow, but right now. Jacob had stood in the hall of Kingsgrant that night, knowing what was going on upstairs, watched by the terrified eyes of the colored servants. Harriet was upstairs doing the best she could, but what was needed was a doctor. The other servants were standing in the doorways around the dimly lit hall, watching Jacob.

"Ben," Jacob had said, quietly, and Ben, who was then a slender boy of twenty, came out of the shadows.

"Yes, Mr. Jacob?" he said.

"I'm going in to South Harbor," Jacob said. "I need another man because somebody's got to keep that boat off while I run and get Dr. Field. Do you want to come?"

"I'll come."

For a few minutes that night, when Jacob had succeeded in finding Dr. Field and the two of them had managed to get back to where Ben had kept the boat maneuvering off of the town pier, it seemed very likely that there would be five lives lost. Boats were breaking up all over the harbor, and the *Ethan Kingsgrant* was taking water from every quarter and the storm was literally blinding. Out on the island Maude was unconscious, and neither her body nor the baby's appeared interested in any further efforts at living. But the boat got through to the island, and it was some seven hours after this, at six o'clock in the morning, that Harold Field made his first mistake in some six hundred deliveries. It was only a matter of a slight excessive pressure on the baby's right shoulder with a pair of forceps, but it was done. It was excusable. The doctor was an old man, the struggles in the waves and the hailstones had left them all shaken and desperately tired, it was an extraordinarily difficult labor and delivery, but nevertheless it had happened.

Late in the afternoon of the next day Maude was conscious, and asked for the baby to be brought to her. The storm was over, and a nurse who had come out that morning brought Patrick to her. Maude had lain there in the bed, loving him and admiring him, and then she had said, not terribly worried at first, "Jake, why isn't he moving his right arm?"

Jacob had stood there, not having slept, and he had looked out through the window, seeing the calm waters that had been so explosive last night. He tried to explain that Dr. Field had done his best, about the ice storm, that there was a good chance that the arm wasn't going to be too bad.

"Who did it, Jake?" Maude said, her eyes flashing and far more color in her cheeks than he had thought possible so soon after the ordeal. "Who did it? Did I do it or did Dr. Field? Who *did* it, Jake!"

"Everyone did wrong except you, darling," Jacob had said, turning from the window and looking down at the two of them. "Everyone did wrong except you and Patrick." Then tears had come out of his eyes and gone down his cheeks.

They never had any specific discussion about leaving Kingsgrant. Maude never said in so many words that it would not have happened in New York, that the island frightened her now, that she dreamed night after night that the child had wandered away from the house and drowned, but Jacob and Rolly Grindall had a talk, and Jacob wrote some letters, and within six weeks they were living in New York. Jacob assumed that Maude would never want to see the island again, but he was wrong. After a couple of years she started going back on vacations, and when she found out she was going to die, she said that she wanted to be buried there. Jacob was never sure if she really wanted to be buried at Kingsgrant, but that was what she said, and that was where she was buried.

Jacob opened his eyes a little wider. The train was pulling into a station, and he bent his head down a little and looked out the window. Fulton Street. Check. Jacob held on to the enamel handle until the car stopped, and then he walked quickly out the door and onto the platform.

v

Bill Bench stood up and stripped off his sweatshirt, and walked along the side of the pool toward the place where the starter was standing. The noise of the crowd in the stands on either side of the pool rose echoing to the concrete ceiling high above, but it began to quiet down as the officials announced the next race. He passed by the officials, and stepped up onto the raised end of the pool and walked to a spot opposite Number One lane. He could see the dark stripes on the bottom of the pool, rippling and turning because of the waves on the surface. The two men from Yale were standing just behind their starting marks now, too, and Bill looked over at his teammate, Cy Marks, and smiled. This was it. In a few seconds he and Cy would be in the water racing the two men from Yale, and in another two minutes the 220-yard freestyle would be over, and all four of them would be hanging against the end of the pool, half dead.

Bill watched one of the Yale men lean over the edge and scoop up some water to slap across his face and chest, and he found that his thoughts were coming quickly and clearly. This was the last time that he would swim for Harvard, and the sad part about it was that he already knew that he was sure to come in fourth. The two men Yale had in the 220 were going to the Olympics next year, and they would come in about twenty yards ahead of Cy, and then he could come in about ten yards behind Cy, and there wasn't a thing he could do about it. Bill smiled a tight smile.

"On your marks, gentlemen," the starter said. Bill hitched

up the brief black trunks and advanced to the edge of the pool, setting his feet down with the toes just curling over the edge. There was just one thing on his mind. He was going to swim and swim and swim, and he knew he was going to come in behind, but he was going to swim and swim and swim. He was going to give it everything he had, and if one of the Olympic prospects got a cramp, then he would come in third and make a point for Harvard.

"Set!"

Bill bent forward, his hands out and behind him.

Blam! The gun went off, and even before the echoes came down from the roof, the four of them had hit the water with a crashing splash and Bill Bench was swimming his last race for Harvard.

VI

Snowjob Porter rarely got upset on behalf of another human being, but right now he was sitting in his room, completely incapable of seeing the page in front of him, because of what had just happened. He and Patrick had been sitting in the living room, discussing some notes that were still in his hands now, and the radio had been on. Bill and Tall Man were the only two who ever bothered turning on the radio, so one of them must have left it on when he went out. Patrick had been saying something, and then he had held up his hand. Snowjob had stopped talking, and they had both listened. It was just a fast little news item, saying that there had been a train wreck near Bryn Mawr, Pennsylvania, and that several people had been hurt. The news announcer had gone on to something else, and before Snowjob knew what was happening, Patrick was frantically thumbing through the pages of the telephone book.

"What are you looking for?" Snowjob asked.

"Boston *Globe*," Patrick said in a preoccupied tone, and a moment later he had them on the line. "Hello. Can you give me the names of the people who were hurt in that wreck down near Bryn Mawr? Sure I'll wait. Hello. Can you give me the names of the people who were hurt in that train wreck down near Bryn Mawr? The one I'm interested in is van Neerdaam. V A N new word capital N double E R D double A M. What? Thanks." Patrick put down the receiver.

"He said there weren't any names like that on the ticker."

Snowjob had finally put two and two together. "I'm glad," he said.

"So am I." Patrick got up and went into his room, and as Snowjob sat in the living room, he thought he heard Patrick pacing around. Finally Snowjob had come back into his own bedroom and was sitting here at the desk that he shared with Tall Man. Patrick's controlled, tense tone of voice was still in his ears, and his relief when he found out that Anna was not in the crash. But why would he think she would be in the first place? Snowjob asked himself. Never mind, the answer came back, the point is that he thought she might be. He didn't know. That's the whole trouble. He doesn't know where she is, or what she's doing. And I guess it kills him.

Snowjob tried to concentrate on the sheaf of notes in his hand, and finally his mind focused on them once again. It was a paper he was writing for his course in International Understanding, which he was taking to fill out his distribution requirements. This paper was really a combined Leverett D-32 product, although Tall Man had only been able to give it moral support. Snowjob had put forth one of his favorite ideas in this paper, which was, now that almost all the elements in the United States had been sold on international cooperation, the

U.N., and foreign aid programs, there might be an even more violent isolationism than that of the 1930's if the people of the United States felt that they were being rebuffed and financially hoodwinked by the very people they were trying to assist. The second part of his paper was devoted to a description of things that might happen, the United States telling the French all right, we *will* go home, and we'll take our Air Force and our Army and our Navy along with us, and see if you really like it so much better that way. There were several examples of this, and then a projection into a future wherein the Western Hemisphere was a completely independent unit, made that way by pouring into South America all the money that had been formerly poured into Europe. Snowjob's real field was social relations, but Patrick and Bill Bench had been interested in the whole idea of this paper, and helped him with it. Bill had given him all the facts he needed, and Patrick had given him the title. "The Chromium Curtain." That was what the United States was going to retire behind. Patrick had written the first paragraph, and then corrected all the punctuation, and although Bill in particular was critical of the underlying idea of the paper, still they were both helping him get it done. Snowjob loosened his tie a little more, and kept on rereading his paper, pencil in hand.

VII

"I don't know," Allston Hunt said. "I used to go along with the theory that writers are volunteers, but I'm not so sure any more. It seems to me that you're drafted into it, just by the things inside you. That is, I'm not sure there really is a choice."

"Well, sir, all I mean is that if you're a writer I think it's perfectly fair for the world to consider you as a person who's sticking his neck out."

"Let's go in the next room." Hunt stood up from the dinner

table in his house on Ellery Street, and motioned for Patrick to precede him into the little living room. They had had dinner together on this April evening, and they had been sitting with their elbows on the table, just talking, since they had finished their coffee twenty minutes before. "Sit down," Hunt said, dropping into an armchair. "Well, you do get my point about the fact that the thing may run you, rather than you running it?"

"Yes, sir. I think I do. All I mean is that if you're a good healthy ditch-digger willing to work, then the world owes you a chance to make a living, and if you can't make a living, then there's something wrong with the society in which you live."

"But if you're a writer, then it's different?"

"I think so. There's the world, and the world's work. If you're willing to do the world's work, the world owes you a living. If you have the egotism necessary to be an artist, then you stand up and say, my work comes first and the world's work comes second — " Patrick stopped and smiled. "In that case, I don't think the world owes you anything. If you've got what the public wants, you'll make some sort of a living out of your art. If you haven't, you won't."

"I regret to say that I agree with you on that. The world doesn't owe an artist a damned thing," Hunt said, and then he sat sprawled in his armchair looking toward the ceiling. "Patrick," he said slowly, turning his head, "what the devil is all this about you and the Law School, anyhow?"

Patrick straightened up. "Well, I made my father a promise to go for a year, at least. When I made it I really thought I wanted to go. But I know if he made me a promise, he'd keep it."

"But you don't want to keep it."

"I don't know."

Allston Hunt straightened up in his chair. There had been

an almost anguished tone in Patrick's voice just then, and Allston decided that he was pressing too far. "I liked the last section you handed in," he said, trying to get on something that was more strictly within his province, "but there was one thing I wanted to talk over with you. It's that passage on masturbation. It just won't go. You can write a whole book on homosexuality, but one scene involving masturbation and you can't get a publisher this side of Paris."

"Well, I don't expect 'Technical Jones' to be published anyhow."

"Never mind about that. You've got to write it as if it *is* going to be published. I think your problem is simple on this thing. If you keep the passage in, and I'm not saying there's anything wrong with it, you won't get the book published. Since I think it's better to have it published with that passage out than not have it published at all, I'd take it out, if I were you."

"I suppose you're right," Patrick said. "But anyhow, I don't think this book is going to get published."

"Look, Patrick," Hunt said, turning in his chair, "you've got to get over this idea that books are written by supermen. Every year I come up against the same thing in my class, and it's very understandable. You people look at a book, and because it *is* a book, and it looks impressive when you hold it in your hand, you're inclined to think that what's in it is a little more authoritative than it is, and that the author is some sort of person way up there." Hunt pointed a finger toward the ceiling and kept staring at Patrick. "Authors are just you and your classmates, a little bit farther on down the line."

Patrick couldn't think of anything to say, so he just nodded.

"How do you feel about your book?" Hunt asked in a softer tone. "Is it shaping up more or less the way you had it in mind?"

"Well, I find that some of these characters of mine sort of

develop a life of their own. I had it all planned for my Bostonian girl to throw over Leapingdeer, but they're getting along so well that I'm going to have a hell of a time breaking them up."

Hunt smiled. "That's a good sign," he said. "Whenever a character of mine runs away with me, I just let him keep the bit in his teeth. There's plenty of time to revise later on, and it doesn't happen that often." Hunt looked at his watch. "I hate to throw you out of here," he said, standing up, "but I've got some work to do tonight. For Harvard, not for me."

"Well, all things be to the greater glory of God," Patrick said lightly, standing up too. The second he said it, he felt like a complete ass, but Hunt did not seem to notice. "You sure there isn't something I can help you with around here, sir?"

"No thanks. My housekeeper's already done the dishes, and that's about all there is."

"Well, thank you again for a wonderful dinner."

"I enjoyed it," Hunt said. "Good night."

"Good night, sir. Thank you again." Patrick went down the steps into the April evening. It was a little chilly, but he felt a glow right through him. Just the idea that Hunt would have him to dinner was enough. Patrick turned over that concept of being drafted instead of being a volunteer, decided that he still didn't quite see it, and went on under the streetlights and the trees.

VIII

Eileen came out of Best's with a package under each arm, and headed up Fifth Avenue. It was the third day of May, and the world looked good. Eileen could hardly believe that she was buying things to take to Europe, but that was what she was doing. She and her friend Patsy Snelling had their passage booked for the twentieth of June, and she felt as if it were tomorrow. There were a million things to do, and then all in one week she had to pass her exams, go up to Cambridge and see Patrick graduate, and then streak for New York and the boat.

She crossed the street to the block on which St. Patrick's stood, and decided to go in for a visit. She hitched the light silk scarf she had around her neck up so that it covered her head, and went into the cathedral.

The springtime was in here too. Eileen went pretty far up, toward the altar on the right-hand side where the Blessed Sacrament was displayed, and knelt down in a pew. She felt a tide of excitement moving within her. It was May in New York, and it would be June on the Atlantic, and it would be summer in France. The only thing that worried her was something that she had been thinking about for the last few days. She had been realizing that Patrick and her father were going up to spend at least part of the summer at Kingsgrant, just the two of them, and that the two of them had not been together for any length of time without her being there, ever. A few of the worse fights over the years had paraded through Eileen's mind, but she had decided that all she could do was hope for the best. She had been Miss Buffer State for a long time, and someday she was going to leave completely, to get married, so they might just as well learn right now how to get along. She was going, and that was that.

Eileen looked up at a statue of the Virgin Mary, and another disturbing thought crossed her mind. She and Patrick had had quite an argument about the Blessed Virgin when he had been home on his Easter vacation this year. It had all happened one night at dinner, and Eileen couldn't remember how it started, but there was Patrick with his face red, saying he was *not* trying to minimize the influence of the Virgin Mary, but it was

his position that first things came first, and the Trinity came
a long way ahead of the Virgin Mary, and he was sorry to
tell Eileen that he thought a lot of Catholics were giving the
Virgin Mary almost as much attention as they gave to Christ.
She had flashed back with something, and then her father had
said something, and she and Patrick had both turned as one
person and told their father to please keep out of it, and he
had blown up and stalked away from the table. It had not been
too pleasant, but it had certainly livened up the place for an
evening.

Anyhow, Eileen said silently, half to herself and half to the
statue before her, If you love enough, there's plenty of faith
and devotion to go around. Plenty. She said an Our Father,
and then a Hail Mary, and went back out into the sunlight on
the street.

IX

Three days before his first final Patrick knocked on the door
of Allston Hunt's office and after a moment the door opened.
The room was dark and in the corner someone was working
a machine that gave off a red light.

"Come in, Patrick."

"Thank you, sir."

Allston Hunt closed the door behind Patrick. "Just photo-
stating something," he said. "Sit down."

Patrick sat on the battered leather couch over by the wall
and watched the outlines of Hunt and the other man as they
bent over the machine.

"Well, I'm going away tomorrow until graduation," Hunt
said, coming over and sitting down beside Patrick in the darkness, "so I suppose this is good-bye." The machine kept going
slam-click.

"Yes, sir. Good-bye until next year, anyhow."

"Yes." Hunt stood up. "I've got your last section of manuscript here somewhere." There was a sound of a drawer opening, and after a minute he was back. "Might open this envelope when you get outside — make sure it's the right one."

"Yes, sir." They sat there, both silent for a few seconds.

"I liked that part about the Civil War in this last section — the idea that this generation of American children think that the Civil War was fought by a lot of old men because so many of the statues are bearded."

Patrick smiled in the darkness.

"I hope you finish this thing, Patrick."

"I think I'll have to."

"Well, that's good. I don't usually do this, but anytime you get it finished and you want to try and get it published, why don't you give it to me, and I'll hand it to a couple of my friends."

Patrick sat there for a moment. For the first time in the whole year it came through to him that Allston Hunt really thought there was a chance that *this* novel, not some future novel but this novel, could be published. He tried to open his mouth to say something.

"Well, thank you very much, sir. Thank you very much for everything."

Hunt stood up, and Patrick stood up too.

"Incidentally," Hunt said as they were walking toward the door, "you're getting an A for the year."

"Well, that's very good to hear."

"You deserved it. But it isn't the grade that matters. Grades are just a way of keeping score as long as you're in school. Maybe in Civil Service, I don't know."

"Well — " Patrick said, and then the door was open and he and Hunt shook hands.

"I wish you luck, whatever it's going to be. Let me know how you're doing, Patrick."

"Yes, sir." Patrick felt the whole inconclusive thing between them, between himself and the future, between himself and the past. "Thanks again, sir," he said, and walked off toward the stairs, hearing the door close behind him.

X

Tall Man was standing over by the couch, the telephone receiver in his hand. He was not going to stay around for the graduation ceremonies. He was all packed, and Snowjob and Patrick and Bill were standing around awkwardly, waiting for him to finish this conversation with a professor who had called up with some last-minute scheme.

"I appreciate it very much, sir," Tall Man said, "but I'm already signed up for this thing. I certainly do appreciate it, and I'd be very much interested in doing it when I come back. Very much. Yes, sir. OCS for the Marines. Well, thank you. Good luck to you too." He hung up and smiled at them. "It never rains but it pours. Possibility of being a Junior Fellow." He shrugged his shoulders.

"I'll bet you've forgotten something," Snowjob said.

"I guess I'd better take one more look." Tall Man went into the room that he and Snowjob had shared for the past years, and Patrick looked away when he saw that Snowjob's eyes were a trifle wet. That was the thing about Snowjob, Patrick thought as they all stood there, hearing Tall Man clomp around his room one more time. Snowjob was usually so composed on the surface that it always came as a surprise to find that he had a heart.

"Here," Tall Man said, coming out with an alarm clock in his hand. "I got this up at the Coop freshman year. I don't

196

know why, but it still rings." He put it down on the table in the middle of the living room. "It's all yours," he said to them. "I'm going to sleep for the next three weeks, and after that I'm damned sure I won't need any alarm clock."

There was a knock on the door. "Here's my ride," Tall Man said. "The only other guy at Harvard that comes from Arizona." He opened the door. "Be with you in a minute, Glenn. Right there."

"Take care of yourself, Tall Man," Bill said. He stepped up to Tall Man and they shook hands.

"I'll walk you down to the car," Snowjob said.

Tall Man looked at the three of them. He wanted to say something, but he knew he was just going to walk out of here. They all talked about home, and going home. What he was going home to was a guardian who would have him for dinner one night, and maybe let him have his old room or maybe tell him he'd better try the Y, his married daughter was living with him now and there wasn't as much room as there used to be. He would sit around Flagstaff for a couple of weeks, and then thumb his way back east to Quantico. These three were the best friends he had ever had, and he knew it never could have been any better by getting closer to them. He had got as close to them as he wanted to, and you should never get any closer than that.

"We'll have a Concrete Kimono reunion one of these years," Patrick said, shaking his hand.

Tall Man nodded his head.

"I'll see you guys," he said, and picked up his bags.

XI

Jacob sat at the desk in his office at Cutter, Kingsgrant, and Lee. It was late afternoon, he was tired, and there was a client coming in in a few minutes. His hand was resting on a smooth stone from Hurricane Island. It was a paperweight of his, and just now, looking at the stone that came from an island in Penobscot Bay, the sadness that he had been feeling all this past week welled up in him particularly hard. He and Eileen were going up to Patrick's graduation tomorrow, and although he was proud and pleased and looking forward to being there, at times this past week he had found himself wishing so much that Maude was alive, and could see her boy graduating from Harvard.

You're tired, Jacob said to himself, staring down at the flat stone. It was a circular stone, and he flipped it over, stared at that side, and then flipped it back again. The front of his mind was making a note to get the *Virginia Law Journal* for the first quarter of 1944 out of the firm's library tonight and read it at home in connection with a case he was preparing, but the back of his mind was taking over. He kept staring at the stone and wishing that Maude could see Patrick graduate, and, slowly, the worst of Jacob's memories descended upon him, so that after a minute there was nothing left of Jacob in that office except a good-looking middle-aged man in a business suit, staring at a stone. The outward man was there, but his mind was in a private, unhappy place.

It had all seemed so impossible to Jacob. Maude had become pregnant for the third time in the spring of 1937, and although it had seemed to Jacob that she was having an unusual number of visits to doctors, he put it all down to her worries that there might somehow be a repetition of what happened to Patrick's arm. When he tried to point out to her that she had had remarkably little trouble having Eileen, Maude just nodded in a preoccupied way.

He came home one afternoon late in April, quite pleased

about a case that he had settled out of court that morning, and he heard Maude talking to someone. Her voice was coming from the bedroom, and it said, "But Dr. Harris, people don't *die* when just one blood vessel in the brain breaks, do they?"

Jacob froze in the hall.

"Believe me, Mrs. Kingsgrant," he heard Dr. Harris' voice saying in a strained way, "I've made every check there is. I certainly wouldn't tell you if it was just a possibility. Every one of these tests showed an aneurysm. You've got to tell your husband."

Jacob had walked into the bedroom then, and there was Maude, dressed in street clothes, sitting on the edge of her bed. She looked up at Jacob as he came through the door, and they just stood there for a moment, Jacob and Maude looking at each other, and Dr. Harris sitting in a chair, staring down at the carpet. Then Jacob sat down beside her and took her hand.

Maude smiled. "Don't worry, Jake," she said. "It'll work out."

Jacob's first reaction had been a couple of days of stunned disbelief, gradually crystallizing into a solid resentment of the medical profession. He ran through four sets of specialists in New York, and a trip with Maude to Johns Hopkins and back, searching for a doctor who would tell him that it was a false alarm. It was no false alarm. What Dr. Harris had hated to suspect from the way that Maude's vision had been occasionally blurring on her recently was true. They had diagnosed it correctly up at Presbyterian. She had a congenital berry aneurysm of the brain, only now announcing itself, and at any moment the thin wall of the vein where it was located might break, and she would die. It might not break for twenty years, or it might break three seconds ago. Most of the doctors told Jacob that in cases of this kind it happened sooner rather than later.

"Look, Jake," Maude said one day when Jacob was sitting

in his armchair across from her in the library, his head in his hands, "if this thing is going to happen, I don't want my last days to be with a furious bull moose. I just hope I have time enough to have the child." Jacob had looked up at her as she stood there, still marveling at how a person could have something that would leave them looking all right until one morning they were dead, and then he had met her own slow smile with a weak effort of his own. There was something about the way Maude said certain words, and the way she said "furious bull moose" was adorable.

"All right, Maude," Jacob had said, standing up and putting his arms around her gently, "I'll try to get used to it."

That May they walked in Central Park, and no one would ever know exactly what went through Jacob Kingsgrant when he watched Maude reach up and pick a blossom from a tree, or lean down and give a peanut to a squirrel. Finally, in June, Maude suggested that they go up to Kingsgrant. They spoke about going up for the summer, but behind their conversation Maude was telling Jacob that she thought she was going to die this summer and she wanted it to be at Kingsgrant, and Jacob was telling her that she needn't die at Kingsgrant to please him. But Maude insisted on going up, so off they went on the steamship to Bar Harbor, Jacob and Maude and Patrick and Eileen.

It seemed to be an especially pleasant summer. The winds that crossed the island were warm and soothing for once, and the gardens bloomed beautifully. Jacob and Maude took long, slow walks, around and across their island, and one thing that he particularly hated to bring up with Maude was his conviction that the children should be told about what might happen. He was planning to ask her what she thought about telling them, and one day before he got around to it, she took the children for a walk. When the three of them came back, Patrick and Eileen knew. No two of them ever spoke about it, but it was perfectly clear that they knew. The only thing Maude ever said to Jacob was that she didn't want the children to see her body. She wanted them to remember her alive.

And then one afternoon. Jacob and Maude had come in from having a walk and a long conversation about where Patrick should go to preparatory school when the time came, and what they would name the child she was bearing now if all went well, and Maude walked into the library while Jacob took off his hat and hung it in the hall closet.

"There's some tea here, Jake," Maude said from the library. "Want some?"

"Sure," Jacob said, bending down to pat Ben's dog Stephen. Then he straightened up and went in. Maude was sitting there in her chair by the fireplace, the tea steaming in front of her, but she was not leaning forward to pour the tea. She was sitting back in the chair, her head forward on her chest, and she was dead. Jacob picked her up, almost as if she would break, and carried her out of the living room and up the stairs. Patrick was standing at the top of the steps, and he stood there by the banister, watching them come, but Jacob did not see him at all. Jacob went on past him, carrying Maude, and took her into the bedroom and laid her down on the bed. She still had on her coat from walking around outdoors, and her cheeks still had the high, healthy pink that comes from walking in the salt air.

Patrick stood there for a minute on the landing, and then he turned and walked into the nursery and found Eileen.

"Eileen," he said, sitting down next to her, "Mother's dead, just like she said she would."

That night Jacob sat down in front of the empty fireplace. He had poured himself a drink but it sat untouched. Occasionally he heard a noise from upstairs, where the undertakers from Bar Harbor were working. The priest would be out tomorrow morning, and they would bury Maude in the ground that she had chosen. Jacob sat for hours. He had an idea that Rolly had been there, but he wasn't sure. He heard the undertakers leave, and about midnight Harriet brought him something to eat.

"Mr. Jacob?" she said tentatively when she came back to take away the tray.

"Yes, Harriet?"

"We were wondering if it would be all right if we went and paid our respects now."

For a minute Jacob stared at her, not knowing exactly what she was talking about. "Oh, yes," he said finally. "Yes, Harriet." He sat there and heard the servants go upstairs, and about twenty minutes later he heard them come downstairs again, with Ben crying in a deep, elemental sob of hurt and grief.

Finally, at about a quarter past one, Jacob stood up from his chair and started up the stairway. He walked toward the room where he knew Maude would be, and then at the doorway he stopped in complete astonishment. Maude was lying in the casket, set between two large candles and before a bank of flowers, and in front of the casket there was a prie-dieu. Patrick was standing on the prie-dieu, and he had lifted Eileen up so that she was sitting on a corner of the coffin, her pajama-clad legs hanging down its side. Eileen and Patrick were both looking at their mother's face, and Patrick was gently touching her forehead, stroking Maude's forehead over and over again. Eileen had her fingers in Maude's hair, and she was curling it around her fingers in the candlelight. Jacob's eyes blinded with tears, and then he walked into the room.

Eileen looked up and saw him.

"Hello, Daddy," she said. "Mother's gone to heaven, just like she said."

XII

Patrick got a little loaded the night before his graduation. He and Jacob and Eileen had dinner at Joseph's, and then Patrick went up to the Club when he got back to Cambridge, and found a party going on there. Finally he came back to Leverett D-32, ready to go to sleep, and even before he opened the door, he heard singing noises inside.

" 'Oh, the monkeys have no tails in' — where's it they don't have tails, Bill?"

" 'Oh, the monkeys have no tails in Zamboanga,' " Bill's voice sang back.

Patrick opened the door. "Where's Zamboanga?" he said, smiling, and then he saw that Snowjob was wearing the dress whites of an ensign. He had been commissioned a couple of days before. "You look *great*, Snowjob!"

"Thanks, old bean," Snowjob said, passing into a not at all bad British accent. "Admiralty asked me to take a gunboat round and blast the bloody natives, don't you know." He pointed to a bottle of scotch on the table. "Have some. We've been having plenty."

"Plenty," Bill said. He was in khaki pants and a T shirt, and his books and clothes were all over the place, and there were cardboard boxes around, and open suitcases. "Packing," Bill said, weaving a little.

Patrick looked at the bottle. It was a good two-thirds gone.

"Add water and drink," Snowjob said, pointing toward the bathroom. "Don't even add water if you don't want to."

Patrick went into the bathroom, got a tumbler, filled it about half full of water, and came back out into the living room. "Where'd you go in your uniform?" he said, pouring some scotch into his glass.

"This is a private showing," Snowjob said. "Thought I'd

dress up and impress my roommates."

"I'm impressed," Patrick said, sitting down.

"Now what I say," Snowjob said gravely, looking at his nearly empty glass, "is that for a monkey, for a monkey, mind you, it must be pretty damned important if you have a tail or if you don't have a tail." Bill had gone into his room, and Snowjob raised his voice. "Don't you think?"

"Yes!" Bill shouted back from the bedroom.

"Don't you think?" Snowjob said, peering at Patrick. "Don't you think?"

"Unquestionably," Patrick said.

"Remember," Snowjob said, "things always look darkest before the storm. And why shouldn't they, for God's sake?"

Bill came out of his room. He had put on his academic gown, one of the ones from the Coop that they had all rented for tomorrow morning. "Dress up and impress my roommates," he said, an idiotic smile on his face. Patrick and Snowjob started laughing, and then Snowjob's face became serious, and he peered at Patrick.

"You know something?"

"No."

"You're sober."

"No."

"That's all right, PK," Bill said. "You be sober if you want to. You be drunk if you want to. You're my brother. Romulus and Remus. And the wolf."

"The wolf is in Arizona by now," Snowjob said. He looked in his glass for a second, and then got up and poured what was left of the bottle into his glass. "Any objections?" he said.

"Never touch the stuff," Bill said.

"Well, good night, men," Patrick said, standing up and knocking off what was left in his glass.

"G'night."

"G'night, Patrick," Bill said. "Be in in a little while."

"Good night," Patrick said. "God bless you." He stopped at the door. "Oh, and Anchors Aweigh."

"Permission granted," Snowjob said, making an exaggerated salute.

Patrick's face grew serious as he stood by the bureau, undressing. All along he had known that Snowjob was in the ROTC, and he had seen him take off for drills in his uniform often enough, but still it was something to see him sitting there, an officer in the Navy. Patrick knew plenty of people like himself, who were going to go to the Law School, or Medical School, or the Business School, but basically this class was moving out to go to the Korean War. There was nothing dramatic about it. They were just going. They had been exempted until they had finished their formal educations, and now most of them had finished their formal educations, and they were going. Patrick stood there thinking about it, and looking at his face in the mirror.

"Listen," Bill's voice said from the living room, "how would you like to buy twenty-seven books on international relations?"

Patrick smiled, turned away from the mirror, and switched off the light.

"Yes, Father," Patrick said over the telephone. "Yes, Father. I'll meet you at the gate right after the ceremonies. Yes. All right. And if we should miss each other just come down to Leverett. Right. No, we're going up to the Baccalaureate Sermon in a minute. Yes, I'm wearing it right now. It fits all right. O.K. See you there." He hung up and smiled at Snowjob, who had come out of the bathroom, wearing his black gown too.

"I can tell you one good practical reason these things went out," Snowjob said, closing the bathroom door behind him. "Where's Bill?"

"I finally got him up about ten minutes ago," Patrick said, "but he's coming along pretty fast."

Bill came in, chewing a doughnut and pulling on his gown. Their three mortarboards were sitting on the table, around the empty bottle of scotch.

"Well, here I am," Bill said through the doughnut. "What's left of me."

Snowjob put on his cap, and then Patrick put on his.

"I understand I was a credit to nothing last night," Bill said, putting on his mortarboard too.

"Well, gentlemen," Snowjob said, "since we all look equally silly, shall we go?"

And they went.

10

ONE OF THE Kingsgrant elms finally let a little morning sunshine through its foliage and into Patrick's window, and Patrick woke up. He lay there for a couple of seconds, staring up at the ceiling, feeling that same quick, unpleasant thought that he had had the first thing every morning for six months. No Anna. It just took a moment, but it was there every morning. I've lost Anna.

The thought receded, and Patrick sat up against his pillow. On the chair next to his bed was the manuscript of his novel, tucked in a manila folder, and Patrick smiled as he looked at it. He had been working on it again for the last few days, and last night he had decided to read some of the early part before he went to sleep. It had been a long time since he had read the earlier part of his own novel, and, lying in bed before he went to sleep, it had come to him as an agreeable surprise. He saw plenty of mistakes, and things that he would change, but there were parts of it that he had forgotten about, parts that he read again and liked and believed were good. He had read about fifty pages of the hundred and fifty that he now had, and then he had turned off the light and smiled in the darkness.

Patrick got out of bed, put his feet into his slippers, and went into the bathroom. As he brushed his teeth half a dozen thoughts flipped through his mind, none of them occupying him for very long. He was figuring out that Eileen would be landing in Europe today or tomorrow. He and his father had seen her off the week before, and then Patrick had come on up here to Kings-grant. Jacob would be along in another ten days, to begin his three weeks' vacation.

A minute later Patrick was in the shower, soaping himself and loving the warm water on his back, and he almost started to sing. It had been a pretty happy week up here. Finals and Generals seemed mercifully far behind, and all this past week people in South Harbor had been congratulating him on graduating, as if graduating had been some particular feat that none of the other hundred thousand men who had gone to Harvard since 1636 had been able to accomplish. It was pleasant to sit out here and play at being lord of the manor. He got up when he felt like it, he dropped in on Mr. Grindall when he felt like it, he dropped over to the cannery when he felt like it, and this past week he had been writing, and writing a lot. Usually it happened in the afternoon. He would come back from looking over the silent cannery with Luther Allen, and there would be his typewriter on the desk in the living room. Patrick would circle around it, and then he would sit down and pick up where he had left off, and the next thing he knew it was seven o'clock and Harriet was insisting you've got to have some dinner, Mr. Patrick.

Patrick turned off the shower and stepped out into his day. He was feeling hungry, but he knew that Harriet would have the scrambled eggs and coffee to fix that.

II

Eileen sat at a table in the big orange café at the Rond-Point of the Champs-Elysées and smiled across the table at her friend Patsy Snelling. There were two boys with them, friends of

Patsy's who had just graduated from Yale, but her smile was just for Patsy at the moment, and Patsy smiled back the same secret smile.

The secret was just being in Paris. Eileen had been walking around the city for three days, looking at it and looking at it and looking at it. Paris was one of the few things that was even better than you thought it was going to be, and now here they were at midnight, drinking white wine under the chestnut trees. In a few days she and Patsy were going to rent a car and take off for the Riviera and Italy, and eventually they would report to their junior year group at Grenoble, but that was years away. Right now it was midnight and the Yale men were talking about Scott Fitzgerald and a French sailor walked past the café, a French sailor with a little red pompon on his hat, and smiled at Eileen. Eileen did a double-take, and then she smiled right back. The Yalies were still talking about Scott Fitzgerald.

III

Patrick walked up the trail toward the old quarry high above Penobscot Bay. It was such a beautiful day that it was hard to believe. It was not one of those days that shoot the works in the morning and turn into a hazy business in the afternoon. This day had been a real champion, holding back plenty so that now, in the afternoon, it was a combination of warm sunshine and mild breezes, with a few clouds and not a trace of haze or fog. Patrick had been working hard on his novel for almost two weeks now, and when he saw the weather this morning, he had decided to vote himself a holiday. He had got into Chrissy and whipped over to Bucks Harbor, but all the boats there were already out in the Reach, so he had decided to come over here and walk and think and sit in the sunshine. It was the same place where he and Anna had gone walking once, in the days before they first kissed, and he had not been back since.

He came through the last of the spruce trees at the very top, stepping over a six-inch cleft in the huge granite formation that jutted out over the Bay, and, pulling a branch aside, walked onto the bare space that revealed the best view of the Bay. There was the rocky beach down below, and Deer Island, and the rest of the Bay out beyond Deer Island, and a vast hush hung over all of it. There were sails on the water, and some wind in the trees behind him, but it was all one great uncanny hush. Patrick stood looking down at the man-made shelves on the face of this high hill. Once they had been sharp and clean, but now the spruce and the moss and the wild blueberry bushes had had their chance at the rock once again, and, looking up from a sailboat, you would never know that there had been a quarry here. At first glance it seemed an unlikely place to cut granite, but that was only if you were thinking in the twentieth century, thinking of how far back toward a road it must have been, and how difficult to carry out the stones. What had actually happened in those 1870's and '80's and '90's was that the great pieces of granite were lowered almost vertically into the holds of the four- and five- and six-masted schooners that came alongside at high tide, and when they were not taking on granite they were taking on ice, run through the quarry on a series of sheds that started over in Walker's Pond. And there would be a Kingsgrant taking his percentage of it all, as Kingsgrants had worked the fisheries from their island when living on an island was a matter of defense from the Indians, and as Kingsgrants had taken their share of lumber when lumber was the thing, and today blueberries, when blueberries were as much of a thing as there was.

Patrick stretched, gazed at the level granite under his feet, and decided to do a couple of push-ups. He got into the position, face down and his hands on the rock on either side of him, did a couple of push-ups, and then turned over and just sat there in the sunshine. It was one more funny thing about his right arm.

He could do push-ups as well as the next man, but he could not chin himself.

Slowly, sitting, he began to think about Anna. It was all so different this summer. Everything was the same, and everything was different. He drove through the wooded countryside in Chrissy, he walked up to the post office in South Harbor, and nothing had changed and everything had changed, and he didn't see that there was one damned thing he could do about it.

Patrick passed his hand across his face. All right, he said to himself. It was good while it lasted. It was more than that, a voice inside him came back. It was the only girl that had ever meant a damned thing.

He sat for quite a while, looking out over the water and the islands. He thought about Anna and about his friends. This was a hard place to realize that a war was going on. Tall Man was going to be reporting to Quantico any day, and Bill Bench said that his draft board had him earmarked for some time in September. Snowjob Porter was on a destroyer in the Atlantic. Some young men were getting killed, but many more young men were wondering how they were going to do in their next tennis match, or whether dual carburetion was really going to improve the performance of their cars all that much. Patrick stood up and took a final look around. Then he walked off this topmost shelf of granite and started making his way through the hunched trees that kept low to stay alive in the wintertime winds. He was thinking about his novel again. It was all laid in Cambridge, with Technical Jones and Leapingdeer and Leepingdeer's Bostonian girl and her parents, and now he was wondering if somehow he couldn't get in a scene somewhere around here, so that there would be some real open country, and some real weather, instead of Cambridge and Boston. Patrick started down the trail away from this highest point, and although his feet kept reacting to what his eyes showed him in the trail ahead, his mind was all on the novel. These past two weeks here were the first time in his life that he had just done writing, and the difference was tremendous. Instead of having to cut it up with three college courses, you could just turn it over in your mind when you were not working on it, and when you were working, you didn't have to stop at a given hour to get ready for a quiz in some other subject. It was a marvelously satisfying experience, and even though he circled around his typewriter for a long time before he sat down at it, when he finally did sit down, it started to come. Just one sentence, and the next sentence was right there in his mind, and the next thing, it was seven o'clock and Harriet was asking him if he wouldn't like some dinner. Patrick would look at her out of the mists, and say yes, that would be very nice. After an afternoon like that he could remember standing up at times, to go to the bathroom, or just to pace up and down, but basically, once he had joined combat with that typewriter, he was always there, and if he got up and walked around the room, it was only to gather strength for the next rush. Even as he came down this trail in the sunshine, his mind was already back at the island, sitting on the corner of the type-writer and waiting for his body to come across the water and join it.

IV

"Do you want a cigarette?"

"No thanks," Anna said to the young man. "I don't smoke." She let her chin go back on her hands and lay there on her stomach in the Saturday afternoon sunshine, looking at the children splashing in the Tuxedo Club pool. She and her mother were staying with their cousins for the summer, and Anna had taken a job at the library during the week. It was all very nice to lie here in her bathing suit beside the pool on week-ends, but

Anna kept wishing that something would happen. And nothing, but nothing, was happening.

A little girl did a bellyflop into the pool, and Anna smiled, remembering little Mary Preston. The Prestons had asked her again this summer, and she had said thank you so much, but I can't. I'd love to, but I can't. And I really can't, Anna thought, looking out over the surface of the pool, feeling the concrete under her arms. She closed her eyes and pretended that she was going to sleep, but she knew that she wasn't going to make it. She had never fallen asleep in broad daylight before, and there was no reason that she should start now. Visions of Maine danced before her, and when she opened her eyes and saw the pool water, it just made her shut her eyes all the harder and think of the bright crystal clearness of Walker's Pond.

Walker's Pond and all that went with it. Anna thought for a moment of getting in touch with the Prestons and saying that she'd be up. All she had to do was go up there, and Patrick would find out that she was there, and then somewhere up there they would most certainly meet. Most certainly. And there wouldn't be any particular obligation on her when they met.

You liar, Anna's inside yelled at her. You're trying to hedge. You're trying to see him without facing the music.

Anna turned over on her back, closing her eyes to the sun.

"Anna, I'm going to get a coke or something. What do you want?"   .

"I don't think I want anything right now," Anna said. "Thanks anyhow."

v

Patrick had driven over to Bar Harbor in Chrissy to meet his father, and now the two of them were sitting at dinner on the island. Jacob was in a good mood, and his face seemed to relax more and more as he looked around the white dining room in the candlelight.

"I don't think you can imagine what a local country this was in nineteen-seventeen," he was saying to Patrick. "At Plattsburg every time you went around the corner you ran into somebody you knew. And if you hadn't met them, you still knew about them. Very different."

Patrick nodded and took a drink of his burgundy. The roast beef was good, and he didn't know exactly how Harriet had done the potatoes, but they tasted wonderful.

Jacob finished his roast beef and drank some of his wine. "Tell me," he said, that absent-minded look on his face that indicated that he was feeling for the buzzer under the carpet, "have you read any of the books on that list the Law School sent you?"

"No, I'm afraid I haven't."

"You'd better get at it." The kitchen door swung open, and Harriet came out and began to take off the dishes. "I was hoping you might decide to do a little clerking for Rolly Grindall this summer."

"I hadn't thought about it."

"Um." Jacob nodded his head, and took another sip of his wine.

"I've dropped over there a few times. We always have a very interesting talk."

"I'm not so interested in the interesting talks. I just think if you did a little work for him you might get the feel of the kind of problems that lawyers have to deal with."

"I guess so," Patrick said, studying his wineglass.

"Apple pie and hard sauce," Jacob said, beaming at Harriet when she came in with the dessert. "This is really a welcome home in the best tradition."

"I hope you like it, Mr. Jacob."

"I know I'll like it," Jacob said, and began to eat.

Patrick lay in his bed later that night, and sleep seemed to be a thousand miles away. The last two weeks up here had been good, and suddenly he felt guilty and everything was wrong. Tonight, after dinner, his father had been sitting in the living room reading, and Patrick had stared at the typewriter on the desk and not gone near it. He felt as if he might be able to write something tonight, but with his father sitting there he just didn't want to go through any explanations about what he was doing.

Patrick turned over on his side, and there was an expression on his face as if he were tasting something bad. He was thinking about the books he was supposed to read for the Law School. Patrick twisted over again in the bed and then he sat up. As if the mists were clearing, suddenly he saw why he had not read the books for the Law School, and why he had never thought of clerking for Mr. Grindall this summer.

The truth was that he wasn't one damned bit interested in the Law School, or Mr. Grindall's law office, or the law. Patrick stood up out of bed, switched on the light, and sat down hard in the easy chair in his room. It had been staring him in the face for so long, but he had never seen it as he was seeing it now. People asked you what you were going to do with yourself, and you said, I'm going to the Harvard Law School in the fall, and they clapped you on the back, and that was that.

Patrick's mouth tightened. He was thinking of his father, and his father's happiness at the idea that he was going to be a lawyer. He remembered the evening when he promised that he would try it for a year, and the evening seemed a million years ago. Everything was coming at him fast now, the promise, and Allston Hunt, and the last two weeks, sitting writing, whereas the whole free summer was predicated on the idea that he was going to the Law School. Patrick shook his head and sat in the chair for a long time, staring at the wall as if he was expecting to see the answer written there.

VI

"What's the matter with you, Patrick?" Jacob asked. Twenty-four hours had passed since they had had the welcome-home dinner with the roast beef and the apple pie with hard sauce, and now they were at the table again. It was the same room, and the same hour, but Patrick had been hopelessly nervous all day. He had stayed away from the house as much as he could, and right now his face was in an unhappy concentration as he made little gestures toward eating his food.

"Nothing," Patrick said, lifting some of the lamb stew to his mouth. "I'm all right."

There was some conversation during the next ten minutes of the meal, but it might as well have all been silence. Jacob remarked that some more rain and fog would be a good thing for the blueberries, and Patrick agreed with him. Jacob said that Bertram had told him there was a sparrow hawk seen in South Harbor, and Patrick said that he hadn't heard about it. Patrick sat at his place, feeling his heart beating, and he knew that he had to say what was on his mind.

"Father?"

"Yes?" Jacob put down his fork and looked at his son's face in the candlelight.

"Look, Father — look." Patrick sat there, his face working for a moment, and then he opened his mouth again. "I can't do it."

"Do what?"

"Go to the Law School."

Jacob grew taller in his chair. "You promised."

"I know I did," Patrick said. "I know I did."

Jacob stood up, and then he sat down in his chair again, as if everything had gone out of him. "All right," he said, "perhaps you shouldn't be a lawyer." His voice sounded tired. He looked over at Patrick. "What do you want to do instead?"

"I want to write," Patrick said after a moment, hearing his voice come out weak and scared.

"What do you mean?"

"I mean I want to be a writer. I want to write fiction." They were both speaking in low tense voices.

"Do you have any reason to suppose you can support yourself doing it?"

"No." Patrick shook his head miserably. "No."

"Patrick — " Jacob took a deep breath. "I can't let you do it. Look around this place. It's *yours*. You've got responsibilities, Patrick. This place is yours, but you've got to hold up your end. You'll have to sacrifice this idea about writing."

"Father, I've got to try it," Patrick said. "I've got to try it."

"No, you don't have to try it!" Jacob was breathing hard. "Just deny yourself something for once. You're not any better than anybody else. You're not any better than all the people that have held this place together. Just give it up, Patrick. Just give it up."

"I've got to try it," Patrick said. "I'm not saying I can do it, but I've got to try it."

"Well, you're not going to sit here while you do it." Jacob's voice was low and choked with anger. "You're not going to break your promise to me and then sit here writing deathless prose."

"I don't blame you," Patrick said quietly. He was feeling sick. They both looked at each other as if they could not understand what was happening. "May I be excused?"

"You're excused," Jacob said, his voice dry and broken in his throat. Patrick got up from the table, and Jacob sat there, staring down at a point on the mahogany table where a candle's light was reflected.

VII

When Patrick got up the next morning, he started packing. He didn't know what else to do. His father had remained downstairs after dinner, and Patrick had just stayed in his room until he finally fell asleep lying dressed on his bed.

Patrick jammed all the clean shirts he had into his suitcase, and then, as he was making another trip back to his bureau, he heard a knock on the door.

"Come in."

Jacob came through the door. He was wearing his old blue dressing gown, and neither one of them had had any breakfast. His face looked haggard, and he sat down hard in the chair near Patrick's bed. Patrick looked at him for a moment, and then went on with his packing.

"Where are you going to go?" Jacob said after a minute.

"I don't know."

Jacob nodded his head, and was still sitting in the same position when Patrick came out of the bathroom with his toothbrush and shaving things.

"Take anything you want to," Jacob said. His voice was terribly tired. "Take another suitcase, and take that typewriter of yours. And take that car."

"That's kind of you." Patrick kept putting the shaving things in his suitcase.

"It's not kind." Jacob got up. "I'm going downstairs and get some coffee."

Half an hour later Patrick finished having a cup of coffee out in the kitchen, and went into the front hall. His two suitcases were there, and his typewriter, and his topcoat, looking rather unnecessary hanging over one of his suitcases in the summer sunshine in the hallway. His father was coming down the stairs. Jacob had put on a gray suit and a tie, but he had not shaved.

"I told Bertram to bring the station wagon around," Jacob said. He sounded sick.

Patrick nodded, and picked up the two suitcases. Jacob picked up the typewriter and the topcoat, and they went out and down the steps. The battered station wagon was sitting there, with Bertram at the wheel, and they got into it. The car moved slowly down the driveway between the rows of elms, and Patrick suddenly wanted very much to get out and go up to his mother's grave and say good-bye. He looked over at his father, who was staring straight ahead. He knew his father wouldn't mind, but they were in the car already, and he could see Ben down by the launch. Then the station wagon stopped near the pier and they were walking down the ramp to the float where the *Ethan Kingsgrant* was sitting.

"I didn't say good-bye to Harriet," Patrick said.

Jacob nodded. "Do you want to go back and say good-bye?"

"No. I mean I just didn't."

Jacob nodded again. "I'll square you with everybody."

Patrick stood there for a moment. "Well," he said, "thanks for everything."

"Sure." Jacob watched Patrick get his things into the motorboat. Patrick put his coat down on the seat, and then he nodded to Ben, and Ben cast off the bowline and Patrick cast off the stern. The boat moved out onto the water, gathering speed. It was a beautiful morning, with a brisk wind and little flecks of foam on some of the waves. Jacob stood watching the figure standing in the cockpit of the boat as it got smaller on the water, and then he sat down on the end of the ramp and put his face in his hands.

VIII

Patsy and Eileen checked in at the hotel in Florence late in the afternoon, and Eileen said that she would go over to American Express and pick up their mail. She walked out of the hotel and down beside the Arno, asking her way until she came to the American Express Office. Patsy had a stack of mail, but there was just one letter for Eileen. Her newly tanned hands tore open the envelope with her father's handwriting on it, and then, as she began reading, she drew in her breath. Patrick had left home. Jacob hoped that Patrick would see that he was chasing after a foolish illusion, an illusion that he could not allow Patrick to develop by giving even tacit consent to it.

Eileen closed her eyes for a second, and then she went back out onto the street. She recognized the Ponte Vecchio from its pictures, and she saw that there was a place out there on the bridge where people were just sitting, looking at the river. She needed a place to sit right now. Eileen cut blindly through the traffic of small cars and motor scooters that were buzzing along the road by the river, and a couple of minutes later she was walking past the shops that lined the sides of the road across the ancient bridge, the letter from her father in one hand, and all of Patsy's mail in the other.

At the center of the bridge the wall of shops on her right opened up, and Eileen went over to the low wall that revealed a view of the river and the bridges upstream. She got onto the wide top of the wall and sat there with her back to the traffic on the bridge, looking at the pink sunset on the water. The first emotion that she felt, now that she had got over the surprise, was one of anger. The two of them had done it within three weeks of the time she had sailed from New York. All right, Eileen thought. I'm not going home. This isn't going to change my plans one bit. Then she sat for a long time, oblivious to the sounds of traffic on the bridge, and the remarks of the young Italian men walking past behind her. All her anger at Jacob and Patrick evaporated, and her face was sad. She knew she wasn't going to go home, but when she thought of the two of them, neither of them evil people, neither of them wanting to hurt anyone, her face looked as if she was in pain. After a long while she swung herself down from her perch, and walked back toward her hotel, walking home like a little girl who has lost her doll.

IX

It was a stifling hot day, and it was no cooler in the New York State Employment Office than it was on the baking sidewalks below. Patrick sat on a bench between a middle-aged colored woman and an old man who kept clearing his throat, and from time to time he pulled a handkerchief out of his pocket and mopped his face. He had just been doing a little arithmetic on the top of the first page of his *New York Times*, and what it added up to was that he had damned well better come through with something today. He had been down here for four days, and he had forty-six dollars left. All he kept thinking of was that it had been a good thing that he had been able to sell Chrissy. He had tried to sell it to the garage at South Harbor, but they had shaken their heads and said they couldn't handle a convertible, not at any price, got no call for convertibles. He had driven Chrissy over to Ellsworth and gone in there scared to death. He had just a couple of dollars in his wallet, and he had already made up his mind to get to New York if he possibly could. He had gone into the place in Ellsworth, knowing that he was going to sell the car to them for exactly whatever they offered him, and they had offered him a hundred dollars. Patrick had not dreamed that they would give him more than seventy-five, and he had taken the hundred and got on a bus for Portland

and Boston before they had a chance to change their minds. He had taken the train from Boston to New York, and he had spent most of the trip down on the train looking at jobs, in a copy of the *New York Times* that he had bought in the South Station, and looking for places to live. As the train had come on down, with Patrick wincing every time he thought of how it had all ended up there, and scared every time he wondered what was going to happen to him now, he had made a few discoveries. There were Help Wanted ads for experienced drill press operators, and experienced automobile salesmen, and experienced shipping clerks and admin. ass'ts, whatever they were, but there were no Help Wanted ads for experienced English Majors. Most of the ones that did say Coll Grads sounded as if you were letting yourself in for a long course of training, involving stuff to read at home and night classes and so forth, and as far as Patrick was concerned, that was not the idea. He didn't want to walk into some advertising agency or brokerage firm, all bright-eyed and bushy-tailed, and tell some personnel man that he wanted a career with this particular company. All he wanted was something from nine to five to feed him so that he could write from eight to eleven. And he had better get it soon, because after the trip down, and the first week in advance at the roominghouse on Eighty-Seventh Street where he was living, and buying an alarm clock, and just buying his meals, he had cut the hundred down to forty-six dollars. But the room was good. The old luck of the Irish had come through on that one. He had picked out the room on the train, and got off at 125th Street, and called up. No, the room wasn't taken yet. Patrick had put the two suitcases and the typewriter and his topcoat and himself into a taxi, and he had promised himself that if 338 East Eighty-Seventh Street was one-third bearable, he would take it. Twelve-fifty a week was probably too much, he didn't know, but he was going to take it.

He took it. It was one big room, and he shared a bathroom with a couple of other people, and there was no shower, just a bathtub, but he took it. Mrs. Charnow said she would change the sheets every week, and she had even brought in a table for him to work on.

"Kingsgrant!"

Patrick stood up and made his way toward the desk. Please dear God let there be something, he said to himself. Anything. I'll take it. Believe me I'll take it.

x

Jacob rarely had too much to drink, but this evening he was standing on the roof at 1120, with a scotch and soda in his hand. It was his third evening back in New York after his saddened three-week vacation at Kingsgrant. He never carried a drink to the roof, but this July evening, after his solitary dinner, he had begun to reread the letter from Eileen that he had found when he came home, and he had had three stiff scotch and sodas in a row. Now he was standing on the side of the roof that over-looked Park Avenue, his eyes gazing at the vast stretch of tenement roofs that extended from beyond Lexington Avenue over to the East River. Eileen's letter said that she had heard from Patrick, and that Patrick had a room on Eighty-Seventh Street between First and Second Avenues, 338 East Eighty-Seventh, and a job in charge of a crew of high school boys delivering free samples of Rice Krispies and Corn Flakes. Patrick was down there somewhere in that expanse of flat low roofs in front of Jacob, and Jacob took another sip of his drink and shook his head. Until he had read Eileen's letter he had been sure that Patrick would come home any day now. Jacob's face screwed up in the same expression it took on when the wound in his leg was hurting. Once again he went over it in his mind. The dreams of youth. By all means, the dreams of youth. Jacob could remember himself as a little boy, raised on a mixture of *The Boys of Liberty* and King Arthur. He had ridden with the Crusades, he had explored new oceans, he had saved Banker Throckmorton's daughter, he had read his history book and refused General Lee's sword at Appomattox. He had done all of it, but then somewhere in there it had faded, just as it should fade, and he had become aware that there was work to be done. But apparently Patrick was still riding on his own private crusade. All right, Jacob thought, lowering his glass from his mouth and staring out over the twilight stretch to the East River. So Patrick may not be a laywer. All right. But this. Eileen says he's leading around a bunch of boys delivering breakfast food, and this nebulous, nebulous writing.

Jacob turned and started pacing around the roof, his glass still in his hand. The shadows were beginning to fall faster now, but still he kept staring at every corner of the roof as if he could see an illumined memory there. Summertime, just before they went off to Kingsgrant, and Patrick and Eileen in bathing suits, playing with the hose for the roof garden, spraying each other with water and making shining, sparkling arches out of the stream. Or winter, and when their nurse Maria did not take them to the Park, when there was an epidemic or when the weather was just too bad, there they would be, building snowmen or snow tunnels, or cheerfully sending one snowball after another whistling down at the taxis cruising Park Avenue. But still, Jacob thought, but still. Even granting that this roof was a good place for a boy's imagination to grow, there were limits. And Patrick was out beyond the limits.

Jacob whipped around in the midst of his pacing, and marched to the eastern edge of the roof. For a moment he looked as if he were going to bellow out to Patrick to come home and stop this nonsense. Then, standing at the iron railing, looking out over the evening lights of this part of the city, his face softened. I hope to God you're all right, Patrick, he said to himself, and then he turned away from the ledge to go downstairs to his empty apartment.

11

PATRICK STOOD at the bus stop at Second Avenue and Eighty-Sixth, reflecting on the deceptive coolness of the city at this hour of eight in the morning. It was nearly the end of July in what had been a scorching summer, but every morning as Patrick stood waiting for the Second Avenue bus there was little more than a hint of the heat to come. He stepped to the curb and looked up the avenue. A bus was visible about three blocks away and Patrick dug into his trousers pocket for the fare. Every morning at about this time Patrick's one emotion was anger at the fact that Mr. Kelly, the foreman, insisted that he and the other three crew leaders wear neckties, while the boys who were the crew members changed into company-supplied and company-laundered blue cotton shirts, open at the throat. Company policy, Mr. Kelly would say. Put that tie back on, Kingsgrant. Mr. Kelly would sit there in his car, his sports shirt open at the neck, licking at an ice cream cone, and watch Patrick put his necktie back on and pat down the wringing wet collar of his shirt. That's better, the fat little man would say. Keep 'em moving, Kingsgrant. Then he would adjust the car fan so that it cooled his fat face more effectively, and drive off. Patrick would go on leading his six boys down the hot street, standing on the sidewalk while they went into the buildings and hung the little paper bags each containing a sample package of Rice Krispies and a sample package of Corn Flakes on apartment doorknobs.

Patrick got into the bus and found a seat. He sighed, pushed the coming hot day on the pavements out of his mind for a minute, and thought about what he had done on the novel last night. It had been a good night, an evening when everything he wrote seemed to spring and move easily from thought to thought, and he had racked up nine pages before he went to bed at midnight. The story was moving along, and he had two hundred and fifty pages now. It represented more than two-thirds of the total action of the book. He had broken the back of the job. It was coming. Some nights he felt that he was playing over his head. He would get into a scene and it would go better and better, but he would pretend to himself that he could really write this well, and then he would come to the end of the scene and read it over and there it was.

Other nights it was not so good. Hot nights, sweltering hot, and the characters in the book sounded as if they were saying polite little speeches to each other. He would sit there glaring at the page in the typewriter, looking at the page as if he were thinking of how to outwit it. And then he would say the hell with the golf course scene, have the guy remember what happened on the golf course as he's riding the commuter train the next morning, and the page of idiotic dialogue on the golf course would go into the waste paper basket, and Patrick, dressed in shoes, socks, a T shirt and shorts, would continue hammering into the night.

The bus came rolling into Fifty-First Street, and Patrick swung down and started walking toward the warehouse that was their base of operations, taking a moment to look at his watch as he swung along. In a minute he saw the big rented truck out in front of the warehouse, and Kelly's car. The advertising firm that was conducting this campaign had another unit working way uptown, and there was a set of crews working the West Side, but for all practical purposes Mr. Kelly's set of four crews was an independent vessel, and Kelly was Captain Bligh. Mico the truck driver was tossing one case after another of the bagged samples onto the truck. This was his only hard exercise for the day. After this he simply cruised around behind Kelly, stopping to let the boys from the crews load up again when their outsize mailmen's bags became empty. Mr. Kelly was standing beside his car, his dumpy little figure bent over a map that he had spread out on the fender. As always, he had a stub of a cigar in his mouth. In the three and a half weeks that he had been working for Kelly, Patrick had never seen him with a fresh cigar in his mouth. Sometimes, standing on the street, waiting for the six boys who were his crew to come out of the houses where they were delivering, Patrick wondered if there might not be a store someplace where Kelly bought his cigars, pre-stubbed.

" 'Morning Kingsgrant," Mr. Kelly said, not looking up from his map.

"Good morning, Mr. Kelly," Patrick said.

Kelly kept looking down at his map. "Paper says it's going up to ninety-six today."

"I believe it," Patrick said, and went over to help Mico throw a few of the cases of breakfast food onto the truck.

II

Bill Bench crossed under the Third Avenue El and walked down Eighty-Seventh Street, past the post office. He came down the street in the first relieving coolness of the August evening, his white linen suit in contrast with the gray stained sidewalks and dirty brick housefronts. At the corner of Eighty-Seventh and Second Avenue he paused for the light to change. One thing that struck him was that there were an awful lot of people living down here. The side streets were dotted with boys playing stickball and pushball, and at every third window a fat middle-aged woman in a cleaning dress or a slip sat motionless, gazing at the street below.

The light changed, and Bill cut across Second Avenue. He moved down the right side of Eighty-Seventh Street and began looking up at the numbers painted on the dark glass over the doorways. The old men in black suits and black hats passed him, smoking pipes and speaking German. Three thirty-two, 334, 336. Three thirty-eight. Bill stood at the bottom of the brown stone steps for a moment, looking up at the front door. It was painted a dark green, and the paint was pretty well flaked off. He went up the steps and opened the door, and then went through a second door and found himself standing in a dim yellow hallway.

Bill remembered that Patrick had told him over the telephone to come on upstairs, and after he had looked around curiously for a minute, he began to climb up the narrow stairs. The yellow wallpaper had a trace of a pattern on it, but it was so faded that it could have been either flowers or ribbons. As he came up onto the first landing, under the dimness of the small light bulb over his head, he heard a door open on the floor above.

"Hi." Patrick looked over the banister on the floor above.

"How are you, boy?"

"Come on up."

"Coming." Bill trotted up the next flight of stairs, and they shook hands. "How've you been?" he said.

"O.K." Patrick smiled at him. "What got you to Larchmont?"

"A boat."

"How long are you down for?"

"Just a couple of days."

"Well, I'm damned glad you called up. Come on in." Patrick led the way, and a few moments later Bill was looking around his room. It was a room about ten feet by fourteen, with a closet and a good-sized bed and a table. There was a chair at the table, and Patrick's old typewriter sat there, surrounded by manila folders and piles of manuscript. Patrick pulled the chair away from the table, and motioned Bill to it.

"Mind if I take off my coat?" Bill asked.

"Of course not. I haven't had a jacket on all summer, practically."

"Well, tell me about this gag job."

"It may be a gag," Patrick said, "but it's keeping me alive."

"What do you make?"

"Forty a week. The government takes out three fifty. I tell them I need it more now than I will when I'm sixty-five, but that's a waste of time."

Bill smiled. "But what do you do?"

"Well, let's see." Patrick was smiling as he sat on the edge of his worktable. "I'm in charge of these six boys distributing free samples of Rice Krispies and Corn Flakes, and what I really do is tell them what streets to work down, and when they come back up the street I check off the street on my map, and then we go on to the next block. They have to work about four times as hard as I do."

Bill nodded. "What do you do for laughs?"

"Not very much." Patrick was smiling that defensive smile that Bill knew so well, the one he put on when he was trying to pretend that he was all right and not hurt. "I don't know, Bill. I tried taking out a couple of the girls I used to know, but it costs too much money. I mean it. I know the kind of evening they expect, and I just can't afford it."

"Well, wouldn't they just be willing to settle for the movies?"

"I suppose so. I don't know. I don't really care too much.

All I wanted was the company anyhow."

So it's still Anna, Bill thought. "Do you see many of the guys from college?"

"Uh-uh. I tried having lunch with a couple of them on the week-ends. That costs too much too." Patrick smiled again. "You know, they make quite a production out of lunch in this town. I always thought lunch was just a meal until I saw the way some of these guys go at it." He straightened up from his perch on the edge of the table, and smiled at Bill again, but it was the real smile this time. "What's going to happen to you, big boy?"

"Well, the way it looks right now the draft board is going to nail me about the end of September, and I looked into this Army OCS thing, and I think I'll enlist a little before they draft me."

"How does it work?"

"Well, you enlist and then you take sixteen weeks of basic training. They don't give you any guarantees, but anyhow after your basic training either you go on as a Private or if you make OCS you go there. I guess OCS takes about five months, and then you're a Second Lieutenant. They say you have a lot better chance for it if you enlist. Instead of being drafted."

Patrick nodded. "That makes sense. How about dinner?"

"Great."

"I hope you like German food," Patrick said, "because believe me, that's all they've got around here."

Bill looked at him earnestly. He wanted to ask Patrick what had happened with him and his father, but he decided to let it go. "How's your book coming?"

"It's coming. I sent Professor Hunt a big hunk of it a couple of weeks ago, and he's coming down here on business in about a month, and we've got a date to have lunch and talk about it."

"Good. When do you think it'll be done?"

"Maybe in another couple of months."

Bill nodded again. He was thinking that, back along the line somewhere, somebody should have told them that things might work out like this. Somebody should have told them that you might have to drop everything and go into the Army, or that you might have to go off on your own and write a book. Somebody should have let them in on it.

"Let's go eat," Patrick said.

"Great." Bill put on his jacket again, and they went out into the hall.

III

Patrick sat on a bench in the Mall, listening to the Goldman Band as it played one of its outdoor concerts. He had tried to work after dinner, but the night had been so hot that finally he had half staggered out into the street. All that was on his mind was that it might be cooler in the Park, and then, walking around in the Park, he had heard the sounds of music, and come to hear the concert.

As he sat listening, a lump came into his throat. Somehow the music released a vision of a better, happier world than this world of walking the pavements endlessly in the steaming heat, and of twisting in bed at night. A great yearning came up in him, just to belong again, to be somewhere where there was a common interest and a common goal, and where there were friends and laughter.

It's your own fault if you're unhappy, Patrick said to himself. He shook his head. I don't know. He sat half sprawled there on the park bench and a tremendous desire came over him just to go up to 1120 and ride up in the elevator and ring the bell and his father would come to the door.

If you did that you'd be finished, a voice said in Patrick's mind. You'd never be a good lawyer, and you'd never be a good writer. Patrick nodded his head vigorously, but there was still the lump in his throat, and a moistness in his eyes. The music came sweeping to the last bars of the last piece on the program, and the audience on its many hundreds of park benches, drawn up in a vast semicircle about the outdoor stage, applauded for a full minute. Patrick straightened up and clapped hard.

"Thank you, ladies and gentlemen," the conductor said. He said a few other things to which Patrick did not listen, and then he said, "and now, for an encore, we shall play for you Victor Herbert's always lovely melody, 'A Kiss in the Dark.'"

The orchestra began to play. Patrick listened and now the tears were real tears, standing in his eyes. He was back in that restaurant in Philadelphia, and Anna was beside him, and the violinist was playing. Then they were dancing at the Stork Club, that first evening that he had met her family, and when the orchestra swung into a Charleston, the dance that she had taught him by the lake, Anna had smiled and said, "This is no drill, Patrick. This is the real thing." He had not thought about that one for a long time, and now he smiled, a smile on his lips while the tears were in his eyes. And then the concert was over and he was walking home alone in the crowd.

IV

They turned the corner of Fiftieth and Third, walking slowly in the shimmering heat of the afternoon. Patrick's boys were straggling behind him, their blue uniform shirts half black with sweat. They were to do this side of the street, the east side between Fiftieth and Forty-Ninth, and then "T" in down Forty-Ninth, coming back up to Third again. Patrick's eyes opened wider as he saw the awning halfway down this block. The legend on it read FABIEN'S. As the boys started going into various doorways of the houses facing Third Avenue, Patrick stopped one of them.

"Give me a sample, Battagliola," he said.

"O.K." The boy stopped and took one of the little paper bags out of his canvas bag.

"Thanks," Patrick said, and walked toward the awning, straightening his tie. Crew leaders shall personally deliver the sample to grocery stores and restaurants. Patrick smiled and walked through the doorway of one of the best restaurants in New York.

It was cool inside, and quiet, and dark. A waiter advanced frowningly upon this young man in shirtsleeves who was standing there holding a small paper bag.

"I'd like to see the maître d'hôtel," Patrick said before the waiter could open his mouth.

"Wait here," the little man said, and in a minute another man came over to the space near the bar, where Patrick was standing. "Yes?"

"This is a free sample of Rice Krispies and Corn Flakes," Patrick said, handing the paper bag to the man. The maître d'hôtel held the package in the palm of one hand, and with the other hand he opened the top of the package and peered in.

"I see," he said.

"That's all," Patrick said, and walked through the doors and out into the sunshine. The boys were coming out of the houses where they had been going up and down the stairs leaving the little paper bags at every door, and Patrick led them around the next corner, into Forty-Ninth. He bent down and put a chalk mark on the sun-softened macadam of the street, a white arrow with a K next to it to show that it was his crew, and then watched the boys as they divided, three to a side, and began working their way down.

He was still smiling about Fabien's, but now as he stood at the corner of Forty-Ninth and Third, waiting for the boys to reach the far end of the block and come on back up, he found himself wondering what was going to happen on Saturday. He and

Allston Hunt were going to have lunch at the Harvard Club, and every time he thought about it he found himself getting nervous. There wasn't anything to get nervous about, nothing could possibly be changed just by having lunch with Professor Hunt, but still he found himself getting nervous. His mind ranged over all that had happened to him since he began that book, and finally he saw the boys coming slowly back up the block, treading on the shimmering sidewalks as if they were walking in a dream.

v

Allston Hunt sat across the table from Patrick, and even while he was talking about specific things in the manuscript, there was a debate going on in his mind. The problem was that he had shown a large part of Patrick's manuscript to a friend of his who was a publisher, and the publisher had been quite interested in it. Allston had come down here to the Harvard Club thinking that it might be wise not to mention the matter to Patrick, since it might give him false encouragement, or throw him off his stride in his work. That had been before he had talked to Patrick, but now that he had some idea of how little encouragement Patrick had been getting from any source, and now that he was beginning to understand what a lonely life Patrick was leading, he thought that it might be well to tell him about it.

"Patrick," he said suddenly, right in the middle of one of Patrick's remarks.

"Yes, sir?"

"Excuse me for interrupting you, but there was one thing I wanted to tell you about while I still had it figured out the way I wanted to give it to you. I showed what you gave me to a friend of mine who's a publisher, and he liked it. I mean he was interested in it, and I'm not trying to say he wants to publish it. I wouldn't know about that, but he thinks you're a born writer, just as I do."

Patrick looked at Professor Hunt for a minute, and then a broad grin came onto his face.

"I'm certainly glad to hear it," he said.

"Well, I thought it might give you the encouragement you ought to have. But remember that doesn't have any guarantees in it."

"But still it's nice to hear."

Hunt smiled. "You know, it's quite a responsibility when you encourage somebody else to be a writer."

"I guess so," Patrick said. "But you *are* encouraging me?"

"Obviously." Hunt took a sip of the coffee that had just been set before him. "What are you going to do when you get it finished?"

"I don't know, exactly. I was down talking to my draft board the other day. I come up for a physical about January sometime."

"I was under the impression you were Four-F."

"I've never been sure about that. I've never taken a physical."

"Well, do you think you might pass it?"

"I might be able to."

Hunt looked at Patrick for several seconds. "Patrick," he said slowly, "you don't *want* to be in the Army, do you?"

Patrick smiled. "I don't think 'want' is exactly the word. I've been thinking about it quite a bit."

"Well, stop thinking about it and get your Four F if you're entitled to it. You wouldn't like the Army."

"No, but I might not like being a Four-F, either."

Hunt put down his cup of coffee. For a moment all he could see was shredded remnants of men, with the desert sand swallowing their blood. "You haven't been out in the sun too much on this job, have you?"

"No. I don't think so." Patrick laughed.

"Good." Allston took a last sip of his coffee, and they both stood up. "My offer still goes. Whenever you get this thing done, I'll try to get you a publisher."

"Don't worry, sir. When it's done you'll be the first to know about it. I'll make some of those changes you suggested." They walked out of the dining room, and then they were in the front hall, shaking hands.

"You know, there's one thing I'd like to explain to you," Allston said. "I like you, but the reason I want to see you published is because I think what you write is worth publishing. I'd want to see you published if you were a son of a bitch."

Patrick smiled. "I understand that, sir. I never heard of any book being published because the publishers thought the author was a good guy."

"You've got the picture, Patrick," Allston said, smiling, and they shook hands again.

Patrick walked toward Fifth Avenue. It was the beginning of September, and the heat was just beginning to lose its grip on the city. He was thinking that Harvard College had made a pretty good investment when they hired Allston Hunt.

VI

Jacob got off the elevator at the twenty-first floor, said good night over his shoulder to Clarence, the elevator man, and shucked his Chesterfield off and folded it over the banister rather than hanging it up as he usually did. Then, his Homburg in his hand, he walked into the library, tall and straight in his dinner clothes, and mixed himself a scotch and soda.

He stood there for a minute, looking at the bubbles of soda rising in his glass, and tried to calm himself. It had all been such a simple-sounding evening. A dinner party with Henry and Barbara Lee. Jacob had been to a hundred dinner parties at the Lees. But this evening there had been a woman there, a widow of about forty-five from Washington, and she had taken one look at Jacob and made a dead set for him. She was lovely-looking, and before the evening was over Jacob understood perfectly well that she had made up her mind to marry him if he displayed the slightest further interest.

Jacob paced slowly across the library floor, the glass golden in his hand, and stopped at the eastern windows, looking out at the moonlit night. This sort of thing had happened to him before. But what bothered him was that this time it seemed quite appealing. Jacob took a sip of his drink. He knew perfectly well what it was. It was loneliness. Always before Eileen had been within a few yards, and if Patrick was away somewhere, he would always be coming home on a certain date. And now Eileen was writing him from Grenoble, and Patrick was not writing from anywhere. And this Mrs. Fredrickson was obviously ready to move right in. And she was very nice, too. She had been born in Maryland and she had a certain number of unobtrusive horses in her background, and she was pretty and intelligent and gay. She was ready for immediate occupancy.

Jacob smiled and took another sip of his drink. He was thinking of how pleasant it would be to come home from work and find something that looked like Mrs. Fredrickson, what was her name, Helen Fredrickson, sitting there. There would be conversation at dinner. Jacob remembered his years of eating alone out at Kingsgrant. It had seemed fine to him then, but it did not seem so fine to him now. In another couple of years Eileen would probably get married, and God only knew where Patrick would be. Then he could sit alone at dinner every night until he died. Jacob took yet another swallow of his drink, and then the strangest memory crossed his mind. They had tried to explain to him what was wrong with Maude, and one day

Dr. Harris had suggested to Jacob that he come up to Medical Center and talk to the neurosurgeon who had been in charge of the last set of examinations.

"Hello, Mr. Kingsgrant," Dr. Harris had said, his face business-like but sad, and they had both walked through the labyrinth of corridors. Finally they had come to a door and walked in. It was a good-sized office, with a view of the spring sunlight on the Hudson River.

"This is Dr. Manning," Dr. Harris had said. "This is Mr. Kingsgrant."

"How do you do, Mr. Kingsgrant," Dr. Manning said. He was a little man with a crisp, efficient air. Jacob shook hands and nodded. "Won't you sit down right here, Mr. Kingsgrant?" the surgeon said, and then he walked over to the window and pulled the shades.

"He's going to show you the X-rays," Dr. Harris said, pulling up a chair and sitting down beside Jacob. The neurosurgeon crossed the darkened room and switched on a plate-glass screen that stood against the wall, two yards from where they were sitting, and then he put the first of the X-ray plates in front of the lighted square.

"This is a view of the patient's brain," the doctor said. Instead of Maude's pretty head Jacob saw an area of shadows. "Now in order to establish the existence of an aneurysm such as this patient has, we inject a kind of dye in to the carotid artery. Then the blood stream carries the dye through the brain as well as through the rest of the circulatory system, and if you are watching the brain closely as the dye comes through, you can see the existence of any abnormalities." The doctor was warming to his subject. He substituted a second plate for the first. "Now here you see the dye entering the brain." His finger pointed toward the top of the plate. "You see the way that the dye brings the network of veins into view." Jacob nodded in the darkness. The neurosurgeon put up another plate. "Now in this one you see the aneurysm. I think you could see it a little more clearly if you came up here." Jacob was only sitting about four feet away from the screen, but he stood up. The specialist's index finger pointed to a small bulbous shape off a straight, narrow artery.

"This is know as a congenital berry aneurysm of the basilar artery," the little man said.

"I see." Jacob pulled himself together. "And when it breaks, that's it?"

The efficiency went out of the surgeon's voice. "I'm afraid so, Mr. Kingsgrant," he said, and switched off the light behind the screen.

"Well, thank you very much, doctor," Jacob said, as the doctor busied himself opening the blinds, and then Dr. Harris was leading him back down the halls.

Jacob stood there, and in front of his eyes he saw that network of veins. Maude's pretty head. He turned away from the window and crossed the room to the table where the mixings for drinks were kept, and put down his half-full glass. Then he picked up his hat and gazed down at it as he held it in his hand. A phrase that Patrick and Eileen sometimes used came through his mind. Thanks, but no thanks. Thanks, Mrs. Fredrickson, Jacob said to himself, but no thanks. Jacob let half a smile cross his face, and then he hit his hat once lightly against the side of his leg and walked on out of the room.

VII

Patrick had not thought that he would get even near finishing the novel that day, but from the moment that he had started work at ten o'clock this Saturday morning it was as if his entire system demanded that he finish it as quickly as possible. He had staggered out for a hamburger at three o'clock in the afternoon, almost dizzy, and been back at work fifteen minutes later. It was rolling. By six o'clock in the evening he had done fifteen pages, and there were only three more scenes to go. Patrick reeled out for another hamburger at seven o'clock, had two of them this time, and plunged back into his work. At eleven o'clock he started the last scene. It was short, it had always been planned as a short scene. Patrick could have written it in his sleep.

At eleven thirty-five it was all over. Patrick sat looking down at the keys of the typewriter. It was 11.35 P.M., September 25, 1951. Patrick pushed back his chair. He stared at the last page as it rested in the machine. He had always thought that when this moment came he would give a great shout of joy, but all he felt was a terrific tiredness. He nodded his head, and deep inside him he felt as if something had clicked into place. He had told his story. He had done what he set out to do.

He got up from the table, picked some change off of his bureau, and went downstairs to the pay telephone in the hall. When the operator answered, he said, "I'd like Western Union." He waited. "Western Union, I'd like to send a telegram to a Professor Allston Hunt, Twelve Ellery Street, Cambridge, Massachusetts. Message is as follows: Just crossed finish line. Hope you will approve of final product. Patrick Kingsgrant." Patrick dropped in the coins that the operator asked for, and then walked slowly up the stairs. He came back into his room and looked around it with tired eyes. The typewriter still had the last page in it. Patrick went over and lifted the page out of the machine. He looked at it for a moment, and then put it down gently on top of the pile of pages that had been accumulating all summer.

The next morning there was a telegram on the table in the hall. It said: DELIGHTED NOW GIVE IT THAT ONE MORE REVISION IT CANNOT POSSIBLY NEED A. HUNT.

12

PATRICK STOOD at the bar of the Lorelei on Eighty-Sixth Street and stared at his reflection in the mirror behind the bar. He took a good swallow of the glass of draft beer that he held in his hand, and then he looked around. The orchestra across the dance floor was about to start playing, and half the young men at the bar were moving toward the tables, where a host of young ladies were sitting. It was an interesting place, the Lorelei. Working girls from every borough of the city came there in the evenings, arriving at about ten-thirty, after they had gone to the movies. They would drift in to the main room in pairs and little groups of three and four, and take a table. They would order some nice smooth after-dinner drink like a martini or a manhattan, and wait to be asked to dance. The good-looking ones never had to wait long. Patrick often came here, just to watch. He had never summoned up the courage to ask one of the girls to dance, but it was occasionally pretty funny to stand in the middle of the eager crowd at the bar, and see how they fared with the girls and the bouncers.

The music started, and after Patrick had watched the dance floor fill, he turned his attention back to his glass. There were a couple of soldiers standing a little way down the bar, and Patrick looked at their uniforms. All summer there had been light-colored khaki shirts and trousers, but now, in October, all the Army was wearing olive-drab wool trousers, and Ike jackets of the same material. Patrick took another swallow of his beer and kept on staring at the uniforms. The two soldiers were too busy drinking and staring out at the dance floor to notice him. Two days before, a postcard had come from Bill Bench, who was suddenly RA12421386 and at Fort Dix, New Jersey. It hadn't said much except that he wasn't very happy.

"You want another one?" the bartender said.

"Sure." Patrick looked at the uniforms again. The last two days, ever since that postcard from Bill, Patrick had been feeling the impulse to get it settled about whether he was going to be in the Army. He was about halfway through the last revision of "Technical Jones" now, and it was almost time to go down there and find out about this OCS. In the telephone book it said that Army recruiting was 39 Whitehall Street.

Patrick picked up his new beer. He gave up looking directly at the two soldiers and looked at their reflections in the mirror behind the bar. Memories were rising up of his years as a little boy drilling in the Knickerbocker Greys, and his winters drilling on the frozen parade ground at Tabor, with the wind howling in off the ice on Sippican Harbor. It was not much fun, standing at attention, but there was something about marching men that always caught at Patrick's heart. He knew that there was nothing finer-looking than men marching off to war, and nothing worse than what happened to them when they got there, but the parade came first. He couldn't help it. Looking at those two soldiers, he wanted to be in there too, and he knew he was going to try it. He knew his arm would keep him out if they got a really good look at it, he was willing to admit that to himself, but he had played plenty of sports and done plenty of things, and if he could just get in there he was sure it would be all right. Patrick finished his beer and looked around the place again. Suddenly he wanted some fresh air, and he put down a quarter beside his glass and walked out into the night.

II

A few people had got off at Wall Street the stop before, and now there was almost no one left on this late morning subway. Patrick sat on one of the wicker seats. His hand was in his coat pocket, touching Eileen's first letter from Reid Hall, her dormitory in Paris, and he was thinking how pleasant Mr. Kelly had been about letting him have the day off. He had been frighteningly ready to dispense with Patrick's services.

The train rolled into the last stop and he stood up. There was nobody ahead of him on the platform as he walked toward the stairs and the sunshine. He forgot about Mr. Kelly and his job for a moment, and thought about Eileen. At least *she* seemed to be completely content with what she was doing. As Patrick came up onto the street he pulled her letter out of his pocket, not to look at it, but to check the address which he had written on its back. He knew it was 39 Whitehall Street as well as he knew his own name, but still he had written it down on the envelope. He looked around, surprised to find himself this near the Battery, and went looking for 39 Whitehall Street.

Thirty-Nine Whitehall Street turned out to be a large, square, red brick building. It had an American flag over the doorway, and on the corner of the building there was a square blue sign with white letters saying, "United States Army Recruiting," and under it, "Air Force Recruiting." Patrick went up the stone steps and through the swinging doors, and found himself in a brightly lit hallway. Everyone in the place was walking around as if they knew what they were doing. Patrick looked at the signs on the wall to his left. Navy, Marines, Air

Force, Army, Army OCS. Army OCS. He walked into the large room to his left. It was partitioned in various places, but a full half of the room was for Army. Down at the far end of the room there was a sign that said "Enlist for OCS." There was an American flag on the wall, and a desk under it. There was a sergeant in an Ike jacket at the desk, and half a dozen young men sat in front of him, on couches made of dark blue cloth and tubular steel. Patrick walked down there and took his place on the couch farthest from the desk. The sergeant was talking to one man at a time, calling each one up to his desk, and Patrick looked around. At the other end of the room there was a sign, "Enlist U.S. Army." The sergeant at that desk was just in his shirt, and there were no blue couches. Several boys who looked about seventeen years old were all huddled close together on a wooden bench, and the sergeant was talking to all of them at once. The boys were wearing leather jackets. Patrick let his eyes come back to his immediate neighbors at this end of the room. With the exception of Patrick's tweed coat, all the young men interested in becoming officers were wearing light tan covert cloth coats, and each one sat a fair distance apart from the others. Patrick thought about that for a couple of minutes, and then he heard a voice say, "Next." He looked up and saw that the sergeant was beckoning to him. He stood up, went over to the chair beside the sergeant's desk, and sat down. The sergeant had a broad, pleasant, Irish face, and he smiled at Patrick.

"What can I tell you about?"

"Well, I'm just interested in learning about this program," Patrick said. "I'm due to come up for a draft physical in a couple of months, and I'd like to know how this works."

The sergeant nodded, and told Patrick just about the same thing that Bill Bench had said. Then the sergeant handed Patrick a sheaf of papers.

"Take these home and fill them out," he said. "That mimeographed sheet on top tells you what you'll need in the way of a birth certificate and so forth. The sooner you get it back here the sooner you can take the tests."

"Fine. Thanks a lot, Sergeant." Patrick stood up with his new load of papers, and walked out of 39 Whitehall Street.

III

Before she turned out the light in her room, Eileen sat on her bed and read Patrick's letter over once again. She was wearing a heavy silk and wool dressing gown she had bought a few days before. It was only the end of October, and the heating in Reid Hall was pretty good. But she still had decided that a heavy robe wouldn't be a bad idea for a Paris winter. She wriggled into a slightly more comfortable position, and kept reading. It was hard for her to believe what the letter was saying. "The part of the physical where they look at your arms and legs was conducted in a big room with all of us standing four deep and some medics halfheartedly looking at us from in front, so I got into the last row and slipped right through. But then, of all bad luck, the psychiatrist noticed my arm when I was going through the short routine talk you have with him, so he walked me back, like a pariah dog in front of the others, to the doctor in charge of the arms and legs place. Fortunately the doctor didn't know what he was looking for, and had me move my right arm around *fully extended*, which of course showed him nothing much. He wrote copiously on my medical report, and I went on. The whole application goes in to Governors Island now, and I ought to know in a couple of weeks whether I am eligible."

Eileen put down the letter and shook her head. He was really trying to do it. She loved him for it, but it was so foolish. Eileen put the letter in the pocket of her new dressing gown, and went over and turned out the light. Then she came back and knelt at the side of her bed, and Patrick was in all of her prayers.

IV

It was late at night when Patrick packed up his manuscript. All of this week-end he had been going over it, page by page, taking out a comma here and putting in a comma there, and finally, after dinner this Sunday evening, he had come to the realization that there was nothing more to do. He had spent the last six weeks rewriting, and he didn't doubt that if he wrote the whole book over one more time it would be just that much better, but if he adopted that philosophy he could still be working on the book in five years. Even after dinner tonight he had gone over the manuscript for another five hours, but all he had done was change one semicolon to a comma and catch two spelling errors. Now he finished clumsily wrapping some brown paper around a cardboard box that Mrs. Charnow had given him. The two big manila envelopes that held the first and second half of the three-hundred-and-forty-seven page manuscript fitted into the box neatly.

Patrick passed some string around the parcel, and tied it up. Then he took the cap off his pen and printed the address, "Professor Allston Hunt, 14 Ellery Street, Cambridge, Mass." and "From P. Kingsgrant — " Patrick hesitated. At the rate his life was moving right now, he might be gone from 338 East Eighty-Seventh Street almost any day. He finally put "South Harbor, Me." Then he sank down in his chair and sat there, looking at the brown package on the desk. He knew he should have made a carbon, but there was no carbon, and that was that. There it sat. His novel. His first novel. He found himself wishing that Anna could see it, and then he shook his head and tried to think about what was going to happen to him now. The job had finally stopped on Thursday. On Thursday for the first time they had seen one of the other crews. They had been working down a street at a quarter to five, and then they had come to a corner and there had been another truck like their own, and other boys wearing the same blue shirts and newly issued windbreakers that Patrick's crew wore, and it had been all over. Everybody in New York City had a free sample of Rice Krispies and Corn Flakes. Mr. Kelly was standing there handing out pay checks, and five minutes later it was all over.

The telephone rang down in the hall below, and Patrick went to the door of his room. A woman from the first floor answered it and began to chat. Patrick came back and sat down. The telephone never rang for him, but he always came to the door.

He put his feet up on the desk, being careful not to touch his package, and his face remained serious while he thought about what had happened Friday. He had gone down to 39 Whitehall, and talked to the broad-faced Irish sergeant. The sergeant had gone through a lot of papers, and then nodded.

"Kingsgrant."

"Right."

"You've got a B profile. You can enlist." The sergeant started to put the papers away, and then he stared at something. "Incidentally, you got one of the highest scores on the OCS mental we've ever had down here." He shrugged his shoulders and put the papers back in the file.

So now all you have to do is enlist, Patrick said to himself. Just close your eyes and enlist. Get it over with. Well, let's see. Today is Sunday. Thursday is Thanksgiving. Wednesday, Tuesday. All right, let's go down and sign up on Tuesday.

Pack up your stuff tomorrow and ask Mrs. Charnow if you can leave your clothes in the basement. For a moment Patrick thought about going up to 1120 and leaving his things there, but he shook his head. He would write his father just before he went. There was some sort of last-minute spot check the day you enlisted, and he didn't want to write his father that he was in the Army until he was damned sure that he was in the Army. Patrick sat in the chair where he had worked so hard, rubbing his chin with the back of his hand and thinking about his father, and about Eileen, and about Anna. It was just a year ago yesterday that Anna had ridden away from him in the Park. And in a couple of weeks it would be his birthday. Patrick thought about that birthday party at Locke-Ober's.

Even with Anna gone, still there had been a warmth that evening, with Eileen there, and his father proposing a toast. Patrick shook his head. He wanted to see his father, but he was afraid that if he did, everything he was doing might topple like a house of cards. He had to believe in this brown paper parcel in front of him, and he didn't want to talk to anybody right now who didn't believe in it. He had thought several times of how it might be if he went up and saw his father, and his father convinced him to take some sort of a job in an office downtown, and talked him out of joining the Army. Patrick was scared enough about joining the Army. He was scared enough about writing. He was scared enough about the fact that all he had at the end of working for five months was twenty dollars.

Let's get out of here and have a beer, Patrick said to himself. He stood up and carefully took the manuscript and put it in his closet. All summer and all fall he had let it sit right out there on the table, in its folders and piles, but now that it was done he was scared that someone would steal it. He couldn't imagine why anyone would steal it, but still he was afraid that someone might. Patrick put it down gently on the floor of the closet, closed the door, and went out.

v

"I think I'll have my coffee in the living room, please, Eleanor," Jacob said to the maid, and stood up from the table. He walked into the hall on the twentieth floor, bypassing the stairway, and turned on the lights of the living room. It was a much more formal room than the library upstairs, and Jacob did not like it much, but it was infinitely more free of memories. Lately he had been using it quite a bit. Jacob sat down and looked around the room as if he were in someone else's house, waiting for the host to come downstairs and receive him. There was an oriental carpet covering the middle part of the room, and some eighteenth-century Italian paintings on the wall, and Jacob could have seen the whole room go up in flames without batting an eyelash. His eyes took in the room again, looking at the marble mantelpiece over the fireplace, and for the first time since he had moved into 1120 he thought about the possibility of moving out. If he was going to be here alone, this was a ridiculous amount of room to have. But look, he said to himself, you were alone in a much bigger place when you were alone at Kingsgrant. Yes, but the land was there, he said back to himself. There's no land to watch over here.

The maid came in with a silver tray on which was a coffee-pot, a cup and saucer, and little silver bowls of cream and sugar. He nodded his head to the maid, and leaned forward to put a lump of sugar and a dash of cream into his coffee. The idea of moving out of here had retreated, and now he was thinking about the fact that in a week it would be Patrick's birthday. Jacob's brow wrinkled as he sat stirring his coffee. He could almost hear the voices and laughter of that evening at Locke-

Ober's a year before. That night it had all seemed so clear, everything had seemed settled, and now here they were, living five blocks away from each other, and those five blocks might just as well be five continents. All right, Jacob said to himself, but he knows where I am. I know where he is and he knows where I am. There's no use going to him unless you're prepared to offer him something. You've got to tell him you're willing to have him live here and go on writing, or you might as well not see him. You'll just fight.

Well, all right, Jacob, he answered himself. But what are you working for? Are you going downtown every morning to keep this place up for two children who aren't here? Now just a minute, Jacob said. I'll tell you why I go downtown every morning. I go downtown every morning because I'm a lawyer. That's what I am. Maybe I wanted my son to be a lawyer and maybe I'm disappointed that he's doing what he is, but I *am* a lawyer. I don't stop working just because he doesn't pan out. I'm an attorney. I do it because it's like breathing, and if you took me away from it I'd stop breathing and die. Jacob sat staring at the oriental carpet, and then he picked up his coffee again.

VI

The recruiting sergeant looked up from his desk and smiled at Patrick.

"All set to go?" he said as Patrick sat down in the little chair beside the desk. Patrick nodded, and the sergeant put a sheaf of forms, interspersed with carbon, into a typewriter and began asking him questions. Name, place of birth, date of birth, names of parents, nationalities of parents.

"Who do you want notified in case of death?" the sergeant asked, still typing out the last piece of information. Patrick sat up a little straighter.

"Mr. Jacob Kingsgrant, Eleven-Twenty Park Avenue."

"O.K." The sergeant typed it out. "Who do you want as beneficiary of your insurance?"

"Insurance?"

"GI insurance. The beneficiary gets ten thousand dollars in case you get killed. They'll explain it to you more upstairs."

"Oh. Well, make it to Miss Eileen Kingsgrant, Eleven-Twenty Park Avenue. That's my sister."

The sergeant nodded and typed it out.

The spot-check physical turned out to be nothing more than an examination to make sure you had not contracted a venereal disease since the last physical. Nobody asked him to look at a chart or do anything with his arms, and it all went smoothly until Patrick came down the line, fully dressed and with all his papers in his hand, to the desk where they were stamping the papers ACCEPTED. The doctor at the desk started to reach for the rubber stamp, and then his hand came back to the edge of the paper as he studied the myriad lines of handwriting and numbers on Patrick's medical report.

"I think you'd better wait here until the chief examiner comes back," the man said. "You can wait in his office." He handed the sheaf of papers back to Patrick and indicated a door. Patrick went inside the office. There was just a desk and a chair, and the walls were of cinderblock. One window looked out toward the harbor, and through the door Patrick could see the line of young men moving up to the desk, hear the rubber stamps fall, and see them move on. He sat on the edge of the bare desk for twenty minutes, watching the line move by. Dear God, Patrick said, let me be in. It's too late to turn back. I don't want to go crawling back. The book's done. All the bridges are burned. Let me be in.

After about half an hour the doctor who had sent him in here got up and came over.

"Why don't you get a meal ticket and eat some lunch?" the doctor said. "He'll be here for sure when you come back."

"Thank you." Patrick handed his sheaf of papers to the doctor, and watched what he did with them. The doctor put them on top of a little pile of papers and departed, apparently to have his own lunch. The line had disappeared, and there was almost nobody in the big room. Patrick got a meal ticket from a bald-headed man who was smoking a cigar, and went downstairs and across the street to the cafeteria run by 39 Whitehall Street. For Tuesday lunch they were featuring a type of hot dog and sauerkraut, and some mashed potatoes that tasted as if they had been dredged out of the harbor. After he had toyed with his food for about fifteen minutes, he drank his coffee and went outside. There was a cold wind whipping across the big open concrete space down here at the tip of Manhattan, but just now it felt good in his face. Patrick walked around for a few minutes, and then he picked a bench where none of the Bowery bums were sitting, and sat down, pulling up the collar of his coat. He was thinking about what was going to happen to him if they stopped him now. He would have to go back there and tell Mrs. Charnow that he was not going to be in the Army after all. She was already showing people his room. It was probably already hired out by now, the rental effective in another couple of days. And he would have to find another job. It might be better than distributing samples of Rice Krispies and Corn Flakes, but still it would be just something to support his writing. And right now he didn't have anything more to say to his typewriter, or to the world, or whoever you were talking to when you were writing. He had put it all in this book, and right now he had nothing more to say. After a few minutes he went back to the building and up the steps. He knew his way around 39 Whitehall Street perfectly by now.

Patrick came into the big room. There was no line just at the moment, and as he came up to the desk, he saw his sheaf of papers sitting there, on top of the pile. There were two doctors standing over by the window having a cigarette, and after a minute one of them, a different one from the one who had told him to wait for the head examiner, came over.

"These papers are mine," Patrick said, pointing toward his papers as they sat on the top of the pile yet to be stamped.

The doctor picked up his papers and matter-of-factly stamped them ACCEPTED.

"Go right on into the office over there," he said, handing the papers to Patrick, and went back over to the window to join his colleague in further conversation. Patrick stood there for a moment, looking at the ACCEPTED on his papers, and then walked quickly into the next room.

Patrick stood at the bar of the Lorelei, grinning crookedly at his reflection in the mirror. It was ten-thirty at night, and he had a pass in his hip pocket, saying that he was a private, Regular Army 12422849, off duty until 0900 the next morning, at which time he was to report to Whitehall Street for shipment. They had sworn him in a couple of hours after that rubber stamp hit his papers, and now he was standing here. Mrs. Charnow was letting him sleep tonight in his bed at 338 East Eighty-Seventh Street, and in the morning he was on his way.

Patrick smiled at his reflection again. Now there was no turning back. The decision-making was over, and he felt a curious way, scared but tremendously interested to see what was going to happen next. The novel was off his shoulders. Everything was off his shoulders. He had bought a hand-warmer at a sporting goods store on the way uptown, because his last card from Bill Bench had mentioned a hand-warmer in it, and he had bought a small canvas bag to hold his shaving stuff and the two sets of underwear that they told you to bring, and this evening he had written letters to Eileen and his father, and that was that.

There were a few soldiers and sailors along the bar, and Patrick smiled at them. I'm coming, gentlemen, he thought. You don't know it, but I'm coming. Tomorrow. His face sobered as he thought about one more decision that he had had to make. They had offered him something called Army Security Agency. A sergeant at a desk that had ASA on it told him that he had scored very high, and since he wanted to be an officer anyhow, it wouldn't make any difference if he changed his enlistment from two to three years so that he could be in ASA. The sergeant said that Patrick could be in OCS within a few months, and that as soon as he was commissioned he would stop serving time on his enlistment and start serving the time of his commission, so why not be an officer in ASA? It was good duty, riding planes with despatches, and code work, and so on. Half of Patrick had balked at the idea of the extra year if he didn't make OCS, but what interested him now that he thought about it was that what had really made up his mind had been that he didn't want to sit at a desk. If he wanted to sit at a desk all he had ever had to do was take his 4-F and forget it.

"Have you got a light?" the man next to Patrick asked.

"I'm sorry, I haven't." He finished what was left of his glass of beer. Well, kid, he said to his reflection in the mirror, this is it. Kiss the girls good-bye. That's a laugh, his reflection said back to him, and Patrick nodded. You're right. Strike that about kissing the girls good-bye. Got no girls to kiss good-bye. For a moment a picture rose in his mind, of Anna leaning over the billiard table that first evening at her house, with the light on her hair, stretching with the cue to make a shot. Patrick cursed himself under his breath, but what he said out loud was, "I'd like another beer, please."

VII

Patrick sat next to the window of the bus, looking out at the flat New Jersey countryside. It was a pretty casual way to go to war. He had arrived at 39 Whitehall at five minutes past nine, thoroughly worried at what might be the consequences of his lateness, and spent the next two hours sitting on one of the Army's blue-cloth-and-tubular-steel couches. After the second hour a husky blond young man with a crew cut had come in from somewhere else in the building and sat down beside him. Patrick had been staring at a large group that had just been herded into the other half of the room.

"Those are draftees," the young man with the crew cut offered.

"Oh," Patrick said, still looking at them.

"You enlisted, uh?"

"Yes," Patrick had said.

"Me too. For three years. How long you in for?"

"Just two years."

"Two years is just the same as you get being drafted. How come you enlisted?"

"Well, I'm interested in this OCS program, and they like you to enlist for it. And if I miss it, I don't want to be in for the extra year."

"I get you," the young man said. He stuck out his hand. "My name's Eugene Schaltenbrandt."

"Hi," Patrick said. "I'm Patrick Kingsgrant." He smiled, and then they sat silently. A few minutes later a sergeant came over.

"Schaltenbrandt?"

"Right here."

"Kingsgrant?"

"Here."

"O'Hara?"

They all looked around. The sergeant shook his head. "Well, there's a good Irishman AWOL on his first day in the Army." He pronounced it *A-wall*. "All right. You two go up to the Port Authority Terminal and take the first bus for Camp Kilmer. I'll give you transportation slips. You're going to carry your own records with you. If you lose them they'll send you back here and you can start all over again. Understand?"

"Yes," Patrick said.

"Are those guys coming too?" Schaltenbrandt pointed at the bunch across the room.

The sergeant did not even bother to look around. "Those men go down there straight from here," he said. "Give them individual transportation and half of them wouldn't show up. We put 'em on a bus right here." He led them to a desk and they both stood there while the sergeant did the paperwork that provided their transportation. "All right," he said. "You might as well get going." He handed them their records jackets, and they tucked them under their arms, picked up their little brown canvas bags, and walked out of 39 Whitehall Street.

"You want a cigarette?"

"No thanks," Patrick said. He smiled a polite smile at Schaltenbrandt, and went back to looking out of the window of the bus. He had not thought about it for years, but suddenly one particular memory from his days in grammar school in New York came into his mind. He and a lot of the other little boys from the Knickerbocker Greys had been present at the farewell review of the Seventh Regiment when it was called into active service. The United States was not yet in the war, but as far as everybody there that night was concerned, they were marching straight out of there and into the war. It was quite a crowd in the Seventh Regiment Armory that night, the wives and the girls of the Silk Stockings Regiment, and the Knickerbocker Greys, wearing their uniforms and wildly excited. Only a Provisional Company had marched, but they had been turned out in the old dress uniform of the Seventh, with their shakos and gray uniform coats and gleaming white duck trousers. The band had come stepping out onto the floor, and then out they came, the spirit of the Seventh, with the bayonets twinkling in the light. Every one of the Knickerbocker Greys would have fallen in behind those ranks and followed them straight to hell, and when the review was over and Patrick saw the men in their dress uniforms taking the young ladies in long dresses up to the second floor, where an orchestra was playing a waltz, he had felt his lack of years like a sword in his heart. Now Patrick sat there on the bus, and as he closed his eyes, he could see the sparkling, marching files, and hear the thunder of the band.

13

THERE WERE no bugles playing at Camp Kilmer. Patrick and Eugene Schaltenbrandt climbed down off the bus and stood there, wondering what to do next. It was a much quieter place than Patrick had expected it to be. A low gray November sky hung over the endless mustard-yellow buildings, and once the bus drove away, the only sound was that of feet on the gravel beside the roads.

"Maybe somebody in here can tell us where to go," Schaltenbrandt said after they had stood for a few seconds, looking around. He went into the waiting room of the tiny bus station, and Patrick followed him. The only man in there was a big soldier wearing a yellow shield with a black bar and a black horse's head on the left shoulder of his olive overcoat.

"Excuse me," Patrick said, "but we're supposed to report here."

"Report for what?" the big soldier said.

"We've just enlisted, and they sent us down here from New York," Schaltenbrandt said.

"You'll be sorry," the soldier said, suddenly smiling, and then he pointed at a car that stood outside. "Take a Post taxi. It'll cost you a quarter, but he'll put you in the right place."

"Thanks," Patrick said, but the big soldier had become interested in a chewing-gum dispenser that hung on the wall.

They sat in the back seat of the taxi, looking out of the windows. The road on which they were traveling was macadam, and it passed by warehouses and railroad sidings and two-story barracks, row on row of two-story barracks buildings, and everything was that same white that had faded yellow, with dull red roofs. The taxi left them off in front of what seemed to be another warehouse. There was a big sliding door that was open just a little bit, and beside the door there was a sign that said INITIAL RECEIVING POINT.

"Well, let's get initially received," Patrick said, and led the way through the opening in the warehouse door. Inside there was a large room. There was a counter cut into the wall at the rear, with several men lounging around behind it. The men were dressed in faded green trousers, with green shirts of the same material tucked into the trousers.

"I wonder what they're doing over there," Schaltenbrandt said, pointing to the forward half of the barnlike room. There were a whole raft of school desks there, and a lot of people in civilian clothes sitting at these desks, apparently doing nothing. In front of the desks there was a blackboard, and a soldier was sitting on a chair beside the blackboard, doing nothing. Everybody seemed quite content. Patrick noticed that this soldier by the blackboard was wearing the same green costume, and he could see what he could not observe about the men behind the counter, that the green trousers ended up by being bloused around the tops of low brown boots that laced up the front. It looked less like a uniform than a very businesslike laborer's outfit.

They came up to the counter, and one of the men behind it pushed pencils and papers toward them.

"Fill in your name and your serial number the way it appears on your records jacket," he said. Patrick looked at his records jacket. Kingsgrant, Patrick. RA12422849. He copied it out.

"O.K.," the man behind the counter said. "Now give me your records jackets. You keep that card with your name and serial number."

A Negro soldier in the other kind of uniform, made of brown cloth, with the Eisenhower jacket and a tan shirt and a dark brown tie, had come in, lugging a big olive-drab duffelbag. The man behind the counter lost all interest in Patrick and Eugene Schaltenbrandt.

"Tole me in San Francisco to repawt here," the Negro soldier said, handing over his records jacket. He was wearing some ribbons on his chest.

The clerk flipped open the big manila envelope and looked at the papers in it quickly. "You're reporting to be discharged here," he said.

"That's what they tole me in San Francisco."

"All right," the clerk said. The soldier who had been sitting up by the blackboard had come back and started talking to the man behind the counter.

"No, all those are US," the clerk behind the counter said. "These two are RA. You can have 'em now."

"Take a seat up there," the soldier who had come back said, and returned to the front of the room. Patrick and Eugene found seats next to each other.

"You should all have a pencil and three different forms on your desks," the soldier in green said, raising his voice as he addressed the group. "The first form is a tag, the second form is a bigger tag, and the third form is a postcard. Has everybody in the room got a pencil, a little tag, a big tag, and a postcard?" Several hands went up, and the private went circulating around. "Yes, that's a postcard," Patrick heard him saying to one of the men. "It doesn't have to have a picture on it to be a postcard."

"All right." The private in green resumed his place at the

front of the room. "Fine. Now put the tags in your pocket. You're going to need them later. Now look at the postcard. You will see on the back of the postcard that it says things, but it also has blanks on it. It says, 'This is to inform you that blank has reached Camp Kilmer, New Jersey, safely, and that he will be here for several days for processing before he is reassigned to another place for Basic Training. He will be available at Recreation Hall Three on blank to see two visitors. This is your pass to see him. Do not lose it.' Now, do not write anything yet. In the first blank you will put your name. Then, in the second blank, put down Sunday, November 28, from 3 P.M. to 5 P.M." He spelled it out on the blackboard. "All right. Do all that now. Your name in the first blank, and this date and time, just the way it is here, in the second blank." A full three minutes of silence. "All right. Now turn your postcard over. Put down the name and address of the person that you want to have come and see you. It can be anybody, but that person can only bring one other person along."

Patrick looked at the front of the postcard. He had not expected to be stumped in this particular exercise, but they had him. Eileen was three thousand miles away. His father? No. His landlady Mrs. Charnow would be very unlikely to want to come running down to Camp Kilmer, but at least he could send it to her if he had to supply a name. Suddenly something hit Patrick. Of course she was in New York. Maybe she wouldn't come, but maybe she would. He picked up his pencil, tried to ignore what his heart was suddenly doing, and wrote firmly, "Miss Anna van Neerdaam, 17 West 11th Street, New York, N.Y."

II

"What county are you from, Pat?"

Patrick looked up from taking his toothbrush and toothpaste

out of his little canvas bag. He had been pushed through a chow line, and pushed through a line to get some bedding, and here he was in a barracks at ten o'clock at night. He had been engaging in an intermittent conversation with this very nice fellow Ratigan in the next double bunk over, and for a second this latest from Ratigan had him stumped.

"Oh," Patrick said after a moment, "near Dublin originally, I think." He looked over at Ratigan, who was lying in the top bunk, the sheets and the brown Army blankets wrapped right up to his chin. He smiled and nodded.

"We're all from County Cork," Ratigan said. He turned his moon face a little more into the pillow. "Are you married, Pat?"

"No, I'm not," Patrick said. "How about you?"

"No." Ratigan gave a very expressive sweep of the eyeballs, in lieu of pulling his hands out from the warmth of the bed. "A lot of these fellows are. Wouldn't you think they could find somebody else? I mean, drafting fathers and all."

"I don't know," Patrick said. "Somebody has to do it."

"You think you're going to like the Army all right, don't you?"

Patrick turned around, a bit surprised. "Well, I haven't closed my mind to the possibility."

"I have," Ratigan said. "That's the only thing I'm sure of in this world. I'm going to hate this thing worse and worse every day I'm in it."

"No work tomorrow," Patrick said. "It's Thanksgiving tomorrow. They're just going to feed us turkey all day."

"They can keep their turkey," Ratigan said, and closed his eyes. "Good night, Pat. God bless you."

"Thanks," Patrick said. "Good night." He went down the center aisle, between the two rows of double-decker bunks, and into the latrine. He almost dropped his toothbrush in his surprise at what he saw. There was a big Negro, dressed just in a white T shirt, squatting on top of one of the toilet seats. He had one big foot on the seat on either side of the bowl, and this was the rather acrobatic posture in which he was relieving himself. Patrick went over to the sinks and began brushing his teeth. There was a boy sitting on the toilet bowl nearest the sink. He had a box of letter paper on his lap, and he was writing a letter, using the box as a desk.

"Hey, buddy," he said after Patrick had finished his teeth.

"Uh-huh?"

"How do you spell 'lonesome'?"

Patrick told him, and then he picked up his toothbrush and tube of toothpaste and went back out into the big area where the two rows of double-decker bunks were. The lights had been turned out, and as Patrick walked quietly toward his bunk he heard a muffled sob in the darkness. It's been a long day, Patrick said to himself. He sat down on the edge of his bunk and began taking off his shoes.

III

Jacob sat in the library at 1120. It was just past midnight, and he was in his armchair, staring at the letter from Patrick. The letter lay on the footstool, opened and read over a dozen times. Jacob's thoughts kept going around in a helpless circle. Patrick had no business being in the Army. Even if his arm looked normal in a uniform, it didn't have the dexterity and strength to do the things that he was going to be called on to do. Jacob stood up and walked over to the fireplace. There had been a good fire, but now there was just a heap of reddened coals. Jacob gazed at the remnants of the fire. It was just too much, he had no business being in the Army. Jacob closed his eyes, and for a moment he saw Patrick's handwriting, "to tell you that I have enlisted in the Army, and will be leaving tomorrow morning — " Not even drafted. He had to go and enlist, as if it made any difference. They shot up the boys who were conscripted just as thoroughly as the boys that joined. His foot kicked once at the carpet. It was so damned unreasonable. Men came to terms with life. If you had a physical defect, it was too bad, but you accepted the fact. And here he was in the Army. Chuck the Law School, go on some literary goose chase writing the Great American Novel, and then top it off by joining the Army. Jacob strode back to the footstool and picked up the letter. He walked back toward the fireplace, crumpling up the letter in a ball in his hand, and then, just as he was about to throw it on top of the pink coals, he let his hand fall to his side as if the strength had been drained out of him. Jacob's head bent forward. Dear God, he said, I've never asked you for very much. Maybe to keep Maude alive. But I always thought we had to work out our problems for ourselves. But dear God, please take care of Patrick.

IV

The lights went on, and for a moment Patrick lay rigid, his eyelids suddenly open, tryng to figure out where he was. He was aware that it was cold, and he brought his left hand up from under the O.D. blankets and looked at his wrist watch. It said three-thirty. Somebody's put on the lights by mistake, Patrick said to himself. Suddenly there was a humming noise, and the squawk box said, "Get out of bed!"

Patrick lay there for another second. The night was pitch-black at the windows. He looked at his wrist watch again to make sure that it had not stopped. Just then two men in olive overcoats and yellow helmets came striding down the center aisle, one on each side, banging away at the iron bedsteads with billy sticks.

"Wake up! Hit it! Get up!" A stick hit the tubular iron rail behind Patrick's head with a terrific bang. "Hit it! Get up! Get up!" the two yellow helmets yelled, and then they strode out the front door of the barracks and into the night.

There was a sort of stunned silence all around. Ratigan was sitting bolt upright in bed.

"This is the *Army*?" he said, shaking his head. Then he pointed his finger toward Patrick. "Gonna feed us turkey now, uh?"

A pair of white woolen socks came flashing through the air, with Schaltenbrandt, Eugene D., in them.

"Better get in the latrine quick," he said. "Get shaved before the crowd gets in there."

Patrick looked around. At least half the barracks were still lying there, wearing almost identical expressions on their faces. They were awake, but they did not believe what was happening to them. Just then the two yellow helmets came back through the door, and everybody who was awake rolled out of bed, and started fumbling around for their clothes. The two yellow helmets stopped at a bunk near the front door. The man in the upper bunk was still blissfully asleep, although his nose was only thirty inches from a bright, naked light bulb. One of the yellow helmets took the front end of his mattress, and one took the bottom, and they swung the whole business, sleeping man and all, off the bed frame.

"Open the door," one of the yellow helmets said to a sleepy-eyed boy who was pulling on his trousers, and they carried their big bundle through the door and into the freezing night. About ten seconds later, as everybody stood there hypnotized, the occupant of the transplanted bed came tearing through the door, dressed in his underwear.

"Holy God!" he yelled frantically. "You know where I was sleeping? I was sleeping *outside!* How'd I get out there?" One or two of his friends moved forward to soothe him and bring his bedding back indoors, and Patrick went down to the latrine to wash up.

Patrick stood in front of the barracks, shivering. It was the damnedest sight that he had ever seen. There was a row of barracks on this side of the gravel street, and a row of barracks across the way. The huge crowd of men on this side of the gravel street were in civilian clothes, and the men on the other side were in those green uniforms with the field jackets and boots and little engineer's caps. The whole scene was illuminated only by a handful of lights — the lights over the front steps of the barracks. It had snowed during the night, and everybody was standing there in snow at four-fifteen in the morning. Each barracks stood together in more or less of a huddle with an attempt at a front rank along the boards that divided the mud sidewalk from the mud-and-gravel company street. They had been standing there for about twenty minutes now, and absolutely nothing had happened. For the first few minutes Patrick had not noticed the cold because of the extraordinary scene of all these people standing there under electric light in the middle of the November night, but now the cold was beginning to really come through him. It was terribly cold. Patrick stood there and tried to remember if he had ever been as cold. For a moment the thought of swimming in Penobscot Bay among the seals crossed his mind, but he dismissed it. That had been fun, and you could jump out again any time you wanted to. Here it was cold, and when you were cold, it just got colder. Patrick could feel the snow melting around his shoes. In another couple of minutes his feet would be good and wet.

A soldier came walking down the middle of the company street. He had on a pair of brown trousers tucked into those low boots, and a khaki shirt with corporal's stripes on them. That was all. Just a shirt. No cap, no coat. Just a shirt. He took a look at this massive accumulation of men, about eight sixty-man barracks' worth, and went back to wherever he had come from. After another five minutes he came back with another soldier. This man was wearing brown trousers, low shoes, a khaki shirt, and an overseas cap. He had stripes on his arm, three stripes up and a rocker underneath.

"Knock it off!" the sergeant yelled, as he and the corporal bore down the middle of the street. Absolute silence. You could hear the shoes of the two men in the crystal night. "Fall back in your barracks. Not yet!" The movement toward the doors of the warm barracks halted. "When you get in there, make your bunks, sweep the floor, empty the butt cans into the garbage cans behind the barracks, and mop under your bunks. When we yell 'Fall out' on the squawk box, you come back out here just the way you are now. All right, hit it!"

It took about fourteen seconds for the five hundred men to get in out of the cold.

v

Patrick came out of the door of the clothing warehouse, lugging a huge olive-colored barracks bag that was filled with what the United States Army had given him to wear. There was still some snow on the ground, but the concrete loading platform had been swept off, and all the men who had gone through ahead of him had plunked themselves down on top of their barracks bags. Everybody was sitting in the morning sunshine, talking and smoking as they sat on the swollen olive canvas bags. Patrick sat down and let his fingers run across the material of his new trousers. They were brown wool, and the overcoat that he was wearing felt like a combination of canvas and some softer material. It was really a beautiful coat, a real trenchcoat, double-breasted and shiny deep green. He sat there and tried to reconstruct in his mind what they had rammed into his barracks bag. What he was wearing was called a Class A uniform, and he had one more of those in the bag. The Class A was the brown affair with the Eisenhower jacket, and it was worn with the overseas cap of the same material. Then they had rammed in about four of the green jobs, which he had discovered were called fatigues, and two engineer's hats, called caps, fatigue, to go with them. Then they had given him two pairs of the boots, which turned out to be boots, combat, and the shoes he was wearing, which were shoes, low quarter. Patrick mused about the boots for a minute. If they gave them two pairs of boots and only one pair of lightweight shoes, it seemed reasonable to assume that they expected them to be spending a lot of time outdoors.

Schaltenbrandt came through the warehouse door. He had his barracks bag perched confidently on his shoulder, and his uniform fit him as if it had been tailored to his measurements. He was the Army ideal, the mesomorph that never showed up.

"Hi," he said, flipping his barracks bag off of his shoulder easily. "Boy, didn't they give us a load of stuff?"

Patrick looked at Schaltenbrandt. With the barracks bag off his shoulder he looked even better, and now he tugged his coat in back as if he already knew that he looked exceptionally well in his uniform.

"Boy," Schaltenbrandt said. "An overcoat, and a raincoat, and a field jacket." He sounded really excited and happy about all the new clothes that they had given him. Just then Ratigan came staggering through the door.

"This is the goddam end," he said. "You have to sign one of those slips?"

"Sure," Patrick answered.

"Sure, what do you mean sure? You walk in and it rains clothes for fifteen minutes, and then you have to sign a slip that says you got everything. How do I know if I got everything?"

"You can't fight City Hall," Schaltenbrandt said.

"You're right." Ratigan just stepped away from under his barracks bag and let it tumble to the concrete. He sat down on it and shook his head. "They're taking my freedom away from me. I can feel it."

"Didn't you like your turkey?" Patrick asked, smiling.

Ratigan smiled back. "Yesterday was all right. I've got to admit it. I ate turkey, and all the rest I did was stand around and say 'Here. Here.'" He shrugged his shoulders. "Where else would I be?" He waved his fist toward the wall of the warehouse. "You've got me, you bastards, but you're not going to make me like it."

VI

There were nearly a thousand brand-new soldiers milling around in the sunshine outside Recreation Hall Three, straightening their overseas caps or buttoning their overcoats. One or two buses had already arrived, and the young soldiers had taken their families out of the cold winter sunshine and into the big gymnasium.

Another bus rolled in, and Patrick pushed up near the front of the huge olive and brown crowd. The first person off was a very old woman, wearing a black coat with a black shawl around her head, and carrying a paper bag. She stood there for a minute, blinking her eyes, and then a fine-looking young man with olive skin and Mediterranean features came forward and put his arms around her. She smiled when he let her go, and as he took the paper bag he kissed her again on the cheek. Then they walked in toward the gymnasium. Anna was not on the bus. All right, Patrick said to himself. She's not coming. She probably never even got the card. But still he stood there, waiting for the next bus. It came rolling in. Anna stepped down. Patrick stood frozen, and his heart beat quickly. He saw her, but he couldn't believe she was there. She was wearing a tailored black wool coat, and her hair was golden in the sunlight under the blue winter sky.

"What a doll," somebody said, and Patrick pushed his way up to Anna.

"Hello, Anna."

"What are you doing here?" She sounded almost angry.

"Picking up cigarette butts, mainly," Patrick said, beaming at her. "How are you?"

"Fine." Anna looked around at the sea of soldiers. "But how are you, that's the question."

"I'm fine. I think we're supposed to go in this big building here."

"All right." They walked into the gymnasium. Most of the soldiers and their guests were sitting on folding metal chairs, eating food from paper bags that their families had brought with them. One soldier was tipping up a bottle of wine, but nobody seemed to mind. There was a terrific din in the place, and at least half the men were staging affectionate reunions with their women. Finally he and Anna found a couple of chairs in a corner.

"Well," Anna said, looking around, "you've really done it this time."

"It hasn't been bad so far."

"Where do they send you from here?"

"I don't know," Patrick said. "I have to take Basic Training somewhere, and they don't give Basic Training here."

Anna nodded. "I want to get a couple of things straight. Then we can chat all we want to. I heard you were on the outs with your father."

"You could put it that way."

"Then you won't be staying there when you have leaves and things?"

"No."

"Patrick, I want you to promise me something."

"What?"

"If you take this Basic business anywhere near New York, you'll come to town every now and then, won't you?"

"Every time they let me, I suppose."

"Well, I want you to stay at my house when you do." Anna was looking at him intently.

"Well, that's very nice of you, Anna." Patrick could hardly believe his ears. "I'd love to. You sure you really want to adopt me like that?"

"Yes, I am."

"It sounds good to me." Patrick glanced around the hall. "You know, we're allowed to take visitors over to the PX. I could get you a cup of coffee over there. How about it?"

"Fine." Anna stood up, and now her graceful back seemed a little less rigid than when she had arrived. Patrick put on his coat and his brown cloth overseas cap, and walked out into the sunshine behind her. They crossed a big field of packed-down snow, side by side, and occasionally Patrick turned to look at the profile of Anna's face as the breeze tugged at the locks of her hair. Here and there other couples, their arms around each other, feminine civilian-clad arms around the olive-covered backs, were walking in an aimless, almost staggering way, legs and sides bumping into each other in sweet bumps and brushes again and again and again. Parents were taking pictures of their sons. It seemed to Patrick that a lot of these people had more than the two visitors they were permitted. Occasionally a whole clan gathered round, laughing and munching food as they watched a father photographing a son and his girl. Patrick and Anna strode along.

"You sure this snow isn't ruining your shoes, Anna?" Patrick said, looking at the way that Anna's high heels were sinking down into the snow.

"No, I don't think so," Anna said. "Why didn't you wear boots, like some of these other people?"

"Well, you're not supposed to wear them off duty with your Class A's. A lot of people do, though, I guess." They had come to the wooden steps of the PX, and Patrick held open the door for Anna. Inside there was the usual blast of heat. There were lines of soldiers waiting to move up to the various counters set along the walls, and a huge jukebox in the middle of the cream linoleum floor was playing, "Because of You." Anna and Patrick stood in the line that was waiting to get food, and Patrick stood behind her and watched her blond head as she turned it, looking at all the unfamiliar scene around her. A vapor of cigarette smoke rose toward the high ceiling of the large PX, and over the voices of the men you could hear the sound of the song on the jukebox.

"Gee, some of these men have a lot of ribbons, don't they?" Anna said.

"Yes. It's funny. The men who've been in a while don't seem to feel the cold as much. The people who call out the roll call in the morning come out wearing shirts, or even T shirts."

"A T shirt in November?"

"I'm not kidding you. And when I say morning, I mean about five o'clock in the morning."

Anna looked around again. "Do you know what any of these ribbons mean, Patrick?"

"Not yet," Patrick said. Their line had come up to the counter, and Patrick ordered them both a cup of coffee.

At about a quarter to five, Patrick and Anna were standing near the door of the gymnasium. They had had two cups of coffee in the PX, and come back to the gym, then walked around some more, and here they were, with the sun going down and the air really cold now, looking at each other's face in the reflection of this dark December afternoon. In fifteen minutes the buses would start leaving. They walked around the gymnasium once more, and silently came back along the road. The sky was the sudden dark blue of a winter evening. Up by the gymnasium the headlights of buses were illuminating the crowd of olive overcoats and civilian clothes that came pouring out of the bright square doorway of the gym. Anna and Patrick walked along the line of buses, looking in the windows until they found one that looked fairly empty. Anna turned, and her hand squeezed Patrick's arm.

"Let me know when you're coming," she said.

"I will," Patrick answered, and then she went up the steps of the bus. Patrick stood in the midst of the embraces and the tears around him, watching Anna go back through the bus until she found a seat by a window. The buses ahead were pulling out, and then the driver slammed the door in front of Patrick, and the bus rolled out into the night. Patrick nodded to himself, and then he walked back across the snowy area, down toward the PX and the rows of barracks beyond. He could hardly believe that it had happened, but as he found himself believing it, all the long-chained hope in his heart leapt up as he walked over the snowy fields.

VII

"Hey, Pat."

Patrick stopped staring at the mattress above him and looked at Schaltenbrandt. They had spent all morning in a freezing warehouse, shuffling forward in their T shirts, from one inoculation to the next, and now they were back in their barracks and for the moment nobody was yelling at them.

"Uh?"

"How about some chow?"

"I thought I was too stiff to move," Patrick said, swinging off his bunk, "but I think you've just sold me a bill of goods." He picked his field jacket and fatigue cap off the bottom of his bed, and they walked out the front door of the barracks.

"Hey, look." Schaltenbrandt was looking up the company street, and, looking in the same direction, Patrick saw a green-clad crowd all packed around the bulletin board.

"Let's go see what's up."

"O.K."

When they got to the crowd the first thing they saw was Ratigan, smiling and shouldering his way out of the press. He had his arms folded in front of him, and his hands were unconsciously massaging the many punctures that had been put in him during the morning.

"We're getting out of this rattrap," he said, beaming. "We're shipping out."

"When?" Patrick said.

"Oh, whenever they get around to it. But at least they got us in mind, that's what I like." Ratigan walked on. "We're going to the same place, Pat," he said over his shoulder. "Schaltenbrandt's going someplace else."

"Where is it?" Patrick shouted after him.

"Fort Dix, New Jersey, and then some numbers." Ratigan said. "All I know is we're going to the same numbers."

Patrick and Eugene began elbowing in toward the bulletin board, and after two minutes Patrick was in there. He looked down one list, and then another, and then he saw his name. He looked quickly up to the top of the list: For shipment Co. B, 50th Inf. Rgt., 9th Inf. Div., Fort Dix, N.J., for cycle 16 wks. Basic Inf. Trng. Patrick smiled. He was on his way somewhere. The show was about to begin.

14

PATRICK PEERED out of the window of the bus as it swished down the rainy highway. Even after only six days of the Army, the civilian cars and the Howard Johnsons along the New Jersey Turnpike seemed to be a marvelous technicolored, disorganized display. Now they were off the Turnpike and booming along a road that ran through farm country, with an occasional gray house cringing against the flat gusts of rain.

Inside the bus it was all olive and brown. Four rows of close-cropped heads came up out of tan shirts, brown neckties, and brown Ike jackets. In the baggage racks overhead, fat olive barracks bags rolled against each other on the turns. Nobody had much to say. They had been up too long for that. It was eleven in the morning, and they had been up since four. They had waited for breakfast in the endless lines of men at Camp Kilmer, and waited to hand in their bedding, and waited for ever in a huge parking lot where buses pulled in and pulled out again, taking loads of men to Georgia, to Mississippi, to Indiantown Gap, Pennsylvania, and Fort Dix, New Jersey. They were somewhere in the middle of the rain, in a bus, in the hands of the Army, absolutely, totally in the hands of the Army, and that was all they knew. They had been told Fort Dix, and not one of them would have been surprised to see a sign saying "City Limits,

Albuquerque, New Mexico." Some of them were asleep. The boy next to Patrick had stuck out his hand when they sat down in the bus.

"My name's Adams," he had said, smiling out of a large, square, strong blond head. "I come from Kentucky."

"I'm Patrick Kingsgrant. I'm from New York."

"Pleased to meet you, Brother Kingsgrant," Kentucky Adams said, and five minutes later he was asleep with his head on Patrick's shoulder, and he was still asleep after all the rainy miles.

The bus was slowing down as they came into a little town, and Patrick pressed his nose right against the glass. The town seemed to be strung out along one main street, and the street consisted of a long row of bars. Behind one or two of the glass fronts he could see the window displays of stores that sold insignia and ribbons, and then the row of bars and stores ended. There was an MP standing in the rain with his white cap wet and his raincoat glistening, and then they were moving past a mustard-yellow building that had some buses beside it. Patrick debated on waking up Adams, and decided to do it.

"We're here, I think."

Adams woke up in one effortless motion, sitting straight up, leaning across Patrick and staring out.

"The Ninth Infantry Division welcomes you to Fort Dix," he read, and Patrick saw the sign. It was in the middle of a green plot of grass, beside an old howitzer that was painted gray. There was a certain cheerful, unlikely quality about the sign by the cannon in the rain. "That's friendly of them," Adams said. They were going around a traffic circle now, and Patrick saw the other buses strung out ahead. A minute later they were moving along a rainswept road. The ground was flat on either side of them, and what trees there were seemed to be low and scrubby against the wide stretch of dark sky. Patrick stared out, trying to see some signs of life. There was nothing. It made Camp Kilmer seem like a collection of skyscrapers.

Suddenly the buses slowed down until they were creeping, and in a moment Patrick saw the reason. Coming along on either side of the road was a file of men. There was a little flag hanging limply from a staff carried by a man at the head of the line, and on they came, slopping in the rain and the puddles by the side of the road. Rain was dripping from the brims of their helmets onto their shiny dark ponchos, and they had their rifles slung so that the muzzles were pointing down and the butts were sticking up under the ponchos. The whole line looked like a string of miserable scarecrow hunchbacks, and they were all making obscene gestures toward the recruits in the buses, and yelling things that were swept away in the blasts of rain.

"What were they mad at us for?" a boy behind Patrick said.

"I imagine because we're riding," Patrick said.

"That's the right answer, Brother Kingsgrant," Kentucky Adams said. "If I was with them I'd be giving us the finger too."

The buses slid down a road toward a little city of yellow barracks, and then they were stopping in what seemed to be a back alley between some sort of sheds. The bus door opened, and the first thing in was a red helmet. There was a man under the red helmet, and he started yelling.

"All right, grab your barracks bags and move out! Don't leave nothing on the bus! Move out!"

Patrick pulled his full barracks bag out of the rack and staggered down the aisle. It was one shoving mess. His overcoat was too hot, and everybody was blinded by everybody else's barracks bag, and if you tried to reach up and straighten out your cap the barracks bag would start to slip off your shoulder. Patrick dropped a glove and tried to bend down and get it and somebody stepped on his hand and then somebody bumped into him from behind and he fell sprawling in the aisle of the bus with the barracks bag on top of him. He got up with his face red and finally he got his glove and got his barracks bag up on his shoulder and staggered down the steps of the bus.

"All right, young soldiers!" somebody in a red helmet was yelling from some distance away. "Put it in four ranks right here!" Patrick stumbled after the man ahead of him, and for a minute everyone was running under the heavy barracks bags. Then the barracks bag in front of Patrick stopped abruptly and did a left face. Patrick did the same thing. There were some more collisions, and then everything was quiet except for the sound of the rain.

There was a big fat man in a red helmet facing them.

"At ease!" the red top yelled. The way he said it indicated that it had nothing to do with being at ease. "All right. Take your barracks bags off your shoulders. All right. For your information you belong to Baker Company, First Battalion, Fiftieth Infantry Regiment. The barracks across the way belong to Able Company, and the barracks down there belong to Charlie Company." He waved his hand toward the barracks across the hundred yards of sandy dirt, and kept staring at the new recruits. "All right. Now these barracks here belong to you. These little houses like, down to my right, that's the Baker Company Day Room, the next one is the Baker Company Orderly Room, and the two houses on either side of where you came in are the Mess Hall and the Supply Room. All right. In a minute I am going to assign you to barracks. When I yell your name, you yell 'Here Sergeant!' and pick up your barracks bag and move into your barracks. All right. Turn around." Everybody shuffled around so that they were facing into the rain. There were four barracks there. They were the same two-story barracks that they had at Kilmer, but even in the rain, these looked neater and more businesslike.

"Starting from the left," the sergeant's voice came yelling in over their shoulders, "is the First Platoon, next is the Second Platoon, next is the Third Platoon, and all the way on the right is the Fourth Platoon. In case you get lost there's a sign hanging over the front door of each one. All right. Turn around." Everybody shuffled around. Patrick could feel rain starting to come down the back of his neck. "All right. For your information my name is Sergeant Stone. I am your Field First Sergeant. You are going to hate me and I don't give a shit. Your soul belongs to God, but your ass belongs to me." The sergeant paused, evidently expecting a laugh. After a couple of seconds the big fat man pulled some papers out of his pocket. "All right. First Platoon. Accacio!"

"Here!"

"Hold it! Come out here, soldier. Yes, you, Accacio." A short boy came forward as fast as he could, carrying the heavy bag on his shoulder. "Put the bag down," Sergeant Stone said. The boy put down the bag and stood there uncertainly, about twenty feet from the sergeant. "I told you to call me Sergeant. You know what a push-up is?" The boy nodded his head. "Give me fifteen push-ups." The boy looked at him. "Right now!"

The boy got down with his feet together and his hands spread out on the muddy ground. For some reason Patrick could feel himself blushing as the boy got down. The boy began lowering his whole front down to a few inches off the ground and raising it up again. After about five push-ups his cap fell off. "Let it lay there!" the sergeant bellowed. The boy got through the fifteen push-ups in front of the silent ranks and stood up slowly, picking up his cap and putting it on his head. His face was flushed. "All right, move out!" the sergeant said. He brought the papers back up in front of him. Adams!"

"Here Sergeant!"

"Aguilar!"

"Here Sergeant!"

"Allen!"

"Here Sergeant!"

The Commanding Officer of Baker Company was a diminutive man named Captain Hare. It was the first evening, and the hundred and sixty men of Baker Company sat on the bunks in the Fourth Platoon, or sat on the floor, or stood silently in the spaces between the double bunks, and listened as Captain Hare answered their questions. He had been answering questions for about twenty minutes.

"Sir, when can we go home?"

"Passes will start after your fourth week of Basic."

"Sir, I've got a kid, and my wife is sick, and I had an appeal still in front of the draft board, and — "

"We can't do anything about that from here, soldier."

"Sir, my father's sick. Can I go home if he gets real bad?"

"That has to be handled through the Red Cross. I want all of you to get that. If you have an emergency at home, tell them at home to call the Red Cross. They'll make an investigation, and then we'll get orders to let you go home for three days or whatever the case gets. Don't come to me."

"Sir, I just live in Trenton. Do I have to wait four weeks?"

Patrick thought the captain was going to explode, but he just smiled.

"You have to wait four weeks just like everybody else, soldier. You people came in at a bad time. You're going to be here for Christmas and New Year's, and there's nothing I can do about it." The captain cleared his throat. "That's enough questions. I want to tell you what you're up against. This is the most serious thing you're ever going to do. Maybe I can make you understand how serious it is when I tell you that before the weather gets really warm again some of you will be wounded in action." Patrick looked around. Everyone was quiet, with their eyes on the little man who stood on the strip of brown linoleum that ran down the aisle between the two rows of bunks. The captain pointed a finger at the crossed golden rifles on the lapel of his Class A's. "You men don't know what this means yet. It means Infantry. The roughest, the toughest, the cruddiest, and the best. The training manual for Field First Sergeants in this regiment says, 'The primary mission of this regiment is to produce an aggressive infantryman who is willing to engage the enemy and kill or capture him.' That's you." Captain Hare folded his hands behind his back. "You soldier, you do your best, you'll be all right. You try to give us a hard time and you'll wish you were dead. What you want to do is to get out of this alive, and the best chance you have to do that is to pay attention while you're here. That's all."

III

Bill Bench looked up from where he was bending over polishing the brass rail that conducted water into the long trough-like urinal.

"I'll be goddamned!" he said.

Patrick grinned and stepped down into the latrine of Bill's barracks. They shook hands violently, and Bill slapped him on the back. Bill was wearing a T shirt, fatigue pants, and combat boots. "What are you doing here, anyway?" Bill said, grinning at Patrick.

"Same thing you are, I guess," Patrick said. "How are you, Bill?"

"I'm O.K." Bill stepped back to look at Patrick in his Class A's and overcoat. "Reasonably sharp for somebody who hasn't been here long enough to put on his Division patch," he said, grinning. "What outfit are you in?"

"Baker Company, Fiftieth Infantry Regiment."

"When'd you get here?"

282

"Just today. Left Kilmer this morning."

"I'll be goddamned."

"Hey Bill," Patrick said, jerking a thumb in the direction of the big main room outside, "what's going on?"

"GI party," Bill said. "Didn't you have to GI tonight?"

"Uh-uh." Patrick took another look at the long room. All the double bunks had been shoved over on one side of the linoleum center piece, and the big tall metal lockers had all been brought over to one side as well. The trunks called footlockers were up on the bunks, along with a fantastic array of helmets and shovels and canteens and overshoes. On the half of the floor that had been left bare, there were a couple of dozen men dressed like Bill, down on their knees and scrubbing furiously. "How come you're not there slopping around in the water?" Patrick asked.

"I'm a squad leader," Bill said. "Listen, Patrick, have you started Basic yet?"

"No. In a few days."

"Well, when they ask for men with previous experience, previous military experience, go up there and say you've had some. I said I'd had four years of military school, and they made me a squad leader. You get out of KP and Weapons Pool, and you get at least as many passes as anybody else."

"Sounds good," Patrick said.

Bill stood there for a few more seconds, smiling at Patrick. "I'll be goddamned," he said.

IV

By four o'clock the next afternoon Patrick was an expert on the various types of New Jersey soil. A bunch of them from the Second Platoon had been sent out on a truck to one of the vast, sprawling rifle ranges, and they had been digging target pits all day.

"What are you digging so hard for?" a rugged giant named

Forlenza said. "They got to take us in when it gets dark no matter what."

Patrick nodded. "I guess you're right." He looked around. There were three of them in the big hole, standing in it up to their waists, and the whole scene had only one touch of bright color. There was a red flag waving up by a tower about a quarter of a mile away. The rest was a dark gray-black winter sky that looked as if it might rain or snow at any moment, and the long flat stretch of sandy dirt off to the woods, half a mile in the other direction. They were in the middle of a vast brown desert, little figures in green fatigues and brown boots, digging, and on the range next door the sharp, cracking rifle shots that had begun at eight in the morning were still whacking away.

Patrick put his little entrenching shovel on the edge of the hole and took a deep breath.

"You are tired?" the other man in the hole said.

"Yes." Patrick smiled and looked at him. He was a snub-nosed young man named Stanislaus Kurna, and he had escaped from Czechoslovakia. He had told them a little about it when they had gone back in to the Company for lunch. The Army was accepting enlistments in Europe from men who had escaped under the Iron Curtain. You signed up for five years, and at the end of the time you were discharged in the United States, as an American citizen.

"Here." Forlenza was holding out a pack of cigarettes, and Patrick shook his head.

"No, thanks. I don't."

"Wish I didn't. Costs too much." Forlenza leaned back against the edge of the hole, his powerful shoulders and his heavy jaw under the green fatigue cap outlined against the light of the darkening sky. He lit his cigarette. "What's wrong with your arm?" he said matter-of-factly, tossing the match over the edge of the hole.

"It was hurt when I was born." Patrick felt his face getting red, and he looked down at the silvery blade of his shovel. "Is it very obvious?"

"Nah," Forlenza shook his head. He was at least six-foot-two. "But we been working together all day."

"Will you go to be an officer?" Kurna said suddenly, to Patrick. He had stopped digging too. His features looked like those of a snub-nosed American boy, but his skin was a leathery yellow.

"I hope so," Patrick said. "I have to take these sixteen weeks first."

Forlenza picked up his shovel again. "You go to college?"

"Yes."

"That figures," Forlenza said, speaking with the cigarette in his mouth as he lifted a shovelful of loose muddy sand over the edge. "What college?"

"Harvard," Patrick said, and smiled.

"What are you smiling for?"

"I don't know."

"Harvard's a good school," Forlenza said. He shoveled out some more. "It's an important school."

Patrick nodded and picked up his shovel again. Even under the big dark Army gloves he could feel the warmth of his palms, where the blisters were starting to form. It was getting terribly cold, and he was hungry. As he jammed his shovel blade into the sandy dirt, he started thinking about the life he had so lately left, where you could usually get a cup of coffee when you really wanted a cup of coffee. He thought about how nice a cup of coffee would be, and then he thought about Anna.

"You dig too hard, Kingsgrant," Forlenza said. "You got to dig easy."

"I'll freeze if I don't keep digging," Patrick said, and the rifle shots kept ringing out a hundred yards away, under the gray sky.

V

Finally Patrick came to the head of the line. He had been shuffling forward for twenty minutes toward the door in the back of the little Supply Room building that held the Armorer's Room and the rifles. Sergeant Stone was standing by the door with a sheet of paper, and the one other cadreman, a tremendously tall Negro named Woodrow Wilson, had another sheet of paper. A couple of trainees like Patrick were inside the Armorer's Room, passing out the rifles. Nobody knew where the Armorer was.

"Name," Sergeant Stone said.

"Kingsgrant, Patrick."

"Serial Number."

"RA one two four two two eight four nine."

Sergeant Stone looked up for just a second when Patrick said RA, and then looked down again.

"One nine seven six three eight two," one of the trainees said, handing a rifle out the door to Patrick.

"Man, you goin' too fast fo' me," Woodrow Wilson said.

"One–nine–seven–six–three–eight–two," the trainee said.

"That's right," Wilson said, smiling as he wrote it down. Patrick took two steps to the right, the rifle in his hands, and was given a bayonet. Then he followed off behind some of the other men who were wandering back to their barracks, looking down at their rifles.

VI

"All right. As long as you're down there, give me ten more." Patrick started doing push-ups again. His stomach ached and his arms ached and he felt the cold of the frozen ground right through his gloves. It was a bizarre scene, Sergeant Stone's pre-breakfast calisthenics. The lights from the windows in the 5 A.M. winter darkness illuminated this weird picture of the big fat man standing in the middle of the area in front of the barracks, surrounded by a farflung circle of trainees in fatigues and field jackets, doing push-ups.

"All right! On your feet! Left face! Double time, ho!" Patrick began trotting around the great circle, feeling his legs dead and stiff under him. "Halt! Right face! Drop down and give me ten!" Nobody groaned any more. They were saving it all for the push-ups. Just get through the push-ups. "All right, soldier!" Stone strode to one side of the circle and pointed at a man. "You look tired. You come out in the middle and take a rest. Maybe when these men are eating breakfast you'll feel like doing some more push-ups. All right! On your feet! Left face! Double time, ho!" Patrick plodded forward. He was thinking that if they could have this much torture under Sergeant Stone and Woodrow Wilson, it was going to be a real vale of tears when the three other cadremen arrived. The rumor was that they were going to arrive pretty soon, and then Basic would begin. "Halt! Right face! You want some more?"

"Yes!" That was the prescribed answer. A wildly enthusiastic affirmative chorus.

"I can't hear you! You want some more?"

"Yes! Yes! Please!"

"I can't hear you! Sound off like you got a pair! You want more?"

"Yes! Oh, please! Yes!"

"All right. You want it so bad, give me fifteen!"

Patrick got down slowly. O.K., he said to himself, give him ten. Slowly Patrick cranked out the ten, going all the way down on his stomach every time and using his knees.

"Hey, soldier!"

Patrick looked up, fully expecting to see Sergeant Stone pointing at him, but the fat man was pointing at a trainee who was
just lying there. "You sick or something, soldier?"

The trainee got up on one knee and shook his head. "I don't
know, Sergeant."

"Well, I'll tell you for your information. You're not sick.
You're not sick until you puke. Everybody on your feet! Left
face! Double time, ho!"

How can you throw up before breakfast in any case, Patrick
said to himself, as he moved forward at a stumbling trot, breathing hard. I hate that bastard. He couldn't do a push-up if he
tried. I hate that fat, unattractive bastard. Suddenly a buzzer
went off.

"Halt! Right face! Fall out and head for chow!"

Patrick turned and started trotting toward the Mess Hall for
breakfast. There was still not a trace of light in the sky.

Right after breakfast Patrick was standing next to his bunk on
the upper floor of the Second Platoon, trying to improve on his
job of bed-making by tightening his blankets, when a soldier
came up the stairs. He was wearing Class A's, and he was
carrying a barracks bag in one hand, and a red helmet in the
other. He had on a pair of sparkling combat boots, and he had
a handsome Latin face, with a neat black mustache. There was
one chevron on his sleeve, and a silver paratrooper's badge on
his left breast. He kicked open the door of the little room at the
back of the second floor, back by the top of the narrow stairway,
and disappeared inside.

"Gentlemen," Patrick said, in a low voice to the two boys
nearest him, "I think we've met our platoon sergeant." They
all stood looking at the door through which the paratrooper had
disappeared. In an astonishingly short time the door opened
and he reappeared, dressed in fatigues, field jacket, and the

plastic liner of his red helmet. He wore the red helmet liner so far forward that you could hardly see his eyes, and there were stitched paratroop wings over the left breast pocket of his field jacket.

"You men," he said in a hushed, husky voice, "I want a meeting downstairs right now." He swung to his left with a light, graceful step, and disappeared down the stairway. Patrick and the others filed down the steps behind him. By the time they got downstairs the paratrooper was standing there near the water fountain by the wall that separated the downstairs main room from the stairway and the latrine. Patrick and the others from upstairs stood crowded in between the door to the latrine and the stairway and the racks holding their newly issued rifles. The men from downstairs were standing in the aisle between their bunks, and they were all staring at the red-helmeted paratrooper as he stood erect in front of the white wall.

"My name's Rodriguez," the soldier said. "I'm cadreman for this platoon. I'm a Pfc, but you *will* call me Sergeant Rodriguez. That's not for rank, but for discipline." He looked around. "Anybody here have any previous military training?"

O.K., Patrick said to himself, here goes nothing. He stuck up his hand. Four other men stuck up their hands.

"O.K.," Sergeant Rodriguez said. "You five line up." The five of them lined up shoulder to shoulder on the lineoleum strip in the aisle.

"What experience have you got?" he said to the first man.

"I've been in the National Guard for a couple of years."

Rodriguez nodded and went on to the next man. The next man said that he had been in the Navy for eleven months at the end of the war.

"Too bad you didn't make it twelve, and you wouldn't be here," Rodriguez said.

"You're telling me," the man said.

"Shut up," Rodriguez said.

Rodriguez came opposite Patrick, and Patrick drew himself even straighter.

"Four years of military school."

The red helmet nodded slightly, and a minute later Rodriguez stepped back from the short rank of prospective squad leaders. "Get me five rifles," he said over his shoulder, and a dozen men stumbled all over themselves getting five rifles out of the racks. "Give 'em to them," he said, nodding toward the rigid little line, and a moment later they were standing with rifles at their sides.

"Right shouldeur, arms!" the platoon sergeant yelled, and Patrick executed right shoulder arms. Thank you, Knickerbocker Greys, thank you, Tabor Academy, he said to himself. The rifle was heavy, but he knew he had got it up there in fairly respectable fashion.

"Ordeur, arms!" the red helmet snapped, and Patrick brought the rifle across his chest and down to his side. Sergeant Rodriguez came walking up to the man on Patrick's left. "Bullshit," he said, in that low hushed voice. "You haven't even been in the Boy Scouts. Drop out." Then he turned and walked up to the head of the line. "O.K. You National Guard man there, you take the weapons squad. That's the fourth squad. You'll be upstairs. O.K. you two," he said, pointing at Patrick and the man who had been in the Navy for eleven months, "first squad and second squad. Navy man first, you second. You two take the top bunk on either side, down on this floor by the front door. Got it?"

"Yes, Sergeant."

VII

Patrick was running across the road in formation, his rifle at port arms, when suddenly he felt something give in his left shoulder. It was a sudden stab of pain, followed instantly by the sensation that something was tearing vertically, from top to bottom. He stumbled from the sudden blow of pain.

"Count cadence, count!" Rodriguez yelled, trotting along beside the double-timing column of twos.

"One two three four, one two three four!" they shouted. Patrick had recovered the step, but his face was grave. The pain was gone, but it felt hot back in there, hot and sort of sticky. Still, the pain was gone, and Patrick straightened up as he ran along with his rifle out in front of him. He and Geremski, the squad leader of the first squad, were at the head of the Second Platoon. The last men in the First Platoon were about twenty yards in front of them. They used this column of twos formation a great deal in moving around, and Rodriguez had been directing a lot of his yelling at Patrick and Geremski, telling them they had to pivot correctly, telling them they had to keep the distances right. Patrick was on the right of Geremski, so the position of the platoon depended on Patrick.

"Column right, march," Rodriguez yelled, and Patrick turned the corner as if he were making a slow cut for a pass in football. His head was up, and he and Geremski trotted along side by side, their rifles held across their chests at a forty-five-degree angle.

VIII

Jacob sat at his desk in his office. He had just finished dictating a couple of letters concerning the probate of a will, and now that the stenographer had left the office he had pulled out the letter he had received last night from Patrick. He was just staring at it as it sat there in its envelope with the Ninth Division insignia on it. He had read it so often last night that it was memorized. It was a pleasant, simple letter, saying that Patrick was at Fort Dix, that he was a squad leader, and that he would not know about OCS for quite a while. There was not a word in it about coming home.

Jacob dropped the letter on his desk and shook his head. On top of everything else, he thought for the thousandth time in the last eighteen hours, he has to land up in the Infantry. And I know how those programs work, Jacob said to himself. If he doesn't make this OCS they'll just look and see what he's trained for, and by that time he'll be trained to be an Infantry private, and off he'll go just that much sooner. Good Lord.

He stood up and walked over to the window. Down below him in the street people were walking against the December winds, and the sky was overcast. Well, if he's in the Infantry he's in the Infantry, Jacob said to himself. Maybe he'll be all right. It seems hard to believe but maybe he'll pull it off. Jacob straightened up, and a funny little smile came onto his mouth, and an expression that was half pride and half fear came into his eyes.

15

PATRICK LAY in his upper bunk, halfway between sleep and a sort of nervousness that would not allow him real sleep. The first ten days of Basic were rolling around in his mind like a ball in a pinball machine.

Men, this rifle you been carrying around the last few days is the M-1. A huge Negro master sergeant, Sergeant Carter. You been learning how to carry this rifle, now we're gonna start getting you ready to fire it. First, this is a rifle, it is not a gun. It is a rifle. It fires, it does not shoot. You fire your rifle, you do not shoot your gun. This rifle is the best military rifle in the world. It's the best friend you've got. You take care of your rifle, it'll take care of you. Now get out your notebooks. This is the U.S. rifle, calibre thirty, M-1. It is clip-fed, it is air-cooled, it is gas-operated. It weighs nine and a half pounds without the bayonet, and ten and a half pounds with the bayonet.

Good Morning, men!
Good Morning, sir!
All right, brush off the snow from those benches before you sit down.

Men, some of you are under the mistaken impression that
the bayonet is obsolete. It is not obsolete. A first lieutenant,
very snappy, very sincere, Combat Infantry Badge, Silver Star,
Purple Heart. Supposing you come up a slope and jump into
the enemy's holes. You've been moving fast the last twenty-
five yards, firing, you've expended your clip and you haven't
had a chance to put in a new one. You jump in the trench
and there's a Chink. No time to get out a clip. No time
for anything but stabbing him with that knife on the end of
your rifle. Or maybe you were careful, you got in a clip just
before the last few seconds of the assault, and you jump in
there with four rounds left in your weapon. The weapon
jams. Or you just plain run out of ammunition. Gentlemen,
the bayonet is not obsolete.

Hut four, hut four, hut two three four
Dress it up and cover down
   Dress it up and cover down
Forty inches all round
   Forty inches all round
Am I right or wrong?
   You're right!
Am I right or wrong?
   You're right!
Sound off
   One two
Sound off
   Three four
Break 'em on down
   One two three four
   Onetwo threefour!

The singsong cadence receded from the front of Patrick's
mind, and he lay on his left side, looking at the dim row of

double bunks that held his squad. From underneath him came the snores of a colored boy from New York named Lish Jones, Jr. In the next bunk over, Stanislaus Kurna was downstairs, and in the top was a tough boy named Maple, who looked like a shorter, tougher version of Brian Donlevy. From beyond came the restless sleeping sounds of the rest of the squad, Forlenza's deep bass snore among them.

"Hey, no," a voice in one of the bunks in Geremski's squad across the aisle said. "Hey, no!" The sleeper twisted in his bed. "Hey, no!"

"You will man, you will," a voice on Patrick's side said, in that quick, elusive Virgin Islands manner. Patrick smiled in the darkness. He had two coal-black boys from St. Croix in his squad. Emilio Encarnacion and Clareford Jakes. They both were still walking around in a daze, and Patrick could hardly blame them. One month ago they had been on the beach in the tropical sunshine, never having worn shoes in their lives, and the next thing they knew they were falling out onto a snowy parade ground at Fort Dix at four in the morning, wearing combat boots.

Patrick sat up in his bunk and let his right hand go up under the long wool underwear that they wore constantly. His hand explored the region between his left shoulder blade and his spine. After that one stab of pain crossing the road that day, there had been no more real discomfort. It had felt as if a big fist was forming in there, tight beside the shoulder blade, and the fist was still there, but there was no pain. Patrick had thought about going on sick call for it, but they made it an awful nuisance to go on sick call, and you missed training, and then he had no desire to let a doctor get a look at his right shoulder if he could help it. He slid down again in the bunk, and, as he closed his eyes, Anna came upon him, the whole thought of her standing there in the snow at Kilmer, the blond hair and the blue eyes against the clear darkening blue of a crisp winter sky. The flush of her cheeks. Patrick closed his eyes even tighter and shook his head. It was no way to get over something. He had conscientiously walked away from his memories of Anna, conscientiously never called her, never written her, for months, never even really hoped, and then he had torn it all down with that one card the first day at Kilmer, and Anna walked the land. Patrick shook his head again. You'll get your first pass whenever you get it and go right to her, won't you? You'll go right to her. That's right, Patrick answered himself. That is absolutely correct. And then he was asleep in the troubled night of the barracks.

At breakfast the next morning there were wild rumors. There had been no Sergeant Stone out there at the reveille formation, and Woodrow Wilson had just stepped out, taken the report, and sent them down to the Mess Hall without any calisthenics. You could have your choice of rumors. Sergeant Stone was sick. Sergeant Stone was dead. Woodrow Wilson was the new Field First. Sergeant Stone had been court-martialed. Sergeant Stone had been assassinated. There was a new Field First, just back from Korea. Sergeant Stone had been promoted to lieutenant.

They came out of the Mess Hall, went back to their barracks, gave the floors a last sweeping, and then put on their brown helmet liners, snapped on their canvas cartridge belts over their field jackets, and took their rifles out of their racks. At the warning buzzer the two squads that lived downstairs formed into a tight little knot in the narrow hallway between the two Supply personnel bedrooms on either side of the front door. When the Fall Out buzzer went off, they banged through the door, raced across about twenty yards of frozen ground, and came to a halt in four rigid ranks.

"Dress right, dress!" It was a new voice coming at them from the gray mist, a sharp, clear voice. The arms swung up, and the lines inched themselves into a straighter position.

"Readee, front!" The arms snapped down.

"Second, Third, and Fourth Platoons, parade rest! First Platoon, open ranks, march!" Patrick stood there with his feet apart and his rifle out at the Parade Rest position, and every head in the Second, Third, and Fourth Platoons turned a little bit, to see the man in front of them as he bore down on the First Platoon. He was tall, taller than Sergeant Stone, and a great deal thinner, and he walked effortlessly. He started down the first rank of the First Platoon, and Patrick got a good look at him. He had a straight, almost beautiful pink face under his red helmet. He had the chevrons of Sergeant First Class on his sleeves, and his right earlobe was missing.

"It's hopeless," the sergeant said half to himself as he came to the end of the first rank he had inspected, and he broke off his inspection and walked back out into the middle of the area. "First Platoon, close ranks, march! First Platoon, parade rest. Company at ease!" He smiled. It was the first time that Patrick had seen anybody smile, standing in front of a company. "I understand this company has been doing a lot of push-ups and not much soldiering," he said in a pleasant tone of voice. He didn't seem to be speaking loud at all, but his words were sharp and clear. They seemed to be bouncing off the barracks behind the formation. "In the first rank I inspected," he went on, still smiling, "I saw two pairs of unshined boots, three poor shaves, three non-regulation sweatshirts under fatigues, and a *gray scarf*. What do you people think this is? Valley Forge?" Patrick smiled, and he could see Geremski's shoulders starting to shake with suppressed laughter in front of him. "Now it seems to me you people are not very well washed, considering the amount of water that's available." The sergeant's starched, faded, light green fatigues seemed to crackle as he spoke. "Tonight at nine o'clock I want every man standing at the foot of his bunk freshly scrubbed. The uniform for this inspection will be a clean white T shirt, a clean white pair of shorts, and shower clogs on your feet."

Somebody laughed. The sergeant just looked at them.

"You people think that's funny," he said. "Well, you are funny. You don't know what a sad-assed little bunch you are. Companee ten-hut!" They snapped to attention. "Right face! Sling arms! First Platoon leading platoon, column of twos from the left, forwaard march!"

That night, after they had been dismissed and were piling into the barracks out of the cold, one of the men who worked in the Supply Room came out of his little walled-off bedroom that opened on to the center aisle just by the front door. He was a rotund man named Scarpa, and since Patrick's bunk was next to the wall of Scarpa's little bedroom, they had occasionally exchanged a smile when they collided near the front door.

"I was watching you guys march in," Scarpa said. "What did that guy do to you? You marched like you was West Pointers."

"I don't know what it is," Patrick said, nodding in agreement as he took off his helmet liner.

"He is good," Kurna said, nodding vigorously. "I will put your rifle away, Patrick."

"Thanks, Stanley," Patrick said. They had all decided that the only way to pronounce Stanislaus was Stanley, and Kurna loved it.

"What's his name?" Scarpa said.

"Somebody told me it was O'Reilley," Patrick said.

"That's right," Maple said from where he was hanging up his cartridge belt on the foot of his bunk. Maple always spoke in an excited, compulsive way. "Clerk in the Orderly Room told me Stone's going somewhere else to be a cook.

That's what he was the whole time. His MOS is for cook."

"O.K.," Scarpa said, "but what's with this Sergeant O'Reilley? What's his secret?"

"It's just he isn't cruel," Lish Jones said.

Patrick nodded and looked at Lish. He was developing quite an admiration for this colored boy from New York. He was extremely neat and efficient, and every time he said something he went right to the heart of the matter.

"That's the Truth," Geremski said from across the aisle. "He isn't a prick. You can tell."

"Mail Call!" somebody yelled, and suddenly there was a thunder of feet on the floor above, as the third and fourth squads came tearing downstairs. Patrick strode toward the big circle that had formed around the mail clerk. Men were standing up on the footlockers, and the mail clerk, laughing and smiling, brushed a couple of men off a footlocker and got up on the brown trunk himself.

"Encarnacion!"

"Here man!"

"Johansen!"

"Here."

"Gridley!"

"Here!"

"Interlicchio!"

"Here."

"Interlicchio!"

"Here."

"Interlicchio again!"

"Here, here."

It was a joke in the platoon. Interlicchio was in Patrick's squad, and now that Ratigan was in the Fourth Platoon, Interlicchio had taken over as the bitching expert where Ratigan had left off. He always got five or six letters, and he never cracked a smile as he took them.

"Kingsgrant!"

"Here!"

"Here's another one, Kingsgrant."

Patrick took the letters and turned away. One was from Allston Hunt, and one had Anna's handwriting. He walked back to his bunk and sat down on his footlocker. Save the best for last, he said, and opened the letter from Allston Hunt. His face became grave as he read it. Hunt had sent his novel to a publisher, and it had been rejected.

"They said they believed that you could write a first-rate novel in the future," Hunt's typing said, "but they can't use 'Technical Jones.' They made a great many complimentary remarks about the style and pace of your book, but I gather that their primary objection is that they feel that the story is a limited and specialized one. As you know, I do not agree with this, and I have already sent the manuscript on to Dyer. I will let you know how things go, and I urge you not to be discouraged. I wish you all the best in the Army, and do let me know how you are. Sincerely, A. Hunt."

Patrick sat there for a few seconds, looking at the letter, and then he opened the one from Anna. Several people were going by him, out the door, but he did not even look up. Anna said that she was looking forward to having him stay at her house on his first pass, and that she wished he would tell her what kind of a Christmas present he would like. "Some people say that fur-lined slippers are the thing somebody in the Army most wants, and then others say that fur-lined slippers are a useless waste of space. So you tell me, please, PK." Then she went on to say that she had gone up to 338 East Eighty-Seventh Street and got his clothes. "Now they are all out of boxes and neatly hung up and moth-balled," Anna's script told him, "and I've sent your gray suit to be cleaned and pressed for your first pass."

"You're coming to chow, Patrick?"

Patrick looked up. Stanley was standing over him.

"Not right now, Stanley." He kept on reading, but that was really all. Love, Anna. Patrick stood up and put both the letters on the brown woolen blankets of his bunk. Then he stepped over to one of the windows along the wall of the big room where all their bunks were, and looked out. Not much of a view. Frozen grassless ground, and the First Platoon about twenty-five yards away, with its garbage cans behind it. There were a few men on the walk, going down to chow in their fatigues with the engineer's caps on their heads and a knife, fork, and spoon in their hands. Over it all there was a dull winter sky. Inside the barracks it was quiet. Everybody had gone to chow. What's she doing? Patrick asked himself. What's she doing? She feels sorry for you, he answered. Maybe she wants you back. Maybe this is what she'd do for any old friend.

"Who the hell knows?" Patrick said into the darkening squad room, and went to his wall locker. He opened it from one of the keys that hung on his neck with his dogtags. He took his knife, fork, and spoon from the shelf at the top, and shut the tall, uniform-filled locker. For some reason the news about the novel didn't bother him right now. It all seemed part of a world that was remarkably far away, and he had never really believed that this novel would be printed, not even on the hottest summer nights, when you had to believe that there was some good reason why you were sitting there alone with a typewriter.

But goddammit, there *will* be another novel, Patrick said to himself, turning and looking down the empty aisle of the long twilit room, with the helmets on top of the lockers and the bunks flat and the bayonets in their scabbards hanging from the belts on the bedsteads. You *will* write it, and they *will* publish it, and people *will* read it. Then he turned and went

out into the cold air, heading toward the long huddled green
mass of the chow line.

II

"On guard position. Ho!"

Patrick snarled and snapped his rifle into the On Guard
position, the point of his bayonet aimed at the throat of Gomez,
the leader of the third squad. Gomez was part Indian and part
Spanish and part Negro, and he looked like Joe Louis. He
was the most gung-ho, ambitious boy in the platoon, and his
shining coal eyes glared back over his own bayonet as he and
Patrick stood like statues, some eight feet apart.

"Short thrust and hold. Ho!"

The two ranks of men gave a concerted growl and stepped
sharply toward each other, so that their bayonets crossed like
rapiers.

"Recover."

Patrick stepped back, still measuring the distance to Gomez'
stomach under his field jacket, the distance to Gomez' brown
throat as it came up out of the brown sweater they wore
under the fatigues.

"Long thrust and hold. Ho!"

Gomez' bayonet came whipping in to a point about sixteen
inches from Patrick's throat, as Patrick's own lunge brought
his bayonet in front of Gomez' face.

"What's the spirit of the bayonet?" the instructor screamed.

"To kill!"

"Recover!"

Gomez' tense face receded. This is a great way to spend
the morning of Christmas Eve, Patrick said to himself, lining
up Gomez' throat over the tip of his bayonet again. It was

strange, the effect this bayonet training had on you. Every now and then you had a terrific temptation to keep on going through the man opposite you.

"Vertical butt stroke and hold. Ho!"

"Yaaah!" Patrick yelled as he swung the butt of his rifle up toward Gomez' jaw.

"Kill!" Gomez yelled in the middle of the growling, and they stood there, looking into each other's eyes over the shiny worn butt plates of their rifles.

Most people would have thought that the Service Club, with its sign, "Service Club Number Eight Welcomes You to the Fiftieth Infantry Regiment," would be the place to go to locate a trainee, but Jacob parked the car he had borrowed from Joe Cutter, and went into Regimental Headquarters. Inside the door of the low little office building, his eyes flicked across the various desks, and the moment that he saw the desk with a wooden plaque on it saying "Sergeant Major" he walked toward it.

"Sergeant?" he said quietly.

The old soldier looked up and saw a tall straight man in an overcoat, with a Homburg in his hand.

"Sir?" he said.

"I'm looking for a soldier named Kingsgrant. He's in Company B."

"Do you know if he's cadre, sir?"

"He's a recruit."

"Just a minute." The soldier picked up the telephone on his desk while Jacob studied the six stripes of Master Sergeant that were on the man's arm. "This is Sergeant Connor, Regimental. Have you got a trainee named Kingsgrant available down there?" He waited for a minute. "Well, when they come in, you tell him he has a visitor at the Service Club. Just a minute." He turned toward Jacob. "You don't want him brought in out of the field, do you, sir? They're all coming in in a few minutes anyhow."

"That's fine, Sergeant," Jacob said.

"Send him over when he comes in," the sergeant major said into the receiver, and hung up. "The Service Club is just down the road."

"I saw it coming in. Thank you again, Sergeant."

"Yes, sir," the soldier said, and turned back to the work on his desk. Jacob went down the steps, got into his car, and drove down to the Service Club. He parked in the lot beside the big cream-colored frame building, and got out. The Christmas sky was gray, gray clouds hanging low over the little barracks city across the road from the Service Club. Jacob stood looking at the sheds and barracks and the abbreviated spire of the chapel beyond Regimental Headquarters. He reached back inside the car and pulled out a package, and then he heard something. There was a woods about a quarter of a mile away, across a large field, and there seemed to be some shouting going on in there. As Jacob watched, a man with a flapping dark guidon came striding down a path in the woods, and a column of twos came straight behind him. The men were wearing their green fatigues and field jackets, with their helmet liners and their boots looking dark in contrast to the fatigues, and they were carrying their rifles slung over their shoulders. As Jacob watched, a man in a red helmet came walking out of the woods beside them. The man in the red helmet would shout something at the column of men, and they would shout something back at him. This column swung briskly out of the woods, and then another platoon in a column of twos came along about twenty yards behind, flanked by another red dot of a helmet. Jacob stood there even straighter than usual, and watched them come toward him. There were four platoons in view now, swinging along, and Jacob could hear the words in the singsong shouts.

"GI beans and GI gravy," the cadreman sang out.

"GI beans and GI gravy!" the platoon roared back.

"Gee I wish I'd joined the Navy!"

"Gee I wish I'd joined the Navy!"

"Am I right or wrong?"

"You're right!" the platoon yelled, hitting it with their right feet.

"Sound off!"

"One two!"

"Sound off!"

"Three four!"

"Break 'em on down."

"One two three four. Onetwo — threefour!"

The platoon went by and the next platoon came along.

"I've got a gal in Kansas City!" — a tall cadreman, strutting.

"I've got a gal in Kansas City!"

"She's got a pimple on her titty!"

"She's got a pimple on her titty!"

Jacob smiled and watched the column of men as they brought their rifles to port arms and ran across the road, just to the left of where he was standing. These four platoons passed by, and then Jacob saw another company coming across the bare field.

Rodriguez yelled "Count cadence, count!" and Patrick and Geremski, at the head of the platoon, bellowed with the others, "One two three four. One two three four!" They were marching across the field toward the barracks city, marching fast and willingly because they were heading for food and this Christmas Eve afternoon off. They came toward the Service Club, and Patrick noticed a lone civilian standing in the parking lot, beside a car. Then suddenly his eyes focused on the civilian, and his heart gave a jump. He straightened up even harder, and he and Geremski marched past Jacob.

Sergeant O'Reilley had gone into the Orderly Room after leaving them in formation at ease, and now he came back down the steps of the little building, some papers in his hand, and cracked, "Ten-hut!" The ranks snapped their rifles in to their sides. "Parade rest! At ease." The ranks relaxed. "The following EM," he read, standing in front of Baker Company, "will report to Weapons Pool at fourteen hundred hours. Ascanio, Baker, Bernardo, Botticelli, Cleary, Dzurak, Edwards, Ehrlich, Ericson, Farmer, and Forlenza. Private Gomez will march the detail to the Weapons Pool." Sergeant O'Reilley folded up that piece of paper and looked at a smaller piece of paper. "Private Kingsgrant is ordered to report to the Service Club. You have a visitor. Probably a lot of the rest of you have visitors over there too." O'Reilley looked at his men. "Well," he said, making a little ball out of the smaller piece of paper, "except for the men on Weapons Pool and KP, you people are off the rest of today and all of Christmas tomorrow. There *will* be a roll call out here tomorrow morning at nine o'clock. That's all. Ten-hut! Platoon sergeant dismiss your platoons."

O.K., Patrick thought, yelling as he ran into the barracks a minute later with his rifle at port arms, you *will* go to the Service Club.

Jacob was standing outside the Service Club when Patrick got there.

"Well," Jacob said, and stuck out his hand. Patrick took it, and they both stood there for a minute, shaking hands, and looking at each other. "Merry Christmas, Patrick," Jacob said, holding out the package that he held in his other hand.

"Well, thank you," Patrick said. "Merry Christmas. I'm afraid I didn't have time to get you anyth — "

"Open it," Jacob said. "And — we don't have to go back in there, do we?" He pointed toward the Service Club with his thumb. "It's awfully crowded."

"I'll bet it is," Patrick said, opening the package. It was a rifle-cleaning kit for a .30 caliber rifle, from Abercrombie & Fitch. It had a cleaning rod that broke down into three parts, and some oil and patches and a bore brush and some solvents. Patrick's face was one delighted smile.

"I remembered we never used to have enough rods to go around," Jacob muttered, "and the ones we did have got broken."

"My God," Patrick said. "It's perfect. We never get enough of any of this stuff. It's perfect." He handed the package back to Jacob, and screwed the three parts together, handling it as if it were a foil or a fly rod. "You don't know how many people have to share the rods we *do* get."

"Well, you'll probably have to share this one too."

"The hell I will," Patrick said, still admiring the cleaning rod. Jacob looked at him and smiled. They both began strolling around the field across which Jacob had seen the two companies march in half an hour before.

"How're the bugs?" Jacob said.

"What bugs?"

"Vermin. Lice."

"We don't have any. At least I haven't heard about them."

"If they had any, you'd have heard about them by now. You don't know how lucky you are." Jacob looked at his watch. "You didn't get lunch before you came over here, did you?"

"No, Father."

"Is there a place we can go together?"

"Well, there's a place called the PX cafeteria. I haven't been there myself, but I understand it's a lot better than we can do anyplace else around here."

"Why don't we go there?"

"Fine."

They both turned and headed back toward the car that Jacob had borrowed for the day.

Patrick stared into the darkness just after the lights went out. From the latrine came the sounds of two harmonicas making their way through "Silent Night." Patrick lay in his bunk, thinking about his father. Jacob had left at the end of the afternoon, but Patrick still felt his presence. They had eaten at the PX cafeteria, and then they had come back to the Regimental Area and walked around. Patrick had shown him the PX, and the chapel, and they had come to the barracks. The rifle racks had been unlocked to let some of the men clean their weapons, and Patrick had handed Jacob his rifle.

Jacob had wrapped his hands around the rifle and studied it for a moment.

"Is this the action?" He took his right hand off the rifle and pointed at the operating-rod handle.

"That's right," Patrick had said.

"Do I have to take the safety off?"

"Either way."

Jacob had nodded and pulled the bolt back with a quick, controlled motion, and then stood there, looking the whole rifle over, tilting its butt upward toward the electric lights to inspect the bore, turning it over to look for rust particles in the two swivels that held the sling, and then handing it back to him.

"You keep it pretty clean," he had said, and Patrick had beamed. Now he turned in his bunk, still looking up at the ghostly white wood of the ceiling in the darkened barracks room. It had all gone much better than he would have dreamed it could. There had been no talk about the past, and no talk about what he was going to do with his life, and no talk about coming home. They had compared notes on their letters from Eileen, and, since he saw that Patrick was really interested, his father had told some stories about the Army that he had never told before. And then he had driven back to New York.

Patrick felt the need to visit the latrine before going to sleep, so he slid out of the tight blankets and swung his legs over the side. Then, sticking one foot against the wall of Scarpa's room, he lowered himself quietly, so as not to disturb Lish Jones. He put on his shower clogs and scuffed his way down the linoleum aisle as quietly as he could. Despite the heavy wool underwear, it was freezing cold in the barracks.

As he came into the latrine, the two harmonica players gave up on Christmas carols, and one of them swung into "Lay That Pistol Down, Babe." There was a boy sitting on top of one of the bowls, writing a letter, and Rodriguez was in there brushing his teeth.

"Merry Christmas, there, Kingsgrant," Rodriguez said, when Patrick came over to the sink to dash some water on his hands.

"Merry Christmas, Sarge."

Rodriguez smiled and wiped his face with an olive-drab towel. It was a study in olive: the towel, and an olive under-shirt that he had acquired in his Army travels, and the muscles rippling under the olive skin of his arms as he wiped his handsome face.

"O.K.," he growled at the harmonica players, looking at them in the mirror, "let's put it away for tonight, huh? And Merry Christmas."

"Merry Christmas, Sarge," everybody said, and they all trailed out of the latrine, except for the boy who was sitting there, writing a letter.

III

By about ten o'clock of the Friday morning after Christmas, Patrick was so fed up with the M-1 rifle that he felt like weeping. They had been coming out to the rifle range every day of the week, starting off in total darkness and spending the days lying on the frozen ground in the biting wind. The week had been one long unhappiness for Patrick. The first day out here the pain from that stab inside his left shoulder had come back again, and it had not left him since. There was that, and the incessant wind flaying the long line of prone men in pale green, and there was his rifle. His rifle would not fire semi-automatically. Everybody else's rifle fired every time you pulled the trigger, but even after the Armorer had looked at it, his had to be cocked before every round.

"Ready on the right. Ready on the left." The words of the loudspeaker on the tower faded in and out on the wind, and Patrick got down in the kneeling position for this exercise. "Ready on the firing line." There was a pause. "Lock and load one clip of ball ammunition." Patrick began struggling to get his clip into the rifle. It was terribly hard for him, because he did not have enough strength in his right hand. It was such a simple thing, just hold back the bolt with the back of the hand, and ram the clip down with the thumb into the weapon against the pressure of the springy metal bridge, but it was hard for Patrick.

"You have thirty seconds to complete the exercise. The flag is up, the flag is waving, the flag is down. Commence firing!"

All of the targets came up out of the pits, two hundred yards away, and a blast of fire greeted them. Patrick was still struggling to get his clip into his rifle.

"Go get 'em!" the cadremen were yelling, and the rifles were blazing away. Patrick finally got the rifle loaded and brought it up. He located his target, lined up the bull's eye on top of the front sight post, tried to center the whole picture inside the circle formed by the aperture of the rear sight, held his breath, and squeezed off the round. Then he whipped his rifle down off his shoulder, and cocked it again, while the men on either side of him kept slamming away, never taking their rifles down. He had fired three of the eight bullets in his clip when the range officer's voice came over the loudspeaker with a long drawn-out, "Cease fiyah!"

There were the inevitable one or two reports just after the command, and then silence along the firing line.

"Alibis," the voice from the tower said. "You have fifteen seconds to complete this exercise. Commence firing!" Patrick brought his rifle up to his shoulder, and squeezed off a round. His shoulder was hurting badly, with an inflamed feeling in the area between his shoulder blade and his neck, and little flaming strings that went up into his neck, and out to the point of his shoulder. He had sweat in his eyes, and he was teetering in this kneeling position that required you to sit on your heel, but he got his target lined up and fired, and cocked and fired again in one timeless controlled rage, and when the command "Cease firing!" came, he squeezed off the last round even though he wasn't sure he had any sight picture at all, and heard the clip go *ting*-ing out of the rifle as the weapon threw it away.

Woodrow Wilson was standing behind Patrick.

"That don' look much like the correck kneelin' position," he said. There was no rancor in his voice.

"I've got a bad knee," Patrick said. "I can't get my heel all the way up under."

"You're *all* screwed up, ain't you?" Woodrow Wilson said in that same dispassionate voice, and made his way on down the line.

IV

Jacob was not angry about a damned thing. That's what he told himself as he walked through Central Park after the early din-

ner that he had had at the University Club. It was dark, and
Jacob was not given to walking in Central Park at night. He
had gone into the University Club and up to the dining room
and then, just about halfway through his meal, he had started
to get angry. It had come to him, as it might come to a man
from the State of Maine, by thinking about practical things.
He was sitting there at the University Club, eating alone as he
had a hundred times before, about to go home to an apartment
where he had lived since 1930, when suddenly he had become
furious. First of all he thought about the maid who was sitting
at home, perfectly ready to cook dinner for him except that for
some reason he had decided it might be more pleasant to eat
down here, and his conscience bothered him about that. Then
he thought about the apartment, two whole floors sitting there
to receive him for a few hours tonight and release him tomorrow
morning, and he winced again. Somehow this brought him to
Patrick, and he thought about how things were with Patrick,
and there was no comfort there. Eileen was in Europe having
a good time. She was very good about writing, and Jacob was
glad that she seemed happy. Then, just as he finished his
entrée, Jacob realized what was wrong. Everything was wrong.
He didn't like rattling around in the apartment. He had moved
into that apartment with Maude and Patrick, and he had lived
there with Maude and Patrick and Eileen, and they had all left
him: Jacob had very rarely felt sorry for himself, but right
now, striding north across the Mall, his rage was simmering
down into an acute case of missing Maude. That autumn after
she had died, he had often walked in the Park. Sometimes he
would walk for hours where they had walked together, and
every step of the way he felt like crying. Eventually he had
been able to think a few thoughts, and even thoughts about
other things. That had not been feeling sorry for himself.
That had been grieving, the dog still looking for its dead master,

and there was a world of difference. Within a year or two
Jacob had been able to enjoy the Park for itself again, but
tonight he was moving through it as if he hated everything
around him. Jacob never thought about whether he was having
a good time, or a bad time, or a mediocre time. He had his
work, and he had Patrick and Eileen, and that was that. Now
it was being borne in on him, all at one moment, that he
was having a damned bad time. He was unhappy, and he had
been unhappy for quite a few months, not just unhappy about
Patrick's view of life, or unhappy about Eileen's absence, but
fundamentally, all the way around unhappy.

Jacob crossed the road at the end of the Mall and began
walking down to the pond where people sailed their toy boats
in the summer and in the spring. His pace was slowing down
a bit, and he was trying to be reasonable with himself. He
was asking himself, almost as if he were an amnesia victim, how
it happened that he, Jacob Kingsgrant, should be walking from
a solitary dinner downtown to a quiet, nicely decorated apartment best suited to the needs of a family of at least four people.
He went right back to the beginning. Maude. Maude plus
Patrick's arm. Then they came to New York. Maude and
Patrick at home, and Lee and Cutter and some of the others
downtown. Jacob was walking along beside the sailboat pond,
his eyes taking in the reflection of the lights on the ice. He
realized that that was really what had kept him unquestioningly
riveted to 1120 Park. He wanted to be near Maude, or rather
he wanted to be where he had spent so much time with Maude.
That plus something in him that often said, That which is, is
good. But tonight that which is was no good, and even though
Jacob had slowed down to a leisurely pace as he went over the
bridge at Seventy-Ninth and headed around behind the Museum,
he kept turning his dissatisfaction over in his mind. You're
angry at nothing, he said to himself. Maude certainly didn't

want to leave you, and Eileen is only gone for a year, and Patrick, well, Patrick has to work out things for himself. You're getting into a stew about nothing, he said to himself as he kept on walking home, but one part of Jacob's usually unanimous thoughts kept whispering, I'm not convinced. Of course you're probably correct, but I'm not absolutely convinced.

Jacob woke up and lay there looking at the white ceiling of his bedroom. He blinked his eyes once or twice and then kept on staring upward, trying to remember the dream from which he had awakened. He and Ben had been fixing something on the boat. Jacob thought for another minute, and then he decided that that was all there had been to the dream. He and Ben had been fixing something on the boat, and Ben had been smiling and laughing. Jacob lay on his back for another minute, and then he sat up, pulled the pillow up behind him, and leaned against the headboard. He just sat and let the sudden knowledge of what he was going to do hit him and engulf him. He was going to get rid of the apartment. That was simple. The management of the building had been dying to get this apartment and cut it up into two apartments. Then he was going to remove Kingsgrant from Cutter, Kingsgrant, and Lee. That was going to be harder. Jacob realized, looking at the window across the room, that that was going to be his one regret in leaving New York. It was going to be harder, and occasionally he would miss the big fees and the big cases and the big clients, but it was going to be. Then he was going back to Kingsgrant, and practice law with Rolly Grindall.

"My God," Jacob said out loud, grinning into the darkness of his bedroom. "My God." He snuggled down happily into his bed and fell asleep a few minutes later, a peaceful smile on his face.

V

Patrick woke up and looked at his wrist watch. It was two o'clock in the morning, they were out on bivouac, it was freezing inside the pup tent, and he had to go to the latrine. He began the acrobatic feat of getting out of his sleeping bag without knocking down the two little tent poles that separated him from the sleeping form of Interlicchio. Finally he was out of the sleeping bag, and, like a great crab, he turned himself around so that he was crawling on all fours past Interlicchio's feet to the entrance of the tent. He felt in the darkness for his combat boots and got them on, fumbling with the laces. He was so cold that his teeth were chattering and he was shivering, not goose-pimple shivering, but big, body-shaking shivers. Finally he had his boots laced halfway up, and then he began feeling in the darkness again. He had been sleeping with his field jacket on, but he still needed to find his rifle, cartridge belt, and helmet. He rolled the helmet out under the tent flap at the foot of the tiny tent, and threw the cartridge belt after it. Then, hugging his rifle close to him, he crawled out under the tent flap, onto the frozen earth. Patrick stood up in the cold fog, put on his helmet, hooked on his cartridge belt, and, slinging the rifle over his shoulder, started the two-hundred-yard walk to the latrine. The whole bivouac was tactical. That meant that you carried your rifle in the chow line, and on your way to the latrine, and you kept it with you in the stands during the outdoor classes. They said rifles will be carried at all times, and they meant at all times.

Patrick made his way carefully down the foggy avenue that separated the tents of the first squad from the tents of the second squad. The other night he had knocked over the tent that belonged to Forlenza and a new transfer named Hetzler, and although they had been remarkably pleasant about it, he didn't want it to happen again. Patrick smiled even through his shivering as he walked past the low, snoring little tents. It was a little too much to say that they all loved each other, but it was certainly true that out here, three miles straight out into the pine woods from anywhere, they were all trying to help each other. The only exception was Jakes, one of the two Virgin Islanders in the squad. Jakes had been far from eager even back in the barracks, but out here he had been hopelessly un-cooperative, never cleaning his rifle and always moving in slow motion. After the first two days of it Patrick had seen the squad watching him. Squad leader was an unofficial rank, and another squad leader could be appointed in your place at any time. Patrick had given Jakes a direct order to clean his rifle, and when Jakes had hesitated, Patrick had reported him to Rodriguez. Rodriguez had taken Jakes for a little walk, and when they came back Jakes could hardly wait to clean his rifle.

Patrick passed by a sentry who was walking around the Mess tent, the bayonet on the end of his rifle a weird white spike in the foggy night. He was on the trail through the bushes to the latrine now, and as he walked along his shoulder ached in the dampness. This week the shoulder had been worse than it was on the rifle range, shooting a variety of pains at him at unexpected times. Sometimes he could do twenty push-ups without any real pain, and then, just twisting open the stopper of his canteen, a blade of pain might hit him and leave him gasping. The hell of it was that his left shoulder was his good shoulder, so that there was no question of favoring it.

"Who's there?" a voice said on the trail in front of Patrick. Patrick had been lost in a sort of shivering dream, and now he looked up from the trail and saw that the little wooden latrine building was in front of him.

"Kingsgrant," he said.

"It's me, Pat," a voice came back. It was Ratigan, just

coming out of the screen door of the little hut. "Colder'n a witch's tit, huh?"

"You're damned right," Patrick mumbled. He needed to go to the latrine badly, and he brushed past Ratigan and went inside.

VI

Anna stepped out of the taxi and walked up the steps of her house, feeling pleasantly self-righteous. She had taken a volunteer job in the afternoons, reading to sick people at hospitals, and she had spent the last couple of hours reading to an old woman in a ward at Lenox Hill. There was television in most of the wards, but some people still preferred a person who read aloud.

Anna opened the door with her key, and walked into the hall. She saw a letter on the table, a letter with a big square of initials and numerals in the upper left-hand corner, and her heart beat faster. She took off her coat, and then scooped up the letter and walked into the living room. The big room was dark in the winter afternoon, and she turned on the light beside the sofa. Then she sat down and tore open the letter. "Dear Anna," Patrick's handwriting said, "this letter is really an act of love. We are out on bivouac, sleeping in pup tents, and I'm writing this in the combined light of a can of Sterno, one candle, one flashlight, and the shiny teeth of Private Interlicchio, who shares this tent with me. Until you have seen two full-grown men clean two full-grown rifles at night in a tent seven feet long, three feet high, and four feet wide, you haven't seen anything. We have everything in the tent with us, packs, gas masks, sleeping bags, rifles, shovels, the whole works, and it is no place for a man with claustrophobia." Anna sat there, alone in the high-ceilinged room, and shook her head as she read on. "Anyhow, I am going to give this to the truck driver who is our one link with civilization, and hope that he will mail it. The stamp I got, of course, from Stanley, who is the man that has writing paper, foot powder, and a *nail file* out here with him in the bush. We stay out here for three more days, running through field problems and listening to lectures from five in the morning until ten at night, and then they're going to walk our remains in on Saturday morning. If all goes well, I'll be in New York by five that afternoon, still ready to take you up on the offer of staying at your place, if that's agreeable with you. I was wondering if you could arrange for me to see a doctor late Saturday afternoon, or Sunday afternoon, or almost anytime over the week-end. Love, Patrick."

Anna put down the letter and stared straight ahead at nothing for a minute. Something's wrong. Don't be silly, it could be some extra something he needs for his OCS application. No, something's wrong. Well, at least I can get him a doctor. Anna looked down at the letter, looking at it as if she could learn something more from it just by staring at the paper. He's coming. All right, Anna said to herself, he's going to be here and you want him here, but then what? I don't know. Well, it's your *business* to know, part of her mind snapped back. You can't just start this thing up again irresponsibly. All right, Anna said back, I don't know why I want to see him, but I want to see him. I tried to forget him and it didn't work and I just want to see him, that's all. I just do.

Anna's mother came into the room.

"Oh, there you are," she said, turning on another light. "Would you like some tea, dear?"

VII

Jacob had had no idea of what his resignation was going to do to his two partners. They had practically suspended getting out their work, and they had been cross-examining him all week. The first phase of running around like chickens with their heads cut off had subsided, and now Henry Lee was pacing up and down Jacob's office with an injured look on his face.

"Jake," he said for the hundred and tenth time in the past five days, "there must be something you're not telling me."

"No, there isn't."

Henry Lee stopped and looked at Jacob. Jacob was sitting at his desk as he had for the past twenty years, except that now he was reading a memorandum on one of the last matters that he would be handling for Cutter, Kingsgrant, and Lee. "I can't believe it," he said. "People just don't do things like this."

Jacob put down the little typewritten sheet he was reading. "For God's sake, Hank," he said, his expression halfway between impatience and a smile, "I'm an attorney. You don't have to live in New York to be an attorney."

"How do you think you're going to like arguing two-bit cases up there?"

"I think I might like it pretty well," Jacob said, leaning back in his chair.

"Well, leave your practice out of it, then. Everything you've got is here."

Jacob smiled and shook his head. "You're wrong about that, Hank. Everything I've got is not here."

16

PATRICK CAME OUT of the Port Authority building as if he
had been shot from a gun, and jumped into the first taxi he saw.

"Seventeen West Eleventh Street," he said, settling his AWOL
bag beside him on the seat, and the taxi moved away from the
curb and out onto the rainy avenue. He put his nose next to the
window and kept feasting on the color and variety of everything he saw, feasting as he had at the window of the bus that
had brought him up from Fort Dix.

"That's a Ninth Division shoulder patch, i'n it?" the driver
said, as they started the slow trip across the crowded midtown
streets.

"That's right," Patrick said.

"I had a cousin in the Ninth Division," the driver said. "They
was a pretty tough gang. How long you been in?"

"About six weeks," Patrick said, still staring at the neon lights
and the streetlights and the mannequins in the windows.

"You look like you been in about six years."

Patrick smiled at the face that was scrutinizing him in the
rear-view mirror. "I'm in training," he said.

"I believe it," the driver said. "You even got a tan."

Patrick toyed with the idea of explaining that he meant Basic
Training, not training for a team, and then he let it go and went

on looking out of the window of the cab. It had started raining just as they were knocking down their pup tents and making their packs, and the whole thing had been a nightmare of cold hands trying to buckle wet, sandy, canvas straps around wet, sandy, blanket rolls, and Rodriguez yelling "Saddle up! Saddle up!" It was the same rain that was still falling, but in the meantime he had marched in with his shoulder flaming under the pack, and changed, and taken the bus, and here he was. To be inside and warm and dry. It seemed a small thing to ask, until you were outside and soaked and freezing.

Patrick smiled as he thought of how he had begun this particular day. Sergeant O'Reilley's whistle had cut through the defensive waves of sleep around his brain, and he had reached up inside his sleeping bag to pull the inside zipper. Interlicchio had bailed out of the tent in about two seconds, and Patrick had found the zipper stuck. He had lain there twisting inside his sleeping bag, listening to footsteps running down to the reveille formation on the road behind the Mess tent, and then all had been silent outside as he struggled with the zipper. Finally it had come, and he had arrived down at the edge of the woods still buckling on his cartridge belt, to see the company standing at attention. Sergeant O'Reilley had turned as though sensing a straggler, and told him to drop down for fifteen. But Patrick still had to smile when he thought of himself writhing inside that sleeping bag as the last footsteps went pounding past his tiny tent.

"Here y'are, buddy," the driver said, and Patrick looked out of the window and saw the front door of Anna's house. Here he was, all right. Patrick reached into his pocket and brought out three quarters and a dime and a nickel. He gave it all to the driver. It was too much, but it didn't make any difference. He had his month's pay of sixty-eight dollars in his pocket, and he didn't care how fast he spent it.

"Thanks a lot," the driver said. "Good luck."

"Thanks." Patrick went up the brownstone stairway in the rain and rang the bell. He felt a tightness in his throat.

The door opened. Anna was standing there, smiling. She was wearing a dark brown wool dress, and her hair was shining.

"Hi," she said.

"Hello, Anna."

"Come on in."

"I will."

He walked into the warmth of the house, and took off his coat in the hall. Then he followed Anna into the living room, feeling a carpet underneath his feet for the first time in six weeks.

"You look wonderful," Anna said. She looked at him in his uniform almost as if she had never seen him before. "You've lost some weight, and you've got a terrific color in your face."

"You don't look so bad either," Patrick said, smiling at her. He sat down on the sofa and Anna sat down in an easy chair, tucking her feet up under her. It was dim in the room, and her hair glowed a soft dull gold in the rainy afternoon. Patrick kept looking at her, and he felt a strange sadness. It was so quiet in the room.

"Would you like a drink, PK?" Anna said after a minute.

"I don't think so, Anna. Not until after I see a doctor, if you've been able to get one for me."

"I've got one, all right." Anna looked at her watch. "We might as well get up there. He's up at Lenox Hill."

"You don't have to come."

"I'd just as soon," Anna said, and stood up.

The doctor examined Patrick, and then sent him in to be X-rayed. When Patrick came out, slipping his dogtags on their little chain around his neck again, he said, "What do you think it is, doctor?"

"Well," the doctor said, "of course the X-rays might conceivably show up some bone injury in the neck or in the spine, but as far as I can judge you've torn just about everything there is to tear from the cervical spine area — " he put his hand on the side of Patrick's neck, "right out to the point of your shoulder." He paused for a second. "You probably overloaded your left side those first few days of digging and things to compensate for your right arm, and then you gave it that one first pull, and I think you probably tore a couple of things right off your spine, and that fist you were talking about — you remember mentioning that fist in there?" Patrick nodded soberly. "Well, I think that fist is a combination of the torn muscles tensing up, and the muscles around it tensing up to try and protect the torn ones. What something like this needs is absolute rest."

Patrick smiled. "Well, I'm not in a very good place to give it that."

The doctor pursed his lips. "Look. I'll send you the X-rays, but right now I think I ought to shoot some Novocain in there. It might relax those torn fibers and give them a chance to heal. Just sit down over there."

Patrick sat down in a white metal chair, and the doctor began to prepare the hypodermic.

"Do you think you could give me some pills for the pain?" Patrick said.

"I'll give you something. How bad has the pain been?"

"Pretty bad, sometimes. I've never felt anything worse."

The doctor nodded. "I'm not sure you ought to be in the Army in the first place, with that lack of development in your right arm."

"Well, I'm in."

"Enlisted, I suppose?"

"As it happens, I did."

The doctor nodded again and came toward Patrick with the hypodermic.

"Well, I hope they can do something for you down there," he said. "There's only so much we can do for you from here."

After he had taken a long shower in water that got hot and stayed hot, Patrick emerged, dried himself off, and marched to the closet where Anna had hung up his civilian clothes. He ran his hands over the soft material of the gray flannel trousers and his two sports coats, and finally he decided to put on his gray worsted suit. The house was quiet, and down below dinner was being prepared. Patrick looked around the room. It was high-ceilinged, like all the rooms downstairs, and he had his own closet, and a bathroom of his own. Across the hall there was Anna's playroom-study, with bookshelves and phonographs, and a soft couch. It was like having an apartment of your own. There was a shower running on the floor below him. That would be Anna, getting ready to dress for the evening. Patrick went over to the window and looked out, just standing in his T shirt and shorts. It had stopped raining. Even though he was out of it now, indoors, he was glad that it had stopped. He went over to a bureau, opened a drawer, and found all his civilian shirts lying there. He picked a fresh-looking white one, and put it on. It felt light and soft. Then he slipped into the trousers. They felt soft and loose-fitting, like something a Turkish prince would wear. In a couple of minutes Patrick stood in front of the mirror, fully dressed. He had had to buckle his belt two notches tighter than before he had gone in the Army, but the whole effect looked pretty good to him. Standing there, staring into the mirror at the gray suit and the dark patterned tie, he was swept by a wave of nostalgia for what had been before. How little he had appreciated it. On the rifle range ten days before, at a moment when they had been doing squat jumps with their M-1's over their heads because somebody had decided that they looked a bit idle, the boy next to Patrick had gasped, "Jeez, and

I used to complain when my mom sent me down to the corner for a loaf of bread." Patrick looked into the mirror for another moment, seeing a montage of Harvard and Kingsgrant and 1120 Park Avenue, comfortable rooms, warm rooms, warm showers. He turned out the light in the room and started down the stairs. Halfway down the first flight he heard a vague jingle, and then he realized that he was still wearing his dogtags. He smiled into the soft light of the stairway and went on down. Mrs. van Neerdaam was mixing herself a drink in the living room.

"Patrick," she said, smiling, and they shook hands. "Don't you look well."

Patrick mumbled something which came out eventually as yes, he'd love a scotch and soda. They both fussed around making his drink, and when Patrick put it to his lips he thought it was almost worth not drinking for six weeks, just to have the first one taste that way. He could taste every bit of the scotch, all the way through, and the tickle of the bubbles. It was quite something after all the wholesome milk, and the Army coffee.

"Wow," he said, aloud, and Mrs. van Neerdaam saw him grinning at his glass and laughed. There was a rustle at the doorway, and Anna walked into the room. She was wearing a black dress. Of course she'd wear a black dress, Patrick thought, of course she would.

"You look terrific, Anna," he said, and she smiled and bowed her head. Mr. van Neerdaam came in a moment later, and he and Patrick shook hands.

"Army doesn't seem to be hurting you a bit," Mr. van Neerdaam said. He had spent the Second World War with a Navy staff at Pearl Harbor. "Damn good branch, the Army," Mr. van Neerdaam went on, as if it were tacitly understood that the Navy and Marines were superior, and now somebody had to say something to the Army man in the corner. "Not too much *esprit de corps*, but they get the job done."

Patrick was trying to think of what to say to that when dinner was announced.

"Bring your drink to the table, Patrick," Mrs. van Neerdaam said, and a minute later they were seated in the dining room, Mr. and Mrs. van Neerdaam at opposite ends of the table, and Patrick and Anna across from each other. A blonde in a black dress, Patrick was thinking. There ought to be a law.

"Going to be an officer, Patrick?" Mr. van Neerdaam asked.

"Well, I've got an application in for OCS, sir."

"Do they have any direct commissions these days?"

"None that I've heard of, sir," Patrick said, and addressed himself to his soup. Every time he looked around he felt that somehow the room was sparkling. There were flickering shadows from the candles on the table, and the silver and the linen seemed to glow. Patrick finished his soup and saw Anna smiling at him. She was smiling, but she had no idea. She had no idea of how cold he had been, and how sleepy, and how tired. He wondered if the one scotch and soda was making him drunk. It was perfectly possible. He decided to make the treacherous thought drop down and give him twenty, and then he noticed the extra crystal glasses at each place. Mrs. van Neerdaam saw him looking at the goblet before him.

"I thought we'd have champagne for the returning hero," she said. Some hero, Patrick thought. For a moment he saw himself again, stuck inside his own sleeping bag as the footsteps went on past, and he smiled.

"That's terribly nice of you, Mrs. van Neerdaam," he said.

At about ten-thirty that evening Patrick was sitting at a table in the Stork Club. After dinner he had held his breath, waiting to see if Mr. van Neerdaam required a game of billiards, but evidently that had been taken care of earlier in the day. Anna had asked him if he wanted to stay at home or go out, and Patrick had answered that he wanted to go out. He wanted to take Anna to the Stork Club and dance and have a million scotch and sodas, and he was doing just that. A minute before, a friend of Anna's had asked her to dance, and Patrick was sitting at the little white-covered table alone, smiling down at the tablecloth. It was all as he remembered it from the days when he had come here during his vacations. The mirrored walls, the fast music, the good dancers, the pretty, well-dressed girls. The orchestra was playing a South American rhythm, and Patrick was glad not to be out there on the floor, attempting it. He took another swallow of his drink, smiled at Anna's half-finished bottle of beer, and looked at her as she swung around the floor in the arms of whoever-he-was. I don't see how she drinks beer and still looks like that, Patrick said to himself, and then he looked away again, around the well-dressed crowd at the tables in the bright, gay room, and shook his head. It was too much in one day. Seventeen hours ago he and Interlicchio had been knocking down their tent in a violent rain and separating it into the shelter halves that would serve as the outside of their blanket rolls. Patrick took the last swallow in his drink, and pointed at it to a waiter who nodded and went off. For the first time since he had left this afternoon, he began to think of the men who had to stay there. Only half the men of each squad could go on pass, and it was understood that the squad leader was one of them. Patrick had been puzzling over whom to let go, when Emilio Encarnacion and Clareford Jakes, the two boys from the Virgin Islands, had come up to him. They had said to let somebody else go, let somebody who could get home go, and then a minute later Stanley had come up to him and said to let somebody else go in his place too. That was the damnedest thing about the Army, Patrick thought as he looked down at his empty glass. Just about the time that you decided that the Army was the negation of everything you considered worthwhile, along came something. A man gave up his first pass out of Basic so somebody else could go home. Or Lish Jones came up and said, Man, you sure cut those corners sharp. Sharper'n Geremski. Or you saw Stanley staring at a beaten-up snapshot of a girl as he lay on his bunk just before Lights Out. You asked him who it was, and he said it was his girl. He loved her, but he was not going to be drafted into the Communist Army in Czechoslovakia. She said she would wait for him until Czechoslovakia was free. So maybe that night taking your rifle apart and cleaning it and putting it back together again made a little more sense than it did some of the other nights.

"Hi," Anna said. The young man had brought her back to the table, and she slipped into the chair beside Patrick. "How's it going?"

"Fine." The waiter brought his new drink. Patrick sat looking at her. He felt that same sadness he had felt in the quiet of her living room, the same sadness mixed with excitement that she was there. She was there, all right, flushed from the dancing, with her blue eyes sparkling and her lovely back straight in the black dress. Patrick took a sip of his drink and kept looking at her. The fairest lady in the land, he thought. And little does she know.

"Do you see Bill Bench much down there?"

"I've only seen him a couple of times. I thought we'd be getting together all the time, but we're both too busy, and then I suppose when he does get a week-end he heads for Boston."

Anna nodded, and Patrick looked at her again. He wanted to open his mouth and tell her she was with him in his thoughts, that she had been with him every day and every night of the past year. What he said was, "How about another beer?"

"Love it."

The bus was silent. Nobody on the bus wanted to be going back to Fort Dix on Sunday night. Their bodies were being carried back to the fatigues and the rifles and tomorrow morning's five-o'clock reveille formations, but their hearts and their minds were back with their families and the warmth of Sunday night supper in familiar surroundings.

Patrick's shoulder was aching. The Novocain that the doctor had given him had worn off during the day, and now that broken feeling back in there was with him again. He looked out of the window as the bus sped past a big gas station on the Jersey Turnpike. A glimpse of the plate-glass restaurant behind it, lights, and then they were in the darkness again. Patrick sat and thought about the week-end. Last night when they had got home he and Anna had sat up in her den across the hall from the guest room he was using, and they had talked. Just about little things. They were not trying to solve the world's problems, or question the necessity for the Korean War. He told her about the men, about Stanley and about how Lish Jones's wife had had to go home to her mother in North Carolina when he was drafted, and about how funny Interlicchio and Forlenza could be, with their sudden feuds and sudden reconciliations. But underneath everything had been his deep desire to take her in his arms and kiss her and maybe cry. So he just sat there, wanting to kiss her but wanting even more not to foul the thing up, and eventually she went off to bed. Patrick sat on the bus, alone with the ache in his shoulder, and thought about the good food and the good lights of the week-end. He looked down at his olive coat, and he could hear the Army coming at him.

Lock and load one clip ball ammunition   The flag is up— the flag is waving

The bus cruised through Wrightstown, still neon-bright at twelve-thirty, and then past the MP's at the gate. Everyone was standing up and buttoning Ike jackets and putting on their overcoats. Patrick reached up into the rack overhead, pulled down his brown canvas bag, and stood there in the aisle, wedged into the crowd of olive coats. Nobody said a word. The bus rolled into the asphalt space behind the mustard-yellow terminal, and a minute later Patrick stepped down into the cold starry night.

II

The pain rarely kept Patrick from sleeping, but the morning of the Thursday after his first pass his shoulder woke him up at about four o'clock, and kept him awake. Patrick lay in his bunk, feeling the coldness of the barracks on his face, and feeling his shoulder throbbing with the hot, unrelenting fist in there. He lay with his face impassive, and after a while he made up his mind to go on Sick Call. He had not been on Sick Call yet, but this was getting to be too much. Never mind if they had to drop him back to another company. He had to get this thing fixed. It was like another mouth to feed, carrying this pain around with him. It sapped his energy, and it took a lot of aggressiveness out of him. The other day when they had been throwing practice grenades and then falling face down into the snow after they had thrown them, one of the instructors had yelled at Patrick that he was hitting the dirt like a little old lady. Patrick was sure he was right, and he was sure that the instructor would hit the so-called dirt the same way if he was trying to avoid a sharp thread of pain inside his shoulder.

The front door of the barracks opened, and a moment later the Charge of Quarters switched on the lights. Patrick sat up.

"Get up," the CQ was saying as he walked down the aisle. "Rise and shine. Cold as hell outside." He disappeared up the stairs to wake up the second floor. All the men were sitting up in their bunks, each man a small stunned statue in long woolen underwear, the most enterprising of them were already beginning to creep out from under the covers. Patrick looked around once more. Then he swung out into the bitter cold of the barracks.

There was a wind whistling through the empty panes of the front
door. This was a direct result of the cadre encouraging them to
fall out so fast that they knocked the windows out of the door.
The cadre said, "Wanna see you coming out so fast you knock
out them windows," and when they obliged, Captain Hare said,
"All right, if you trainees want to be funny, you can just live
without glass in those doors." So they patched them up with
paper, and the first rain or snow took care of the paper. The
cold came up from the floor right through the woolen socks that
Patrick had worn all night in bed, and he shivered as he pulled on
his fatigue pants. As he pulled on his sweater and then buttoned
his fatigue shirt over it, he was trying to organize his thoughts.
When he made up the list to hand in to Rodriguez in twenty
minutes, he would have to remember to put himself down after
the KP's and so on, as going on Sick Call. Then he had to tell
Stanley that he was in charge of the squad for the morning.
Then he had to remember to get out the X-rays, which had
arrived by mail on Tuesday morning, and take them along to
Sick Call with him.

He sat down on his footlocker and started putting on his
combat boots. All over the barracks everyone was at about the
same stage in their dressing. Left boot tied and the trousers leg
bloused over it with a garter, boot comes down, *clunk*. Right
boot a minute later, *clunk*. All over the barracks there were
these clunking sounds, and then heads began popping up as men
got off their footlockers, opened them, grabbed their shaving
stuff and a washcloth, and started walking toward the latrine.
Interlicchio reached up on top of his footlocker, unscrewed a
bulb that hung from the ceiling, and plugged in the tiny radio
that hid in a laundry bag during the day. Everybody in the
squad except Patrick had chipped in for the radio, and Patrick
had never regretted his decision not to contribute. The music
came blaring on, Mario Lanza singing "Be My Love," and

Interlicchio gave one of his rare smiles. His face in profile was like one of the sallow-faced Venetian doges, complete with a hooked nose, while Forlenza was one big, healthy, handsome ox. They both nodded their heads appreciatively at the music, and headed for the latrine.

"How you feelin', Kingsgrant?" Lish Jones asked.

"This damn thing in my shoulder's hurting me worse than usual," Patrick said.

"Never min', Kingsgrant," Lish said, in his soft voice. "You'll be an officer pretty soon."

Patrick looked at Lish to see if he was kidding him, but Lish was just nodding his head as he finished buttoning up his fatigue shirt.

"If I do get to be an officer, I'll put in for you and make you a cook." Lish had mentioned more than once that he had been a cook on the outside, and he was sure he could cook better than what they were getting if they'd give him a chance. "That'd be fine," Lish said, grinning, and Patrick went on down to the latrine.

Evidently there was no provision for any kind of heat in the Fiftieth Infantry Regiment Dispensary. Patrick and the others from Baker Company stood in the cold linoleum-floored aisle of the little whitewashed building, while the doctor in the office at the far end took them one at a time. A couple of the medics were walking around wearing brown sweaters and fatigue shirts under their white uniforms, and one of the patients standing in front of Patrick had kept the hood of his field jacket up around his head, even though they were indoors.

The man in front of him came out, and Patrick went in, carrying his big envelope with the X-rays and the letter that had come with them. There was a Negro doctor sitting at a desk. He was tall, with captain's bars on his overseas cap, and he was wearing his overcoat rather than the white coat that hung from a peg on the wall. Patrick explained about the pains he had been having, and handed the doctor the X-rays, and the explanatory letter that had come with them.

"You shouldn' go to a civilian doctor," the captain said. He sounded angry. He took the X-ray plates out of the manila envelope and held them up to the window by his desk, one at a time. He turned them upside down, and looked at them on both sides. "I don' see nothin' anyhow," he said.

"No, sir," Patrick said. "In that letter the doctor says that if it's a tissue injury, as he believes it is, then nothing would show up, and that nothing has shown up."

The doctor took the letter out and read it. "You shouldn' go to a civilian doctor," he said again. "We'll take all the X-rays you need right here."

"Yes, sir," Patrick said. "I'm sorry, sir. It just seemed like a good chance to get it looked at."

"We'll have to take some X-rays now to proteck ourselves," the doctor said. He stood up. "Take off you shirt."

Patrick stripped to the waist and stood there, hoping that the doctor would not notice his right arm. He needn't have worried. The doctor gave him a few probes in the left shoulder with his thumb, and told him to put his shirt back on.

"You go down to the Post hospital and get X-rayed," he said. "Sergeant Singer out there can give you the slip. You ask him for some sodium salicylate too. We'll let you know if anything shows up."

Patrick stood there. Here was a man who had just seen one set of X-rays that showed nothing, and read a letter from a doctor saying that Patrick had a soft-tissue injury that would not show up on an X-ray, and all he was doing about it was sending him down to have more X-rays that would show nothing, and telling him not to come back unless there was something visible on the plates.

"Next," the captain said, not looking up from his desk. Patrick turned around and got out. He was thinking that this sodium salicylate had better be good.

III

"C'mon, tell me some more," Kentucky Adams said. He and Patrick were lying on a poncho on the BAR thousand-inch range, the automatic rifle between them. It was freezing cold, and they were holding up the firing while the instructor explained something to the cadre. Between a couple of earlier exercises, Patrick and Kentucky had been talking about one thing and another, and Patrick had mentioned his interest in writing. Kentucky had asked him about it, and now Patrick was telling him about his novel. It was surprising how easy it was to talk about it. There was no gamesmanship and no pretensions, just an honest curiosity about something a little out of the ordinary.

"Well," Patrick said, "finally the father of the girl from Boston has a real knock-down-drag-out fight with his daughter about Leapingdeer, and then she goes to Leapingdeer, and for a minute there, if he was decisive enough to elope, he could have her, but he's not that sure, and he says, look, why don't we just try to calm things down and they'll come around, and he's lost her right there. She agrees with him, but that's his highwater mark right there." They both had their heads down near the ground. "She goes back to her family, and I hope at the end you get the impression that she's licked. It was her one chance to break out of the pattern, and she was strong enough to do it if he had really supported her, but he was too young and didn't have much money, and so on."

"That sounds like a good story to me," Kentucky said. "I think it sounds just like it might happen."

"Well," Patrick said, smiling, "of course I can't give you much of an idea of it here."

"I think I get the idea," Adams said. "I like that Indian."

"So do I," Patrick said.

"Is he real?"

"I roomed with him."

"No shit," Adams said. "You think he'd take up with a girl like that?"

"I don't know," Patrick said. "I have to admit he never did."

"You got a girl?" Kentucky said, suddenly.

"Sort of."

"What do you mean, sort of?"

"I'll be damned if I know what I mean," Patrick said. "I mean I've sort of got a girl, sort of."

"Well damn, Brother Kingsgrant," Kentucky said, grinning, "I'd either have me a girl or not have me a girl."

"You've got a point," Patrick said. He was smiling as he looked out at the small paper targets twenty-six yards in front of the gun. Adams was quite a guy. He had managed to get a couple of years of college somewhere, and he had been in the merchant marine, and here he was, ready to try his hand at being a lieutenant. He and Patrick had talked over what they still had to do for OCS, but what had impressed Patrick more than anything else was the way Kentucky handled the BAR. When Kentucky was coaching and Patrick was firing, Kentucky had done everything but look through the sights for him. He had changed the clips and done everything to compensate for Patrick's awkwardness, and then, when they changed positions, Kentucky had fired the weapon as if it were a part of him. All Patrick had had to do was sit there and watch. Now he lay beside the gun, half closing his eyes against the icy wind. This cold was like his pain. In the evening, in the barracks, it was impossible to believe that it had been this cold. When the pain was quiet, and all you had was a slight inflamed feeling, as if it was broken in there, it was hard to remember how it felt when it was like a light blue neon line of pain along the edge of your shoulder blade.

"In the next exercise — " a lieutenant began yelling, and Patrick and Kentucky Adams, like dumb, frozen animals, turned their heads into the wind to hear him.

IV

Bill Bench got off the Post bus at Service Club Eight, and started walking toward Patrick's company area.

A lieutenant came around the corner, his gold bars bright in the dusk, and Bill snapped his hand up to a salute.

"Good evening," the lieutenant said, bringing his hand up sharply.

"Good evening, sir." Bill had a glimpse of the lieutenant's ribbonless chest, and then the lieutenant was gone in the evening. No Combat Infantry Badge, Bill was thinking. A lot of the people who had been overseas dispensed with wearing their ribbons around the Post, but any man who had the Combat Infantry Badge wore it. It was a light blue horizontal bar, with a silver frontiersman's long rifle on it, and it was what showed whether you had been in combat. A corporal at Fort Dix with the Combat Infantry Badge got a lot more respect from the trainees than a lieutenant without it, and it was what every trainee unconsciously looked for when he saluted an officer.

You may be sporting one of those yourself, kid, Bill said to himself as he turned the corner into the tarred street that Patrick's company was on. He was coming over here to say good-bye. It had all happened pretty fast. His company had finished Basic, and then two days ago they had told him that his application for OCS had been turned down. No explanation, and a little form letter thanking him for his interest in the OCS program. Then today his orders had come in. To Fort Lewis, Washington, for March shipment FECOM MOS 1745 Rifleman. He had two days to clear Post, a week's leave, and then back to Fort Dix to catch the troop train for the West Coast.

There was a chanting of cadence from the Baker Company Area, and suddenly the guidon bearer came out from beyond the Supply Room and did a sharp turn to the left. A double file of men came swinging out behind him in the gathering darkness. They were wearing fatigue caps, and their faces were blackened with soot. They're going on a night problem, Bill thought. Just my luck. He kept walking toward where the men were coming out. They kept coming, dead silent in the evening, with strings tied around their pants legs to keep them from flapping, and their canteens and first-aid packages removed from their cartridge belts to cut down the noise. The First Platoon went by, the only sound that of their boots hitting the tar of the road, and then the Second Platoon came out. Bill saw Patrick raise his right hand, and when he dropped his hand the platoon swung into a column left. The cadremen were marching along in the middle of the road, and the column was moving on the right-hand side of the road, so Bill started cruising along beside it, a couple of yards down the dirt bank. He looked just like somebody minding his own business, headed for the cleaner's, or the Telephone Building. He looked up. Patrick had seen him.

"You certainly look funny with your face black," Bill said in a low voice.

"Damn minstrel show," Patrick said, turning his head slightly.

They both walked along for a couple of moments, and Patrick tugged on his rifle sling to bring his rifle up to the vertical.

"I'm shipping out," Bill said, still keeping his voice hushed.

"Where to?"

"FECOM."

"No chance of another shot at OCS?"

"Nope. I just got orders this afternoon."

Patrick was silent for a moment. Then he said, "Gee, Bill."

"I've got to clear Post, and then I'm going home on my leave, so I thought I'd better get over here and say good-bye."

"It was damn nice of you to come over, Bill."

"You getting out of here this week-end?"

"We're on some damn thing called D-Force. We haven't had any passes for two weeks."

"That screws that," Bill said. "Too bad you've got this problem tonight."

"It certainly is," Patrick said.

"Cut out that chatter up there!" a voice snapped from behind them in the darkness.

"I'll see you, Patrick," Bill said.

"Take it easy, Bill," Patrick said. "Good luck."

"Thanks," Bill said, half to himself, and then he stepped all the way down the bank and let the column go on by.

v

By the second course of this particular lunch, Allston Hunt was feeling very unhappy. His friend Alfred Dyer had called him up. He was in Boston on business for his publishing house, and could Allston give him some time to talk about the Kingsgrant book? Allston could, and now he was sitting here in the downstairs dining room of Locke-Ober's, his right index finger idly pushing away at the base of a glass of beer. They had had a couple of drinks at the bar, and they were going through their beers pretty fast, and Allston had an idea that he might be getting drunk. Right now he didn't care.

"Well, look," he said, "there's no chance at all you people can see your way clear to publishing it?"

"Listen, Allston," Al Dyer said, "do you think I'd be here if I didn't think the boy had something? I say we cannot publish this book. *This* book."

"But look," Allston said, "I mean, do you think that talent will always out? I don't think this boy is going to keep on banging his head against a stone wall for ever."

"I don't know," Dyer said. "That's his problem."

"Don't be so sure. It's our problem too."

"I'll buy that," Al Dyer said. He lit a cigarette. Neither one of them was enjoying his food. "The thing is, if we brought out this book I doubt that we'd sell more than two thousand copies. I doubt that we'd sell even that. We can't afford to do it. It's as simple as that."

Allston took a swallow of his beer, and looked down at the tablecloth beside his plate. Then he brought his head up. "I want to see this book published," he said. "I don't care how, or where, or who. I think he's a good writer, and I think he's going to be important if he stays with it. Do you think it's going to be the same story everywhere?"

"You mean other houses? Yes, I do. It's a cliché, Allston. Upper middle boy falls for middle upper girl. Upper middle boy doesn't get middle upper girl. Violins, exit everybody, sadder but wiser."

"Rats," Allston said, and looked down at the tablecloth again.

"I don't see why you have to turn this into a personal matter, Allston," Dyer said, stubbing out his cigarette.

"It's not personal," Allston said, looking across the table again. "I think he's an artist. I think this book is a good book. I think it deserves to be published."

"Allston," Dyer said gently, "he is good. He is good. But if you wept for every unpublished writer you'd put the Atlantic Ocean out of business."

"Be tough," Allston said. "Go ahead, be hard-boiled about it.

This kid can be made tough too, but I want to see him be a tough writer, tough on himself and tough on his talent and tough on his work. We can turn him into a tough businessman who looks into his glass every now and then and wonders what happened, but I'd rather not."

"Goddammit," Dyer said, starting to get angry too, "this is where you people drive me crazy. We have to be idealistic all day long with you people, and enthusiastic with our salesmen, and efficient with the wholesalers, and eat, too. You can blast me for not publishing this book if you want to, but if I went around looking the facts in the face and then closing my eyes and bringing out books like this one, we'd be out of business in a year. Nobody any good would get published that way. None of them."

"All right," Allston said. "Just give me back the manuscript, will you?"

VI

It was 2.45 A.M., and Patrick was walking on guard out by an ammunition dump near the rifle ranges. He was walking along in the freezing moonlit night, tramping slowly past the low barbed-wire fence that bordered the dump. Occasionally he caught a glimpse of Stanley, who was guarding the two demonstration tanks that Fort Dix possessed.

He came to a corner and gingerly switched his rifle from his right shoulder to his left, and kept on walking down the next side of the enclosed area. The little corrugated-iron huts with the ammunition in them shone white under the moon, and a wind whistled in the stand of pine trees nearby. Patrick had the collar of his overcoat turned up, and he was wearing a sweater under the shirt of his Class A's, and his long woolen underwear, and a T shirt under the long woolen underwear, but it was all no good. The night was a freezing crackling clear February night, and the cold came down the rifle as if it was a conductor of cold, right down the rifle and through the palm of his glove and into his hand, like an icy stream. His face felt tight from the cold, and still it was a beautiful cloudless night, with the moon full and beautiful. Patrick had said quite a few prayers as he walked around under the moon, a prayer for Bill, and a prayer for his father, and one for Eileen, and half a dozen for Anna, not all of them just for Anna, but prayers that it might work out between them. Now he had stopped praying, and as he walked along, his ears listening for anything that was not the sound of wind out here on the lonely nighttime desert that spat rifle fire in the day, he was thinking about the past week. In the past week he had had his OCS physical, and his OCS interview. In the physical he had managed to keep his arm out of the way. The bone man had just been sitting at a desk, and when he asked Patrick if he had any defects Patrick said no, hoping to God that the fact that he was taking another physical meant that the New York one was outdated. The bone man had just nodded, and Patrick had gone on. In the interview there had been a major and two first lieutenants, and it had all gone pretty well, as far as he could see. They were pleasant, and, as a matter of routine, they had asked him if he had any physical defects, or if the training gave him any trouble, and he had said no, and they had gone on to ask him other questions.

He came to the next corner, brought his rifle down to port arms, looked around, did a left face, put his rifle up to right shoulder arms, and moved on again. He had a clip in his rifle, and orders to shoot anybody who kept coming toward the ammunition dump without identifying himself. So you've perjured yourself, he said to himself as he walked along, flexing the fingers of his left hand to keep them from getting stiff in the cold. I had to, he answered. If I'm making a try for OCS I have to make a real try.

Patrick thought about it. After this physical he had an A profile, instead of the B he had had from 39 Whitehall Street. Theoretically he was qualified to apply for paratroops. Here he was with an A profile, and the muscles in his left shoulder were hurting him worse than ever. This past week his neck had started to stiffen up on the left side, and there was a little clicking in there every now and then, and his fingers often got numb, even in the barracks.

There is one more thing you can do, a voice said in the back of Patrick's mind. Just withdraw your application for OCS and go down there and show them your right arm. Let them have a good look at it and they'll let you out of the Army. Even if they don't let you out, they'll give you some sort of a desk job and then maybe this thing can heal. I don't *want* a desk job, Patrick answered. I want to be a second lieutenant. I don't want a desk job, and I'm not going to show them my right arm. I volunteered for this thing and I'm not going to back out.

But the pain, another voice protested. That's all right, Patrick answered, you went looking for this thing, now you're stuck with it. But you have a point about the pain. He thought about the two weeks since he had made his one appearance on Sick Call. He had used up the sodium salicylate, which seemed to do no good at all. He wanted to go on Sick Call again, but he didn't think that doctor was going to do much good, and he might spot the arm. I think I can take the pain, Patrick said to himself. Yes, another thought said, but my God, this isn't a battlefield somewhere. This is seventy-three miles from New York, and if a man is suffering from a pain, they ought to be able to fix it.

Suddenly Patrick heard a sound. It was a motor, off in the night, and it was coming closer. In a minute Patrick saw a pair of headlights bounce off the road and into the area. He took one quick look over toward the demonstration tanks, their hulls silhouetted in the night.

"I am here, Patrick," Stanley's voice said from somewhere. Patrick smiled. That was Stanley. Right on the ball when you needed him. He was going to cover while Patrick did the talking. Patrick brought his rifle to port arms. The headlights swung to one side, and the vehicle stopped about ten yards away from him. It was a jeep.

"Officer of the Guard," a voice said, and Patrick recognized it as the voice of the Filipino lieutenant who had inspected them at Guard Mount ten hours before. He brought his rifle to present arms, and then back to port. The short officer came up to him.

"Everything quiet here?"

"Yes, sir."

"Where is the other sentry?"

"Back there, sir."

"Keeping me covered, uh?" The lieutenant smiled. "It's Officer of the Guard, sentry," he said, raising his voice.

"Come on out," Patrick said. He was thinking that he never would have thought of covering Stanley the same way. Stanley came out with his rifle at port arms, the bayonet blade catching some of the light from the headlights of the jeep.

"Do you have any special orders on this post?" the lieutenant said.

"Sir, if anything unusual happens, I'm supposed to call the Guard Hut on that telephone on the side of the Quartermaster storehouse over there."

"I see. Who guards the storehouse and the tanks?"

"That is me, sir," Stanley said.

"Do you have any special orders?"

"Sir, if there is trouble I call by the telephone that is on the warehouse side."

The officer nodded. "Carry on," he said. Patrick and Stanley came to present arms. The officer saluted, got back into his jeep, and drove off.

VII

Jacob stood in the stripped-bare library at 1120, his gaze traveling over the unfamiliar expanse of uncarpeted floor. The grass-cloth wallpaper was still on the walls, and the bookshelves stayed, but otherwise the room was empty. A gray afternoon light came in through the uncurtained windows. He had his coat on and his hat in his hand, and he was taking a last look around. The thing that had surprised Jacob was how simply it could all be arranged, once he had made up his mind. The owners had leapt at the lease just as he had thought they would, he had sold half the furniture, and the rest of his possessions were traveling north toward Maine in a moving van. He had given Eleanor, the maid, and Mary, the cook, three months' wages, and been rather amazed when Eleanor had mentioned that she had always known that he would be going back someday. He had slept last night at the University Club, said good-bye down at the office this afternoon, and now here he stood. All he had to do was give his keys to the doorman, attend the dinner that Joe Cutter and Harry Lee were giving for him, spend the night at the University Club, and fly out for Bar Harbor in the morning.

Jacob stood there, in the place where he had spent most of his married life with Maude, and then he began walking through the apartment. He went into Eileen's room and stood near the door, thinking about how it had been his and Maude's room until Maude died, and then he had traded rooms with Eileen, who loved the big bedroom. Jacob paced across the floor, hearing his footsteps loud in the room, and stopped by the windows, looking out at the view of the East River. Then he turned and looked at the room, thinking about how sweet Eileen had been about his wanting to move out. He had written that he was seriously considering it, and Eileen had written right back, saying that she thought she'd enjoy the dormitory life at Barnard next year. Jacob walked out of Eileen's room, through the bathroom and into Patrick's good-sized bedroom, the one with the southern exposure. He smiled as he walked through the room. It seemed as if there were still echoes of Patrick ringing through it, Patrick energetically banging away at a snare drum when he was a little boy, Patrick listening to the Hit Parade on Saturday night when he was at St. Bernard's, Patrick shouting something to Eileen through his bathroom door as they both dressed to go to dances at Christmastime. Jacob went out the far door of Patrick's bedroom, into the little hall that swung back around to the elevator vestibule near the door of his own room. He started to go down the stairs to see the dining room, and then he stopped. Just let it go, he said to himself. He stepped into the vestibule, and closed the door carefully behind him. He tried it once to make sure that it was locked, and then he put his hat on his head and pressed the elevator button.

Ben and Bertram were both waiting for Jacob at the airport. They bundled him into the station wagon, with Bertram driving and Ben sitting behind, and they both began talking at once. Mr. Grindall was sorry he couldn't come over, but he was in court. He'd be over tonight. The moving van had gotten there all right. Mr. Grindall had gotten Eaton's lobster boat to carry things out, and Eaton had set up a crane out on the pier at Kingsgrant, and between the launch and Eaton's boat they had gotten everything out there fast. Everything was in the barn, just where Mr. Jacob wanted it. Except for the books and the boxes of clothes. They were already unpacked, just like Mr. Jacob said. Mr. Grindall would be glad to see Mr. Jacob. They were glad to see Mr. Jacob. Everybody would be glad to see Mr. Jacob.

"You're not going away any more, Mr. Jacob?" Bertram said, as if it was not enough to have seen it in a letter.

"I'm back to stay," Jacob said, looking through the windshield at the snow-hung spruce branches along the winter road. "Maybe a few trips, but I'm back to stay."

Bertram smiled at Ben, and Ben smiled back, and they both relaxed against the seats of the station wagon as it carried them toward South Harbor.

Jacob spent a few minutes in the kitchen chatting with Harriet, and then he said he thought he'd take a look around the island. He went out into the hall, hung up his overcoat, and put on his old sheepskin-lined coat. As he sat on a chair in the hall, buckling on his overshoes, his eyes took in the piles of books from New York, unpacked and lying on the living room floor, waiting for him to put them where he wanted them. He stood up, put on his hat, and walked out the front door of the house.

There was only a little snow on the wind-swept ground, and Jacob walked across a field, through the spruce grove that held the little cemetery of his ancestors, and up through the trees that climbed the side of the bluff. His pace slowed a little as he came toward the cleared space in the woods, and he took off his hat about twenty yards before he reached Maude's grave. He came up to it and stood looking down at the mound of earth with the light frosting of snow on it, and the gravestone.

Jacob went a step forward, and took off his glove. He put his hand gently on the corner of the gravestone.

"I'm back, Maude," he said, staring down at the mound of earth, and after a minute he put his gloves and hat back on, and started up to the house.

17

BAKER COMPANY was marching out to the Bazooka Range, and suddenly the pain became unbearable for Patrick. It was a clear, sunny February morning, and most of the men were walking along with a spring in their step. For Patrick there was suddenly the flaming string, which he knew and could endure, and the long thin vertical blade. But then out of the pain on the edge of his shoulder blade a new pain started, horizontal razors that began whacking away at every step he took, as if every step was actually tearing a fiber loose in there. Our Father who art in heaven, Patrick said to himself. Our Father who art in heaven. As he marched along, carried by the swift pace of the platoon behind him, he took off his glove and fumbled in his field jacket pocket for the bottle of aspirins he carried constantly these days. Usually he took a couple at every ten-minute break for the pain, washing them down with water from his canteen, but there was no time for water now. He unscrewed the top of the bottle, marching along unevenly, and shook a handful of the white pills into the palm of his left hand. One or two fell into the sand on the side of the road, but he got his hand up to his mouth, and began chewing the pills. He chewed the bitter pills savagely, feeling the horizontal blades keep whacking in, like axes felling a tree. He could feel himself getting weaker. Dear God. Dear God, please stop it. What did I ever do to deserve this? He tried to think of other things, trying to remove his mind from his body, from what was suddenly happening to him. He tried to think of the fine people he had known, the heroic people, but it did no good. This twisting flame was here and now, and what he wanted to do was lie down by the side of the road and cower there until it went away. As he kept moving he tried to think of greater pain, of pain so bad that his was insignificant by comparison. Think of cancer, he said to himself. Think of Christ on the Cross. Yes, part of his mind screamed back in the cloud of pain that was beginning to form in his brain, but Christ was only on the Cross for a few hours. This thing has been stabbing me on and off for weeks. How dare you think you've had more pain than Christ on the Cross? I DIDN'T SAY THAT, I DON'T CARE, IT HURTS IT HURTS IT HURTS.

"Close it up there, Kingsgrant," Rodriguez said. Patrick stumbled forward to try to close up nearer to the tail end of the First Platoon. The green line of men twenty yards ahead blurred for a moment, and then they were back sharp, striding always unreachably ahead. If only we could get to where we're going. All right, something said to Patrick, if something is tearing up back by your spine, it'll tear up, that's all. It'll tear up and then — SHUT UP. Patrick was marching in a blind way, staggering forward. The whole area across his shoulder and into his neck was hot now, and there was a grating pain on the point of his shoulder, and he was trying not to swing his left arm at all as he marched. He hung on to his cartridge belt with his left hand so that his arm would not swing, and still the razor blades kept striking, and the cleats in his neck were aching now, but mostly it was the razor blades.

"I told you once, Kingsgrant," Rodriguez said, cruising alongside. "Close it up."

"Yes, Sergeant," Patrick heard his voice say.

He had no idea of how much time had passed, but suddenly they were turning off the road and marching into a cleared space in the woods, behind a wooden grandstand. The pain was throbbing, hot and throbbing in his shoulder, and a good sharp blade of it was moving down the outside of his upper arm. Like a man drugged, Patrick halted when Geremski halted, and stood there, marking time with his rifle slung on his right shoulder, while the third and fourth squads swung out of the column of twos and came up on his right.

"'Toon, halt!" Rodriguez was sounding off in his husky bark. "Ordeur arms!" Patrick reached with his left hand for the rifle sling on his right shoulder, and a huge claw suddenly hit right underneath the shoulder blade. It closed and locked, and Patrick staggered and pulled back his hand as if he had come into contact with fire. He looked over his shoulder at Stanley.

"Get my rifle off my shoulder," he said, and Stanley's capable hands brought it down and alongside him.

"Leyuft face!" Patrick turned to the left, and then he found himself walking out of the formation toward Rodriguez, who watched him come with a fascinated expression on his face.

"Sarge," Patrick said out of his ashy throat, "my left shoulder is hurting me terribly. I've got to get some help."

Rodriguez' expression turned to one of disappointment and distaste. "Go see the Field First," he said, and Patrick stepped away from him, toward where Sergeant O'Reilley was standing by a low tree.

"Sergeant," Patrick said, coming up to him, "my platoon sergeant sent me over here. I've done something to my shoulder, and I have a very bad pain." Patrick had noticed the company commander standing a few feet away, and just then Captain Hare came over.

"Man says he pulled a shoulder muscle on the way out here," Sergeant O'Reilley said.

Captain Hare took a look at Patrick's face. "I believe it," he said. "You go back in on the Mess truck, son. It'll be making its first trip out here pretty soon."

"Yes, sir," Patrick said. The claw was gone, but it felt all hot and throbbing and sticky inside there.

Patrick lay face down on a table in the Fiftieth Infantry Regiment Dispensary, feeling the heat lamp above him starting to loosen the scramble of tendons on his left side. He had arrived back in from the field after Sick Call was over and the doctor had gone, but Sergeant Singer had put him under this lamp about half an hour before, and the pain was subsiding under the heat. As he lay on the table, he was beginning to know terror for the first time in his life. He had been scared at times in the past, but what had happened out there this morning was the beginning of terror, the little animal running screaming away from the big thing hunting him down. Patrick lay with his face pressed into the white sheet on the table, feeling like a man suddenly and unexpectedly washed up on a beach in the middle of a shipwreck. For a moment the waves seem out of reach, but there is always tomorrow and the jungle.

You're better, a voice inside Patrick's head said.

What do you mean I'm better? You mean just for the moment the pain's better.

All right. That's what I mean.

But what's going to happen?

I don't know. What scares me is that you might lose your mind. This pain has got you worn to a frazzle, and all it takes is telling the wrong person to screw himself, and you're in the Stockade.

All right, just leave me alone. Tomorrow morning I'm going on Sick Call, and maybe they can do something. I hope to God they can do something.

. . .

"Captain, this is the man I was telling you about, came in yesterday all cramped up with pain," Sergeant Singer said to the Negro doctor as Patrick came forward into the room.

"You're the one went to see a civilian doctor, aren't you?" the doctor said.

"Yes, sir." Patrick's face was drawn. All night his shoulder had been throbbing in a painful knot, and the fingers of his left hand were numb.

"Well, what's the matter this time?"

"Sir, my company commander sent me in from the field yesterday because he thought I was in too much pain to stay out there."

"Take off your shirt," the captain said. Patrick stripped down quickly. "What's the matter with your right arm?" the doctor said as he stood up and stepped behind Patrick.

"Just a birth injury, sir," Patrick said, taking a deep breath. "It's all in my medical records. But it's the left side that's hurting me."

"I was goin' to say," the doctor said, examining Patrick's left shoulder, and never said what he was going to say. "Well, I can't see a thing," the doctor said after he had pushed away at the left shoulder for a few seconds. "We'll send you down to the hospital and get some X-rays."

Patrick stared at him. He wondered whether the doctor was aware that there were already two sets of X-rays, plus a written explanation that what was wrong with him was not going to show up on an X-ray, or whether the doctor was playing with him, or whether the doctor was really a doctor at all.

"Sir," Patrick said, "is there any chance that I can have a light-duty slip?"

The doctor stared at him as if he was an insect on the floor. "No. Why should you have a light-duty slip?"

"But sir, I've been in pain, and maybe if I could just rest this —"

"Easy — " Sergeant Singer said, trying to head this off.

The doctor stamped his foot on the linoleum floor. "You ain't gonna get no light-duty slip till we fin' out if there's anythin' wrong with you," he said, glaring.

"Yes, sir," Patrick said, and went out of the room.

While they were taking his X-rays down at the Post hospital, Patrick was doing a lot of fast, desperate thinking. Look, one part of him was arguing, you've done your best. Now just show them what's wrong with your arm and you'll probably get a C profile and a desk job. There must be some doctors down here who know what they're doing. Maybe you'll even get a discharge.

No, Patrick answered himself. I got myself into this thing and I'm not going to bail out because it gets a little rough.

All right, the voice said, but nobody could have bargained for this.

As Patrick got dressed after the X-rays, he had reached two conclusions. The first was that he was not going to show anybody his arm, and the second was that he still had to get some help, some rest, something to fix him up. He had to talk to somebody down here. He came out into the hall, buttoning up his field jacket, and a doctor who was a first lieutenant came by.

"Sir?"

"Yes?" The doctor stopped and gave him a friendly smile. Patrick told him the story.

"If I were you," the doctor said, when Patrick finished a minute later, "I'd just turn myself in every time the pain gets too bad. There's nothing I can do for you from here." He smiled again, and walked on.

Patrick watched him go, and then he turned and walked down the corridor toward the main entrance of the hospital. There was a sign that said CHAPEL, and Patrick looked in. The small chapel looked warm and attractive, and he went in and knelt down. He said an Act of Contrition, and then he just knelt, looking down at the warm brown wood of the pews. You've got to get hold of yourself, he said. You've got to get under control, and take it. You've taken plenty, you can take some more. I don't want to take any more, he answered back. I'll stay out in the cold with the best of them, I'll scrub the floors, I'll do any goddamned thing they tell me to, I'll go to Korea, but I don't think I can take many more mornings like yesterday.

He stood up, made the sign of the cross, and walked out of the chapel into the hallway. There was a chaplain coming down the hall, a fatherly-looking captain. He smiled at Patrick, and Patrick stopped.

"Sir?"

"Yes?"

Patrick told him the story, his eyes fixed firmly on the silver cross that was on the collar of the chaplain's uniform.

"I can't do anything for you," the chaplain said. "You'll have to go through the dispensary in your regiment."

"Thank you, sir," Patrick said, and walked on. He went out onto the porch of the hospital, putting on his field cap, and then stood waiting for a Post bus. That's it, he said to himself. Your company commander can't do anything for you without a slip from the Dispensary, and that Dispensary isn't going to do anything for you. You're stuck, kid. Good luck. Patrick nodded his head, and kept on waiting for the bus.

II

Jacob parked the station wagon behind the courthouse in Ellsworth and got out, feeling as nervous as he been all the way over from South Harbor. It's just another case, he told himself, taking his briefcase from the front seat and shutting the door of the car. But I wish Rolly was here. Jacob started walking toward the building, thinking over the one or two really cogent arguments in his case, while his face wore an intense expression. It had been Rolly's case right from the beginning, but Rolly had insisted that he come over here and argue it on appeal. "Got to see if you're up to snuff, Jake," he had said, smiling, and Jacob had told him that it was a splendid welcome-home present.

He went up the steps and through the door of the building. It was a new courthouse, and Jacob wandered around for a minute, a tall figure in a gray suit under his New York overcoat, and then he found the courtroom. The expression on his face was still tight.

He opened the door of the courtroom, took off his hat, and walked down the center aisle. He went to the table for appellant's counsel, took off his coat, put his hat on top of it, and started pulling papers out of his briefcase and arranging them on the surface of the table.

"Jacob Kingsgrant?"

Jacob looked up and saw a man who had the unmistakable look of every Clerk of Court in the world.

"Yes," Jacob said. "I was going to find you in a minute, as soon as I got set here."

"Don't worry about that, Mr. Kingsgrant. I wasn't talking about checking with me. Judge Arnold wants to see you in his chambers."

Jacob nodded his head and followed the clerk through a door on one side of the bench. New courthouse, new clerk, new judge. For a moment he thought of how he had assumed it would be, everything just the same, and the knot in his stomach became a little tighter. He couldn't help the way he felt about this case. It was no good telling himself that he had handled cases of twenty times the importance of this one every week of the last few years. This was where he had started, and this was where his father had sat on the Supreme Court, and he wanted this one. He had worked on this case, and now he wanted it. The look in his eye was like a boxer so keyed up that he would beat in the side of a locker if he was told the bout was off, and still he was scared at how different it was from the old days over here, when he knew everybody around the courtroom and they knew what he could do. Counsel for the appellee was a young man from Bath who had been about ten years old when Jacob last argued a case in the State of Maine. He had a good reputation.

The clerk opened the door, and ushered Jacob in.

"Mr. Kingsgrant, Your Honor."

There was a bald-headed man about forty years old sitting behind the desk. He put on a pair of steel-rimmed glasses, stood up, and came around the desk with his hand extended.

"It's a pleasure, Mr. Kingsgrant."

"Thank you, Your Honor."

The judge looked at his wrist watch. "If you don't mind, I'll put on my robes while we talk."

Talk about what, Jacob thought, watching the man go to the black gown that hung in a little bureau closet against the wall. The last time that a judge had called him into his chambers without counsel for the other party had been in 1926, for the purpose of telling Jacob to stop making a fool out of the plaintiff's lawyer on procedure and just go ahead on the merits of the case.

The judge took out the black robe, and Jacob stepped over to him.

"Permit me, Your Honor."

"Thank you."

Jacob helped him into the robe, and gave it that one final

tug needed to settle it down across the neck and shoulders.

"Thank you," the judge said again, and turned around to face Jacob while he hooked up the front of his gown. He seemed shy. "You know, Mr. Kingsgrant, we've heard a lot about you in my family. My great-uncle was up at Augusta with your father."

"Justice Arnold," Jacob said. "Joseph Arnold. I remember my father speaking of him often."

The judge nodded his head and smiled. Jacob nodded his head too. "A very able judge," Jacob said. Now *that*, he was thinking, is a little piece of information that Rolly damned well ought to have told me.

"Well, Mr. Kingsgrant," the judge said, going back over to his desk and picking up some papers, "I just wanted to tell you that all of us around here are glad you're back."

A smile broke across Jacob's face.

"Well, Judge Arnold, that's very kind of you to say."

"You're not going away again, are you?"

"No," Jacob said. "No, I expect to stay in practice with my partner Roland Grindall."

"Grindall's a good man," the judge said. His expression changed a little. "I'd like to talk to you about that antitrust suit some time."

"Any time, Your Honor," Jacob said. "Of course, that was the work of many men."

"That's what I'd expect you to say," Judge Arnold said, and looked pointedly at his wrist watch.

"If Your Honor will excuse me," Jacob said, and smiled at the judge again.

"Of course." The judge nodded. "Well, we're glad to see you back."

Jacob inclined his head slightly, and then walked out of the room. As he strode back toward the courtroom, his fierce expression had disappeared, and there was just a trace of a smile on his face. His stomach felt perfectly calm, and he sat down and finished pulling his papers out of his briefcase as if he had been sitting in that chair since the courthouse was built. The hearing was going to begin in three minutes, and all he wanted was to get to work.

III

"Just a little more to the left," Patrick said. "That's it." The platoon was through with its Friday night GI party, and Patrick was lying on his bunk while Hetzler gave him a massage.

"Still not hurting?" Hetzler asked.

"Uh-uh," Patrick said. "Just keep it light." He smiled as he relaxed under Hetzler's hands. He had bought a heat lamp at the PX a few days before, and now it was screwed into the light socket over his bed, sending down a golden warmth while Hetzler worked on his shoulder during this time before Lights Out.

The barracks was quiet. The floors were still moist from their scrubbing, and in Patrick's squad Interlicchio, Forlenza, and Maple had gone off to some sort of dance that was being held at the Service Club. Jakes and Encarnacion were in a crap game that was being held on the gray concrete floor of the latrine, and Stanley was sitting on the edge of his lower bunk, his straw hair and snub nose bent over the combat boot that he was polishing, holding it between his knees as if it were in a vice. Lish was lying on his bunk below Patrick, reading his Bible, and across the aisle came the low sound of Gridley, who could neither read nor write, dictating a letter home to Geremski. One or two of the other men in the first squad were finishing up on their rifles.

"How are you, Patrick?" Stanley said, without looking up from his shoe shining.

"O.K." Patrick smiled. It was amazing how much Stanley could put into asking you how you were. Stanley always smiled when he asked you how you were, as if it was some big and important joke between the two of you.

"I've got some tape," Hetzler said. "Do you think we ought to try to tape it up?"

"I don't think so," Patrick said. "I've tried it a couple of times, and it doesn't seem to do much good."

"O.K., sir."

Patrick put his head down into the O.D. blanket folded at the foot of his bunk. It amused him when some of the men called him "sir," but right now he found himself thinking about one of the other squad leaders.

The leader of the fourth squad was a seventeen-year-old kid named Frank Gross, and God only knew how he got his men to work for him. Any one of them could have broken little Gross in half, but Gross heard bugles that no one else could hear. He had wanted to get into West Point, and he had been turned down for some physical reasons, so he had enlisted in the Army. Any time he got you alone he explained that he was going to put on more weight, and his eyes might get better living outdoors in the Army, and he was going to try to get into West Point on the enlisted-man quota from the Army. There was something so determined and sincere about him that everybody liked him. They called him Gung-Ho Gross, and when you saw him marching along with his rifle almost as big as he was, and his head lost inside his big steel helmet, but always out front, always ready to volunteer, you wondered if maybe the people at West Point had better not take another look. Rodriguez had picked him out to replace the original leader of the fourth squad, a policeman from Buffalo who was trying to sell his squad their passes. And, in the last analysis, the reason that the Second Platoon got fantastic scores like 94 on the Saturday morning inspections of the barracks was one Julio Rodriguez, late of the Eighty-Second Airborne Division. "Either a rifle is clean or it's filthy," he would say, walking up and down in front of the ranks, his dark brown eyes sparkling sharp from under the brim of his red helmet liner. "There's no in-between." He had been thrown out of the paratroops because his shoulder kept dislocating on jumps.

"I think that's enough," Hetzler said, giving Patrick a final slap in the middle of his back.

"Thanks an awful lot," Patrick said. He sat up on the bunk, and put on his T shirt, and the top of his long woolen underwear. Stanley was lying on his bunk now. He had taken the snapshot of his girl out of his footlocker and was lying there staring at it. "Stanley, do you want to go on pass tomorrow?" Patrick asked.

"No thank you," Stanley said, lying there and continuing to stare at the picture.

"You've got one coming," Patrick said.

Stanley smiled. "Give it to Leesh," he said.

"I don't know if I can do that," Patrick said. "You went last time, didn't you, Lish?" Patrick leaned over the edge of the bunk and looked down at Lish, who was still reading his Bible.

"That's right," Lish said, his teeth showing in a big sudden smile. "But I sure would like to go again, Kingsgrant."

"Well, I'll get out the list tomorrow and see how we work it out," Patrick said. He took his fatigue shirt in his hands, and got up in a kneeling position on the bunk. Then, using his fatigue shirt as a mitt, he unscrewed the hot golden bulb, and, putting it down on the top of his wall locker, he replaced it with the regular bulb. He sat there on top of his bunk, summoning up the strength to go down to the latrine and brush his teeth. It had been a grueling day today. In the afternoon there had been some snow, and they had been out there learning how to crawl under barbed wire. The barbed wire had been simulated by low strings, but still it had been unpleasant, crawling around in snow that turned to water as you cruised through it. And he wasn't much at crawling with a rifle. If he used his left hand to carry the rifle, his right didn't do much of a job of helping to pull him ahead. If he held the rifle in his right, he described a great arc like a crab. Even cradling the rifle in both arms wasn't much good, because it slowed him down a lot. Patrick shrugged his shoulders and dropped over the side of the bunk. As he opened his footlocker and took out his toothbrush and a towel, he began thinking of the weekend ahead. Last night he had waited for an hour at the Telephone Building, clutching the card that assigned him a number that one of the two women behind the desk would eventually call out, and finally his turn had come. He had gone to the booth the woman had told him to go to, and two minutes later there was Anna. Yes. Yes. Yes. Fine. Three minutes later it was set, and he would be seeing her Saturday unless something unforeseen occurred. Now it was Friday night, the barracks were spotless, and Patrick took a deep breath and smiled as he thought about the pass that he was entitled to give himself tomorrow. He wandered down toward the latrine.

"Hey, Kingsgrant?"

Patrick stopped. It was a boy named Joshua, from the first squad.

"Hey, Kingsgrant, you think this rifle's all right?"

Patrick took the rifle and inspected it. He nodded and went on into the latrine. The crap game was still going on.

IV

"I don't know," Patrick said. He and Anna had come back from the Stork Club a few minutes before, and now they were sitting on the sofa in the little study across the hall from his room. "I think dictators are the only people who have ever understood that this country really wants peace. They understand it perfectly, and they count on it, and they always have us at a disadvantage because they know we mean it."

"I think you're right," Anna said. "We really want peace, and everybody's screaming that we're warmongers. It does seem sort of a paradox." She poured some more beer into her glass. They had both made themselves a nightcap downstairs when they had come in, and brought the drinks up here.

"I don't know." Patrick stared down into his drink. "The whole damn thing has elements of a paradox. Fifty-two nations or whatever it is stand up in the U.N. and say, We condemn aggression. So how do you implement that laudable idea? You go to Brooklyn and pick a couple of hundred boys off the street, give them sixteen weeks of Basic, and send them to Korea. It's great."

"How many do you really have from Brooklyn?" Anna said.

"A hell of a lot." Patrick smiled and shook his head. "You know the guy from Brooklyn is a stock figure but, believe me, he exists. I told you about a couple I've got, Interlicchio and Forlenza — they'd fit into Bill Mauldin any day in the week." That was the thing, Patrick thought as he took a long swallow of his drink. Clichés got to be clichés because they were so damn true. You read about pack straps cutting into your shoulders, and the difficulty of walking on frozen ruts in the roads, and then you put down the war novels and got there yourself and by God, there they were, pack straps and frozen ruts and the whole works.

"How's your shoulder feeling right now?"

"All right." Patrick stood up and walked over to the victrola. He had resolved not to tell Anna about the day the pain got so bad, but he had weakened and told her all about it. He looked through the stack of records beside the victrola, and there was "A Kiss in the Dark." He looked at it for a couple of seconds, and then took the record in his hands. He had had quite a few drinks at the Stork Club, but he wasn't drunk. On the other hand, he wasn't sober. If you accepted the Rodriguez Filthy Rifle philosophy of life, he was drunk.

"Do you play this thing often?" Patrick said, turning toward Anna. She was still sitting on the sofa.

"Which one is it?"

"Guess." Patrick took another sip of his drink as he held the record out in front of him.

Anna smiled, expecting him to fill in the information, but Patrick just kept staring at her, and the word "guess" hung in the room.

"A Kiss in the Dark," Anna said finally.

Patrick nodded and put it on. He sat down in an armchair near the victrola and listened to it. He wanted her to hear it. He wanted her to get it straight, about the nights he had spent twisting and aching and thinking of her. He wanted her to be with him in the hot nights in New York last summer, and out there hearing this song as he sat on the Mall. To some people the song might sound like soup, but to him it was all steel, unhappiness and independence and Anna and no Anna all tied up in one. Right now, as he drank, it was all the novels that didn't get published, it was Bill Bench on a transport somewhere in the Pacific, it was all the things that didn't work out.

He looked over at Anna. She was looking down into her beer. It seemed to Patrick that once or twice she took a deep breath.

The record stopped.

"Why don't you come back and sit over here?" Anna said.

Her voice sounded funny. Patrick sat down and she came into his arms as he sat down and they were together, not kissing, but just with their cheeks against each other.

"Oh, God," Patrick said in a whisper.

"PK," Anna said, leaning back against the sofa while her hands stayed on his arms. Her eyes were closed. "What are we going to do, PK?"

"I don't know." Patrick had his arm on the back of the sofa, and now he put his head down on his arm.

"What's wrong?" Anna said after he had been sitting that way for a minute.

Look, a voice inside Patrick's head said to him. You've got to move. You've got to think. You've got to say something.

"I'll be all right." He felt her hand on his right arm. A minute before, when the song was playing, he had wanted to throw his glass against the wall, or grab her hard, or do something to make her go through this past year with him. Now that he had touched her he just sat still, with his head on his arm, feeling his heart hammering.

"I don't think you understand," he said slowly, lifting his head and looking at her. He said it slowly, as if it was important to get the words exactly right. "I don't think you understand what I've been through over you. I don't think I can take it if it hurts again."

Anna started to cry. It was a funny way she cried, just sitting looking at him and crying, not looking away and not lifting a hand to her face. Patrick turned his eyes away.

"Patrick," Anna's voice said after a little while, as her hand tugged at his sleeve, "I don't want to hurt you, Patrick. I never wanted to hurt you." Then she started crying again.

"I'm sorry," Patrick said, not knowing what he was sorry for, not knowing anything, and then suddenly he was afraid that he was going to cry too, and he stood up and walked to the door.

"Good night," he said. As he closed the door he saw Anna, turned away from him and still crying.

At nine o'clock on Sunday evening Patrick hung his gray suit in the closet and started putting on his uniform. Somehow the day had worked out all right. He had gone up to Mass at St. Ignatius by himself, and then he and Anna had met for brunch at the Madison. Brunch there was always good for a few laughs, with dancing and door prizes and so on, and then they had gone for a long walk in the Park. Once or twice they had kissed as they wandered along in the wind under the bare trees, but there had been no more tears, and no discussion of anything except things like who Zelda would have married if there hadn't been a First World War. Then they had gone to dinner at Milly Briggs's place. Milly was a friend of Anna's, and Milly's family lived in an exceedingly sumptuous apartment at Seventy-Third and Fifth. It had all been very pleasant, and after dinner Milly had sent them back to Anna's house in her family's Cadillac. The car was waiting downstairs now, ready to take Patrick over to the Port Authority Terminal.

Patrick finished packing, pulled on his overcoat, and walked out of his room. Anna was sitting on the sofa in the study, and she stood up and walked toward him. Patrick put down his little brown canvas AWOL bag and Anna walked up to him and they kissed, a sweet soft kiss.

"I'm coming over there to see you off," Anna said, tilting her head back.

"Good," Patrick said, and kissed her again.

"You know I've missed you, don't you?" Anna looked into his eyes. "All I was waiting for was something like that card from Camp Kilmer."

Patrick felt a little faint and then he put his cheek against hers. Slowly they moved apart, and started down the stairs, hand in hand.

The chauffeur put a pearl-gray lap robe over their knees, and Patrick smiled as he thought of what a contrast it was to where he was going. His hand found Anna's hand under the car blanket, and they sat tight against each other as the car made its way through the city's traffic. It was quiet in the gray felt interior of the big limousine, and even though there was a panel of glass separating them from the chauffeur, neither of them said much. Patrick just felt her hand in his, and for the moment that was enough. Other things were on the horizon of his mind, the Army and what he had been thinking about at Mass this morning, whether Anna had come nearer the Catholic Church or gone farther away, but all of it was on the horizon this evening. Her hand was in his, it was the last few minutes of his pass, and he was damned if he was going to face all the facts that needed facing.

The Cadillac pulled up in front of the entrance to the huge bus terminal, and Patrick turned his head toward Anna. Her head was turning toward him just as quickly, and then her lips were against his. He wanted to get out of that car and go to Fort Dix about as much as he wanted instant death. He started to open the door, and the chauffeur, who had come around, opened it the rest of the way.

"Take care of yourself," Anna said.

"Don't worry," Patrick said, getting out. "I'll let you know when I'm coming again as soon as I know myself." The chauffeur closed the door, and a moment later the car was pulling away into the heavy traffic. Patrick turned to go into the terminal and there was Forlenza, standing on the sidewalk with his mouth open. Forlenza had seen it all, the chaffeur-driven car, the beautiful blonde, the whole thing.

"Hey, Kingsgrant," he said, "what'd you do, win a quiz program or something?"

v

As they formed up after eating chow out by the Infiltration
Course, Patrick kept feeling that God had intervened directly in
his behalf an hour before. He had taken one look at the Infiltration Course and known that he was cooked. It was a piece of
ground about the dimensions of two-thirds of a football field,
and it was covered with barbed wire and logs and hummocks.
Down at the far end several .30 caliber machine guns were
mounted on little sand-bagged islands, and they fired just over
your head as you crawled toward them up the course. Patrick
had a pretty clear idea of how much his right arm slowed him
down when he was flat on his stomach carrying a rifle, and he
took one look at this miniature battlefield and realized that he
would never make it. If he made it at all it would be after the
rest of them had got through in front of him. They probably
would all stand down there by the machine guns and watch
him come in, panting and far behind. He had been standing
there, waiting for the inevitable to happen, when Captain Hare
had come along and told Rodriguez to have the first and second
squads of his platoon stack their rifles, because they needed to
have some rifles for the Night Firing Course tonight, and the
rifles that went through the sand of the Infiltration Course
wouldn't be able to work for another twenty-four hours. So
Patrick had gone through the practice run before dinner without his rifle, and got through all right. Now it was after chow,
and they were going through again, but this time the machine
guns would be firing.

"Ten-haught!" Rodriguez yelled, and Patrick snapped to.
"Dress right, dress! Readee front!" Rodriguez looked up and
down his formed-up platoon. "Paraade rest! At ease! Squad
leaders, check your squads!" This was an informal command.
It meant that Patrick and Geremski and Gomez and Gross were

to wander down between the ranks and make damned sure that everybody was there. The machine guns were firing a few test bursts now, and as he stepped out to go down the line, Patrick saw that most of the men were smiling. It was a funny, contagious smile of excitement. They were going to try something new, and they were not sure how it would go, but they were going to do it and the machine gun bursts told them that they were going to do it pretty soon. The first person on Patrick's left was Stanley, and Stanley gave him a broad grin.

"Now we go, Patrick," Stanley said. Patrick moved on down the line, past Forlenza's big smile, and past Lish's even broader smile, and past Encarnacion's unbelievably wide smile. They were like a bunch of little boys, and at the same moment something in Patrick kindled up, and it could only be called a fascinated pride. They had been out here since early morning, firing carbines and directing machine gun fire from tanks and hitting the dirt on half a dozen different courses. They had eaten a lot of manure out here all day, and now night was falling and they were going to have a nice interesting manure dessert with tracer bullets, and the thing was that they were all looking forward to it. Looking at their faces as he came back up the line, counting heads, Patrick realized that if Sergeant O'Reilley yelled out that the exercise was off, they would be disappointed.

"Ten-haught! Reeport!" Patrick slid into place at the extreme right end of the platoon, facing out toward Rodriguez. Geremski's hand flashed up to a salute.

"First squad all present or accounted for!"

Patrick saluted. "Second squad all present or accounted for!" He stood at attention as Gomez and Gross reported, thinking about his squad. These were the boys who had been crying in the darkness that first night at Camp Kilmer, and now they were coming back from passes with special paratroop boots that were not issued and not required. The boots had harder toes and harder counters so that they could be made to shine more brilliantly, and the men bought them in New York and in Wrightstown for thirteen dollars of the sixty-eight dollars they were paid a month. It was a pretty quick adjustment. Three months ago Lish had been a short-order cook in Harlem, and Forlenza had been working in a warehouse in Brooklyn. Emilio had been a waiter in a café in St. Croix, and Jakes had been unemployed, to put it mildly, on a beach nearby, a beach from which he had not the slightest intention of moving, ever. So here they stood. These weren't people looking for trouble. They hadn't been breaking down the doors to join the Marine Corps. They just stood here, wondering how it would be to have bursts of machine gun fire coming at them eighteen inches over their heads, and they were the Army.

"Rieet face! Forwaard march! Double time, march!" They trotted in behind the three platoons that had their rifles with them, and finally came to a halt beside the Infiltration Course. There was no doubt about it, the thing looked like a battlefield. Under the lights from the tower on the opposite side, the whole business looked like a supercolossal Hollywood set, and the extras were coming into action right now.

The platoon ahead of them entered the trench that was the starting line, running bent over their rifles. As they ran along, the machine guns at the other end began hammering away. It was quite a sight, the red tracers flashing over the trench and on into the high sandbank beyond. The First Platoon were in place now, all stretched out on the slanting pine logs that formed the front of the trench, and all looking to the right. Someone down at the right blew a whistle and gave that wave of the hand that means "forward" in any language, and they all crawled up over the edge and started wriggling across the sandy, log-studded, barbed-wired area.

"Listen to those machine guns," Maple said from where they were watching. "Them guys are experts."

Patrick listened. The machine guns were taking turns firing. One would play *Shave-and-a-haircut-two-bits*, and the next one would play *Go-down-to-the-levee, I-said-to-the-levee*, and then the whole chorus would come in with straight firing.

"You're right," Patrick said, looking at Maple. They had all put their chinstraps down instead of leaving them hooked around the backs of their helmets, and Maple looked more like Brian Donlevy than ever.

"Listen," Rodriguez yelled, "you start going up a little mound, get off it. That's where they got the fixed charges. You start going uphill really fast, roll back down." Just then one of the charges that simulated artillery shells went off out on the course, as if to reinforce Rodriguez' statement. There was another flash, on the top of another little mound, and then another.

"O.K., move out!" Rodriguez yelled, and the crowd of spectators snapped back into four ranks. Just as if he were a jumpmaster, Rodriguez slapped Geremski on the shoulder and Geremski took off running, with his squad behind him. Rodriguez moved over next to Patrick, and as the last man of the first squad went by, Patrick felt Rodriguez' hand on his shoulder and took off, practically running up the back of the man ahead of him. They slowed down and then an Infiltration Course cadreman led them into the trench, running again. The man in front of Patrick stopped abruptly and flattened down on the pine logs, and Patrick followed suit. It was a strange light out here under the one searchlight, like the light at a night baseball game, but dimmer. They lay side by side in one long line, and Patrick's first emotion was one of disappointment. He had thought that somehow the bullets flying over his head would sound very special, but it sounded just the way it did when you were working the targets on the rifle range, except that this was a little louder and a lot faster. Suddenly a whistle blew, and

Patrick felt the whole line move forward. He crawled over the top and then he was crawling up a slight incline, with one man already pushing ahead of him. Another came in from another side, moving faster, and, looking ahead of him, Patrick saw a boot sole three inches from his nose. The boot sole kicked sand in his eye and then moved ahead. It was all action now, the bullets cracking past, the big fixed explosives on the hummocks going off and shaking the ground, and above all the lonely consciousness of self, right arm and left knee ahead, then left arm and right knee, then a log looming up, take the log by rolling over it and rolling on into a little hollow, sand in your mouth, crawl out the other end of the hollow, barbed wire, turn over on your back and hold up the barbed wire while your feet kick you through. About halfway through Patrick could feel himself gasping for breath, but he kept on, going through this queer flat world of faded green lizards propelling themselves forward through the night, and suddenly he was under the muzzle of one of the machine guns on its little island, and then he was up on all fours, crawling down the little runway between two of the guns. He got up on his feet and followed some of the other men on a brief panting sprint to the line of trees that was the finish, and then he lay there among them, fighting for breath and glad to be through with it.

"I could do it again right now," Patrick heard Forlenza gasping. "I'm not kidding ya, I could do it over right now."

"O.K., Superman," Interlicchio's voice wheezed back, "but couldnya just settle for a few push-ups?"

VI

Eileen was baby-sitting for a friend of hers whose maiden name had been Mary Pease. Mary was a wiry brown-eyed girl who had been a good basketball player at Brearley, and it had come to Eileen as a distinct shock to find that Mary Pease was living in Paris, married to a French doctor thirty years old, and with a child named Jean Pierre Pease Fournier. Once she was used to the idea that Mary Pease was Madame Fournier, they had all got along very nicely. Mary and her husband Pierre had Eileen over for dinner about once every two weeks, and Eileen baby-sat with Jean Pierre most Thursday afternoons. Jean Pierre was a beautiful little boy with reddish-brown hair and a delicate coloring that even Eileen's skin was hard put to match. He had blue eyes, he was two years old, and he was simultaneously charming and destructive. The truth was that Eileen preferred him to his parents. She was sitting here now, a book open on her lap, staring at the March rain that was beating against the window. Jean Pierre was playing with a good-sized rubber ball. His hair was cut short at the back sides, and the rest of it was allowed to grow in a great auburn mass. He was playing with a serious and concentrated look on his face, and Eileen kept staring at the grayness beyond the window. Her face was looking unhappy, because she was doing a little fact-facing, and she didn't like the conclusions at which she was arriving. Here it was only March, and she was pretty fed up with her year abroad. She had been in Paris ever since her group had come up to Reid Hall from Grenoble in September, and the unspoken code among all the Americans in Paris, the Foreign Service Officers and the ECA people and her fellow students, was that Paris was the center of the universe, and there was nothing better than being in Paris. Eileen had gone along with all this, convinced that because she was here, ergo, she was having a good time. Now she was not so sure. There was no doubt in her mind that she had had many pleasant days and pleasant evenings since she and Patsy Snelling had arrived last summer, many interesting excursions and stimulating conversations, but right now she was feeling homesick and a little fed up with a lot of what she had been encountering. For the first few months she had listened politely to the Embassy people at cocktail parties telling her that really America had no culture of its own, that Paris and Rome were the only truly civilized cities in the world, and that America was basically just a brawny young industrial giant without a soul. She had listened even more politely to the Frenchmen, because after all it was the French people whom she had come here to meet and to understand. The French people had a few points to make, too. They said, smiling and inviting you to agree with them, that America's architecture was influenced by its bathrooms, that Americans were socially naïve and politically inept, and that after all, any country that had parades with drum majorettes must have a long way to go. Eileen had nodded at all of it, and tried to ignore the combination of avarice and contempt that spread across the face of the average waiter or taxi driver when he saw an American coming. Whenever she was overcharged, or the taxi driver made a scene in the hope of getting another hundred-franc tip, she had put it down to the fact that she was a foreigner, and if something was wrong, it was her fault. Now, just in the last few days, it had occurred to her that maybe these people were not really quite as good as they thought they were.

I don't know, Eileen said to herself, standing up and walking over to the window. After all, you came here of your own free will. Maybe you just haven't penetrated far enough. I've done my best, she answered herself. I like *coq au vin* just as much as all the Foreign Service Officers and all the young Frenchmen, but hamburgers and ice cream just aren't that bad. For a moment she thought of a conversation that she had had with a French boy who had taken her to dinner the other evening. He had said that American aid to Europe did not really represent the American people, who did not care about Europe at all. Eileen had pointed out that the dollars in the aid programs came out of the taxes of American farmers and plumbers and grocers, just like any other dollars in the possession of the American government. The French boy had been really stunned. It was obvious that it had never occurred to him that that was where the aid dollars came from, but after a minute he had begun speaking about spheres of influence and self-interest, and Eileen had let it go.

She turned away from the window and smiled down at Jean Pierre. He looked up at her thoughtfully, and after a second he smiled and rolled the ball toward her. Eileen knelt down and rolled the ball back toward him, and Jean Pierre laughed as he pushed it back toward her once again.

VII

"You really admire toughness, don't you?" Anna said.

Patrick nodded. They had gone to the movies, and now they were sitting in P. J. Clark's. The little bar was still crowded at one-thirty in the morning, and Anna and Patrick were sitting at a small marble-topped table in the Nineties atmosphere of the back room. He had been telling her about Sergeant O'Reilley.

"I guess so," Patrick said. "It seems to come in handy for the people that possess it. Not just in the Army. Anywhere." He took a big swallow of his scotch and soda. Anna was sitting across from him, and things were right with the world. Her hand was on his arm, and they had had dinner together at a French restaurant over on Sixth Avenue, and then they had seen a revival of *Pygmalion*, and here they were. A tribe of head-hunters could have been sitting at the next table, and Patrick would never have noticed. Anna's hand was on his sleeve, and she was looking at him, just him, and that was all that mattered.

"Toughness always seems a negative quality to me." Anna's fingers moved a little on his sleeve. "I mean, it seems a purely defensive quality."

"I don't know," Patrick said. "It seems to me that toughness and efficiency can often go hand in hand. I mean somebody like Sergeant O'Reilley never raises his voice. He just knows his job, and he knows he could knock you flat if he needed to, and that's it. It's amazing, Anna. He just walks toward a chow line and the line opens up — they give him a hole about ten yards wide."

"I guess I don't understand much about it." Anna took a sip of her beer.

Patrick looked at his watch. It was twenty-five minutes to two. Anna was wearing a navy wool suit, and she looked wonderfully clean and pretty, and when she moved her fingers on his arm he felt happy. This past week had been a hard one, but now he was here, and in a few minutes he was going home to stay at Anna's house.

"How about going?" Anna said.

"O.K." Patrick caught the attention of a waiter, and a minute later they were walking out. His eyes were looking at Anna's warm soft-gold hair as she walked in front of him, and when they got in the taxi and he had given their address, she put her head on his shoulder. He turned and kissed her hair and then they sat with their heads close together. Patrick could feel himself breathing deeply, and then he kissed her, and her arms were hard around his neck, and the traffic outside the window of the taxi was far away.

Patrick knelt in St. Ignatius. The choir was singing the Agnus Dei, there was a faint smell of incense, and Anna was sitting beside him. She had appeared when he was about to go out the door, and said that she'd like to come too. Patrick was glad that she had come, but now, kneeling in the church where he had received First Communion and been confirmed, he was wondering about Anna. Religion had always seemed to Patrick to be a terribly personal matter, and the last thing he wanted to do was to pump Anna on the subject of her religious convictions, but he had to get some idea of where she stood. Thus far, since that day that she had come to Camp Kilmer, he had been so eager just to keep things going again that he had avoided talking about anything that might lessen the happiness of these week-ends. But if she was going to up and come along to Mass with him, she ought not to consider it an imposition to ask her why she was doing it. Patrick decided that he would talk to her about it after Mass, but even as he looked at her, as she knelt beside him, a cold sensation came over his scalp. She looked so lovely in that dark coachman's coat that he had always liked, with her white gloves and the little dark hat that sat close to her head, that it scared him. Last night when they had come in from that taxi ride they had kissed, stretched out on that sofa, and even now, kneeling in church, he could feel the warmth of her body against his, feel it as if they were still back there. Patrick's mouth formed in a hard line for a moment as he got his attention back to the Mass.

After Mass, they went for a walk. They entered the Park at Eighty-Fourth, and wandered up behind the Museum and then across the road and along the Reservoir, both of them moving by a common impulse to walk along the opposite side of the Reservoir from the place where Anna had ridden away from him that morning. Patrick strolled along, and for quite a while neither of them said anything. He was thinking that if you saw them, a young man and a young woman, strolling along on a cold sunny morning, the last thing you would think was that the young man was studying the terrain for cover, and deciding where he would set up a .30 caliber to get the best field of fire. But that was what he was doing, doing it half consciously as he walked along in his civilian clothes, carrying his gloves in his right hand. It was inevitable after some of the field problems they gave you. You might be walking along, tired and sleepy, and suddenly a machine gun firing blanks would open up on you from nowhere, from fifty feet in front or fifty feet to one side of that turn you had just come around. You began to look for cover without fully realizing that you were doing it.

"You seem so well this week-end I haven't thought to ask you how your shoulder feels," Anna said. Her voice came soft and vital and lovely after the silence of their walking by the water. The wind had died down.

"It feels all right. It still aches and there's that inflamed feeling, but none of the really bad pain, thank God. Not recently."

"That's good." They kept on walking quite slowly, not touching, but very much aware of each other's feet on the fine sandy black gravel of the path.

"Anna," Patrick said, and then he hesitated, and gave a smile because he didn't really know how to put it, and he was unsure of himself, " — what do you sort of feel about the Church these days?" He had tried to say it lightly, and tried to make it sound like a bantering comment, and he was ashamed of himself now for putting it like that, in that tone, but it was out and they were still walking.

"I don't know exactly," Anna said. "I lost interest after — well, after we weren't seeing each other any more."

Patrick took a deep breath and nodded. He wanted to spin her around and ask her how they stood, but he was scared. These week-ends were almost the only thing in his life, getting off that Post and coming up here and seeing her and staying with her. It was all good, much better than he could have hoped for, and he didn't want to mess it up. But still he had to know something.

"Look, PK," Anna said suddenly, "we're seeing each other, and we care about each other, and isn't that good enough for right now?"

"I guess so," Patrick said. He felt as if he had been on thin ice, that all it took was pressing it and she would say, then we'd better not see each other any more, and that was the last thing he wanted. And in an odd way the one thing he didn't want to discuss at all was why she had broken off with him the first time. He didn't want even to think about it, or about how he had missed her. He wanted somehow to believe that that part of it had never happened, that she had never rejected him even once, and that they were seeing each other as they always had, and that Anna had never sent him away. As he walked along, suddenly he found himself blushing. In the midst of his relief that they weren't about to part again, he felt a sudden emotion of shame rising in him. He felt ashamed that he was taking it as she dealt it, but he kept walking. He studied the folds of the land, the bushes that even in their wintry state would break up the lines of a man if he jumped behind them, and the banks that would put you out of sight if you flattened out in the right place, and after a while he stopped blushing.

VIII

Bill Bench sat on the troop train for Yongdongpo, his back against the hard wooden seat, and his feet up on his barracks bag. The train was crawling past a crossing now, and Bill looked out of the window at a machine gun emplacement near the track, put there to discourage guerrilla activity. The train moved on, past some people in white working in a field. The stench of the field came into the car, and Bill did not even bother holding his nose. He was getting used to it. At first he had not believed that they used human defecation for fertilizer, but he was beginning to believe it.

"You want one?"

Bill turned from looking at the paddies. One of the two replacements sitting facing him was holding out a pack of cigarettes. The other man was asleep.

"No thanks, I don't," Bill said.

"Sure don't look like much," the replacement said, taking a cigarette out of the pack and indicating the countryside with a nod of his head.

"You're right," Bill said.

The man lit his cigarette, looked as if he was going to say something to his dozing buddy, and then just sat there.

Bill went back to looking out of the window. He was thinking that this was the first time that anybody had spoken to him except in line of duty for about twenty-four hours. Everybody was clammed up, and he was clammed up too. It had started at Camp Drake. Until then there had been a chance that they might stay in Japan. They had all talked Korea, but each man knew that he was the one who was going to stay in Japan. But when they issued new M-1's and trucked everybody out to a range to zero them in, all the talking stopped. All the talking. They had clammed up, and they were still clammed up. It was a simple facial expression. It read: I'm stuck. It also read: I'm coming back alive. They're not going to get me, that's all. I'm stuck, I'll do it, but I am strictly on loan, and if you look cross-eyed at me I'll break your teeth.

The man across the way took a deep drag on his cigarette, looked at Bill as if there was something he wanted to say, and then exhaled and stared out of the window as the train rattled north.

18

ANNA KNELT in St. Patrick's. It was evening, and she had come up here after having dinner with her mother and father and being beaten in three games of billiards. She supposed that there were other Catholic churches nearer, but she knew where St. Patrick's was and she had walked up here in the cold darkness of the March night. It had rained during the afternoon, and the streets were wet and the walk was nearly two miles, but she had wanted to walk.

It was quiet inside the church, and the light made an interesting combination of colors, dull gold rays falling on dull gray stone. She was kneeling just off the center aisle, up near the main altar. Off to her right there was a red light burning in front of the side altar where the Blessed Sacrament was kept, and there were quite a few people kneeling over there, but Anna stayed where she was. Please, dear God, she prayed, help me out. Help me about Patrick, to know how I feel. Help me to know how I feel. Her clasped hands tightened, and then she put her head down on her hands. She could hear a few of the rustling echoes from people walking down the side aisle, and occasionally there was a faint noise from the traffic on Fifth Avenue. Please show me what to do, Anna said. I just want to know if I love him or if I don't. I've tried to forget him and it hasn't worked at all, and I care about him, and I love it when he touches me, but I just don't know. Please help me.

II

Patrick had finished scrubbing off the coal dust that they had used on their faces for a night problem, and now he had cleaned his rifle and was lying on top of his bunk, letting his heat lamp try to loosen up his shoulder. His shoulder had ached pretty badly lying out there in the bushes in the coldness of the night, but tonight had been fun. They had been good working as a squad tonight, cutting some simulated barbed wire right under the noses of the men who were defending it, and topping it off by capturing some of the cadre who had tried to tag on to the end of the squad as they returned to the platoon's assembly point in the darkness.

"This all right?"

Patrick opened his eyes and saw Jakes standing beside the bunk, holding out his rifle. Jakes had given him a lot of trouble, but Jakes was learning to play it cool. If Rodriguez came downstairs now, as he occasionally did, and started pulling rifles out of the racks at random, inspecting them, and then shouting out the numbers of the rifles that did not meet his approval, Jakes could say that Patrick had approved it, if his rifle came up. Patrick sat up under the heat lamp, took the rifle, and slammed it open. Then he reversed it so that the chamber was right under the bulb, and looked at the bore.

"That's O.K.," he said, turning it around again after this superficial examination, and releasing the bolt and pulling the trigger. He handed it back to Jakes and stretched out again on the O.D. blankets. It was ten days since he had walked with Anna by the Reservoir, but as he closed his eyes he saw her as clearly now as if she were right beside him. Boy I wish she were, he said, feeling the heat on his back and on his shoulder. Boy I wish she were. He closed his eyes a little harder as he thought of the warmth of her breasts when he kissed her, and of lying stretched out with her on that couch in the den, both of them breathing hard, and the feel of her heart beating against him. Patrick opened his eyes again and looked at the barracks. Stanley was lying on his bunk, looking at the picture of his girl, and down the way Hetzler had his rifle apart on his bunk, and was polishing each piece with a rag until it shone like jewelry. For a moment a vision rose up in front of Patrick, a sudden vision of the millions of hours that must have been spent in cleaning rifles. It was so many man-hours that it was staggering, and the war movies managed to pass over the manual labor part of warfare pretty quickly. Thirty-six-hour passes and successful landings, that was what the movies showed you. Patrick sat up and picked up his T shirt. As he got up to unscrew the heat bulb, he was thinking that all those man-hours put end to end must equal a good many centuries. Add all the boys cleaning their rifles on both sides from 1914 to 1918 to all the boys cleaning their muskets in front of Richmond, and all the men on both sides at Waterloo, and you probably had somebody running a ramrod down something every three seconds since Horatius stood at the bridge. Patrick started to unscrew the big gold bulb, holding the T shirt between his hands and the hot glass, so that it would not burn him. His right arm was awkward at the unscrewing, but he got the bulb out and had it balanced in his left hand, on top of the T shirt. Suddenly he felt it slipping. The bulb got away from him, and, even as Patrick lunged for it, it fell onto the steel bar at the end of his bunk, and broke with a terrific pop and crash. The glass sprayed down all over the bunk where Lish Jones was. Patrick looked over the edge, a horrified expression on his face as he moved in the silence that followed the crash. Everybody was standing frozen. The particles of glass were all over Lish's pillow, but Lish had been curled up at the other end of the bunk, reading his Bible. Lish just sat there and looked at him. Patrick's eyes turned away, and he looked around. Everybody was staring at him as he knelt on the edge of the upper bunk, and there was a shocked, accusing silence in the barracks.

"Nothing explosive," Patrick said. He got down off the bunk. "I'm terribly sorry, Lish," he said, feeling the tension behind him dissolve back into the clicking of rifle parts.

"That's all right," Lish said, in a tone that showed him just how not all right it was.

"I'm terribly sorry," Patrick said. "I'll clean it up." He got his steel helmet down from the top of his wall locker and began brushing the pieces of glass into it. Lish sat there for a minute, and then started helping him pick some of the pieces of glass off the floor.

"You didn' hurt yourself, did you, Kingsgrant?" Lish said after a minute. Patrick looked at him to see if he was kidding. Lish was not kidding.

"No," Patrick said. "No, I'm all right. But I realize I could have hurt you badly, and I'm terribly sorry." They both finished picking up the particles of glass, and then Patrick put on a sweater and walked down the aisle, past the others, carrying the helmetful of broken glass out to the garbage cans behind the barracks.

III

"How about it?" Rolly Grindall said, pushing his chair back from his desk and standing up.

"Just a minute." Jacob made a notation on the paper in front of him, a deed for the sale of sixty acres of blueberry land, and then he stretched, pushed back his chair, and stood up, too. They both put on their overshoes, coats, and hats, and clomped down the wooden stairway, leaving the door shut but unlocked behind them.

The winter light of noon was weak in the street outside. It was a true March day, a true day of the most unseasonable month in Maine. Gray clouds and fog pushed oppressively low over the Bay and the shore, and the combination of water and snow on the street underfoot promised that if you disliked today's slush, you would despise tomorrow's ice. The two men walked silently up the quiet street, and three minutes later they were stamping up the front steps of Roland Grindall's yellow frame house. Rolly stepped inside the door and sniffed the air.

"Will pork chops do you, Jake?" he said, taking off his hat.

"Just as long as Margie doesn't mind how many I eat," Jacob said, smiling, and the two of them took off their coats and overshoes. It was an old ritual, coming to Rolly's for lunch, and Jacob had fallen back into it as if he had never been away. They walked back through the dark hallway to the kitchen, carrying their wet overshoes in their hands. Rolly's wife Margie was standing at the stove, wearing a flowered apron over her blue linen dress, and she smiled without looking up from her surveillance of the peas that she had cooking.

"How are you, Jacob?" she said quietly.

"Fine, Margie," Jacob said.

"It's pretty slippery out there," Rolly said, and then silence, a companionable and functional silence, fell upon them while Jacob and Rolly put their overshoes beside the legs of the big black wood-burning stove. The men went into the dining room, and seated themselves at the table. Jacob was holding his little surprise for later. He ate lunch with Rolly and Margie almost every day that he was not in Ellsworth or Bangor, and at least three days a week Margie asked him if he had heard from Patrick. Most of the time since he had come back he had had to say no, but yesterday he had received a pleasant short note from Patrick.

He had answered it last night, and said nothing about it to Rolly during the course of the morning, so that he could have it all for when Margie asked him.

The door from the kitchen opened, and Margie came in, carrying a platter of pork chops and a bowl filled with fried potatoes. She went back into the kitchen while Rolly and Jacob pitched into the chops and potatoes, and came back with the peas and a pot of coffee. The three of them moved into a steady, silent destruction of the meal.

"Heard anything from Patrick?" Margie said after about five minutes. She had always understood that Patrick had gone down to New York last summer because there were libraries and things that he needed down there for reference in writing his book.

"Fine," Jacob said. "I just got a letter from him yesterday. He said they were working with something called a fifty-seven millimeter recoilless rifle. You remember anything called a recoilless rifle, Rolly?"

"Can't say as I do, Jake," Rolly said, taking another pork chop from the platter in the center of the table. "How many weeks of that training has he had?"

"He's in his twelfth week now."

Margie's smile faded for a moment. "There isn't any chance he's going overseas, is there?"

"I don't know." Jacob rolled his palms upward once, and then let them roll back onto the white tablecloth, palms down.

"Jake, you ought to see that that boy doesn't get sent overseas," Margie said, looking down at her plate.

"Jake'll do whatever he thinks is right, Margie," Rolly said, passing his napkin across his mouth. "Nothing you say is going to make any difference."

"It's not my business to interfere," Jacob said.

"Jacob, he shouldn't be on hard service at *all*," Margie said, and then looked down at her plate again.

IV

Except during the times when Mass was being said, the Blessed Sacrament was kept in a tiny room behind the altar of the Fiftieth Infantry Regiment's chapel. It was the Friday night at the end of his twelfth week, and Patrick was kneeling before the altar in this little side room. The nave of the chapel was darkened, and the only light was from the red vigil candle on the small wooden altar back here. Patrick was dead tired from a day in the field and a GI party in the barracks, but when they had finished scrubbing the place at ten o'clock he had felt the need to come over here. They were restricted for the week-end, and they had started making up their full field packs this evening. On Monday morning they would get under the packs, heavy packs complete with shovels and sleeping bags, and carry them eighteen miles to their first bivouac area. All week Patrick had been worrying about the march, and this morning he had gone on Sick Call. He had not been down there for six weeks, simply because he was sure that doctor was never going to do anything for him, but finally he had decided to go on the off-chance that they might give him something better than sodium salicylate for the pain. As Patrick knelt here now, praying that if he had pain it would not be too bad, memories of this morning came back to him. There had been a new doctor, some sort of civilian with a German accent, and he had thrown the two men in front of him out of the office, yelling, "You should go to Mental Hygiene! You're not sick, you are sick in the head!" On that encouraging note, Patrick had stepped into the office, explained that he had had pain in his left shoulder for twelve weeks, that he was about to go on an eighteen-mile hike, and that he would like something for the increased pain he would probably have. It must have been Patrick's evident willingness to walk out of the office that did it. The doctor had given him a slip for some sodium salicylate, and then, as Patrick said, "Thank you, sir," and started to walk out, the doctor had said, "Joost a minute."

Patrick had stopped.

"Yes, sir?"

"You have these troubles for three months?"

"Yes, sir."

"Sergeant Singer, get this man an orthopedic appointment."

So Patrick had been given an orthopedic appointment. It was for the first day of his sixteenth week, so that he would have all the joys of two separate weeks of bivouac, the thirteenth and fifteenth, before his left shoulder was examined. Nonetheless, it was nice to think that it might get looked at and even fixed, and all he had to do now was pray that there would be no pain as on that one terrible day. People with nothing wrong with them had occasionally passed out on some of their speed marches to various ranges, and you could certainly pass out on an eighteen-mile hike if a real spike of pain got started and kept going. It would drain you out in a few miles, and then there would be nothing left of you.

Patrick shifted slightly before the altar. It's too late for God to withhold the pain, a part of his mind said. If God were going to withhold the pain this coming Monday He would never have allowed your shoulder to be torn in the first place. You're praying for a miracle. I'm not praying for a miracle, Patrick answered. I'm praying for as little pain as possible. I'm going on the march. I just want as little pain as possible. He said three more Our Fathers, and then made the sign of the cross and rose from where he had been kneeling before the tiny altar. It was warm in the room, warm and quiet, and the red candlelight seemed cheerful in the darkness. Patrick made the sign of the cross again, and went out through the main aisle of the chapel and into the cold night air.

The barracks was quiet when Patrick came through the door. The lights were out, and almost everybody was asleep. Patrick took his towel and his toothbrush and toothpaste, and went down to the latrine. Maple was sitting on the steps, polishing his combat boots.

"CQ been around?" Patrick asked, going over to the sinks.

"Yeah," Maple said, not looking up. He was one of the hold-the-shoe-in-your-hand school of polishers, and he had one of his hands inside the boot while he cheerfully whacked away at it with a brush held in the other hand.

"Did he say anything about me?"

"No. You know they don't check any more. He just came through and said lights out."

Patrick nodded and put some paste on his toothbrush.

"Where you been, anyhow?"

"In the chapel," Patrick said.

"How come it's open at ten o'clock at night?"

"I don't know. It does seem funny."

"You wouldn't catch them leaving their machine guns unlocked," Maple said. He held up the boot and studied it in the light from the naked bulbs overhead. "They got that Weapons Pool locked up like it was Fort Knox."

Patrick nodded, and began to brush his teeth. Two minutes later he was back at his bunk. Just as he was starting to undress, he heard a sob. For a moment he thought it was Lish, and then with a sensation almost of terror he realized that it was Stanley. Patrick went over to Stanley's bunk, convinced that he must be in the throes of some terrible illness. Patrick bent down and reached out his hand gently and tentatively, feeling the rough wool of the blanket under his fingertips.

"Stanley?"

"Yes?" There was an icy, empty tone in Stanley's voice.

"You all right?"

There was another sob, this time more subdued, as if Stanley was strangling the noise in his throat. Patrick put both hands down on the cot firmly, and leaned down farther, trying to see Stanley's face in the darkness.

"What's wrong, Stanley?" Patrick said.

"All right. I will tell you." Stanley sat up and got out of his bunk. Patrick watched, and then, when he saw Stanley walking toward the area by the front door, the little hallway between the empty cadre room and the room where Scarpa slept, he followed him. Stanley was in his socks and long woolen underwear, and the tear paths on his face were illuminated by the electric light from outside coming through the glass panels in the top half of the door. As Patrick came alongside him, he tried to speak, but he couldn't make it. They looked at each other.

"There was a letter after chow," Stanley said. His voice was soft and even. "It was from my aunt."

Patrick nodded. He knew that Stanley's aunt was the link between Stanley and his family. The whole correspondence was apparently a tricky and risky business, and Stanley had received only one letter in the seven months since he had escaped.

"There was a letter from my girl," Stanley said. His voice was barely audible, and he was looking out of the panels in the door, his face in profile to Patrick. "She said — she says we must see it is impossible. She will marry a carpenter. I know him. I am a kid to cry."

Patrick closed his eyes for a second.

"Jesus, Stanley," he said. All Patrick could think of was that Stanley could have had the girl. All he had to do was stay there and be drafted into the Czechoslovak People's Army like ninety-nine and forty-four one-hundredths per cent of his contemporaries. Instead he was an RA at Fort Dix, New Jersey.

"I am not mad," Stanley said. "I am just sorry." He tried a smile, but it never got off the ground.

Patrick felt stunned. He was trying to think of something to say, but all he could think about was Stanley at night, in those few precious moments before lights out, when the other men were either asleep or writing their families, lying on his bunk staring at the snapshot of his girl until the CQ came in the barracks and turned off the lights.

"I think maybe she is married now," Stanley said. "I think maybe she is married for two weeks."

Patrick shook his head and put his hand on Stanley's shoulder. Suddenly Stanley opened the door of the barracks and stepped out into the March night. Patrick stepped out onto the tiny porch behind him, and as Patrick closed the door he saw Stanley sag against the wall of the barracks and then slide down until he was sitting on the boards, his back against the barracks wall, staring at nothing as the wind of the night flapped his woolen underwear. Patrick went inside the barracks, got the blanket folded at the bottom of his bunk, and went back out. He put the blanket around Stanley, and then sat down on the low red-painted wood railing of the tiny square porch.

"Patrick, you have a girl?" Stanley said after a minute. He did not look up. He just kept staring across the area to the lights hanging over the front doors of Able Company.

"Yes," Patrick said. He looked down at Stanley on the boards of the porch. Stanley usually stood so straight that it was shocking to see him sitting there, huddled under the blanket, with the silvery paths of the tears on his face.

"I am a kid to cry," Stanley said again, and then he put his head on his hunched-up knees.

Patrick ground the heel of his combat boot into the boards of the porch. He was thinking that he would like to hurt Stanley's girl, hurt her badly.

"It's cold," he said after a minute.

Stanley nodded his head, and held out a hand toward Patrick. Patrick leaned down and helped him up. Stanley felt as limp as a rag. Patrick opened the door, and stood there in the aisle, watching Stanley as he made his way down to the latrine, the blanket around his shoulders and trailing behind him down the aisle.

v

Somewhat to the surprise of Baker Company, the buzzer sounded right after chow on Sunday evening. Patrick put on his field jacket and field cap and raced out to the formation. He had a terrible feeling that the march might be starting right now instead of in the morning, and his whole body felt light and sick when he thought about how bad it might be.

Sergeant O'Reilley was standing there. After the platoons had formed up, he gave the signal to break ranks and gather around him in a large semicircle.

"I just want to say something about these next few days," he said. He was wearing his red helmet liner, and he stood straight and tall, with his feet a little apart. "Anybody can soldier when you're living in the barracks. These next few days will be a little different." He looked around at them, his blue eyes seeming to look at each individual. "Now I want to give you a slogan that's carried me through the Army. Don't fight the problem. Some of you goddam people are still fighting the problem. Don't fight it. Unless you people are very lucky, a lot of you are going to get orders for FECOM, and that means a lot of you are just a few weeks away from being in combat right now. Even if you've just been along for the ride so far, try to pay attention these last couple of weeks, because it might make the difference between getting through it all right and coming back in a mattress cover." He kicked at a pebble with his foot. "Now," he said, an expression of distaste on his mouth, "this route we're going out on tomorrow is across country, and if a man drops out he's going to sit there for a long, long time. This is a tactical march. There aren't going to be any ten-minute breaks, or any of that shit, and we don't have any way of picking up stragglers. If you fall out you're just going to lie there. Now I know some of you can't make a march like this. For instance Ciaccio. There's nothing wrong with Ciaccio that can get him a C profile, but he hasn't got the strength for a march like this. It's not his fault, but if I was his platoon sergeant in Korea I'd get rid of him pretty damn fast. You're one of the KP's tomorrow, Ciaccio. You'll go out on the truck. All right. The rest of you are dismissed, and I want to see anybody up here who doesn't think he can make it."

The company filed back into the barracks, and Patrick stood there, undecided. There were about twelve men up there, talking to Sergeant O'Reilley. Patrick thought about it. Here was the reprieve. Here it was. He set his face and walked over to the little group.

"They still haven't given you a pair of combat boots that fit?" O'Reilley was saying to Botticelli. "All right, go out on the goddam truck." He turned to Patrick. "What's yours?"

"Well, Sergeant, I've had this pulled shoulder muscle all through Basic, and I just don't know if I can make it. I'd like to try the march, but I just don't know."

"If you can't make it, we can't have you along," Sergeant O'Reilley said. "Go out in the truck." He swung his attention to the next man.

Patrick turned, his face set and sour, and walked back toward the Second Platoon. Inside, some of the men from the fourth squad were lugging a machine gun and a bazooka upstairs. For twelve weeks they had simply been Gung-Ho Gross's fourth squad, but now they were discovering that the fourth squad was the weapons squad, and had to carry out a machine gun and a bazooka along with most of its other equipment. Down the line there were shouts of "Holy God!" as the Fourth Platoon discovered that it was the Weapons Platoon, and had to carry out handy little items like 60 mm. mortars, 57 mm. recoilless rifles, and a couple of machine guns and bazookas.

"Hey, Kingsgrant," Hetzler said, "who's gonna carry our BAR?"

Patrick looked, and sure enough, there was a BAR on Interlicchio's bunk.

"I hadn't thought about it," Patrick said. "I think maybe Forlenza."

"Hey, no!" Forlenza said.

"You're the biggest man in the squad," Interlicchio said.

"Man you *will* carry the BAR," Jakes chimed in, chuckling.

"Hey, no," Forlenza said, but the smile on his face showed that he knew he was the biggest and strongest man in the squad, and that as long as everybody admitted that, he would carry the BAR.

"I will carry it," Stanley said, suddenly. Everybody looked at him. They knew something had happened with Stanley, but they didn't know what it was.

"O.K., if you want to," Forlenza said.

"Look," Patrick said. "You two switch it back and forth. One carries a rifle for a while, and then he gives his rifle to the BAR man and takes the BAR for a while."

"That's good," Stanley said, and wandered off.

"Will you be carryin' a carbine or somethin' special tomorrow, boss?" Emilio asked Patrick.

"No," Patrick said. He looked down at the BAR. "As a matter of fact, Sergeant O'Reilley told me to go out in the truck."

They just stood there. None of it was lost on Patrick. It wasn't that they were mad at him. They knew he'd had troubles. It was just that they were walking, and he, their squad leader, was riding out in a truck. It was as if a chasm had opened up between himself and the rest of them. Nobody was angry. They were making the march, that was all. Patrick's face tightened, and he went over and tried to find something that needed straightening out in his wall locker. His pack, rolled and ready to go, lay in the corner by the edge of his bunk.

Later in the evening Rodriguez called him up to his room at the head of the stairs. Patrick knocked, came in, and shut the door behind him.

"Eighteen miles isn't so far, Kingsgrant," Rodriguez said. He was sitting on the edge of his cot, wearing his fatigue trousers and an olive undershirt.

Patrick stood there. The white-painted room held a wall locker, a footlocker, a bunk, and the two of them. "Sarge," he said, "believe me, I want to make the march. Maybe, if I could do it without a pack."

"No squad leader of mine is gonna march without a pack," Rodriguez said. "I'd rather have you go out on the truck." He stood up, opened his footlocker, and took out his shaving things. He picked up an olive towel from the bottom of his bunk, and hooked it around his neck.

"I'm sorry, Sarge."

"I know you can't help it if you got something wrong with you, Kingsgrant," Rodriguez said, "but eighteen miles isn't so far."

"I think I'd better go on the truck, Sarge."

"O.K." Rodriguez went past him, opened the door, and went down the stairs to the latrine.

At three o'clock in the morning Patrick was still unable to get to sleep. He knew that Stanley was awake too, lying in the darkness with his eyes open. Patrick clasped his hands behind his head. Every time he tried to get to sleep he thought of how he was going to feel tomorrow, looking up from setting up the Mess tent out in the wilderness, and seeing his company coming down the road. He closed his eyes and saw them coming toward him, the green-clad forms in lines on either side of the road, coming toward him steadily, helmets, full field packs, rifles, the works. Patrick had had a haircut at the barbershop in the PX a couple of days before, and the barbers had refused to believe it when he told them that they were carrying out their sleeping bags on top of everything else. Nobody carries out their sleeping bags, they said. The sleeping bags always go out in a truck. Just watch us move out Monday morning, Patrick had said, smiling, if you're up that early.

Patrick rubbed his clasped hands against the back of his head as he stared up at the dimness of the white wood ceiling. Dammit, he said to himself, yesterday morning you thought you had to make the march, so you were ready to make the march, and if you fell on your face, all right, you fell on your face. His face grew taut as he thought about his twelve-week education in pain, the hot aches that came on him when he did something even as simple as polishing his boots, and then the real pain, that slicing light blue knife back there that came in almost accompanied by weird violin music, the pain that was like another mouth inside you to feed. And on top of everything else, he said to himself, one of these days you might be dead. It had just been occurring to him recently that he might actually get killed. All it needed was for his application for OCS to be turned down, and he was on his way in the pipeline to Korea. You asked for it, he said to himself, his lips pursing in the darkness, and you might really get it.

He turned over under the tight sheets. The thought of Anna came up in the night, rising as if there were some blond wind forcing it in upon him, leaving him helpless in front of it. He would be seeing her this week-end, and all he wanted was to be on that bus for New York right now. Instead he had a week before him of getting up in the darkness every morning, just standing up in the predawn darkness, knocking down his tent, and packing up to walk to a new place. And the pain. Anybody can soldier in barracks, he heard Sergeant O'Reilley's voice saying. Anybody can soldier in barracks. He thought about O'Reilley and then he thought about what a good-looking couple Sergeant O'Reilley and Anna would make. He shook his head at the thought, and then Anna was alone with him again. Maybe she can take it the way it is, Patrick thought, turning in the bunk again, but I want to get this thing straightened out. As he lay there he heard Kentucky Adams' voice on the BAR range again, Well damn, brother Kingsgrant, I'd either have me a girl or not have me a girl. Then he heard Sergeant O'Reilley's voice saying "Stand up, lad," as he sometimes did. He would say "Stand up, lad" and the whole company would stand tall, taller than tall. That was O'Reilley. Sometimes he would march them around the big square at the half-step, looking them over. At the half-step everything could become exaggerated, and you stood taller and made your flank movements sharper. Then Patrick was away from the square, seeing those lines moving toward him through the woods tomorrow morning, and his eyes were still open when the night went gray at the windows.

It was right after breakfast that Patrick knew he was going on the march. The men were all standing around the barracks, stuffing toilet paper from the latrine into the pockets of their field jackets, and adjusting each other's packs, when Patrick knew that he had to go. He had to march out of here with them, and if he was lying in a ditch somewhere by noon, all right, then he was lying in a ditch somewhere by noon. He got his rifle out of the rack, walked over to his bunk, and got his helmet down from the top of his wall locker. Then he picked up the forty-pound pack, with the blanket roll around the top of it and the shovel on it and the sleeping bag in the cargo pack under it, the whole strapped-together thing. It took a good yank just to get it off the floor.

"Hey, Stanley, help me on with this thing, will you?" he said. Stanley had just finished hooking two of the forward straps of his pack on to his cartridge belt. He looked at Patrick and smiled for the first time in three days.

"You are sure, Patrick?"

"I'm sure." Stanley held up the pack like a tailor helping a man into a jacket, and Patrick stuck his arms through the pack straps, right arm first. Stanley pulled and pushed to get it sitting properly, and then stepped away to view his handiwork. Patrick pushed his head back. The top of the blanket roll was right against the back of his helmet, riding high, just the way it was supposed to be.

"That's good," Stanley said.

The buzzer sounded. Patrick put on his gloves, snatched up his gas mask bag, grabbed his rifle off his bunk, and walked out through the door. The whole company was coming out of their barracks, walking heavily under their packs, pulling on their gloves and helping each other get their gas masks hanging properly at their sides. Patrick moved to his position at the head of the second squad and stood there, wishing to God that it would start. Geremski stepped into his position ahead of him, and then turned around and looked at Patrick.

"I thought you were going on the truck," he said.

"I changed my mind," Patrick said. There was a big brown truck sitting near the Orderly Room, looking strange and huge in this area that only saw men on foot. The truck looked as big as the little Orderly Room building. Men were running in and out of the Orderly Room, and there was a feeling of excitement in the air. Up and down the ranks everybody was shifting their feet on the hard ground, and the packs were already feeling heavy on their backs. Patrick felt a tap on his shoulder. Lish was standing there.

"Why don't you go out on the truck?" he said.

"No, I'm walking," Patrick said. He wished to God they would start.

"Hey, look," Forlenza said, coming up with the BAR on his shoulder. "You can still get on the truck."

"Go ahead, get on the truck," Geremski said.

"What the hell, Kingsgrant," Interlicchio said, stepping out of his place down the line. "O'Reilley told me I could go on the truck, I'd be inside there right now."

"Ten-haught!" Rodriguez had come out of the Orderly Room. He had the same pack on his shoulders that the rest of them did, but no rifle. "Squad leaders, reeport!"

"First squad all present or accounted for," Geremski said.

"Second squad all present or accounted for," Patrick echoed, and he saw the way that Rodriguez' head suddenly turned in his direction. At the end of the reports Rodriguez put them at ease, and came over to Patrick.

"You're coming with us, huh?" he said.

"Yes, Sergeant," Patrick said. Rodriguez looked at him for another moment, and then went back out in front of the platoon. Sergeant O'Reilley had just stepped out of the Orderly Room. He came across to his place in front of the company, giving one sour look at the little knot of men clustered around the truck. Then he snapped into place, facing the company. He stood there tall and straight, and somehow the pack did not look very big on him.

"Ten-hut!" he exploded. "Right face! Sling arms! First Platoon leading platoon, column of twos from the left, forwaard, march! Route step, march!"

Baker Company marched out of the area and down the tarred street, carrying the BAR's and the machine guns and the bazookas, moving quietly in route step, each man marching his own way. There was no yelling of commands, just the sound of the company moving down the street. Up ahead the guidon slapped in the March breeze. The cooks and clerks turned out along the street, and the KP's from the different company Mess Halls came and stood by the side of the road, watching them go past. In a few minutes they were out of the Regimental Area and moving across a big field. Way up in front Patrick could see Captain Hare and Sergeant O'Reilley. Captain Hare let Sergeant O'Reilley take the company out to the field most of the time, but whenever there was going to be a really good shoot-em-up Captain Hare stopped signing things in triplicate and put on his helmet and came along. He was walking along with O'Reilley on his left, O'Reilley tall with the pack looking light on him, and the short captain looking as if the pack were going to drive him right through the ground. Captain Hare put up his hand, and a little wedge of scouts fanned out from the first platoon and went trotting ahead to be the point of the column. Sergeant O'Reilley gestured at one of them and the man looked back over his shoulder. Then he nodded and took out his bayonet and put it on his rifle. On a tar road off to the right the Mess truck hummed past, and then the column moved into the woods on a dirt road.

As they passed the area where they had bivouacked in their fifth week, Patrick was smiling. It was a little early to say that the miracle had happened, but his shoulder felt fine. It was a good morning for March, and there was a smell and a taste of early morning in the woods, and there was a cool breeze. He and Geremski were swinging along close together on the narrow dirt road, right behind Rodriguez. Up ahead the Second Platoon appeared as a double file of big square packs with helmets rising above them. They came around a turn and out onto a broad flat dirt road that stretched as far as the eye could see.

"Watch O'Reilley goose it up," Geremski said, his hands pulling the pack straps on his chest down a bit. Patrick nodded. He was thinking about the way that they were rigged out, each man with his own shovel and his shelter half. In effect, you had your house on your back. Patrick's mind was wandering over it all as he swung along behind Rodriguez' red helmet. He was thinking that maybe life was harder in other armies, but in any army it could be cut down to the bare essentials. Here was a man, he had his shelter on his back, he had water in his canteen, he could carry C-rations in his pack, and he had his weapons on him. You could turn him loose in the outdoors for at least twenty-four hours just as he stood, an eminently self-sufficient unit.

"I don't know what O'Reilley thinks we're gonna be using for gas in another ten miles," Geremski said. Patrick could feel the pace going up, and he could see Rodriguez' sparkling paratroop boots stepping into the longer, faster stride. He tugged down on his pack straps, and debated about taking off his gloves. His hands were sweating inside the heavy gloves, but it was a cold day, and the gloves helped you keep a comfortable grip on the pack straps and your rifle sling. Patrick hitched his rifle up a little nearer to the vertical. The pack extended almost out to the edges of his shoulders, and it was particularly hard for Patrick to make his rifle rest easily when he was wearing the full pack, because the lack of development of the muscles right at the point of his right shoulder gave him about an inch less shoulder out there, and the inch would have come in handy for giving the rifle sling a better purchase. He debated switching the rifle over to his left shoulder and decided to keep it on his right. If his left shoulder was getting along without extraordinary pain this far, it was probably a good idea to leave well enough alone.

"You are all right, Patrick?" Stanley's voice said from behind him.

"I'm O.K.," Patrick said, not turning around. "So far." He looked at his wrist watch. It was eight-thirty. In about half an hour Anna would probably be waking up. She might do a little shopping, and meet a friend for lunch, and then go and read at the hospital during the afternoon. It was funny to think of Anna still being asleep. You've got to get it straightened out with Anna, Patrick said to himself as he moved along. He could feel a nervousness rising in him when he thought about this coming week-end. He knew that even though he might fight against it, he was going to have to get some sort of a statement out of her. Watch it, boy, the more cautious part of Patrick said. Watch it, watch it, watch it. If you press her hard it may be just like putting a knife across your throat. All right, PK, he heard her soft lively voice saying, if it's got to be yes or no, it's no, but why can't we go on this way? That's what she'll say, Patrick said to himself, I'm telling you, that's what she'll say. Maybe, Patrick answered, but this deal is up in the air, and it's got to make a landing. A landing is one thing, the cautious part came back, but being shot down in flames is another. Dammit, Patrick yelled at all the factions in his head, it isn't doing me much good the way it is. This girl has been in my mind for nearly two years, and I want it to amount to something.

POPOPOPOPOPOPPOP POPOPOPOPOPOP POPOPOP POPOP POPOPOPPO POPOP POPOP OP

Patrick hit the ditch right beside Stanley, hunched down with his chin on his chest. A moment before there had been a long line of men moving forward on either side of the road, strung out for three hundred yards, and now the road was empty. Patrick stuck his head up. The machine gun was off somewhere to the right of the bend in the road forty yards ahead, and the First Platoon was already crawling out of the ditch on the right-hand side of the road and into the bushes to assault the machine gun.

Rodriguez came sliding in from nowhere.

"Get your squad out into those bushes and go for that gun," he said.

Patrick gave one wave of his left hand, picked himself up, and moved out of the ditch and into the brush, his rifle in front of him. Stanley was beside him. The gun was hammering away up ahead of them, and they started toward the sound, crouched low. There was a crashing sound in the bushes behind them, and Geremski and the first squad, who had hit the ditch on the opposite side of the road, had come over to join them. Up ahead of him in the woods Patrick saw people from the First Platoon moving forward in a hive of activity, one man picking himself up from behind a tree and sliding in behind a bush, and then another man, on another angle, moving forward six or eight yards before throwing himself flat. Suddenly the ground underfoot became spongy and then it was water. Patrick had a confused impression of freezing water in his combat boots, men up ahead moving like jack rabbits, looking over to see if his squad was spread out to the right of him, being amazed to see that it was, and then suddenly the gun stopped firing and a crystal silence fell on the ambush swamp. A whistle sounded from back on the road, and Patrick turned and started wading back toward drier ground.

"That was damn smart," Maple said, coming alongside. "They put the machine gun behind some water. Damn smart, boy."

"What the hell," Patrick said, breaking through some bushes and clambering up the side of the dirt road where it dropped off into the marsh. The First Platoon was already moving forward, their fatigues covered with dark stains of mud and water, and Rodriguez was waving at the Second Platoon to fall in and come on along.

"They only killed about half of us before we got that gun,"

Geremski said, trotting into place abreast of Patrick, across the road.

"I never even saw the gun," Patrick said.

"Well, I guess the First Platoon saw it all right," Geremski said.

"Hey, Gridley," Hetzler yelled across the road, "how was that for a burst of six?"

"Fire a burst of six!" Gridley yelled back, smiling. It was his favorite expression, and he used it on all occasions. The platoon chuckled once at Gridley, and moved on behind Rodriguez.

By about the eighth mile out the sun was warm. Everybody had taken off their gloves and stuffed them into the pockets of their field jackets or hung them on their bayonet hilts, and a grim determination had settled down upon the column. Nobody was doing much talking.

Sergeant O'Reilley came walking back down the line, moving on the inside of the road, between the lines of men. The Fourth Platoon had been fired upon a few minutes before by a concealed machine gun that had let the entire column pass before opening up with its belts of blank cartridges, and the Third and Fourth Platoons had dealt with it while the First and Second sat in the ditches on either side of the road, some of them grabbing a quick smoke. Presumably O'Reilley was going back there to ask the platoon sergeants how it had been. He came back, moving between the two advancing lines, walking straight and tall, his face impassive and his stride as quick and smooth and jaunty as if he were moving from the Orderly Room to the Mess Hall. He stared for a second at Patrick, and then, just as they were passing each other, his lips moved.

"How you doing, Kingsgrant boy?"

"O.K., Sergeant," Patrick said, and then O'Reilley was gone on down the line. Kingsgrant boy. Kingsgrant boy. A great happiness leapt up in Patrick's throat, and he pulled his rifle a little nearer the vertical.

"Air attack!" It was Captain Hare's voice, unbelievably loud, considering how far ahead he was. Patrick looked up at the sky with a reflex motion. There was nothing in front of him, and he turned his head. All around, helmeted heads were jerking about in bewilderment. There, right on top of them, so big that it hardly seemed real, was a Piper Cub that had come sliding in over the trees behind them with its engine off. It seemed to be hanging above them. Patrick grabbed his rifle off his shoulder and ran off the road. He went about ten yards into the woods and flung himself down behind a tree. All around there were the sounds of men crashing flat into bushes and piles of leaves. There was a patch of snow where Patrick had landed, and he wriggled away from it as he looked for the plane. Suddenly its engine came on, and it soared like a bird above the road and the treetops. The plane shot down the road and then turned, a tight sudden turn, and came flying back the other way. One moment it was just a little plane way ahead of the column, and the next second it was right there, even before Patrick had his rifle set on his shoulder. Patrick could see the pilot. The man was wearing an overseas cap and sunglasses, and he was smiling. The plane roared past, lifted up over the end of the column, and came back again. This time Patrick had his rifle up, and, leading the plane, he squeezed the trigger of his empty weapon two or three times. The plane whizzed by, waggled its wings once, and flew off toward the horizon. Patrick stood up, feeling stunned at the suddenness with which it had happened. He had had no idea of how fast a plane could close in and move away. As he walked up onto the road he saw a broken paper bag of flour nearby. So the plane had been dropping bombs, too.

"Hey, can ya imagine what it's like when a jet does that to you?" Forlenza said, coming up on the road with the BAR held in his hands as lightly as if it were a golf club. Patrick nodded and smiled, and, hitching his pack up higher, began walking forward again.

It was about an hour after this that Patrick began to realize that he was likely to make the whole march. They had just been through a gas attack, marching along with the hot, choking masks on their faces, and when Rodriguez yelled "Take 'em off!" Patrick took his gas mask off and felt the air cool on his face. The sky was blue, and the air was cool on his face, and suddenly he was pretty sure he could make it. Nobody was saying an unnecessary word. Although it was most certainly a group activity, a mass movement of men, each man was marching along silently, each man locked with the problem, each man marching his own eighteen miles, thinking his own thoughts. As the company mounted a long bare ridge, the sun of the day beginning to be hot on them in their field jackets under the packs, Patrick began thinking of how little he had understood the nature of warfare before he had come into the Army. Before he had come into the Army the fact that wars were fought outdoors had escaped him. It must have been a result of having all your ideas of war piped into you while you sat in a nice air-conditioned movie theater. Somewhere he had always had the idea in the back of his mind that at the end of the day you retired from the field to a nice camp where you talked big man-talk during the evening and your equipment cleaned itself. He had never grasped the fact that you ate where you fought and defecated where you fought and slept where you fought, and if you slept at all, you woke up to another day of the same thing if you were alive. All Patrick's daydream warfare had been conducted under blue skies at a temperature of seventy, and he had never comprehended that when it was thirty below or a hundred and twenty above the generals kept the armies right out where they were, and that any weather was perfectly acceptable killing weather. He had never understood that wars were manual labor. Killing somebody was a physical matter, and a good mechanic was likely to be better at it than a good Latin teacher simply because he was likely to be a lot better with his hands.

"Look at Kingsgrant," Rodriguez' voice suddenly came to Patrick's ears. "He's makin' it, you can make it."

"Yeah, but I got the BAR," Forlenza's voice said.

Patrick turned. "Can you take it for a while, Stanley?" he said to the sweating face behind him.

"I will take it," Stanley said, and dropped back to switch weapons with Forlenza.

"My feet are getting hot," Geremski said.

"Shit man, I don't feel my feet at all no more," Encarnacion sang out, smiling, his teeth whiter than ever in the gray dust on his black face. Patrick smiled. Emilio was a child, but he was a good, well-behaved child. Jakes was almost sinister by comparison, and yet in a strange way Patrick was beginning to feel that Jakes might not be a bad man to have around when things got rough. Jakes had been bad news all along, but he was an athlete and a good shot, and if he got in a situation where he was convinced that there was no easy way out, he might be all right. Patrick looked over at Geremski and nodded. Geremski just shook his head as if he wanted to be left alone. It was all coming through to Geremski now. He was just staring ahead, his eyes fixed in his dusty face, putting one foot ahead of the other. When he had said his feet were getting hot, he had been saying a lot more than that. He had been saying that he could feel himself near the end of his rope, and that he was scared. But he was still putting one foot ahead of the other. That was all that was left now. Just putting one foot ahead of the other.

A long time later Patrick became aware of a ripple of talk and interest coming down the line. Somehow whatever it was leaped the gap between the First and Second Platoons, and Rodriguez said to Patrick, "Bivouac area coming up."

Patrick's face smiled, a smile cracking in the middle of the cake of dust and sweat. The company was walking downhill around a turn, and a minute later, about half a mile ahead, Patrick could see a big sign of the sort used to mark ranges and bivouac areas. His throat was dry. A couple of miles back he had taken a couple of swallows from his canteen, but now he did not want to use up his strength wrestling the canteen out of its canvas holster on his hip. They were almost there. Patrick kept looking ahead eagerly, watching Sergeant O'Reilley's red helmet and Captain Hare's red and white helmet as they moved steadily toward the sign beside the road. They reached the sign and passed it by. The First Platoon marched by the sign, and then Patrick was marching past the sign, a look of anger and disbelief on his face.

"What is this shit?" Interlicchio said in a loud cracked voice.

Rodriguez just shook his head. "I thought this was the one," he said. The buoyancy had gone out of his voice.

Patrick gritted his teeth and hitched up his pack. All right, goddamit, he had come eighteen miles, they weren't going to shake him now.

"Sergeant O'Reilley forgot somethin', I bet you," Encarnacion's voice floated out, singsong and gentle, "an' we are goin' back to get it. We are goin' to walk aroun' the world an' come into Baker Compahnee from the other side."

Silence closed in all around them, and there was nothing but the road and the dust and the sun. Another sign rose up beside the road, and they marched on past this one. Patrick began to feel himself fading. His shoulder was behaving well, but this was a tiredness like a sleep. He was going down into it like a sleep, and he knew that when he went all the way under he would fall down and that would be it.

"Man I can do no more," Jakes announced, but they all kept

walking under the sun. The road stretched on and on, and they just kept walking, and Patrick felt as if his heart was going to break. They were going to break his heart on this road, and he knew they could do it. Just a little more and they would break his heart. He looked over at Geremski. Geremski's face was working, and it looked as if he was ready to cry. The pace was going up. Back somewhere along the line in the silence somebody finally did let cut a sob, but they kept walking. Patrick could feel consciousness coming in on him and fading out on him, and under it he could feel the pit opening up. It was like passing your thirtieth push-up. You knew you were good for a few more, but you also knew that after a few more there would come a moment when you got down and couldn't get back up, and you would try, with your arms shaking, and then finally just drop to the ground.

There was another sign up ahead of them now, and they all marched toward it, their sweat-drowned eyes blinking as they stared at it.

Sergeant O'Reilley came abreast of the sign, gave a relaxed signal with his left hand, and he and the Captain executed a sharp column left and strode into the road that opened up in the woods, beside the sign. The two files of the First Platoon came together and passed into the woods, and then Patrick and Geremski were close beside each other again, stepping down the pine-needle-covered dirt road with the little patches of snow on it. O'Reilley was standing beside the road, and when Rodriguez came by he fell in alongside Rodriguez.

"I'm tired," Rodriguez said. "We got much further to go?"

"Now don't *you* start giving me that," O'Reilley snapped. "That's all right for these guys, but not from you."

They came out into a cleared space, and Patrick saw the First Platoon come to a halt ahead of them. It was strange. He could see the First Platoon halting, he could see where he was, but he felt as if he was in a dream.

" 'Toon halt!" Rodriguez croaked, and they stood there. Patrick halted and stood there, sweat running down his face in muddy trickles, but he could still feel himself marching forward, one foot after the other. After eighteen miles the forward motion did not stop all at once.

"Ordeur arms!" Rodriguez croaked. "Left face. Parade rest, at ease."

There was a crash, and Patrick looked to his left. Gridley had passed out on his face. The men on either side of him dragged him over toward a little spruce tree.

"O.K.," Rodriguez said. He looked pale. "Everything is still tactical. We go up to our section of the defense perimeter, eat chow up there, and then dig the holes we sleep in tonight. Let's go." There was a Mess tent over to the left, but evidently it did not have anything to do with them just at the moment. The platoon broke up into a big group just following Rodriguez as he walked up a slight slope. Nobody was saying anything. They came to an area with a lot of bushes and low trees, and a road running along at the farther end of it.

"O.K.," Rodriguez said, "that road is the perimeter. Drop your packs."

There was a pile of C-ration boxes and two ten-gallon containers of water in a cleared space, and the men gathered around it and started dropping their packs. Patrick shrugged out of his pack and let it fall to the ground behind him. Then, not even bothering to take off his gas mask bag, he sat down with his back against the mass of his pack. He could feel the big pit that had been opening up under him close again. Some of the men were picking up boxes of C-rations and filling their canteen cups from the big O.D. water cans, but most of them were just sitting on the ground beside their packs, holding their rifles across their laps and looking at nothing at all.

"I am flyin'!" Encarnacion was saying, flapping his arms like wings, and they all laughed. It was an immense sensation to take off the pack after four and a half hours' walking under it. You felt light as air. Lighter than air.

"O.K.," Rodriguez said. He had taken off his pack too, and he had his helmet off as he stood in their midst, scratching his head. "I've got to have four men on guard up on the road while the rest of you eat. Who's it gonna be?"

Patrick felt his hand going up in the air. He got to his feet. Stanley was getting to his feet too, and slinging his rifle on his shoulder.

"All right all right all right," Gung-Ho Gross said, getting up off the ground in a sort of lurch. Gomez was standing up too, his mouth working as if he was trying to get rid of the dusty dirty taste of the march. Gomez looked like Joe Louis after fifteen rounds, and Patrick smiled as he saw him. Gomez was even more tired than he was, and Patrick got a weird satisfaction from staring at Gomez and knowing that it was true. Patrick looked down at his sprawled-out squad.

"Don't look at me, boy," Interlicchio said. "I couldn't get up if I wanted to."

"Nobody's looking at you," Patrick said.

Rodriguez led them to the edge of the road.

"You guys can just lie here," he said. "It's just we've got to have some people along the road. Gomez and Gross, go down there."

Patrick nodded at Rodriguez and lay down. Stanley sat down slowly, his back against the trunk of a slender birch tree.

"How is it, Patrick?" Stanley asked.

"I guess I'm all right. That's a long way."

"You will be good in Korea, Patrick," Stanley said, and fell into a deep silence, his eyes half closed. Patrick's expression grew thoughtful as he looked at Stanley sitting there against the tree, his field jacket soaked through with sweat at the arm pits. The world was full of things you would never imagine. A Dear John from behind the Iron Curtain. But right now Stanley looked more composed than he had at any time since the letter had come.

"Here," Rodriguez' voice said. Patrick looked up and saw Rodriguez standing there. He had several small boxes of C-rations in his arms, and he dropped one down beside Patrick. Maple was behind Rodriguez, carrying one of the water cans. Patrick got up on his knees, got his canteen cup out from under his canteen, and poured himself some of the fresh, clean water from the porcelain-lined O.D. can. It tasted better than all the iced tea he had had on the hottest summer days of his life. Rodriguez had distributed the other boxes of C-rations to Gomez and Gross, and now he came back and sat down between Stanley and Patrick.

"Think I'll eat with the thirty-year men," he said, taking a GI can opener out of his field jacket and starting to work on a can of hash.

"What do you mean, thirty-year men?" Patrick asked.

"You two guys are in this for a career, aren't you?" Rodriguez said. Patrick looked at him to see if he was kidding. He was not kidding.

"You want some pineapple, Sarge?" Patrick said, holding out a silvery little can from his box of rations.

"No thanks, there, Kingsgrant," Rodriguez said. Patrick started to work opening his main can, which was cold meat stew. Thirty-year man. Patrick was grinning from ear to ear, and he almost spilled the can of stew when he got it open.

VI

Patrick woke up with the back of his head in ice water. He twisted away from it and sat up on one elbow in his sleeping bag. He and Maple had worked hard on pitching this pup tent in the snowstorm last night, but still the water had come through from underneath. Patrick looked at his wrist watch in the darkness. A quarter to five. Maple was snoring, and rain was beating down on their pup tent.

Slowly, Patrick felt around for something dry with which to wipe the water off the back of his head. He got his handkerchief out of the pocket of his fatigue trousers, which he was wearing underneath a pair of canvas field pants, and massaged the back of his head with the handkerchief. He was wondering how much more they were going to have to take. Monday night they had slept in holes, and Tuesday they had maneuvered their way across country to a new place and then had field problems until eleven o'clock at night, and yesterday they had fired on a couple of ranges in a snowstorm so thick that some of the firing with machine guns had to be called off because the targets were invisible at two hundred yards. Nothing was dry anymore. Last night Lish had left in an ambulance, shivering uncontrollably, and Geremski had injured his eye by running into a twig in the darkness, and now it was a new day and it was raining.

A whistle cut through the sounds of falling rain. It blew again, and then again.

"All right, campers," Sergeant O'Reilley's voice rang out across the acre of soaked pup tents. "All out for a dip before breakfast!"

"Hit it!" Rodriguez' voice croaked sleepily. "Squad leaders get those men out."

Patrick wriggled out of his sleeping bag.

"I'm gonna resign my commission," Maple said, sitting up. He had been sleeping with his field cap on, and it was so far back on his head that he looked like some sort of comedian. "This settles it. I'm gonna resign my commission."

"You ready?" Patrick asked.

"Christ," Maple said, getting out of his sleeping bag. "O.K." With one motion they both stood up in the dimness of their tent and knocked it down simply by standing up into the wet canvas. Then they stepped out from under the uprooted shelter halves and let the whole wet canvas mass fall back down on their possessions.

"Crawl on my feet again, I'll knock your head off!" an enraged voice said from inside a tent down the line.

"Don't tell me it's rusty," another voice said from another direction. "I tole ya to put ya rifle in ya sleeping bag."

Patrick stood under a tree, eating his scrambled eggs with a spoon. They were cold, and the rain was falling on them, and rain was dripping off the brim of his helmet and into his food. They were scrambled eggs made from powder, and none too good anyhow, but right now they tasted like cold worms. It was still that grayness before the real dawn, and people were coming out of the Mess tents with their Mess tins looking like ghosts as they moved toward the nearest thing that looked like shelter. Everybody wanted to stay in the Mess tent, but the Mess sergeant kept telling them that there wasn't enough room. Just room enough to come out of the rain on one side, blink like a poor dumb animal at the light in the tent, let them splash your food into the tin, and out into the night on the other side. Patrick studied the box of dry cereal that had been put into the other half of his Mess tin. Ever since his job with Rice Krispies and Corn Flakes he had hated even to look at a box of dry cereal, and most of the time that it had been handed to him in the Army he had skipped it, despite the ferocious hunger that they all always had. Now he looked at the box, tore it open, and shoveled the dry cereal into his mouth as fast as he could eat it.

Sergeant O'Reilley took one look at the company as they filed into the grandstand at the course called "Mock Village," and decided that the time for joking was over. The rain had turned into a cold gray drizzle that hung down over the roofless houses that Baker Company was to assault, and the only sounds coming from the men as they stood in the grandstand was the sound of feet stamping and teeth chattering.

"At ease!" Sergeant O'Reilley stepped forward in front of the grandstands. The men were wearing their ponchos, but it was pretty useless, since everything they had on underneath was already soaked through. The sound of chattering teeth was loud and sharp in the air, and the company stood there, sullen and resentful and beaten. But still they stood there, at a semblance of attention except for the stamping feet, standing because they had been trained to stand until they were given the order to take their seats.

Sergeant O'Reilley was not wearing his poncho, and his fatigues were soaked black like everybody else's.

"You people are pretty miserable," O'Reilley said. "I feel sorry for you. We all feel sorry for you." His light blue eyes looked at them in the drizzling mist. Behind him the unpainted wooden walls of the Mock Village were almost obscured in the wet grayness. "But you might as well get one thing straight. The only man who can bring you in out of here is the Commanding General, and I don't think he's very likely to do that."

Patrick moved one of his feet, and water squished inside the boot.

"You people shouldn't feel so sorry for yourselves," O'Reilley said. "You all know we're going to bring you in on Saturday, and a lot of you are going to be home on pass on Saturday night. Sometimes in Korea we were up to our armpits in mud, and we didn't know if there was ever going to be any relief."

It was the first time Sergeant O'Reilley had spoken of being in Korea. Everybody was quiet, and the sound of the stamping feet died away, although there was still a birdlike clicking of teeth.

"Now we'll get some fires started," Sergeant O'Reilley said, "and when you're not running through this course or the Close Combat Course next door, you can warm yourself up. Remember to get your feet out of your boots as much as you can. All right, stand up, lads." O'Reilley straightened up until he was stiff as a ramrod, and in the rain the men straightened up where they stood on the boards of the grandstand. "Baker Companee — Seats!"

"Two!" they yelled as they had been trained to, and they sat down.

VII

"They'll never get that tree," Forlenza said. "Never."

BLAAM! The 57 mm. nearest them went off again, and they all watched a flash and a geyser of earth jump up about forty yards short of an old tank hull in the chewed up waste that stretched away underneath the hill where they were sitting. It was Saturday afternoon, and this was the last exercise of the bivouac. In an hour they were going back to the Fiftieth Regiment in buses, the sun had been shining all day, and they had nothing to do except sit in the warm sun on the hillside and wait their turn to fire the 57 mm. recoilless rifle.

BLAAM! A flash and a spout of earth went up to the left of the tree. The tree was about half a mile away, and the tank hull was about five hundred yards away. The two little cannons alternated on the targets. There were four men at a time on a gun, and the rest of the company lay sprawled out on the hillside on either side of the two guns, getting sunburns and baking their waterlogged clothes and bodies. The sky was blue, almost hazy from the sunshine, and it hardly seemed possible that only last night another load of men had been taken away in ambulances, shivering and feverish.

"That guy's gonna try," Hetzler said, and they all looked at the nearest gun. The barrel looked almost delicate on its tripod mount. There was a warrant officer coaching the men as they tried the gun, and now he had stepped in and was adjusting the sights. The warrant officer knelt down in the gunner's place, and the rest of them got into position, and the trainee acting as section chief leaned over the barrel and tapped the warrant officer on the head to indicate that the weapon was loaded and ready to fire.

BLAAM! There was a flash right on the tank hull, and the tank gave a terrific jerk as several hunks of metal spun off into the air. Everyone on the hillside clapped their hands politely, and the warrant officer stood up, took off his helmet, and bowed, grinning. Then another crew of trainees stepped in and proceeded to drop their rounds all over the landscape.

The afternoon moved on under the hot sun, punctuated only by the sounds of these two guns in the wilderness. Everybody was just content to lie in the sunshine. Tonight some of them might be in New York on pass, but that was all far, far away. Right now it was just good to lie there, drying out cigarettes on the grass and turning your head toward the sun.

"You know," Interlicchio said after a while, "this must be what the Artillery does all the time. Just sit on their ass an' fire at one thing an' another. Can ya imagine that?"

"Man I *will* accept a transfer," Jakes said. He was lying on his back with his eyes closed. Right next to him Emilio was sitting hunched over, massaging himself around the knees as the sun bathed them.

"Sure," Patrick said, "but it comes the other way too. The Artillery is a pretty high priority target."

"You're a pretty high priority target when you're running up a hill that somebody else wants to keep," Maple said. He was eating some hard lemon candy from a C-ration.

"I found a home in the Army," Hetzler said, grinning. "How about you, Mr. Kingsgrant? You found a home in the Army?"

"I don't think so," Patrick said, smiling and tugging at a small tuft of grass that had come through the winter.

"Man," Jakes said, still lying there stretched out, "when I go back to Saint Croix I am goin' to get a good jail sentence. I am goin' to do somethin' to get a good jail sentence. You go to jail they never touch you for the Army no more, man."

"That's all I ever wanted," Interlicchio said. "I just wanted to be left alone."

BLAAM!

"Ah, what are ya gonna do?" Forlenza said. He was lying on his side.

"I'm not kidding you, I may have to resign my commission," Maple said, smiling. "Gridley and me are gonna fire a burst of six and then resign. I'm sorry but that's the way it is."

"Ah, what are ya gonna do?" Forlenza said. "So we go to Korea. So what?"

"Listen," Interlicchio said, "the Chinese want Korea so much, let 'em have it. The Koreans never did anything for me."

"Wouldn't you rather fight them in Korea than Montana somewhere?" Patrick said.

"Hey, Kingsgrant," Interlicchio said. "You're gonna tell me the Chinese are gonna invade the United States?"

"Maybe not right now," Patrick said, "but if somebody had stopped Hitler about the time he first started taking over countries, he might have given us a lot less trouble in the long run."

"What are ya gonna do?" Forlenza said, sitting up. "These Communists, they think they can grab anything they want. We give 'em a good kick in the nuts, maybe they'll mind their own business for a while." He stretched out again on his other side.

"Hey, Interlicchio," Stanley said. He had been watching the explosions. But now he turned his head. "You know why I'm here?"

"Why?" Interlicchio said, respectfully.

"Because I don't like it under the Communists. It's not good with the Communists. You better fight them in Korea. It's no good when they are the government."

"All right," Rodriguez' voice came down the slope from above them, "what do you say you guys pay a little attention there?"

"What're we supposed to do?" Maple said in a low tone. "Count the shell bursts?"

"What he means is he wants us to look *interested*," Interlicchio said. "You interested?" He poked Forlenza.

"I'm fascinated," Forlenza said, resting his chin on his hand and looking like a gigantic Rodin wearing a helmet. "It's more super-colossal than the movies."

"What the hell," Interlicchio said, looking to see if Rodriguez had gone and then stretching out on his back, "you see one shell burst, you seen 'em all."

Patrick sat there, playing with the tuft of grass, and feeling the sun pour down into the knotted torn muscles on the left side of his back. At the back of his mind he knew that he would be in New York tonight, but he was not thinking about New York. He nodded his head as he looked out over the huge torn field, watching the explosions leap up. So far Forlenza was right. Nobody had hit the tree.

19

PATRICK AWOKE as the bus started down the incline to the Lincoln Tunnel. The Manhattan skyline sat across the Hudson River, neon-bright in the clear night. He looked at his wrist watch. It was almost midnight. They had come in on the buses late in the afternoon, and cleaned their rifles and shovels and shelter halves and the rest of their equipment, and after an inspection at nine o'clock Sergeant O'Reilley had let them go. Patrick had changed into his Class A's and checked out without having time to take a shower, so he still had all the dried grime and sweat of the week in the field on him, and he felt itchy and grubby. He had managed to clean up his face and hands, but that was about it. Now he looked out again at the city across the water as the bus hummed into the lower part of the turn into the tunnel. Over there was Anna, and over there across the water, this week-end, things had to get solved. He was living on the edge of his nerves, with pain, and uncertainty about where he was going and what was going to happen to him, and he had to know how things stood. Patrick's face at the window was hard and young and worried.

The bus plunged into the flashing tunnel, and Patrick turned his head away from the window, turning himself slowly and stiffly in his khaki shirt and O.D. uniform, stiff with pain and fatigue.

"So about two o'clock in the morning she says, 'Oh, I love you!' " a voice behind Patrick was saying. "So I says, 'Baby, I can always take a later bus.' "

Patrick smiled, a soft, sad smile. It was a funny way to get ready to fight a war. For five days you were out eighteen miles from nowhere, no electric light, no running water, sleeping in holes and shaving out of a helmet when you shaved, and then on the sixth day they brought you back in, stuck you on a bus, and dropped you in the middle of the biggest city in the world. Have fun, soldier. We were only kidding. We start kidding again at four-thirty Monday morning. Be with us, won't you?

New York absorbed the bus as if it were a tiny pellet thrown into a huge maw, and a few minutes later Patrick stepped into a taxi outside the Port Authority Terminal.

"Seventeen West Eleventh Street, please," he said, and began looking out the window as the cab pulled away from the curb. The lights of the city had never looked half so bright to him.

The taxi stopped for a light. There was a Spanish-looking girl on the corner, holding up her hand to try and get a cab. She was a cheap, striking girl, and Patrick stared at her. She stared back, the gaze of a young woman who had stared down a lot of people in her time. Patrick just kept on looking, and finally the girl averted her eyes. The light changed, and the taxi moved on. In a store window there was a mannequin wearing a plum-colored net dress, and Patrick stared at the store window and the lights and the plum color. He thought that he had never seen anything so beautiful and so soft.

He paid the taxi when it stopped in front of Anna's door, and then went up the steps in the clear night. The door opened even before he rang the bell, and Anna was there.

"Hi," Anna said.

"Hi." He stood on the threshold and looked at her, and then she was coming closer to him and he had dropped his AWOL bag on the doorstep and he was kissing her. He did not say Look, Anna, or, Anna, we've got to straighten things out. What he said was, "Oh, Anna."

Somehow he was sitting on her sofa and they kissed again, and his coat and AWOL bag must be out in the hall because they weren't with him, and they kissed again.

"Do you want a drink?" Anna said, looking at him after a kiss.

"No," Patrick said, and kissed her again.

"Patrick?"

"Uh?" He opened his eyes and found that she was sitting in an armchair, smiling at him.

"You fell asleep."

"Oh."

"I thought about just letting you sleep there, but maybe you'd be more comfortable in bed."

"You're right." Patrick shook his head.

"I brought you a glass of milk," Anna said after a minute.

Patrick turned and stared at the glass of milk. He was still trying to take in the fact that he had fallen asleep in mid-kiss. Boy, you must be tired, he said to himself.

Anna came over to the sofa and slid into his arms. Her lips were warm.

"What's the matter, PK?" she said after a few seconds. "You look as if something's bothering you."

"Something is," Patrick said. He picked up the glass of milk, and then suddenly he felt so tired that he was afraid he was going to drop it, and he put it down with elaborate care. Suddenly his eyes shut on him. They just shut, dropped down.

He concentrated on opening them again, and the lids went up and they were open again.

"I guess I'd better go to bed, Anna," he said in a whisper.

"Go ahead," Anna said. "I'll just put the milk away and turn out the lights. Don't hang up your coat or anything. Just take your little bag if you want it and go on up."

"All right," Patrick said. He stood up. "I hope you didn't want to go out anywhere."

"I knew we weren't going out anywhere," Anna said, smiling. "It's half past twelve, PK."

"That's not so late unless you're tired," Patrick said. He chuckled as if he had said something very funny, and then he walked out the door and up the stairs. He had forgotten his AWOL bag, and he just kept climbing up the steps, determined, studying the steps and moving toward a real bed.

Patrick tried to concentrate on reading the Sunday *Times* as he sat opposite Anna at the breakfast table, but he could not do it. Mr. and Mrs. van Neerdaam had gone off to visit some friends of theirs in Cornwall for the day, and they were alone in the dining room. Anna was wearing a dark red dressing gown and Patrick had on his gray suit. He looked at his watch. It was half past ten, and if he expected to get up to St. Ignatius for High Mass at eleven he had better get moving.

"You interested in going to church, Anna?"

"It's so late now, I don't think I could get dressed in time," Anna said. She had out the second section of the paper, and was studying the engagements and marriages.

Patrick looked at her, and his mouth turned into a small thin line. The unconcerned tone of her reply still hung in the room, and she was going right on reading the paper.

"Anna — " he said. His heart was suddenly beating hard, and he had to get it straight.

"Um?" She was still reading the paper.

"Do you or don't you?" Patrick said, his voice a cracked whisper over the breakfast table.

"What?" Anna put down the paper and stared at him.

"Do you or don't you love me?" Patrick said slowly, his mouth working hard around the words. He kept looking at Anna, and he saw her face grow still, and then it looked to him as if she was going pale.

"PK," she said, as if she was fighting for breath, and her hand grabbed at a spoon and then let go of it. "Look, Patrick, there's so much that's uncertain. I mean, about religion and everything. Why can't — "

"Never mind about the religion right now," Patrick said. His heart was still beating hard, but his voice was coming back. "The religion is important between us only if you love me. I love you. Do you or don't you love me?" He kept staring at her. When he had said that about the religion he saw her wince, as if he had torn away something she was hiding behind.

Anna sat there, staring down at the polished wood of the table. "I don't know," she said after a minute. Her face looked as if she was going to cry, but she did not cry.

"I'd think you'd know by now," Patrick said. He felt hollow inside, but he couldn't stop what he was saying. "If you were going to love me you'd know by now."

"Patrick," Anna said, her face coming up and a sudden sharp look in her eyes, "I don't think you're in any position — "

"Position to what?" Patrick asked. He could feel an anger coming over him. His body started to shake. He knew exactly what she meant. He was dependent on her for these week-ends, and the food he was eating, and the love he felt, and the hope he had. She knew it, and she was telling him that he was in no position. She was right. He was in no position. He was in no position at all.

Patrick stood up. His face was red, and he could hardly see. He still could not express the rage he felt, rage at the fact that she was right, that she held all the cards, and that she could say to him in that cool voice that he was in no position.

"Are you all right, Patrick?" Anna said, looking at him with wide eyes.

"I'm all right," Patrick said. His voice sounded like a man trying to say something right after coming up from under water. "I'm going."

"I'll see you after Mass," Anna said, placatingly.

"No." He leaned toward her, his hands on the back of the chair in which he had been sitting. "No. I mean I'm going. I'm coming back after Mass and I'm going to get my clothes and I'm going."

"I don't see why you have to do that!" Anna threw down her napkin and stood up.

"No." He was breathing more normally now. "No, you don't see why."

"You don't have anyplace to go."

"Goddam you, Anna," Patrick said. He stood there for a moment, and he saw it happening. He saw the little vertical line form in the middle of Anna's forehead, and he saw her mouth open a little as she took in the fact that he was walking out on her. For two years it had been an article of faith with her that Patrick loved her. Patrick loved her, and would do anything for her, and it was simply up to her to decide whether to pick him up or drop him or keep him jumping through hoops. And now he was walking out.

"Maybe I do love you, Patrick," Anna said, raising her hand toward him.

Patrick turned and went out.

The light changed, and he crossed Second Avenue. He was walking in a stunned dream, but he was doing everything right. At Mass he had stood up when everybody stood up, and knelt when everyone knelt, and now he crossed the street when the light changed. It was strange, walking back here through York-ville, seeing all the streets and all the bars that he had last known in the baking summer. He went down the block, his face set, and went up the steps of 338 Eighty-Seventh and rang the bell.

"Yes?" His old landlady, Mrs. Charnow, was looking at him, and then she said, in a voice going up on a roller coaster, "Mr. Kings*grant!*"

"Hello, Mrs. Charnow." Patrick smiled. There was something about her friendly face that had always made him smile.

"You're in the Army?"

"Yes."

"You look good. You look good."

Patrick smiled again. "I'm sorry to bother you, Mrs. Charnow, but I was wondering if you could store some clothes for me. You know, just put them anywhere."

"Sure. I think I can do that. Come in. You have any luck with the typing?"

Patrick shook his head. "I'm afraid not." He looked around the old familiar hallway. He was thinking that when he had first come to live there it had looked pretty grubby, but after the barracks it looked awfully damned good. "I certainly appreciate your taking the clothes."

"It's nothing," Mrs. Charnow said. "You're doing plenty for me."

"What do you mean?"

"In the Army, in the Army."

"Oh." Patrick looked around again.

"You want a cup of coffee?"

"I wouldn't mind," he said. "I wouldn't mind. Thank you very much."

Patrick came back to Anna's house at about two o'clock in

the afternoon. He had had two cups of coffee with Mrs. Charnow, and then he had gone to the Park and walked beside the Reservoir, feeling the tears of anger and frustration and sorrow just behind his eyes.

The maid opened the door when he rang. Patrick had been standing on the step, his heart hammering, hoping that it would be Anna and somehow it would be all right, but it was the maid who opened the door.

"Miss Anna has gone out, Mr. Kingsgrant," the maid said. "She asked me to help you pack."

"There won't be much," Patrick said. He went up the stairs slowly. At the landing he looked up, hoping that Anna would be standing there and this time she would really love him and believe in him and make him strong, but there was only the empty hall. Patrick stopped for a second with his hand on the bannister, and he knew that now it was over. He knew that if Anna came in the door now, he would get down on his knees and ask her to take him back on any terms at all, but he knew that if he did that, there would just be another Sunday morning and another breakfast like the one he had just been through. And she wasn't coming in the door.

"I'm not going to wait," Patrick whispered in the dim hall, and forced himself to take a step forward.

II

There was an electric light burning in one corner of the Guard Hut, and a fire flickering in a pot-belly stove. Kentucky Adams and Patrick had come in from walking guard on the Motor Pool from midnight to two o'clock, and they were sitting on a bench in the corner, drinking some steaming cocoa that had been brought down from Baker Company in a big enameled dixie. The rest of the men had gone straight to their bunks after coming in out of the cold night, and as the light from one bulb and the flickering stove played across the darkened area, there was only the sound of snores coming from the men as they lay fully dressed on the bunks. Patrick took another swallow of the good hot cocoa and sat there with the cup between his hands, looking over toward Kentucky. Kentucky was leaning back against the wall with his eyes half closed, and the cup of cocoa was steaming beside him on the bench. Kentucky had been acting as Corporal of the Guard during the Guard Mount this afternoon, and he had come down the front rank behind the Sergeant of the Guard and the Officer of the Guard. The Officer of the Guard was a very sharp-looking captain with a First Division Patch, a Combat Infantry Badge, and the Silver Star. He had chewed ass all the way down the line, but when Patrick had executed his usual clumsy inspection arms, resting the stock of his rifle a little bit against his leg in order to help his weak right arm hold the weapon while his left hand slapped back the bolt, the captain had blown up.

"What was that?" he had said to Patrick.

"Inspection arms, sir."

"You're a mess," the captain had said. "Corporal of the Guard." Kentucky had come forward, all sparkling brass and shining boots and his blond jaw square under his helmet liner. "When we fall back into the Guard Hut you will give this man instruction in doing inspection arms."

"Yes, sir," Kentucky had said, and the inspecting party had moved on.

Now it was ten hours later, and during that time Patrick had been doing a lot of thinking. It was as if the scales had been suddenly pulled away from his eyes, and he saw now that he had been taking Basic Training with one arm. He was beginning to realize, for the first time in twenty-two years, that he was crippled. All at once he saw it, in one flash of remembering how clumsy he had been with the BAR and the M-1, and how it had been just good luck that he had got through the Infiltration Course because his group had not had to carry rifles. He was not clumsy, he was crippled. Not seriously crippled, not in a way that would prevent you from leading a normal civilian life and even playing some sports, but this was no place to be crippled at all. And on the heels of reaching that conclusion as he had paced around the outer fence of the Motor Pool with his rifle as the sun went down, he had felt the fear that he had felt a few times before, the vague fear that he might die. He had got a letter from Bill Bench today, and Bill was in it all the way. Bill was in a company on the front line. Patrick had realized that it could happen to him too, that he could miss OCS and be sent to Korea, but he had never realized before what a poor chance he had of surviving in combat. Now it was all coming to him fast, on top of the numbness that he had felt ever since he had walked out of Anna's house on Sunday afternoon. That was three days ago, and they would be restricted this week-end and then go out on bivouac next week, and then there would be a week of processing and they were finished with Fort Dix. It was all one big thing bearing down on all of them, and now Patrick saw no light at all. Until last week he had hoped for Anna, lived to go and see Anna, and when he thought about the Army he thought of himself as Lieutenant Kingsgrant, smashing through to glory while his batman shined his boots. Now he was realizing that he better have a batman to carry his rifle and fire it for him. He had kept thinking that he could make it, that if he just kept his defects concealed he would end up where he thought he should be, fighting the enemy with his nation's army in time of war, but in one fast self-revelation he was seeing that he was all wrong. In these last two hours of walking his post in the darkness one scene had come back over him again and again. Again he had dropped that heat lamp on the iron bar at the bottom of his bunk, again he had heard it explode, again and again he had seen the look on all of their faces in the barracks when they saw how near he had come to hurting Lish. He had dropped that bulb for the same reason that he could not do inspection arms properly after fourteen weeks, and now he was beginning to realize that not only might he get killed himself, but he might wipe out a few of his own side with him.

Patrick stood up and swallowed the rest of his cup of cocoa. Kentucky was still sprawled out on the bench with his eyes half open. Patrick wanted to read the letter from Bill again, and he went over to the upper bunk where his overcoat and helmet liner and blanket were, stepping quietly in the darkness.

"Pat?" It was a whisper.

"Uh-huh?" Patrick said softly. Ratigan was on guard duty with some of the boys from the Fourth Platoon, and he had picked the bottom half of the bunk where Patrick had his things.

"How you doin'?"

"O.K." Patrick got Bill's letter out of his overcoat and bent down toward Ratigan's moon face in the darkness. "I didn't wake you up, did I?"

"No. You all right?"

"Sure. I'm just going to read this letter, and then I'll get some sleep."

"Good night."

"Good night," Patrick said. "God bless you."

"God bless you too."

Patrick walked back toward the bench. Kentucky had awakened and was slowly untying the laces of his combat boots. Patrick sat down, the letter from Bill in his hand, and thought about how he and Ratigan had a special smile reserved for each other, and how they often would drift together at ten-minute breaks. It was all because they had been together in those first days at Kilmer when they were herded around like stunned cattle. If the Army was smart, Patrick said, looking down at the envelope that said "Free" in Bill's handwriting where a stamp normally was, they'd keep you right with the first guys you were with on the first days. Classify you somehow before you ever spent a night in the Army, and then keep you with the first guys. Patrick took the letter out of the envelope. "Dear Pat," Bill's long-tailed handwriting said, "just a belated note to catch you up on where I am. I'm with the Second Division. I got up here and I thought they might give us some more training, but they put us into companies and I'm in it." A new paragraph began. "I don't know what to say about this place. Believe me, Syngman Rhee is just another oriental war lord, and don't let anybody tell you a different story. I've never appreciated my own country the way I have since I landed here. The homesickness is tremendous, but there is no spirit of mutiny or anything like that. Everybody is just sweating it out for the Big R. I get five days R and R in Japan in about three months, but it's the Big R that's on everybody's mind. One thing is for sure, I couldn't be collecting points faster if I tried. I'm a rifleman in a rifle company, so you can pretty well figure out how I've landed up." Patrick turned the page over. "I've adopted a dog, or a dog has adopted me. He was already in this squad, but he seems to have taken a liking to me. We all feed him, and I must say he isn't particular. The other day he ate a cigar. (Not part of his regular diet.) His name is Dean Acheson, and the name is a good deal more dignified than the dog. He doesn't look at all oriental, and at night he gets taken back to the CP and stays warm." Bill's handwriting was closing in on the bottom part of the second page, and he began to crowd it up in his last paragraph. "Take it easy, Pat. I hope you make OCS if that's what you want, but stay away from here. If you get out of this whole deal all right, do what you want to do. Whatever it is, do it. Give your family my best, and let's start planning a massive, Cronin's-type plaster job when I get back. I'll be bringing quite a head of steam into the project. Sincerely, Bill."

Patrick stared at the letter for a moment, and then put it back into its envelope.

"Letter from your girl?"

Patrick looked up. Kentucky was standing sleepily with his combat boots held in his right hand.

"No. Just a friend."

Kentucky nodded his head and yawned.

"Good night, Brother Kingsgrant."

"Good night, Kentucky." Patrick got onto his feet, picked up the plastic cup he had used before, and ladled himself out some more cocoa. He stood with the cup in his hand, and there were sudden tears in his eyes as he thought about his girl. At least there was one thing this time. He no longer really believed that it would work out. Before, when she had ridden away from him in Central Park, he had stayed away from her because she had sent him away, but he had hoped and prayed that somehow it might work out, and that she might love him, that she had to love him because he loved her. Now, since Sunday, he hurt all over, but it was more the feeling that he had had when he realized, about a week after his mother's funeral, that she wasn't coming back. He had thought he understood when his mother told Eileen and him about heaven, but he had thought that at least they would be able to see each other sometimes.

Patrick sat down on the bench. The Guard Hut was silent except for the breathing of the men. He looked at his watch. It was half past two. In another hour they would begin to wake up the group that had been off since ten o'clock, and start them getting ready to go out and relieve the group that was out there now, walking slowly with their bayoneted rifles on their shoulders, guarding Fort Dix as it slept. Patrick took a swallow of cocoa. It was beginning to cool off a little, but still it tasted good. Stand up, lad. He thought about the phrase, and it was almost as if O'Reilley were saying it in the darkness. Just keep going. Maybe they'll take you for Armor OCS and maybe you'll be all right when you've got a tank to go through the Infiltration Course for you. You've kept going for fourteen weeks with the pain. You've kept on doing the best you could. Just keep going and maybe this thing will work out. For a moment a picture rose in his mind of himself coming up a road in Korea. Bill was standing there, and his outfit was coming up to relieve Bill's outfit.

"I'll be goddamned," Bill said, his voice saying it even more wonderingly than the night when Patrick had appeared in his barracks during the GI party. "I'll be goddamned."

Patrick put the cup of cocoa down on the bench, picked up his letter from Bill, and wandered off toward his bunk.

III

"Who?" Eileen said into the humming, hissing, crackling French telephone. For a moment she had had the funniest idea that it was Snowjob Porter.

"It's Snowjob, Eileen," the voice said, more clearly this time. "I'm in Cannes."

"Snowjob! "What are you doing in Cannes?"

"My ship's in Cannes. I'm coming up to Paris for a few days, and I want to see you."

"Wonderful! I'd love to see you, too. Have you seen Patrick?"

"No. I sent him a postcard from Gibraltar the other day, but we haven't been very good about writing."

"Where's Tall Man?"

"I don't know exactly. The last time I heard from him he was in Camp Pendleton, California."

"Where?"

"Camp Pendle — I'll tell you when I see you."

"All right. I'm at Reid Hall."

"I know. I want you to show me the town."

"Fine. I'd love it. What kind of things do you want to do?"

"You know what I want to do?"

"What?"

"I want to sit in a café on the Champs-Elysées and have about five drinks. All right?"

"Got just the place," Eileen said, smiling. "When do you get here?"

"Tomorrow."

"We'll pub-crawl right down the Champs-Elysées. If it's a warm day we can sit outside."

"Just so it's the Champs-Elysées," Snowjob said. "See you tomorrow."

"All right," Eileen said. "Call me when you get here."

"I'd better just come over," Snowjob's voice said. "I don't want to cope with their telephones any more."

"I don't blame you. See you tomorrow."

"G'bye."

" 'Bye, Snowjob."

There was a click, and Eileen beamed as she hung up the staticky little phone. It was as if all of Leverett D-32 had walked in the door. There was sunlight on the window on this last day of March, and spring was trying hard. Eileen looked around, decided that she wanted to take a walk, and went up to her room to get her coat.

IV

The troops sat beside their packs, eating a C-ration lunch in the drizzling rain.

"How'd you like that flamethrower?" Forlenza said to the squad, not looking up from the food he was eating. "Wicked, uh?"

Patrick nodded and kept on eating the cold hash in the olive-colored can. They had been out here three days, and they were tired beyond anything they had felt before. Because of almost incredibly bad scheduling, they had had two hours of bayonet practice and an hour of PT on Monday afternoon, just before the eighteen-mile night march. They had started off the march after chow, already exhausted, but most of them had made it. Since then it had been the familiar nightmare of sleeping in cold sandy wet holes and trudging under their packs from one obstacle course to another. The only improvement was that it was the first week in April now, and the snow seemed to be over. Right after this break for lunch they were going into a twenty-four-hour exercise called "The Company in the Attack." This morning they had had a demonstration of some of the weapons that would be working with them in this exercise, and then they had run through the initial phase of it once without firing, accompanied by the blue-helmeted cadremen from this course.

"That Artillery is for nothing," Interlicchio said.

"If that is Artillery, man," Jakes said, cupping his hands as he tried to get a cigarette going, "I don't want none of it."

"I hope they do better than that, anyways," Lish said. He had been in the hospital for a week, after the thirteenth week bivouac, but he had been returned in time for this one and he seemed to be making it all right.

Patrick took another bite of the clammy hash as they sat in the rain. He was forced to admit that they had a point about the Artillery, at least on the basis of this morning's performance. The company had been in a grandstand that looked out over the chewed-up plateau that they were going to attack and then defend against a simulated counterattack, and they had had a demonstration of a 105. The 105 had come rolling up behind a truck, and as its crew got it ready to fire, a squeaky-voiced lieutenant with a red scarf at his throat had told them condescendingly about the Artillery, how the Artillery could give them the real support when they needed it, and how this gun was about to demolish a concrete bunker four hundred yards away. Then the lieutenant had gone down to the cannon, which was being loaded with much shouting and stamping and counting off by the numbers. Baker Company had sat there like expectant little children, waiting to see the bunker disappear in a puff of smoke. There had been more yelling, and then the gun had started blasting away. After six rounds the nearest shell had come within about fifteen yards of the bunker, and the Artillery had hooked up without another word, and driven off.

"All right, let's get moving there. Leave your packs right there." It was Rodriguez' voice. Patrick got up, hurriedly shoveling down the rest of the cold hash. In a corner of the area he saw a sergeant wearing a light blue helmet. He was passing out bandoliers of live ammunition to some of the men who were gathering around him.

"Smoke if you got 'em," the sergeant said as Rodriguez came up with the platoon following behind him. "All right. You people been through one dry run on this course this morning, so I won't say anything about that. I just want to give you a little practical advice. We haven't had anybody killed out here yet, and we won't have as long as you people listen to what we tell you. The cadre out here are combat veterans. There isn't any chickenshit out here. Nobody's going to harass you. Who's got a cigarette?" Several people offered him a cigarette. "That

one's too wet," the sergeant said, smiling. Finally he picked one.
"Thanks." He lit it in one fast motion. "If at any time you're
in any doubt about what's going on," he said through the first
few puffs, "just stay still. Don't go forward when you're in
doubt. If you go too far forward you'll get it from a bullet or
an artillery shell. If you're all alone, there's probably something
wrong. Try to stay abreast of the people you're with. Above
all, don't fire your weapon when you're in any doubt about
whether you ought to be firing it or not. You men firing BAR's,
that goes double for you." He took a long puff on his cigarette
and stared at them as they stood in front of him, rain-blackened
figures with their rifles slung on their shoulders. "I understand
this is a pretty good company. If you want a high company
score, you've got to keep playing ball for the whole twenty-four
hours. When you take that hill, dig in like you meant it. When
they try to infiltrate you tonight, put up a lot of fire with your
blank cartridges. You'll get the blanks later. Your own cadre
will be with you once the initial attack is over, but during that
attack the men with the blue helmets out here are your boss.
There'll be a couple of blue-tops with every platoon. If you're
in doubt, look around for the blue-top. O.K. Plenty of ammo
for everybody over by that shed. Move out."

WHAAM!
It was twenty minutes later, they were standing on a road
that ran through a weird forest of tree trunks that had had the
bark blasted from them, and the Artillery was slamming away
over the area that was their objective.
WHAAM!
Patrick stood beside the tank that was going to move up with
his squad for part of the way. He had a bandolier of ammunition looped over his left shoulder and running down under his
right arm, and he was chewing some gum from his C-rations.

The tankers were buttoned up inside their silent monster.

WHAAM! WHAAM!

I hope it goes all right, Patrick thought. This morning he had almost collapsed from the effort of going across the half-mile course, running and hitting the dirt and running again. He had got to their objective behind most of the squad. Now he looked at them. They were spread out on either side of the road, Hetzler and Maple and Lish Jones and Forlenza behind him on his side, and Interlicchio and Jakes and Encarnacion and Stanley on the other side. Forlenza had the BAR, and Stanley was back there to help Forlenza with the BAR if he should need it, and to keep an eye on the squad from the rear. They were standing in the drizzle, about five yards apart, smoking or chewing gum or staring at the hull of the tank just ahead of them on the dirt road. Patrick was just a little ahead of the rest of them.

WHAAM!

"Awright," a blue-top said, appearing from nowhere, "lock an' load one clip. Squad leader, check to see they've got the safeties on."

"How about bayonets?" Patrick asked.

"Christ, yes. Haven't you put those on yet?" The cadreman disappeared back into the forest of naked tree trunks.

"Fix bayonets," Patrick said, turning around. There was the sound of the bayonets coming out of their scabbards, and then the sound, just after the clicking of the bayonets onto the rifles, of the bolts being drawn back as everybody put in a clip of ammunition. Patrick slammed in a clip, thinking about how much better he was doing it than those first five days on the range, and started down the line on his side. As he passed each man the man raised his rifle up for Patrick to see that the safety was snapped back toward the trigger, and Patrick nodded and kept going. He stopped by Forlenza. Forlenza grinned at him in the rain, and Patrick grinned back. It was that same infectious smile that sometimes spread through the squad when they were about to do something new and exciting and a little bit frightening.

WHAAM!

"You've got to get those rounds out fast now," Patrick said to Forlenza, as Forlenza held the big BAR out toward him.

"Don't worry," Forlenza said, putting the automatic rifle back on his shoulder. "We're gonna be all right. We got the best squad leader there is."

"Sure," Patrick said. "I was so good this last time I almost didn't get there."

"This thing is a ball breaker, all right," Forlenza said. "Don't you worry. We're gonna be all right."

Patrick smiled, checked Stanley's rifle, and went up the other short file, grinning at Emilio as he went by.

WHAAM!

Patrick checked his own safety again and then stood beside the tank, still chewing his gum, with one hand on his cartridge belt and one hand on his rifle sling. Suddenly he was aware that Emilio was standing next to him. There was a funny look on Emilio's face, as if he had something to say and didn't know quite how to say it.

"How are you?" Patrick said, smiling.

"I go into combat with you any time," Emilio said, and went back to his position in the short file across the road.

The Artillery had stopped. The tank roared with a sudden, ear-splitting racket. The blue-top came out of some bushes up ahead on the road. He didn't say anything. He just waved his arm forward in that old, unmistakable gesture. The tank roared particularly loud for a moment and started forward. Patrick waved to his squad to come on, and got down in a fast crouching trot as he stayed alongside the tank. About seventy yards up the road a path moved off to the left. The blue-top dove off onto this path, and Patrick followed him as the tank kept on along the road.

"Keep going until you hit the first firing line! Open fire as soon as you get there!" the blue-top yelled. He had jumped off the path and was watching them run past. A machine gun was hammering away not far to the left. Patrick broke out of the bushes. The path disappeared, but about fifteen yards ahead of him were the red-painted stakes marking the first firing line. Patrick reached the line and dropped into a prone position. The others came diving in on both sides of him. Patrick knocked off his safety, lined up on a red silhouette target in front of him, and fired. He touched the trigger again, and to his amazement his rifle was firing semi-automatically for the first time in four months.

BAPAPAPAP BAPAP BAPAPAP. Forlenza had the BAR going.

"Move ahead!" the blue-top yelled. Patrick put his rifle back on safety, and got onto his feet. The next firing line was about thirty yards away, and half of his squad was already in front of him.

Patrick jumped into his hole at the end of the course about three seconds after the rest of them had tumbled into theirs. Emilio was in the big foxhole, and Patrick came in beside him, all combat boots and sand and knees. A couple of the men in the squad were already firing at the silhouette targets down in the valley at the bottom of the slope. Patrick got his elbows set on the rim of the foxhole and began firing at a target down the slope. His foxhole was above and behind a couple of the other foxholes. His rifle was working beautifully, and he had never been better at putting the clips in. He felt a hand on his shoulder. It was the blue-top, motioning him to fire at the next target over to the left. Patrick got his face away from behind the sights and saw why. His shots at the other target must have been passing within a couple of feet of Forlenza, who was standing in the foxhole just below, almost in the line of fire. Patrick shifted his attention to the new target and began firing again, feeling relief that he had been aiming carefully before. If he had just fired them to get rid of them, Forlenza might be dead right now. In a second the thought was lost in the controlled frenzy of loading, aiming, firing off a clip, and loading again. Emilio's rifle had become so hot that it had stopped working, and now Emilio was just handing him a new clip every few seconds. Two minutes later Patrick came to the end of the last clip. He put down the hot weapon.

"Get digging!" the blue-top yelled.

"What with?" Patrick shouted back. Their shovels were back with their packs, near the place they had jumped off with the tank.

"Use your steel pot!" the cadreman said. "The Chinks are coming right back up the hill, and you want to have as good a hole as you can!"

Patrick took off his helmet, separated the steel part from the liner, and began digging into the side of the already large foxhole. The rifle fire was petering out, and for the next couple of minutes the only sound was that of men digging.

"Awright," the blue-top yelled. "Here comes the counter-attack."

The few men who had any ammunition left fired their rounds off at the same targets they had fired at before, and the rest of them simulated firing by working the bolts of their rifles.

"Awright," the blue-top yelled after a minute. "Counter-attack beaten off. Clear your weapons and take a break. We'll be tactical again in about half an hour, after you go back and get your packs."

They stood up in the silence. Nobody said anything. They

came up out of their holes and stood at the edge of the slope. It was a sharp slope, and the ground was bare and chewed up. It looked like every newsreel picture of Korea, and the silence after the firing made it seem all the more dramatic, just the big slope, with holes and wires all over the place, and the men walking slowly up to its edge and looking down into the stillness of the valley below. This was it. This was the way it looked.

"Awright," the blue-top yelled. "Put all your brass in your helmets and bring it up here."

"Listen to that," Maple said, turning away from the crest of the hill. "I'll bet when you go into combat there's somebody standing there saying 'Awright, men, let's police up this battle-field.'"

"Boy," Forlenza was saying, "I could hear those bullets going right past my head."

You're so right, Patrick said to himself, and got down into his hole and began picking up the shiny brass ejected cartridges that were everywhere in the dirt.

v

When it happened it did not involve explosives. Patrick was checking his squad in their holes about two hours after chow. It was dark, and the four platoons of Baker Company were dug in on a large circular perimeter, supposedly alert and waiting to repulse infiltrators. Actually most of the men were asleep, and a sound of snoring was in the air all along the slope where the Second Platoon was dug in for the night.

Patrick stood on the edge of Forlenza and Maple's hole. All he could see down there was darkness, and a sound of happy snoring came up out of the hole. He thought about waking them, decided that it would be worth his life if he did, and walked on to the next hole, about twenty yards away. Lish was standing in the deep hole, resting his elbows on its rim, and Stanley was asleep, sitting with his back against one of the hole's sandy sides.

"How's it going?" Patrick said quietly, lowering himself down into the hole.

"All right," Lish said. "I'm awful tired."

"So am I."

"I can still hear all that stuff going off in my ears." Lish rested his chin on top of his folded arms. His rifle was lying on the rim of the hole, operating handle up.

"I can still hear it too," Patrick said, looking around. The night had a sort of luminosity about it. He was thinking about where he could find some water. The top of his canteen had become unscrewed in the attack, and by the time he had noticed it, all his water was gone. The can of pineapple that he had with his C-rations for evening chow had sufficed to give him enough liquid to get the food down, but now he was thirsty. "Where do you think I could get some water, Lish?" Patrick asked, running his hand over the butt of his rifle and brushing away some of the sand that had accumulated on it.

"I don't know. I heard they's some coffee back at the Platoon CP."

"Think I'll go back there and get some."

"Which hole you in, Kingsgrant? Case anything starts."

Patrick pointed into the darkness above them. "I'm in that hole I was digging in this afternoon. With Emilio." He put his rifle up over the edge and started to climb out. Just as he was balanced on the lip of the hole, the entire side of the hole caved in and Patrick fell straight down in a mass of falling sand and dirt. As he landed he could feel his right knee snapping and twisting, and then he was lying in the bottom of the hole.

"What's wrong, Kingsgrant? What's wrong?"

Patrick's helmet had fallen off, and he could feel beads of sweat on his cold face. He felt as if he was going to vomit.

"I don't know yet," he heard himself saying. He sat up and his leg gave him another band of pain. He shook his head, and put both his hands gently on his thigh, near his right knee.

"I know you must be hurt from the way you fell," Lish said. Patrick shook his head again. He didn't have much doubt about what had happened. The doctors had told him never to smash up his knee again, and he had just smashed up his knee.

"Is there anything I can do to help?"

"Not right now, Lish." His knee was beginning to feel hot. He looked around. Stanley was still asleep. The earth that had come down had buried Stanley's boots, but he was still asleep with his helmeted head forward on his chest. "I think I'll try to get out of this hole," he said after a few seconds.

"Lemme help you." Lish lifted him up and put him on his feet. Patrick leaned against the side of the hole with both hands, and gingerly put his right foot down. There was an immediate string of pain that went all the way up into his thigh. He leaned against the side of the hole for another minute, sweat running off his face, and then, with Lish helping him, he got up on the edge of the hole and rolled out and lay there. After a minute he got up, standing on his left leg and using his rifle as a crutch, and tried putting his right leg down again. The pain was not quite so bad this time, although he let out a gasp. After a couple of minutes he found that, although it hurt a lot, he could do an extreme limp if he got his weight off his right foot quickly. Once or twice he sobbed from the pain, but he could limp several yards at a time. The leg felt all hot.

Suddenly Patrick looked up at the cloudy, luminous sky, and laughed, a funny, this-is-too-much kind of laugh. It had just occurred to him that it might be all over. God had watched him get into the Army, perjure himself, suffer pain, head hell-bent toward destruction, and now God had reached down from behind those luminous clouds and put an end to it.

"You all right, Kingsgrant?" Lish's voice said in the darkness.

"I guess so." It had suddenly occurred to Patrick that he had seen an ambulance up near the tower on the road that they had used for their jumping-off place, and that if he went back down that road maybe the ambulance would be there, and they might be able to do something for him. Slowly and painfully he made his way over the crest of the hill, using his rifle awkwardly as a cane.

Half an hour later he was still limping up the tank-rutted road. He had given up using the rifle as a cane because it was too heavy and awkward, and now he had it slung on his shoulder. The moonlight from behind the clouds was ghostly on the road, and even more ghostly when the road went into the forest of white jagged tree trunks. It was quiet in the forest, and occasionally from a distance there would come the sounds of a sudden exchange of shots, or a flare would go up somewhere even farther away. Patrick stopped to rest a good many times along the way, leaning or hanging against one of the silvery stripped trunks beside the road. There was nothing moving anywhere.

Finally he reached the tower. It was a big house-like box sitting up in the air on four long thin legs, outlined black against the silver-patterned clouds, and the ambulance was parked by one of the legs, silent and dark. There was nobody in the cab when Patrick limped up to it and looked in, but there was a snore coming from the back. Patrick hobbled around to the back door of the ambulance and opened it. There was a Negro asleep on one of the stretchers, his wiry hair suddenly silver from the moonlight that shone in when Patrick opened the door. Patrick reached in and put his hand on the man's shoulder.

"Huh?"

"I'm sorry to bother you," Patrick said, "but I've just smashed up my knee, and I'm afraid it's pretty serious."

"Man, I'm just the driver. I can't do nothin' for you."

"Well, isn't there somebody who can?"

"Man, I don't know. You better come back in the mornin'."

Patrick stepped back and closed the door. Then he turned and started making his way back along the road. Some of the clouds had pulled back, and the night was clearer. There was nobody in sight, and after a while as Patrick came out of the forest and onto the flat, chewed-up expanse, there was not even any firing any more. A great quiet hung over the area.

After he had been limping along for a few more minutes, Patrick became convinced that he was on the wrong road. Everything was just flat shell-holed earth, and there were no landmarks at all. A track would cut in here and lead off there, and the moon shone down on all of it equally. Patrick stood still for about a minute, his face tight, and then decided that he would keep going on this road and hope that he was right. He walked faster now, his pain and frustration too deep for cursing aloud. As he walked, he swore inwardly. He swore at the night, and the road, and the man in the ambulance. He swore at everything, but most of all he swore at himself. He swore at himself for joining the Army. He told himself that it was nobody's duty to join the Army, the Army was just a nasty business and it was each man's responsibility to himself to see that he wasn't in it. Somebody had to do it, but let it be somebody else.

Suddenly he saw the platoon command post on the right. It might be somebody else's CP, but it looked encouragingly like his. He kept going, and a couple of minutes later he came to the crest of the slope and saw the familiar pattern of holes that were his command. He crawled into his hole. Emilio had made a good thing of it, spreading their shelter halves across some pine boughs from the other side of the valley to make a roof on their hole. Patrick got himself inside his sleeping bag, drawing in his breath every time his knee hurt. Just as he got himself inside, brushing away a rivulet of sand coming down from the top of the hole, a rattle of blank firing started nearby. It was strange, hearing the real shots superimposed on the ones that were still banging away in his head from the daytime. He had not paid any attention to the shots in his head while he was limping toward the ambulance and back, but now he heard both sets, the present ones and the remembered ones, and he felt too sick and wounded and beaten to do anything about it.

Emilio started struggling out of his sleeping bag.

"Handle it, will you, Emilio?" Patrick said. He lay listening to Emilio work his weapon and fire off the wet blanks that went *phht,* and then to his surprise he found himself going right through the pain and on into sleep. Our Father Who Art in Heaven, Patrick started to say, and then he was asleep.

VI

A lot more than Patrick's knee broke that night. He woke up the next morning, dimly aware that Emilio was moving around, and lay still, looking up at the design of pine bough and shelter half over his head. He could hear the rest of the squad moving around outside, rolling up their blankets and shelter halves and sleeping bags.

He wanted very much not to get up. His knee was a big thing now, stiff and swollen and painful to the touch. He did not care any more about the other people, and he was scared.

"Kingsgrant you better saddle up boss," Emilio said from above the canvas.

"I'm not sure that I can," Patrick said. He raised himself up and started pulling his sleeping bag out from under him. It was hard work, but eventually he got it down around his legs. Then he got on his side and pulled his bad leg out of the mass of blankets and sleeping bag. It hurt, but he could move it. He switched himself around like a great crab and came crawling out from under the roof that Emilio had put on the hole.

About ten minutes later, with the help of Stanley and Emilio, Patrick had his pack rolled. He felt terribly hungry, but there was no time for them to eat their remaining C-rations. All over the hillside little packed-up squads were starting to wander from their holes back toward the main assembly area where they had seen the artillery demonstration the day before, and they were going to have to get down there too. It was all too evident that for the moment there was no time for breakfast, and most certainly there was no Sick Call.

Patrick looked around the immediate area, his face bristly and taut and tired. He saw Stanley watching him, and then he realized that he was still in charge of this squad, and they were waiting for him to tell them what to do.

"Stanley," he said, "go back to the platoon CP and ask Rodriguez if he wants us to move out of here. Just give us a wave if he does."

They stood with their packs at their feet, leaning on their rifles as they watched Stanley sling on his pack and take off.

"How you feelin' this mornin', Kingsgrant?" Lish asked.

"Well, my leg's swollen up so it's sort of holding itself together," Patrick answered, trying to smile.

"Bet it hurts," Lish said.

"Whatdidya do, hurt you leg?" Forlenza said.

"I'm afraid so."

"This is no place for a hurt leg." Forlenza shook his head.

"I agree with you."

Stanley waved at them from back by the little hump that marked the CP, and they started moving in his direction.

Patrick tried using his rifle as a cane for the first minute, but it seemed heavier and more awkward than ever. He was limping badly, so that his steps were practically hops instead of limps, and the rest of the squad was pulling ahead of him. The pack felt as if it weighed two hundred pounds.

Patrick saw Captain Hare coming down the rough battlefield road, moving past them in the opposite direction.

"Sir?" Patrick said, stepping off the side of the road.

The company commander stopped. He was obviously in a hurry. "What is it?"

"Sir, I'm afraid I injured my knee pretty badly last night, and I was wondering if there's anything I can do about it."

"There's an ambulance down by the tower," the captain said. "Maybe they can do something for you." He walked on. Patrick turned on and hobbled through the stand of blasted trees, on toward the tower. His squad were way ahead of him. He came to the tower, and the ambulance was gone. He saw his squad going down a road that was a couple of ruts in a scrub-pine wood, and he followed them down it. His leg was burning, and every now and then something in it caught and pinched, a sharp, mean, pinching pain deep inside the knee.

Everyone was sitting in the area just behind the stands when he got there, munching their breakfast of cold biscuits. Nobody said much, and everyone was tired and muddy and unshaven. It was a foggy day, and the cadremen were just as dirty and tired as the men with the rifles. Patrick looked around for Rodriguez, but Rodriguez was not in sight, and a minute later they were filing into the stands. There was a captain there, one of the men who had briefed them the day before. The attack, he said, had been rated Excellent. He was sorry to say that the defense had only been rated Good. This was due to the fact that in several sectors there had been a minimal response to the attempts at infiltration. This minimal response, the captain said in a matter-of-fact way, was because more than fifty per cent of the company had been asleep. The captain said that he hoped they had all learned something from their experience out here, and Baker Company dragged itself out of the stands.

When Patrick came hobbling up, the Second Platoon was already in four ranks, ready to move out. He went up to Rodriguez.

"Sarge," Patrick said, "I hurt my knee very badly last night, and I don't think I ought to walk on it very far."

"You'll have to walk out of here," Rodriguez said. He did not appear to be very concerned.

"I thought maybe I could go on a truck." Patrick was getting scared.

"All the vehicles are gone ahead," Rodriguez said. "Fall in, Kingsgrant."

Patrick stepped back to his place at the head of the second squad, and a minute later he was marching down the road. He was limping badly. Occasionally that deep-in pinch would happen in his leg, and when it did, he would stumble. Anger and fear crossed and recrossed in Patrick's mind. He was afraid that finally they were doing it to him. Finally they were really hurting him. They had caused him pain with his left shoulder, plenty of pain, but still he could move his left arm any way that he wanted to. But maybe right now, right on this march, they were finishing off his leg. Maybe he was going to limp the rest of his life. He thought of what had happened the first time he smashed up his knee. They had taken him in to the field house on a rolling stretcher, and ten minutes later he had been lying on a table with his football uniform off and ice packed all around his knee. This time they had let him spend the night in a hole and then march out with a full field pack. And this time was probably more serious than the first time. If it hadn't been finished off last night, it might easily be finished off by noon today.

Suddenly the knee pinched again, and then again. Patrick let out a sob. Goddam man in the ambulance last night. Goddam company commander. Goddam Rodriguez. They were ruining him and they didn't care. This was too much. This had nothing to do with a bad right arm, or tearing muscles in your left shoulder trying to compensate for a bad right arm. Anybody might have wrenched his knee falling in a foxhole, and this was the treatment they gave you. Patrick pulled up his rifle and sobbed again as he struggled along. You fool, he said, you should have just stayed there on the ground and said you couldn't move. Then they would have had to do something for you. That's what anybody with a brain in his head would have done. Anybody. All you had to do was lie there last night and get Lish to call Rodriguez. Then Rodriguez would have told the C.O. and the C.O. would have told the ambulance driver to take you in, and that would have been that.

"Close it up there, Kingsgrant," Rodriguez' voice said.

Patrick hobbled forward to close up the interval. He was not crying outwardly, but inwardly he was bawling like a baby. He wanted his mother. He wanted the pain to stop, and the march to stop, and this whole grubby sweaty nightmare to stop.

"Come on, Patrick," Stanley said in an exasperated way. Stanley was doing a tap dance under his full pack in an effort to keep off Patrick's heels. Patrick lurched ahead, and then, through the tears in his eyes, he saw a tower up ahead. There was something familiar about the tower, and as they neared it Patrick could see what it was. It was the tower on the range that they had come to in the trucks that morning four months ago, the day he had spent digging target pits with Stanley and Forlenza, before Basic Training had started.

The left file of the First Platoon flanked across the road to join the right file, and a minute later the company was grounding packs in formation near the firing lines in front of the tower, and marching off to begin the exercises.

By about one-thirty in the afternoon several things had happened. Patrick had discovered that there was going to be a Sick Call held in the tower at a quarter to two. Gomez had started to get tough about something with a man in the First Platoon and been kneed in the groin. They had all had a C-ration lunch, and Patrick had had a run-in with Sergeants Rodriguez and O'Reilley combined. Over to one side of the big Transition Range there was a 57 mm. Refresher Course. There were half a dozen of the recoilless rifles there, but these were adjusted to fire a .22 caliber bullet from within their barrels, at a target ten yards away. It was purely an exercise in handling the sight, but it entailed having to kneel down beside the sight. Patrick had told Rodriguez that he did not think he could bend his leg to kneel down.

"All right," Sergeant O'Reilley had said, appearing suddenly behind Rodriguez, "if he can't kneel down then he'll just have to come out here some other day on his own time when he *can* kneel."

"You better kneel, Kingsgrant," Rodriguez had said, good and loud, and finally Patrick had managed to do it by making his left leg be the one that bent, and keeping his right leg stiffly out in front of him. The funny thing was that he had done all right. So far he had not fired the Transition Range, but he was standing with the others, waiting to see if he could get into the various positions for firing at the moving targets.

"Sick, lame, and lazy, right up here!" Sergeant O'Reilley yelled. Patrick set his rifle carefully in one of the racks that stood behind the firing line, and hobbled over to join the little knot of men that was forming around O'Reilley.

"Let's go," the sergeant said when he had them around him, and they walked off behind him, toward the tower. There was an ambulance sitting beside the tower when they got there, and Sergeant O'Reilley passed it and motioned to them to follow him up the wooden stairway that ran up the side of the square concrete tower. Patrick hobbled up the steps behind them, holding on to the banister with both hands, and found them all in a little room. There was a bunk in here, and a couple of pin-up pictures on the wall. A good big stove was going, and the room was comfortable and warm after the raw foggy day outside. Patrick sat down on the remains of a chair that stood by the door. There were two men in here wearing clean fatigues and field caps. One of them, a Negro, was lying on the bunk reading a comic book, and Patrick looked at him and wondered if he was the driver from last night. The other one, a young-looking Pfc, was staring at the teeth of one of the men from Baker Company.

"I'm sorry," the Pfc said after a minute, "but the best I can do for that toothache is tell you to make a dental appointment through your dispensary next week. All I can give you is something for the pain."

Sodium salicylate, Patrick thought, and the medic brought out a little box of sodium salicylate tablets.

"Do I go back now, Sarge?" the man with the toothache said to Sergeant O'Reilley.

"Did you fire the Transition?" O'Reilley said, not looking up from where he had sat down on a little chair beside the stove.

"Yeah."

"You might as well stay and get warm."

Gomez was next. "I fell on a recoilless rifle," Gomez said. "Got me right in the balls."

"Tell him the truth," Sergeant O'Reilley said, still gazing at the feet of the pot-belly stove. "Somebody kicked him there. Nobody's going to court-martial you for having a little fight now, Gomez. It might hold up your orders. Another five weeks and you'll be getting all the fighting you want."

"At least it'll be warmer in another five weeks," a man from the Fourth Platoon said. He and his buddy were taking advantage of the stove. They were filling their canteen cups with water, adding soluble cocoa powder from the C-rations, and heating it while they had the chance.

"It'll be warmer," Sergeant O'Reilley said. He took off his helmet and kept sitting there. His reddish hair was as disheveled as the rest of their heads, and he looked boyish. Suddenly he looked up. "You people are lucky," he said. "You've had a lot better training than I got. I went in at Inchon with a BAR, and I was firing the thing for a week before somebody showed me how to take it apart so I could clean it." Then he went back to gazing at the stove, while the medic looked at the rest of them.

Patrick was last.

"What's your problem?" the Pfc said.

"I smashed up an old knee injury last night."

"Take down your pants." Patrick slid down his field pants and fatigue pants, and then his long underwear. He looked at his leg. The right knee was twice the size of his left, and terribly discolored. The room was quiet except for the fire in the stove. Everyone was looking at his knee.

"What are you trying to do, Kingsgrant?" O'Reilley said after a minute. "Get out of the Army?"

"No, Sergeant," Patrick said.

"I'm taking this man in," the Pfc said. "The rest are all marked duty, Sergeant."

"O.K.," O'Reilley said, standing up. "Let's get going." He put his helmet on his head and walked out the door.

Patrick sat on a stretcher in the back of the ambulance, watching the more populated part of Fort Dix go by. They were taking him down to Dispensary U, which was where patients were treated in the afternoons. His leg was throbbing, but the thing that was worrying him at the moment was what would happen to his rifle and pack. They were sitting out there on the Transition Range. If you left a rifle sitting around you were not very likely to see it again, and trainees were charged in full for lost equipment.

"How you making out?" the Pfc said, turning halfway around in the front seat. The colored private was driving.

"All right, thanks."

"Hurt much?"

"Not too much right now."

The Pfc nodded his head and turned back toward the windshield. Patrick's face was drawn, but expressionless. The Pfc was a nice guy. It was pleasant to have nice guys around you when you were hurt. When you had something broken and painful the fight went out of you and you didn't want to be barked at or have to snap to.

The ambulance rolled into a black macadam area behind a low white building.

"Here we are," the Pfc said as they came to a stop. "Don't move till I come around to the back." He jumped out and opened the back doors a moment later. "Just slide out," he said. "Take your time." Patrick got out, and he and the Pfc went into the Dispensary building. "Get a slip from that girl over there, and then just sit down on that bench," the Pfc said. He went inside another room.

Patrick limped over and gave a civilian girl secretary his name, rank, serial number, and organization, and in five minutes the Pfc came back and took him down the hall to a doctor. The doctor was the same Austrian civilian doctor whom Patrick had seen once before, the one who had told Sergeant Singer to get Patrick an orthopedic appointment down at the hospital. Patrick stood in front of the doctor, wondering if this meant that his orthopedic appointment next week was canceled, or moved up, or lost like everything else, but the doctor gave no sign of recognizing him. He told Patrick to take off his trousers, and then prodded his knee and told him to bend it. Patrick could bend it about twenty degrees. The doctor nodded, and strapped up Patrick's knee with adhesive tape.

"You are regular Army?" he said in his Teutonic accent, looking at the slip that the civilian girl had typed up.

"Yes, sir."

"I give you a light-duty slip for three days. Then we look again at the leg. Go back to where your company is, but no marching."

"Sir, my company's on bivouac."

"Then go back to your bivouac."

Patrick felt like asking the doctor if he had ever been on bivouac, but what he said was "Yes, sir. Thank you, sir."

When they got outside to the ambulance the Pfc said, "Listen, buddy, sometimes you've got to take care of yourself in this outfit. You go back to your company area and show them your light-duty slip. They won't send you back out there. Just don't go back out there now. Go to your company area, got it?"

"Got it," Patrick said. "Thanks for everything."

"Take it easy."

Patrick nodded and limped off toward the road. The first two Post taxis that came by showed no inclination to pick up this dirty-looking soldier who was standing in the middle of Fort Dix wearing a helmet and cartridge belt with bayonet. The third one stopped.

"What'd you do, make a parachute drop in here?" the driver said, smiling.

"Not exactly," Patrick said. "Can you take me to Baker

Company Fiftieth?" He reached down into his fatigues, thanking God that they took their money with them on bivouac so nobody could break open their footlockers and steal it. He brought out a quarter and put it into the meter as he climbed slowly into the cab.

"Baker Fiftieth," the driver said.

"Check," Patrick said, and sat back against the soft cushions of the warm cab.

VII

Patrick came limping down the long linoleum-floored tunnel that connected the various sections of the Post hospital. He was making his way slowly, following the signs that were directing him to the Orthopedic Ward. It was Monday afternoon, and his long-scheduled orthopedic appointment had materialized. Sergeant Singer had called him into his office at the Regimental Dispensary when he was down there having his knee put under a heat lamp this morning, and he had been very brief. "Kingsgrant," he had said, "you're lucky your orthopedic appointment is coming up this afternoon. You better get everything straightened out down there, because if you don't come back with a slip saying you got something wrong with you, I don't want to see you no more."

Patrick turned a corner, following the signs, and his knee gave a hard pinch. He stopped for a moment and cursed quietly. They had all been restricted over the week-end, and even though he had taken it easy, the various pains in his body had become worse. The swelling in his knee had gone down, but the pain had increased. His left shoulder seemed to be stiffening up, and there was a clicking in his neck. He felt whipped and beaten and scared.

Up ahead there were several signs sticking out above the

doorways of various wards and departments, and Patrick looked at them. X-ray. No. Urology. No. Orthopedic. And how. Patrick turned in through the screen doors under the sign, and stopped at the desk.

"What's your name, soldier?"

Patrick looked at the girl behind the desk. She was pretty, but she wore glasses and she had a businesslike air.

"Kingsgrant, Patrick."

The girl riffled through a file, came up with Patrick's appointment slip, and handed it to him. Patrick took the slip, and wandered into the waiting room. Half the men in the waiting room were wearing hospital pajamas. Some of them were in wheel chairs, and there was quite a sprinkling of casts and slings around the room.

Patrick took off his field jacket and sat down. He was glad now that he had put on his cleanest set of fatigues, since all the men in the pajamas looked immaculate. The man next to him offered him a magazine, but Patrick said "No, thanks" and sat there, thinking hard. He was trying to decide what to do about his right arm. He was certainly going to have to show the man his left shoulder, and if the man was any good he was going to notice his right shoulder and arm once he was standing there, stripped down. Listen, the militant part of Patrick's mind lectured him, you're no more entitled to show them that arm now than you were before. But the militant part of Patrick sounded tired and unsure of itself, and it did not repeat the statement. Goddammit, Patrick's flayed nerves answered back, I never bargained for four months of pain and then a smashed-up knee. I never bargained for that. Nobody could bargain for that. It's a wonder I haven't lost my mind.

Patrick was still thinking and staring at nothing when he heard his name called.

"Here," he said, and got up as quickly as he could. There

was a captain standing in the hall, just outside the door of one of the small examining rooms. He was a big man with a round, pleasant face, and he was wearing a tan smock over his uniform shirt and trousers.

"Kingsgrant?" he said.

"Yes, sir."

"You just get undressed in this room here. I have another examination, and then I'll be with you."

"Yes, sir." Patrick went into the bare room and started taking off his boots. Hell, you'll probably come out of here just the way you went in, he said to himself. No profile change or anything. His boots were off, and he took off his fatigues and then sat on the one examining table against the wall, just wearing his T shirt and shorts. He was remembering Geremski's face when they had talked about his coming orthopedic appointment. "I'm not kidding you," Geremski had said. "I been down to the hospital when I got that stick in my eye. It's a whole new deal down there. They really look at you down there. If I was you I'd show them everything you got wrong with you." Patrick thought about the doctor who had told him to come in here. He did seem to radiate the air of a man who knew what he was doing. Patrick tried to straighten out his knee, and was rewarded with a sharp locking pain. He closed his eyes and shook his head.

The doctor came in and shut the door behind him. Patrick got off the table.

"Well, what's wrong with you?" he said.

Patrick took a deep breath. "Well, sir, I got this appointment originally for pains I'd been having in my left shoulder and my neck, and since then I've smashed up an old injury in my knee." His face flushed. "And then I've got a birth injury to my right arm, too."

"You sound like an educated man," the doctor said, coming

around behind Patrick and putting his hands on the outsides of Patrick's arms. "Where'd you go to school?"

"I graduated from Harvard, sir."

"That's about as good a place as any." The doctor smiled and took out a tape measure and put it around Patrick's right bicep, and then around his left bicep. "I imagine you have a hard time moving your right hand out this way," he said, putting his arm in an L and moving his hand in an arc to one side, keeping the forearm horizontal.

"Yes, sir."

"I know the injury," the doctor said. "Hop up on that table and we'll take a look at your leg." He pulled once on Patrick's leg. "Pretty damn loose."

"Yes, sir."

The doctor examined Patrick's leg for another minute, and made him do a few motions with his arms. Then he began writing on a pad.

"I think these'll get you out of the Army," he said.

Patrick stared at him.

"Well, if you don't want a discharge, say so," the doctor said. "You don't have to get out of the Army, I suppose. I imagine they can probably find something for you to do."

Patrick opened his mouth. Deep within him he could feel a lot of things crumbling.

"Under the circumstances, sir," he said slowly, "I think I'd better take the discharge."

20

PATRICK was standing by the door of the barracks on Tuesday morning, watching the company march out to one of its last days of training, when he felt a hand on his shoulder. It was Scarpa, taking one of his many breaks from working in the Supply Room.

"Hey," Scarpa said, "come on in my room."

Patrick watched the tail end of the cadence-shouting Fourth Platoon disappear around the corner of the Mess Hall and into the street, and then he came into Scarpa's little cadre room by the front door.

"I heard in the Orderly Room you came in there yesterday from the hospital with a light-duty slip says you might be getting out." Scarpa stuck out his hand. "Congratulations, kid."

Patrick took the hand, tried a smile, and sat down on Scarpa's footlocker.

"Sit on the bunk," Scarpa said. "Nobody inspects this room."

Patrick got up off the footlocker slowly and sat down on Scarpa's bunk. Scarpa sat down beside him, picked up his low quarter shoes from the floor, and began to dust them off preparatory to shining them. "That's really great," Scarpa said, producing a can of shoe polish and opening it. "How does it work from here?"

"Well," Patrick said, "I have a physical in about ten days, and then I come up in front of a board, and I guess they decide."

"How do you like that?" Scarpa said, applying polish to the shoes. "What do the guys in your squad think? I bet they're so jealous they can't see straight, huh?"

"I haven't told them," Patrick said. "Anyhow, I might not be getting out."

"Maybe not," Scarpa said, "but you're gonna get a C profile out of this thing for sure. For sure. Even if you do go to FECOM, you don't have to come back without a leg or something. Like me. No combat. No matter where they ship me, I've got that C profile."

Patrick nodded his head, and Scarpa looked at him. His hand, with a gob of brown polish on the index finger, stopped moving over the shoe he was holding.

"Say, what's the matter with you? Aren't you glad? Jeez, it was me I'd be drunk for days. Wouldn't be nothing coming out of that Supply Room."

"I'm glad in a way," Patrick said. "I know I'm going to be a lot more comfortable physically."

"Comfortable *physically!*" Scarpa said. "What the hell, you're gonna be free! You want to go around the corner for a beer, you can go. You want to go to the ball game, you can go. You oughta be down there kissing those doctors' asses."

"I know."

"Well, get happy."

"I don't know." Patrick lifted his hands up and brought them down on either side of him. "I just hate to run out on it."

"Don't tell me you're that much of an RA," Scarpa said. "You're so broken down you can't even walk. This FECOM is no joke, Kingsgrant. You think any one of those guys out there wouldn't take a discharge right now?" He pointed with the shoe in the direction of the empty squad room on the other side of the wall, and then went on applying polish.

"Maybe they would," Patrick said, standing up. "I've got to go down to the Dispensary and show them this slip. Just so they know about it."

"Boy, don't let me stop you from doing *that*," Scarpa said. "Just take your discharge if they give you a chance at it. Don't fight the problem."

"O.K.," Patrick said, and limped out into the empty squad room. He went down the aisle, planning to go out of the barracks by the back door, and stopped at the doorway of the latrine. Gibson, a kid from upstairs, was the Barracks Orderly, and right now he was cleaning up the washbasins with some Ajax.

"Mr. Kingsgrant," he said, looking up from working on one of the basins.

"How's it going?" Patrick said. Gibson always worked hard, and he was polishing these washbasins as if their condition was a personal affront.

"O.K. Say, Kingsgrant?"

"Yes?" Patrick was still framed in the doorway, and now he came down the two steps into the room.

"Say, do you know when we get orders?"

Patrick shook his head. "It's supposed to be sometime this week."

"Where do you think we'll go?"

Patrick looked at Gibson. Gibson had a young face, and he was looking at Patrick with a dumb, trusting stare, as if Patrick knew the answer, if he just cared to tell.

"I don't know," Patrick said.

"Maybe we'll go to Germany," the boy said, starting to scrub away at the basin again. "You ever go to Germany when you was at college, Kingsgrant?"

"No. I understand it's good duty, though."

"Boy, I sure would like to go to someplace like that," Gibson said.

"I don't blame you."

"I'll have to go to Korea if they say so," Gibson said, "but I sure would like to go to Germany. I'll never be able to go traveling anyways else. You know if you go to Germany you get your thirty days' leave right there. You could go to Switzerland and see the mountains or anything."

"You're right," Patrick said.

Gibson stood back and looked at the basin.

"Looks good," Patrick said.

Gibson smiled a pleased smile, and nodded his head, still looking at the basin. Then he looked at Patrick. "How's your leg, Kingsgrant?"

"All right. It hurts a little."

Gibson looked at his watch. "I've gotta wax that linoleum upstairs," he said. "Hey, Kingsgrant, you think maybe if I went over to the Orderly Room they'd tell me if there was any orders yet?"

"I don't know," Patrick said. He stepped back up the two steps.

"Maybe I'll go over there later on," Gibson said. "You think the latrine looks all right, don't you?"

"It looks great," Patrick said, and nodded his head encouragingly. Then he went out the back door and started his slow walk to the Dispensary.

II

On Wednesday evening, right afer chow, the buzzer sounded. Nobody had been warned of any formation, and they all trotted out of the barracks, wearing fatigues and field caps.

Sergeant O'Reilley was standing there in his fatigues, with his red helmet on. He had a sheaf of papers in his hand. The orders, Patrick thought, standing at the best imitation of attention that he could do with a leg that was still too swollen to straighten out. The orders. Here it is.

"Parade rest!" Sergeant O'Reilley yelled. There was an electric silence on the parade ground. It was still quite light after chow, and a tiny breeze sent a scrap of paper dancing past on the ground behind Sergeant O'Reilley. "The following EM will report to Fort Lewis, Washington, for April shipment to FECOM. Accacio, Aguilar, Allen, Archer, Ashburn, Ascanio, Austin, Baker, Bernardo, Botticelli, Brown — "

Patrick's mind stopped. Sergeant O'Reilley was reading out the whole company. With the exception of a few holdovers like himself, the sergeant might just as well be reading the Encarnacion, Ericson, Farmer, Favicchia, Forlenza, Geremski, company roster. "— Dunphy, Dzurak, Edwards, Ehrlich, Giaramitta, Gibson, Gomez, Gridley, Gross, Hennessey, Hetzler, Interlicchio, Jakes, Jones — " Patrick's mind closed again, and only opened once more, to register the name Ratigan.

Sergeant O'Reilley came to the end of the list and let the papers fall to his side. "You'll start your leaves Friday evening. You *will* report back here one week from Friday, and take a train from here to Fort Lewis. Any man coming back late will not just be AWOL. Any man coming back late and missing a troop movement on orders to a combat zone will be guilty of desertion in the face of the enemy. If you have any further questions about anything, see the Orderly Room." He paused. The company area had never been so still. Across the way some men from Able Company had gathered, waiting to find out what had happened to Baker Company.

"Ten-hut!" Sergeant O'Reilley said. "Companee, dismiss!"

They walked back to their barracks. It was absolutely quiet. Patrick went inside.

"I didn't hear your name, Kingsgrant," Maple said. "You coming with us?"

"I don't know," Patrick said. "I'm supposed to be one kind of a holdover or another. I'm an OCS holdover, and I'm a medical holdover now too."

"Hey, Kingsgrant?" Hetzler said quietly.

"Yes?"

"Could you lend me maybe a dollar in change? I've gotta call up my folks."

"Sure."

"Well, whadidya expect?" Forlenza was saying to Interlicchio. "You really think they was gonna send you to Alaska or somewhere?"

"Just shut your hole," Interlicchio said, and went out through the back door to join the crowd of men heading for the Telephone Building.

Patrick stood by his wall locker.

"That settles it," a voice from outside said, drifting in through a partly opened window. "I'm getting married next week."

Lish was sitting on his bunk. He had taken his box of writing paper down out of the top of his wall locker and now he was staring at a sheet of paper, trying to start the letter to his wife. Patrick looked around and decided to go take a walk somewhere.

III

Jacob was sitting in the living room at Kingsgrant on Saturday morning when Ben knocked on the door and brought in the mail.

"Letter from Mr. Patrick," he said, coming across the room to the armchair where Jacob was seated, having a cup of coffee and looking at the *Bangor Daily News*.

Jacob stood up quickly and took the mail from Ben. He dropped the rest of the letters onto the armchair and took Patrick's over to his desk. He sat down at the desk and slit the letter open with one stroke of his paper knife. "Dear Father," Patrick's handwriting began, "I have had a medical examination recently, and although I can't be sure of all the results, it seems clear to me that I am not going to go to OCS, and I will never be in combat. I thought you would like to know." Patrick began a new paragraph. "I had a very pleasant letter from Eileen the other day. She saw Snowjob in Paris. Trust Snowjob to get to Paris. She seems to be enjoying her year abroad, and I think it must be a wonderful experience for her." The handwriting dropped down again. "The training here is virtually completed. Ninety-five per cent of the company is going to Korea, and they all start their one week's leave tomorrow. This business of only having one week seems pretty tough on the boys from the Virgin Islands, who can't get home at all, but that's the way it is. A few of us will be staying around, pending assignment, or in my case, medical reclassification. One of the ironies is that Stanley (I think I told you about him. The boy who escaped from Czechoslovakia.) is not going to Korea because, if captured, he might be dealt with much more harshly, and there might be reprisals on his family if they definitely found out he was in our Army. It makes sense, and I am very glad he doesn't have to go, but it seems strange to stop an outstanding soldier like Stanley from going to fight an ideology he really hates." There was one more short bit. "I hope you are well. Give my best to everyone, and if there are any new developments, or any change of address, I'll let you know. Sincerely, Patrick."

Jacob put down the letter. "Thank God," he said quietly. "Thank God." His eyes moved to the picture of Patrick on his desk. It was Patrick as a little boy on the island, wearing shorts and a rumpled-up shirt. The hair that was thinning now had been a great dark waterfall, and there was a faraway look in his eyes, and an amused smile on his mouth. Jacob stared at the photograph for a second, and then began reading the letter over.

IV

It was Wednesday afternoon, all the men who were going to Korea were home on leave, and Patrick was raking the area between the Orderly Room and the Supply Room. All week the clock had been running down. Since the troops had left for their leaves on Friday, everything had been moving at half speed. Nobody would have dreamed of telling anyone to do a push-up. O'Reilley disappeared every morning right after breakfast, and nobody asked where he was. Baker Company was out of cycle, and there would be no more yelling until the new trainees arrived. The few holdovers had all moved down to the Fourth Platoon, and they spent their days pulling details, painting and raking and helping to inventory things in the Supply Room.

Patrick saw something out of the corner of his eye, and then he straightened up, holding the rake in one hand. Rodriguez was walking down the steps of the Orderly Room with a barracks bag on his shoulder, and Stanley was coming behind him, carrying another barracks bag, filled with extra things that Rodriguez had acquired in his travels within the Army. Patrick had known that Rodriguez was going to ship out for somewhere, but he had not known where or when.

"I see you're on your way," Patrick said as Rodriguez came walking across the area where he had been raking.

"Yeah." Rodriguez stopped, the olive barracks bag balanced on his shoulder. His Class A's were pressed razor-sharp, and his brass insignia was glittering. He smiled. "I asked them for a transfer a million times, but I didn't think I'd get it."

"Where're you going?"

"Camp Drum. Thirty days and then Camp Drum."

"Well, good luck, Sarge."

"Thanks," Rodriguez said. "Somebody was telling me you might be getting out."

"There's a chance," Patrick said.

"Listen, Kingsgrant," Rodriguez said, "if you get a chance to get out of this dead-ass Army, you take it."

"O.K., Sarge."

Rodriguez turned under his load and smiled at Stanley, who had come up behind him with the second barracks bag.

"Let me hear from you, both you guys," Rodriguez said. "Just a postcard or something. Just my name and serial number and Camp Drum, New York. It'll get there."

"Right," Patrick said.

"So long there, Kingsgrant." Rodriguez took his right hand away from steadying the barracks bag for a moment, and they shook hands. Then he moved on, his paratroop boots sparkling and his overseas cap cocked forward on his head. Stanley followed behind him, taking the other barracks bag as far as the bus stop.

Patrick stood watching them disappear around the corner of the Supply Room building, and then he started halfheartedly raking again. He was thinking that if anybody had told him, four months ago, that he would be sorry to see the last of any of the cadre, he would have laughed. But that was how it was now, Rodriguez just passing by with a barracks bag on his shoulder, and on out of his life. Filthy weapon. Patrick smiled a sad smile as he thought about Rodriguez, a game cock under a red helmet, glaring his way through a rifle inspection.

"Kingsgrant!"

"Here!" Patrick yelled, even before he turned around. One of the clerks was standing on the wooden steps of the Orderly Room, wearing the usual clerk's getup of combat boots, Class

A trousers, and the Class A shirt with no Ike jacket on top of it.

"Got some papers here got to go over to Regimental Head-quarters. Leave off that for now."

"O.K.," Patrick said, and leaned his rake against the side of the coal bin. He walked slowly toward the Orderly Room, feeling the pain in his knee and cursing the whole situation, cursing clerks and cursing the papers that had to go to Regi-mental Headquarters and cursing a situation in which a man with a smashed knee was the Company Runner just because he was nearest. And way underneath he was afraid of going over toward Regimental Headquarters because the other day, coming down the steps from having delivered some papers over there, he had been seized with a tremendous impulse to walk another two hundred yards to the Telephone Building and call Anna. He had stood on the dirt sidewalk outside Regimental Head-quarters, swaying with the sudden feelings and desires that were passing over him, and then he had come back to Baker Company as fast as his leg would let him, and gone into the Supply Room and asked Scarpa to give him something to do. He knew that this time would be a little easier, and that a day would come when he would go through a whole day without wanting to call Anna, but still he was sorry when they sent him even near the Tele-phone Building.

v

Eileen and a friend of hers named Woody Thomas and half a dozen other people had got in the habit of having tea together at various cafés during these days of the early spring. This afternoon one of Eileen's friend joined them at the Deux Magots carrying some mail for Eileen.

"One from my brother," Eileen said, and opened it up. She began reading, and a smile spread across her face. "He isn't going to get hurt," she said aloud, staring at the page.

"What's that?" Woody said, going on stirring his cup of tea.

"My brother says he's had some sort of medical re-evaluation. He doesn't know exactly what's going to happen, but he won't be in the fighting."

"That's good," Woody said. He was a 4-F because he had asthma. He had had both the asthma and the 4-F for a long time, and he was used to the situation. He kept on stirring his tea, and Eileen kept on reading her letter. "I wrote Father about all this a few days ago," Patrick wrote. "I hope you are continuing to have a good time, and, assuming that you are coming home this summer, I may see you then. I doubt that I am going to be shipped out of the country. Right now I am just doing lots of cigarette-butt picking up around here until they decide what to do with me. I'll let you know developments as they occur. Do write soon and long. Love, Patrick."

Eileen put the letter back into the envelope and sat looking across at the church of St. Germain des Prés. She had the feeling that there was a little more to this than Patrick was telling, but still, the important thing was that he was not going to be in the fighting. For the first time in a couple of minutes the voices of some of the other people at the two tables they had pulled together came through to her.

"I don't see how General Eisenhower can miss," one of them said. "He's knocking them dead right now in those press conferences."

"I don't know," a girl replied. "I think the people will vote for the Democrats. They aren't going to bite the hand that's been feeding them."

"They've been feeding the country inflation with that hand," somebody said.

"I think it'll be General Eisenhower," Woody said. "He's got quite a personality. That's what you need, a strong machine or a strong personality."

Eileen stood up.

"I'll be back in a couple of minutes," she said. She put the letter from Patrick in the cloth handbag she had with her, and started walking across the square to the church.

VI

Late Friday afternoon the troops started coming back from leave. They came with freshly cleaned and pressed uniforms, and even their barracks bags looked as if they had been scrubbed by some industrious mother. Most of the men who were going to Korea would come later, directly to the train depot down near the bus terminal, but these were the ones who had no families coming to see them off, and wanted to get some chow in the Mess Hall before the train left. They ate early and disappeared, and then the holdovers went in and ate.

Patrick and Stanley were eating the noodles and slimy meat that were the main course, and discussing Stanley's assignment to Able Company as a cadreman, when one of the OCS holdovers from the Fourth Platoon came up to their table.

"We better go if we're going to get there," he said.

"Where?" Patrick said.

"Down to see them get on the train. There's a whole bunch of us going down."

Patrick and Stanley both picked up their trays, and a few minutes later the fifteen of them who were holdovers for one reason or another were on one of the Post buses, a little knot of faded green fatigues all sitting together in the back.

The bus left them off along the road near the train depot, and they all started walking along the side of the road.

"Let's square this thing away," Kentucky Adams said. They stopped, adjusting their caps on their heads, and made two ranks. "Squad leaders up front," Kentucky said, motioning to Patrick, but Patrick shook his head.

"I'm still limping too much," he said, and fell in at the end of the little column of twos. They stood tall in the evening, their eyes squinting in the sunset, and then Kentucky Adams stepped out to the side of the formation.

"Forward, march." They stepped off hard, with their heads up and their shoulders square. Kentucky was out in the middle of the road, looking them over, and they were swinging along, feeling it the way it is when everybody has it right and everything is one swinging correctness. Adams began giving them the cadence, good and loud and clear, and they did a machine-like column right into the area by the tracks.

"GI beans and GI gravy!" Kentucky yelled.

"GI beans and GI gravy!" they yelled back. They had never marched straighter or yelled harder. Their heads were up in the sky. There was a train next to the long concrete platform, and the whole company was on the platform, surrounded by their families. When they recognized the column in fatigues they gave a tremendous cheer.

"Gee I wish I'd joined the Navy!" Adams went on as they marched toward the platform.

"Gee I wish I'd joined the Navy!"

"Sound off!"

"One two!"

"SOUND OFF!"

"THREE FOUR!"

A band was marching into the area down by the farther end of the platform.

"BREAK 'EM ON DOWN!"

"ONE TWO THREE FOUR, ONE TWO— THREEFOUR!"

"Detail, halt! Dismissed!"

They broke out into the crowd, the handful of faded green fatigues mixing into the big crowd in their Class A's. The band began playing. Patrick found himself next to Forlenza. Forlenza had a pretty black-haired Italian girl with him, and she was crying and kissing him again and again. Patrick moved away.

"Hey, Pat."

Patrick looked around and found Ratigan standing there.

"I been looking for you," Ratigan said.

"Is your family here?"

"No. They wanted to come, but it was hard enough the way it was."

Patrick nodded. He was trying to think of something to say. The band was playing "There's a long, long trail a-winding."

"I hope you get those bars," Ratigan said. "You're one of the few guys around here I can picture with bars."

Patrick thought of explaining it all to Ratigan, but he just smiled.

"How long are you going to be on the train?"

"I don't know," Ratigan said. "As long as it takes to get to Fort Lewis. I never been West. Maybe we'll see the Rockies, huh?"

"I'll bet you will," Patrick said. There was a terrible lump starting in his throat. An officer got up on the steps of one of the cars, and when the band stopped he began reading the roll call of the men going on the train. It took a couple of minutes, and then the band began playing again.

A whistle blew, and the men started getting on the train.

"Good luck," Patrick said to Ratigan.

"Take care of yourself, Pat," Ratigan said, and then he was gone in the crowd. All the wives and mothers were crying, and some of the men were holding their babies up to their faces and kissing them. Patrick saw Ratigan getting onto the train, lugging his barracks bag. He turned at the top of the steps, gave one almost imperceptible nod in the direction of the waving crowd, and then disappeared into the crowded car. Patrick began looking around for members of his squad, but almost all the men were on the train now. The band was playing "Auld Lang Syne." A little woman with a shawl over her head was standing next to Patrick. She was waving without a hope of being seen behind the taller people, and she was crying.

Suddenly the train began moving, and the crowd erupted in a paroxysm of waving. One or two girls were on the bottom steps of the train, kissing their men, and now they stepped off, hiding their faces in their hands. The band still playing "Auld Lang Syne," and very slowly, with hundreds of hands waving from inside it, the train pulled out of the station.

Patrick looked around. Everyone was turning away slowly, silent and with dazed looks on their faces. Stanley was walking away, and his shoulders were shaking the way a man's shoulders shake when he cries. Patrick could feel tears blurring his own eyes, and then he saw Kentucky Adams. Kentucky was still standing on the platform, looking down the empty tracks. Patrick turned and began walking back toward the bus terminal in the middle of the crowd of civilians.

VII

Bill Bench's squad never heard the mortar shell coming. It was about eleven o'clock in the morning, and the whole sector had been pretty quiet since dawn. The shell was the first round, just an aiming round, and it was remarkable that it landed right in the trench.

For the first couple of minutes Bill couldn't feel anything. He knew his head was deep in the dirt that had fallen down, but he couldn't seem to move and help himself. He heard somebody screaming, and then the screaming turned into moaning, and then it stopped. Just when the shell had landed he had felt as if he had been hit in the stomach with a baseball bat, but all he felt now was that he was choking to death.

A couple of hands came up in the dirt near his face. They were not his hands, and they were like a little animal digging furiously. There was air again, and he gasped.

"You're going to have to work fast on this one," somebody said. Bill could feel himself being turned over. The place where he had been hit with the baseball bat was beginning to get hot.

"Try to get some of the dirt out of his stomach," a voice said quickly. The place where he had been hit with the baseball bat was starting to turn into several stings, and suddenly Bill's vision cleared and the stings were knives. He sobbed.

"Over here," somebody was saying. Bill could feel hands working around his midsection. The knives were cutting around inside his stomach now, but things were blurring again and his eyes closed.

"Have to fix this first," a voice said. Bill opened his eyes. He wanted to reach his hands down toward his stomach, but he couldn't move his hands. There was a face under a helmet in profile in front of him. The face never looked at him. It just kept looking down toward his stomach with a concentrated expression, and Bill could feel hands, and he could feel a needle going into his arm. Then he was being carried somewhere, and for a long time all he could see was the sky lurching above him, and sometimes a pair of helmets ahead of him.

He felt the ground solid under him again, and for some reason the knives were not so sharp. He could see a couple of men moving around, and then a hand came down, offering him a white cigarette.

"I don't smoke," Bill said.

Some men came in carrying a stretcher, and when they put it down on the ground it went out of Bill's line of vision. A man came over to him and pulled his dogtags out of his fatigues and looked at them.

"Water," Bill said.

The man looked at him. "I'm sorry, buddy, but you can't have any water." The man started writing something on a tag. He leaned down and fixed the tag on one of the buttons of Bill's fatigue shirt, and then he went away. Bill felt as if he was drunk, and for some reason he felt quite pleased with his tag. There was a breeze here, and every now and then the tag flipped up near his eyes. He saw a bottle of blood hanging over him, clear against the blue sky, and he wondered when they had put that there. The knives twitched a little, and then they revolved in his stomach, and Bill sobbed.

"Give him some more," a voice said, and Bill felt a needle go into his arm. He felt terribly thirsty.

"Water," Bill said.

A face came down near his.

"We can't give you any water," the face said. "For what you've got we can't give you any water."

Bill lay there. He thought it was bad of them not to give him some water.

A face came and leaned down over his. It was his platoon leader. His platoon leader came from Ohio State and sometimes they had talked politics together.

"You're going to be all right, Bench," the young lieutenant said. "They're going to take you back to a hospital and fix you up real good."

Bill tried to nod. He didn't know if he had nodded or not, but the lieutenant nodded again.

"Get me some water," Bill said.

The lieutenant looked up at one of the men who was handling the plasma, and then he patted Bill gently on the shoulder.

"I guess you can't have any," he said. "I've got to get back."

Bill nodded, and the lieutenant stood up and walked away. Bill lay there and then it occurred to him that it would be nice if the lieutenant could write his family and say that what had happened hadn't hurt at all.

"Lieutenant —" he said.

"He left a couple of minutes ago," a face said, coming down near him.

"Chopper's coming," a voice said after a while. Bill lay still. For a time he had been very much interested in what was going on, but now he felt as if something was draining out of him. He felt it going, and then he had the sensation that he was next to a paper wall, and he was trying hard not to slide through the paper wall, because it would be bad to slide through the paper wall. It was made of gray paper, and it was a good idea to stay on this side of the wall, but he felt less and less as if he could help it and he might have to slide through the paper wall even if he didn't want to.

"This one right here," somebody said, and Bill felt himself being picked up, but now nothing was rough. He was sliding, and the bottle up over his head was swinging against the sky, and once or twice his tag hit him in the face. He liked his tag. In a minute they were putting him down somewhere.

"What's this?" Bill said. A man leaned down near him.

"I couldn't hear you, buddy."

"What's this?" Bill said.

"This is a helicopter. It's going to take you back to a hospital."

Bill nodded. He had seen some of them come up to the aid stations before. They were putting a plastic cover up over his head and the top of his stretcher, and Bill realized that he was going away from these men. He wanted to thank them and tell them he was sorry about asking for the water. He lay under the plastic cover and tried with his eyes to attract their attention, but now he couldn't see any faces at all. Over his head he could see the big blade flashing around. It was going around faster and faster, and Bill wondered whether there was another man in a stretcher on the other side of the helicopter, like the ones he had seen.

The helicopter gave an upward yank, and Bill lay there. He was feeling sad, but every now and then the tag hit him in the face. The tag was waving around, and Bill even smiled at it once. The plane was turning, and now it was going forward. Bill could feel everything it was doing, and now he knew he was going to have to go through the gray paper wall. The knives were there again, and he knew that any second now the knives were going to take the last of everything out of him and then the whole thing would be on rollers and he would roll through the gray paper wall. He felt sad and he thought it might be fun sometime to get bundled up like this with a tag waving if you didn't have that gray paper wall and the knives. He knew he was going to get rid of those knives and he was glad he was going to get rid of them. He felt all alone and he wished there was somebody to talk to. If there was somebody here he might be able to explain about the gray paper wall and they might hold on to him somehow so he wouldn't have to slide through it. Maybe they could take the knives away without having to go through the wall. And then maybe they could even give him a drink of water. Suddenly he knew the rollers were there and he was rolling and he went through the wall.

They took the plastic cover off when the helicopter landed at the field hospital, and a bare-headed doctor in fatigues took one look and then reached for Bill's pulse.

"This one's dead," he said. "Get the other one inside just as fast as you can."

21

"CUPS, canteen, two hundred and one," Scarpa said.

"Cups, canteen, two hundred and one," Patrick repeated, and wrote down the number after the place on the inventory.

"Canteens, steel, one hundred and ninety-four," Scarpa said.

"Canteens, steel, one hundred and ninety-four."

"Covers, canteen, canvas, two hundred and six."

"Covers, canteen, canvas, two hundred and six."

"Ten-hut!" somebody near the door of the Supply Room shouted, and Patrick and Scarpa straightened up, their pencils still in their hands. Captain Hare came walking through the piles of gas masks and shovels and overshoes, looking like a thundercloud.

"Scarpa," he said, "what's this about a missing double bunk?"

"I'm afraid one *is* missing, Captain," Scarpa said.

"Well, how could we lose a double bunk?" Captain Hare asked.

"I don't know, sir."

"You realize I'll be charged for it?"

"Yes, sir."

The company commander stood there. "Scarpa," he said, "I don't care how you do it, but get me a double bunk."

"Yes, sir."

The captain looked around. "That's all," he said, shaking his head at the piles of equipment laid out for inventory, and walked out of the Supply Room.

"Hey, Kingsgrant."

Patrick turned around. The mail clerk had come in from the room where the rifles were kept.

"Letter for you," the mail clerk said.

"Thanks a lot." Patrick took the letter from him. He looked at the envelope. It was from Mrs. Bench, at Pride's Crossing.

"Let's get these gas masks squared away," Scarpa said. "We get this inventory done, we get the C.O. off my back."

"O.K.," Patrick said, putting the letter in the breast pocket of his fatigue shirt. Mrs. Bench was probably asking him to come up whenever he got leave. Patrick bent over and began separating the gas masks into piles of ten.

"Patrick, I don't see you so much," Stanley said. They were both eating the meat patties inside peppers that Baker Company was serving for lunch. Stanley had no duties yet as cadre over at Able Company, but he lived over there and was still attached to Baker Company for rations. Everybody was getting sent all over the place. Patrick and Kentucky Adams were now living in a decrepit affair called the Holdover Barracks down by the Stockade, and they were all leading an intensely boring and vastly disorganized existence. Baker Company had no use for them, but they were still here, waiting to see what the Army would do with them and showing up like faithful hound dogs at every meal, ready to trade rumors about when the new trainees would arrive. At first Patrick and Kentucky and Stanley had made a sport out of seeing whether they could get out of the company area after a meal without being grabbed to empty garbage cans or paint footlockers or sweep out the Orderly Room for the clerks, but now they were so bored that they just dawdled, half hoping that somebody would catch them and make them do something. Kentucky had walked around in a haze for a few days after the troops left and then gone in and withdrawn his application for OCS, but he still had to wait around for the orders that would send him after the scattered men of Baker Company.

"I understand there's a movie tonight that isn't so bad," Patrick said, pushing his metal tray away from him. Even though training was over, they still ate as if each meal might be their last. There was a little Dixie cup of ice cream for dessert, and Patrick went after it and knocked it down in about ninety seconds.

"I will try influence," Stanley said, and disappeared up toward the serving counter. He was back in a minute with two more Dixie cups, and they each knocked down their second Dixie cup without saying a word.

Patrick grunted, smiled, and pushed his metal stool a couple of feet back from the table where he and Stanley were sitting. It was a far cry from the days when the last man in the chow line had just enough time to walk through the little dining room with his tray and out the back door, eating his food as he walked because the warning buzzer for the next formation had already sounded. Now the handful of men sat sprawled out at different tables, having their second and third and fourth cup of coffee, talking about whether it was worth going out to Wrightstown tonight or whether it was better to settle for the movie at the theater in the Regimental Area.

"What movie?" Stanley said.

"I'm not sure. It's got Maureen O'Hara."

"She is the one always with pirates?"

Patrick smiled. "That's the one." He took a swallow of his cup of coffee, and then he remembered the letter from Bill's mother. He took it out and opened it.

480

There was a breeze in the pine trees, and occasionally a dead leaf would go skittering under the grandstand and across the deserted square of sand in the woods. Four weeks ago Baker Company had been out here around the edges of this square of sand, running through sighting practice with the 60 mm. mortar. Now everything was silent.

Patrick sat in the empty grandstand, looking out across the square. He was not at all sure of what time it was. He remembered getting up and walking out of the Mess Hall, and carefully washing his tray in the big garbage can filled with hot soapy water, and carefully washing his knife, fork, and spoon in another can, and now he was sitting here. Sunlight was pouring down on this area that had been cut out of the woods, and several times he had seen squirrels poking along the edge of the pine woods across the sandy area. The letter from Bill's mother was back in his breast pocket, and Bill was dead.

It was evening when Patrick came into the Holdover Barracks. He had sat in the grandstand all afternoon, and then he had gone down to Baker Company and eaten supper. Stanley had asked him to come to the movies, but Patrick had said he didn't feel very well. He had walked the mile from Baker Company to the Holdover Barracks very slowly, feeling the pain in his knee, and the stiffness in his shoulder and his neck.

Nobody lived on the bottom floor of the barracks. There were not even any bunks on the bottom floor. It was beginning to get dark outside, but nobody upstairs had bothered to turn on the lights. There were two men asleep on the little single cots they used in this barracks, and one man was lying on his back, smoking a cigarette and staring at the ceiling.

Patrick sat down on the edge of his bunk. After about five minutes he took off his field cap. He stared at his boots in the twilight. The window behind Patrick's bunk was open, and after a long time he stood up and went over to the window. He rested his elbows on the wood, and gazed out at the barracks in the Stockade. They were just like any other barracks, but there was a tall barbed wire fence between his barracks and the barracks that held the prisoners. Way down to his right there was a tower with a couple of men standing beside a machine gun in the silent evening, and just across the fence, sitting on the back steps of the nearest barracks, there was a boy playing a harmonica. The boy was looking out at the rich dark blue of the sky through barbed wire, and playing "Stormy Weather." Patrick rested his chin on top of his folded arms and listened to the notes coming out of the shadows down there. The boy played "Stormy Weather" with a lot of feeling, and the notes came marching out over the barbed wire. Way up in the evening sky a plane went past, red and green lights winking on the tips of its wings, and then it was gone and Patrick was still at the window and the boy was still playing the song. Ain't no sun up in the sky. Stormy weather. The song stopped being just a song, because the boy was good. The notes said he was sorry he went AWOL, and he wasn't giving any promises and maybe when they let him out he'd go AWOL again, but he still wanted to be out of there.

Patrick stood at the window for a long time. The boy with the harmonica had plenty of time, too. He had more time than he wanted to think about, and he played "Mood Indigo," and "Stardust." He played them slowly and thoughtfully, and the notes kept coming through the strands of barbed wire as the shadows became darkness. There was nothing moving in the Stockade. Just lighted windows and white barracks in the evening. Nobody was going anywhere, and the only sound was this one harmonica. The boy on the steps played "I'll Be Seeing You," and Patrick kept staring out of the window. The thought had come into his mind that he had to write Mr. and

Mrs. Bench, and then suddenly and for the first time he really understood that Bill was dead, and that Bill's body was just something coming back in a box, and that you couldn't talk to what was in that box. Tears started coming out of Patrick's eyes, and he put his face down on his folded arms. After a minute he pulled himself away from the window and lay down on his bunk. In the darkness of the barracks he was back at Tabor with Bill, both of them out sailing on the water of Sippican Harbor, both of them ducking their heads as Bill brought the tiller over, and then he was next to Bill as they whipped up to Pride's Crossing in Chrissy with the top down, and then Bill was across the table at Cronin's, pouring himself a Budweiser and saying for the third consecutive year that this year by God he wasn't going to go out for swimming, and Bill diving into the water and the crash-crash of the limbs going through the water because young men loved to be alive and competing with each other.

II

"Hey, gimme a smoke for later, uh?"

"Just keep walking," Patrick said, and the prisoner turned his head to the front and kept on trudging along the dirt shoulder of the road, five yards ahead of him. Patrick was carrying a carbine, his left hand around the stock, and the crook of his left elbow supporting the butt of the little rifle. It was an unvarying pattern, the muzzle of the toylike weapon pointing at the sky just over the prisoner's head, the slow, half-ashamed and half-defiant gait of a prisoner in Class A's being taken to trial under guard, and the sun beating down on the shimmering road. Patrick loosened his grip on the stock, and then tightened his hand again. It seemed to him that he and this prisoner had been walking forever. All week he had been escorting AWOL's from one place to another under guard. Sometimes he picked them up at the Detention Barracks and took them to Regimental Headquarters. Sometimes he picked them up inside the Stockade and took them to the Fiftieth Infantry Regiment Courtroom to be tried. But always he was walking somewhere, his knee aching and his left shoulder hurting, and always there was a prisoner in front of him. They walked slowly on their way to be tried, and they were always convicted, and they walked even more slowly on their way back.

As he walked under the hot sun a hopeless series of thoughts revolved in and out of Patrick's mind. It had been ten days since he found out about Bill's death, and whenever he thought about Bill it began as an inability to comprehend that he was not going to see Bill again. Then it would come slowly, like something locking into place, and he would be ashamed because he was sitting here, and because the other day he had signed a paper requesting discharge. It had been purely a formality, just a paper saying that he understood he might be eligible for discharge and would take it if he was given it, but still he had been thinking about Bill when he signed it. He had thought about Bill, and about all the men in Baker Company who were probably getting to Korea about now, and he had signed it. The paper had gone away into a great administrative limbo, and maybe one of these weeks he would come up in front of a board that would decide his fate, and maybe he wouldn't. In the meantime he was walking along with his knee aching and his spirit broken. A spurlike pain was developing in the heel of his left foot because he was favoring his right leg, and he was scared and ashamed and disgusted and bored. When he prayed at night he prayed for Bill and he prayed that the Army was not light-dutying him into a permanent limp, and that was all he could think of to pray for.

Patrick passed the back of his right hand across his face, trying to get rid of some of the dust that had settled there. He was thinking that the illusion of isolation was almost complete now, twenty-four hours a day. The new trainees had arrived at Baker Company, and everybody was busy with two hundred scarecrows who kept bumping into each other and losing things and signing things the wrong way. He was alone all day with just an anonymous, docile prisoner shuffling ahead of him, and all he got when he checked with the mail clerk was a few moments of his heart thumping until he found out there was no letter from Anna. There never would be a letter from Anna, and he knew it in exactly the same way that he knew there never would be a letter from Bill. There had been just two letters since the one from Mrs. Bench. One had been from Professor Hunt, saying that his novel had been turned down from one more place. The other had been from his father. His father had said that he could not help but be glad that Patrick was not going to be in combat. He told Patrick that he had done all that he could. He asked Patrick to keep him informed of how he was, and what was happening to him. It had been a short letter, but it had said what Patrick wanted to hear, that he had done all he could. Patrick had been meaning to write his father that Bill was dead but he had not done it yet. He had written the Benches, but this was different. He knew he had to write his father that Bill was dead, and he had to write Eileen that Bill was dead, but he kept putting it off, as if it was not true until he wrote it to his family.

"How much farther we got to go?" the prisoner asked, without turning his head this time.

"Quite a way," Patrick said, and shifted the carbine slightly. He felt absolutely nothing toward the figure ahead of him, neither vindictiveness nor sympathy. It was just his job to slip off the safety of the carbine and squeeze off a round between the prisoner's shoulder blades if he should make a break for it. They were just two men walking together under the sun, and since they were walking, they had more in common with each other than with anyone who passed in a car.

III

Patrick had been sitting in this waiting room of the Post hospital for three hours, and he was rapidly coming to the conclusion that it was the worst three hours he had ever spent. Last week he had taken another physical, and this morning when he was calmly walking past the new trainees to the head of the chow line with Kentucky Adams and Stanley, a clerk had told him that he was supposed to come down here this afternoon for the medical board that was to decide his fate. He had reported here at one-thirty, and it was now four-thirty. Every time a door to any one of the many offices had opened the last three hours Patrick had been halfway out of his chair, but they had called every name but his own. Now he was sitting here, one of the last, and some of the doctors were going home. For three hours he had been silently begging for them to get him in there and settle it. Horrible possibilities had risen in his mind. Private Kingsgrant, he saw a two-star general saying, we have discovered that you deliberately concealed defects to enlist, and that you repeated these falsifications before an OCS board. Off to the Stockade with you. Six months for fraudulent enlistment. Other things had tangled in his mind. A hundred times he had imagined himself saying, Sir, I've changed my mind. I withdraw my application for discharge. I realize I can't do you much good fighting, but I have a perfectly good mind and I feel I owe my country eighteen more months sitting at any desk you name. He imagined himself saying it, but he knew that he would go in there and keep his mouth shut. He wanted out. He was scared, scared of the pain he had had in Basic and scared of the way things were stiffening up in his shoulder. They had yet to even look at his left shoulder, and his knee kept right on hurting him. He wanted to be out and get fixed, and not be on light duty that consisted of walking miles on a bad leg or loading six hundred blankets on a truck. Maybe loading blankets sounded like light duty to the Army, but a bale of blankets weighed as much as a bale of hay.

"Kingsgrant."

"Here, sir."

Patrick stood up, his heart beating quickly, and followed the doctor down the hall. He smoothed down his fatigue shirt, and said one more prayer that the doctor who had sat on his OCS board would not be sitting on this one. That was all he needed, to come in and see the doctor in front of whom he had said that he had no physical defects, and absolutely no difficulty with the training.

Patrick stepped into the room, following the doctor who had come out and called him.

"Come in, Private Kingsgrant," the doctor in the center said. There were a major, a captain, and a first lieutenant, all in smocks, and none of them the doctor from the OCS board. "Private Kingsgrant," the major who had just spoken said, "we have decided to base this discharge purely on the birth injury to your right shoulder and right arm, since that seems to merit discharge all by itself. We know you have some trouble with your knee too, but since we're trying to save the taxpayers some money we're not going to discharge you on the basis of an injury for which we might have to pay you disability as long as we have one for which we do not. You understand that among the papers you've signed is a waiver of disability?"

"Yes, sir." Patrick was thinking that still nobody had done anything for the pain in his left shoulder and his neck, but this was no time to mention it.

"You understand that you can still make a claim with the VA and that this waiver just says you won't claim anything from us."

"Yes, sir."

"Now, we know you have some trouble with your knee, and if you want an operation on your knee, we will be happy to perform it for you. Is that clear?"

"Yes, sir. I'll take care of the knee myself, sir."

"If you'll just strip to the waist, Private Kingsgrant."

Patrick took off his fatigue shirt and his T shirt and stood facing the three doctors.

"He's pretty husky," the major said, "so it shows up pretty clearly."

"I don't see anything wrong," the first lieutenant said.

"The *right* arm, doctor," the major said quietly.

"Oh, I see," the first lieutenant said. "It was just the way he was standing."

"Bring your right arm in as close to your side as you can, elbow bent and palm up," the major said. Patrick nodded and did it. "Now give us all the motion you have outwards." Patrick really tried. "I think that's pretty clear," the major said. "I don't think this man should take even a week of Basic."

"I've been through Basic, sir."

"I don't see how you did it," the major said, smiling and shaking his head as he looked down at some papers. "I see that this knee condition is a complication of an old injury. How'd you get that?"

"Playing football, sir." Suddenly Patrick saw them saying that if he was a football player he could damn well stay in the Army. "I went out for it at college. It was a foolish thing for me to do." He hated himself for adding that.

"I don't think he could defend himself adequately with that arm," the captain said. Patrick's lips tightened a little.

"All right, Private Kingsgrant," the major said. "You'll get your discharge."

"Will it be an honorable discharge, sir?"

The major smiled. "Yes, unless you sock your commanding officer in the jaw between now and the time this thing gets processed."

"Yes, sir."

"That'll be all, Private Kingsgrant."

"Yes, sir." Patrick bent down, picked up his fatigue shirt and T shirt, and walked out into the hall.

IV

Jacob came walking up the driveway from the pier to the house, his eyes feasting on the light green buds that were everywhere in these last days of April. The grass seed that he had told Bertram to plant on some of the bare patches near the driveway was coming up very well, and Jacob smiled at the new whiskers of grass. His glance traveled across the buds on the trees once more, and he took a good deep breath. It was really spring in Maine at last, and as Jacob looked at the house, framed at the top of the driveway in an arch of budding elms, he decided that he might as well have the house painted this summer instead of waiting for next year. The white paint was holding up pretty well, but it had been three years, and Ben and Bertram loved to get out there in the August sun and paint the house. They were good at it, and during at least one or two afternoons Rolly would come out. Rolly would always wear a pair of overalls that were faded bluish white, and Jacob would get into a pair of dungarees and a wool shirt that was so old nobody knew what century it came from, and they would paint all afternoon and then drink some beer on the back steps of the house.

Jacob came into the house. Harriet was helping Moonstone move some furniture so that she could dust it, and Jacob nodded to them.

"Heard from Patrick today," he said. "He's getting out for sure."

"That's wonderful, Mr. Jacob," Harriet said. Jacob saw the question on her face Will he be coming here? but Harriet did not ask the question, and Moonstone just said, "I'm glad he's all right." Jacob walked on into the living room and sat down at his desk. He took the letter from Patrick out of his pocket and read it for the fifth time since it had come this morning. It was a short letter. It said that Bill Bench had been killed, and then went on. Patrick said that he would be discharged in about a week. And that was all the letter said. Sincerely, Patrick.

Jacob stared at the top of his desk. He had known that Bill was dead because Eileen had heard about it in Paris and written him the news in a letter that had come just two days before. Jacob had not been sure of whether to write the news to Patrick, and now this letter settled it. Bill was dead, and Jacob sensed that Patrick was having the same hard time taking it in that he had had himself. He had read Eileen's letter and then it was as if a part of his mind had immediately begun to tell him that if he just ignored it, it would not be so. Several times in the last two days he had known rationally that Bill was dead, but the grass was coming up, and the sky was blue, and it was hard to understand that at the other end of the world your son's roommate was dead.

The smile that had been on Jacob's face when he looked at the new grass was gone now, and he pulled a piece of writing paper toward him and stared at it. He had a great deal to say to Patrick, and as usual he was certain that he would not be able to say it the way he meant it. He took out his fountain pen, wrote down "South Harbor, April 28, 1952," and "Dear Patrick." Jacob stared at the page. He shook his head and then looked around the room. There was Maude's painting on the

wall, and a photograph of Eileen in a Brearley gym suit, and
the little photograph on his desk of Patrick as a boy on the
island. And here he was, sitting alone in the house. "I was
terribly sorry to hear about Bill," he began. "I know that his
death is hard to bear. We used to say that the best people got
killed, and it still seems to be true. All we can do is hope
that he died in a worthwhile cause. Having fought in the war
to end wars, I am more than a little cynical about justifying
sacrifices this way, but still we can hope. If there is anything
I can do, let me know. I am writing the Benches." He hesitated.
"I know that Bill's death compounds your already sensitive
feelings about your present situation. I cannot help it, Patrick,
I am delighted that you are out of there. I don't think you
belonged in there, I think you have done everything you could,
and I think you have come to a situation that you just have
to accept." Jacob thought for a while before he started the
next paragraph. "I have had occasion to think hard about
your interest in writing. Your actions of last summer, and the
fact that you really finished your novel, have convinced me
you mean business about this sort of thing. I will not tell you
I approve of it, but I am no longer sure that I know enough
to either approve or disapprove. I am now prepared to hope
that you will come here upon your discharge, and stay here
for at least the summer, working as you wish. I once believed
that a young man should stand on his own two — " Jacob
scratched this sentence out. "I think now that it is silly for
you not to share in the benefits of Kingsgrant, no matter what
your occupation may be. I would never try to hold you
here, and you could come and go as you please, provided you
continued to work at *something*, which I am now convinced
you will do. Please consider this carefully, Patrick. Eileen is
returning from Europe this summer, and it would be marvelous
if we could have a happy summer here together. I shall hope
to hear from you soon. Love, Father."

He sat back and read his letter over. He wished that somehow it could sound more inviting, he wished that he could sound more enthusiastic about the prospect of Patrick as a writer, but he could not. Jacob sighed, and began to copy over the letter to Patrick.

v

Patrick got off the Post bus in front of the Service Club, and crossed the road. He was in his Class A's, and he had a manila envelope under his arm. It was Thursday afternoon, he was being discharged Monday, and he had been spending the day at Classification and Assignment, signing forms.

"Brother Kingsgrant."

Patrick had been walking along, intent on his own thoughts, and now he turned and saw Kentucky Adams standing there, wearing his Class A's, with a barracks bag on his shoulder. Kentucky swung the bag lightly to the ground.

"Where're you going?" Patrick said.

"FECOM," Kentucky said, smiling. "Goin' home for a week, and I *will* get drunk."

"I wish you luck, Kentucky." Patrick looked at the apple-cheeked young man standing in the late afternoon sunshine. Adams looked like a square-jawed young god, handsome and clean.

"Same to you, Brother Kingsgrant," Kentucky said. He was in high spirits. "Sorry you're getting out. You might have had a lot of excitement in this outfit."

The bus that had brought Patrick into the Regimental Area had turned around down by the Weapons Pool, and now it was coming back up this side of the road. Kentucky signaled the bus. Patrick shook hands with him, and then Kentucky swung his barracks bag on his shoulder and climbed aboard.

"Hey, Kingsgrant!" he said, sticking his head out of one of the windows. The bus was already moving away.

"Yes?"

"You ever write another book, you put me in it, hear?"

"I sure will!" Patrick yelled, and then the bus was gone up the road.

VI

Allston Hunt finished reading the letter from Patrick and sat for a long time, looking out of the window of his office in Warren House. It was a simple letter, starting off with the fact that he was shortly to be discharged from the Army. Patrick said that he had called up his old landlady and asked her if she had a room, and she had said no, "but I got a friend, Mr. Kingsgrant," so he thought he would be living near where he had been the summer before.

But I got a friend. Allston smiled as he looked at the letter. Patrick said that he appreciated all the efforts that had been made for "Technical Jones," but that he was pretty sure that it was never going to be published. He said that he was going to get a job in New York. He thought that pretty soon he would feel like writing another novel. He would write it in the evenings and on week-ends, and maybe this one would be published.

Allston's face moved into a tight grimace. He was thinking of Patrick down there last summer in New York, and Patrick riding off like Don Quixote to the Army. Underneath this letter he thought he felt a deep sadness, but somehow the letter sounded very much as if it had been written by a man and not a boy. Allston tapped the pencil on the desk top, harder and faster. For a moment he was thinking of all the boys who had sat around the table in this office, listening to each other read their work aloud, and then going back to the infinite aloneness of a typewriter and a blank sheet of paper. Every June they passed on, but in the stillness of this room, with a newly green tree pressing at the window, he could almost hear their voices. All the voices, earnestly reading what they had written, trying to impart life, trying to reach each other, trying to communicate. And then, sometimes years later, there would be a book in the mail, compliments of the author, with an inscription that sounded like that boy's voice speaking. Sometimes it would be a magazine with a story proudly marked in it, and sometimes it would be a letter like this one, a letter that said don't count me out. Don't count me out yet.

VII

Neither Patrick nor Stanley set out to get drunk on Saturday night, but they got drunk. They ate chow in the Able Company mess, with Patrick as Stanley's guest at the cadre table, and then they took a Post bus to the main gate and walked out into Wrightstown.

They had come to see a movie, but the movie turned out to be a double feature of a Frankenstein and "Cat Men," and neither of them wanted to see that. They walked along the street, discussing Stanley's platoon in Able Company and talking about the way that Sergeant O'Reilley was whipping the new trainees into shape in Baker Company, and then Patrick realized that this was probably the last time that he would ever be in Wrightstown, New Jersey. He was getting his discharge Monday morning, and he certainly didn't intend to stop here on his way out to New York. This was the last aimless evening in Wrightstown, and there was one place he had always wanted to go. There was a big bar named Baloney Joe's, and Patrick wanted to be able to say that he had been to a place called Baloney Joe's.

So by seven-thirty in the evening they were sitting in

Baloney Joe's, making a well-coordinated attack on two bottles of Budweiser.

"Patrick," Stanley said at about half past nine, when they were working on their fourth round of bottles, "what was it in the letter?"

"What letter?"

"The letter for you at chow. Maybe two weeks ago. Maybe three weeks. After you read it you looked sick."

"Oh. That was about a friend of mine." Patrick was tearing the label off his bottle of Budweiser, and he kept looking at it. "He got killed in Korea."

"Oh. I'm sorry." Stanley took a long swallow of his beer. "Good friend?"

"Very good."

"Was he in the Army?"

"Yes. He was in the Second Division."

They both took a long swallow of their beer. The place around the booth at which they were sitting was filled with uniforms, and girls entertaining the uniforms. It was noisy.

"I feel bad about getting discharged," Patrick said after a couple of minutes. "I know I'm taking it, but I don't feel too good about it."

"You're lucky, Patrick. I would like to be discharged too."

Patrick looked at him. "Really, Stanley?" He had torn the middle of the label off the bottle, and now he was working on the remaining edges.

"I don't know," Stanley said. "I enlist to fight the Communists. But they don't send me to Korea. After five years I take the discharge. You're lucky, Patrick. You will go in the nature somewhere and think great thoughts. Maybe you write another book."

Patrick looked up from his idiot's game of denuding beer

bottles of their labels. He had expected Stanley to say a thing like that about as much as he expected the beer bottle to blow up in his face. Great thoughts, eh? Great thoughts in the woods.

"Let's have another beer, Stanley."

"It's a good idea."

Jacob was just about to leave Rolly Grindall's house a couple of hours after a bean supper when Rolly's number rang out on the party-line phone. Margie came in just as Jacob was putting his coat on.

"It's long distance for you, Jake."

Jacob looked at his watch. It was a quarter past ten, and he was sleepy. He kept his coat on and went to the phone.

"Jacob Kingsgrant?"

"Yes."

"Just a minute for Wrightstown, please."

There was a sudden blast of noise on the other end of the line, and then Patrick's voice came over the din.

" 'Lo, Dad?"

"Is that you, Patrick?"

"Yes. I thought maybe I could get you at the Grindalls', and by God I did."

"Yes, Patrick," Jacob said, starting to smile, "you did. Where are you?" He could hear a couple of the other phones on the party line being picked up, but the racket on the other end held its own.

"I'm in a place called Jaloney — Baloney Joe's, in Wrightstown. You know, next to Fort Dix."

"I see," Jacob said. He was grinning.

"Hey, Dad?"

"Yes, Patrick?"

"Look — I wanted to explain something. I got your letter

this morning. About coming up to Kingsgrant." There was a pause. "Look, Dad. I've got a room in New York. Right near where I was last summer. I think I ought to get a job and get organized. I mean, I'd like to come, but not yet. Do you understand?"

"Yes, Patrick." Jacob was nodding his head, and he didn't care if the whole county was listening.

"It's nothing personal. That's the whole point. There's nothing personal about it."

"I know it," Jacob said. "I know it, Patrick."

"See," Patrick said, "then when I come for a vacation or something it'll be right."

"Yes," Jacob said. "Yes."

"Hey, Dad?" Patrick said. "I want you to say hello to my friend Stanley."

"I'd like to."

There was a sound of a struggle at the other end of the line, and then a voice said timidly, "Hello, sir?"

"Hello, there. Are you taking good care of my son?"

"No, sir. Your son is taking care of me."

Patrick's voice came on again.

"I guess we'd better hang up or I won't be able to buy any more beer."

"Well," Jacob said, "you don't want to have that happen."

"Not yet, anyhow," Patrick said. "Good night, Dad. God bless you."

"God bless you, Patrick," Jacob said, and then he hung up. "That was Patrick. He's all right." Jacob sat down. "Rolly, let's have a drink."

Rolly looked startled, and Margie glanced at the clock.

"All right, Jake," Rolly said after a minute. "What's the occasion?"

"I wish I could explain it to you," Jacob said, standing up

and taking off his coat. "Let's have a drink, and maybe I can."

At two o'clock in the morning Patrick and Stanley were having a serious conversation in front of the Baker Company Orderly Room. The only thing about it was that they were shouting, and once or twice Stanley fell down to add emphasis to his remarks.

"I still think I'm a bastard, and you ought to *agree* with me!" Patrick roared.

"But Patrick!" Stanley yelled, and stood there swaying, with an expression on his face that indicated that he thought he had made an important point and was awaiting an instant rebuttal.

"And that's just one thing!" Patrick bellowed.

"But you are RA!" Stanley yelled. "Nobody can ever say to you!"

"Oh, I don't know!" Patrick screamed. "I don't know about that!"

A window flung open, and Sergeant O'Reilley's voice cut into the night air.

"Kingsgrant, what are you and that Czechoslovakian doing out there?"

"Ten-hut!" Stanley yelled.

"Ten-haught!" Patrick insisted. "Rodriguez *always* said haught. You going to let him down just because he's gone?"

O'Reilley laughed. "We've got a whole restricted company asleep here. You want to wake 'em all up?"

"No!" Patrick shouted.

"No, *Sergeant!*" Stanley said.

"I'm sorry, Sergeant!" Patrick yelled. "I meant 'No, *Sergeant!*'"

"All right," O'Reilley said, "do I have to come out there and knock your pointed little heads together?"

Patrick and Stanley looked at each other, and just a glimmering of real life came through.

"No, Sergeant," they both said, softly.

Stanley stuck out his hand, and they shook hands.

"Breakfast," Stanley said.

"Completely," Patrick answered. Stanley walked off, and then Patrick looked around. Sergeant O'Reilley was still at the window, laughing. "Sergeant?" he said softly.

"What do you want?"

"Can I sleep here 'night? I don't want to go to the Holdover Barracks."

"You couldn't *get* to the Holdover Barracks," the sergeant said. "Try the cadre room in the First Platoon. Downstairs, left-hand side as you come in. Both bunks are empty, so you ought to be all right no matter how you land. Got that?"

"Got it got it got it," Patrick said, and the morning found him asleep in the shower room just off the latrine in the Second Platoon.

VIII

"Hey, let me see what the thing looks like," Scarpa said.

"Sure." Patrick opened the manila envelope and pulled out the big white piece of paper that said, "Patrick Kingsgrant RA12 422 849 Private E-2 Regular Army is honorably discharged May 4, 1952. This certificate is awarded as a testimonial of Honest and Faithful Service."

"Gee," Scarpa said, holding the discharge in his hand as he stood on the other side of the counter in the Supply Room.

Patrick took back the piece of paper. The morning had been a fast whirl of getting his final pay, signing another couple of papers, and then saluting a lieutenant colonel who stood behind a card table and passed out discharges to about a dozen of them from all over the Post. Now Patrick had just finished his last meal in the Army, and he had washed his knife, fork, and spoon very carefully in the hot soapy water in the garbage cans. Scarpa had kept his barracks bag here since he had checked out of the Holdover Barracks this morning, and now Patrick had come in to get his bag and give back the Army their knife, fork, and spoon. Patrick looked at the utensils as they sat on the counter, and then he turned to Scarpa.

"What about my coat?" he said, pointing at his overcoat, which was folded on top of his barracks bag.

"Regulations say you can keep it if the temperature is under sixty the day you're discharged. Let's see what it says." Scarpa came out from behind the counter, and he and Patrick went over to one of the windows of the little building. There was a thermometer just outside the window. It was a gorgeous day, and the thermometer read seventy.

"Fifty-nine," Scarpa said. "Keep your coat."

"Thanks," Patrick smiled. "I don't have to check out in the Orderly Room, do I?"

"No. Captain Hare isn't there. There's just clerks over there. Nobody you want to say good-bye to."

Patrick nodded and put on the coat. He and Stanley had just had a minute before lunch, but they had given each other permanent addresses, and alternate permanent addresses, and then Stanley had straightened his red cadreman's helmet on his head and gone off to take care of his platoon.

"Good luck," Scarpa said.

"Thanks a lot, Scarpa." Patrick shook hands with him, and then he picked up the barracks bag with his left hand, and, carrying the manila envelope with the discharge in it in his right hand, he went through the little front door of the Supply Room. Outside he stopped and propped the barracks bag against the wall of the building. There was one more thing he wanted to do. Everybody had been wearing the Regimental pins when they went home on pass all the way through Basic. They were not supposed to do it, and he was one of the few who did not blossom forth wearing the pretty white enamel insigne once they were on the bus. He had always liked the looks of those pins, and now he wanted to go over to the PX and buy a set of three of them for a souvenir. Patrick started toward the PX, and as he walked, he heard the fall-out buzzers going off. Baker Company came tearing out of the barracks, carrying their newly issued rifles at port arms, ready to march out for the afternoon. A lieutenant came walking past the other way, and Patrick gave him an air-cutting salute.

"Good afternoon," the lieutenant said.

"Good afternoon, sir." Patrick went into the PX. For once the line was pretty short because everybody was supposed to be in formations somewhere, getting ready to move out to the field. Patrick kept the manila envelope tucked under his arm, and a minute later he came out of the PX, putting the three pins into the pocket of his overcoat.

Able Company was just going past as he came out on the steps of the PX, and Baker Company was marching out onto the road at right shoulder arms. Patrick stood at the bottom of the steps and watched Stanley go by with his platoon of Able Company, marching along in the middle of the road, yelling cadence at his men. He was looking the other way, and Patrick just stood and watched him go. Then Baker Company came past. Sergeant O'Reilley swung by, his attention concentrated on the double file of trainees across the road, and in a minute they were all gone by, and their yelling became faint up the dusty road. Patrick stood looking after them, and he was sorry that he had not had a chance to say good-bye to O'Reilley. He knew that O'Reilley would never even notice that he was gone, but still he would have liked to say good-bye to O'Reilley.